THE
SHADOW
COMMISSION

THE DARK ARTS SERIES
BY DAVID MACK

A DARK ARTS NOVEL

THE SHADOW COMMISSION

DAVID MACK

TOR

A TOM DOHERTY ASSOCIATES BOOK
NEW YORK

THE SHADOW COMMISSION

Copyright © 2020 by David Mack

All rights reserved.

A Tor Book
Published by Tom Doherty Associates
120 Broadway
New York, NY 10271

www.tor-forge.com

Tor® is a registered trademark of Macmillan Publishing Group, LLC.

The Library of Congress Cataloging-in-Publication Data is available upon request.

ISBN 978-0-7653-8323-5 (trade paperback)
ISBN 978-1-4668-9086-2 (ebook)

Our books may be purchased in bulk for promotional, educational, or business use. Please contact your local bookseller or the Macmillan Corporate and Premium Sales Department at 1-800-221-7945, extension 5442, or by email at MacmillanSpecialMarkets@macmillan.com.

First Edition: 2020

Printed in the United States of America

0 9 8 7 6 5 4 3 2 1

for all the unsung heroes

Stars, hide your fires;
Let not light see my black and deep desires:
The eye wink at the hand; yet let that be,
Which the eye fears, when it is done, to see.

—William Shakespeare,
Macbeth, Act I, Scene 4

1963

1

FRIDAY, NOVEMBER 22

Haunted by the stench of demons, Brother Tenzin climbed a steep flight of uneven stone steps. After more than twenty years of living in Key Gompa, the Buddhist monk had come to take for granted the sweetness of its air, which washed down from the Himalayas and across the River Spiti to arrive at the sanctuary cool and cleansed. The temple's unsullied atmosphere made any manifestation of evil beyond its hallowed walls seem all the more foul by comparison, like carrion festering in a field of lavender.

He halted at the top of the stairs to palm sweat from his shaved head, and dried his hand on his tangerine-colored robe. A deep breath slowed his pulse—and confirmed the brisk morning air remained polluted with demonic odors. The presence had grown stronger and more putrid in the minutes it had taken him to reach the abode of the temple's longest-dwelling resident.

Tenzin approached the master's door. When he raised his hand to knock, the door swung silently open ahead of him.

"Come in, Tenzin," said the ancient one.

Tenzin stepped inside. Unlike most rooms in the temple, this one was packed with books, scrolls, and a plethora of containers in a range of sizes—some of them copper, others brass, a few of crystal. A large leather-bound grimoire lay open on the sleeping mat in the corner. In the middle of it all stood Master Khalîl el-Sahir. He tied shut his dark gray robe. "You smell them?"

"Every soul in the temple can smell them."

"No doubt. Where is my wand?" The white-bearded magician pivoted left, then right. "Aha!" He pulled his rod of hand-carved yew from a pile of scrolls. "What say the stars?"

"They are full of dark omens."

"As ever." He wrapped his wand in a band of red silk before tucking it under his belt. "Come." He strode toward the door. "To the roof."

Obedient but apprehensive, Tenzin followed his old friend out of the room. "Do you think that's wise, Master Khalîl? If the enemy is moving against us—"

"If they are, they do so in the open." Khalîl quickened his pace. Despite being over five hundred years old, the master karcist was lean and spry. "Let us observe them from a safe vantage inside the temple's wards before we commit to a response."

Key Gompa's narrow passages and winding stairs were infamous for confounding newcomers, who often derided the temple's interconnecting pathways as a maze, but Tenzin found them as familiar as his own reflection. So, too, did Khalîl, who led Tenzin past the temple that crowned the fortlike conglomeration of boxy white buildings, which ringed the peak of a hilltop high above the Spiti Valley.

Tenzin and Khalîl climbed a final flight of stairs to the temple's flat roof. Icy gales slashed at their faces while they surveyed the landscape below.

Sunrise filled the valley with shadows as long as the land was wide. To the south, rugged ice-capped mountaintops stretched across the horizon. Below the monastery, the River Spiti cut a dark and serpentine path through the frosted plain. To the north, behind Tenzin and Khalîl, slopes blanketed with fresh-fallen snow were topped by broad cliffs of black rock. The wind keened as it swept over a landscape as desolate as it was austere.

Green flames blazed inside Khalîl's eye sockets. Out of respect for the monks of Key Gompa, the old master had restricted his exercise of the Art to angelic magick while he dwelled within the temple's walls. Khalîl found the Pauline Art more difficult to practice and less reliable in its results than its dark counterpart, the demon-driven Goetic Art, but the ancient karcist had never complained about or asked to be exempted from the prohibition. With only a few fleeting exceptions, he had been an exemplary guest.

If someone living here for over a century can truly be called a "guest."

With a blink the flames vanished from the master's eyes. "Our enemy is well hidden."

Tenzin wondered aloud, "Spies?"

"Perhaps. They could also be scouts."

Both possibilities worried Tenzin. The monk searched the blank canvas of snow-covered hills for any sign of danger. "Master Khalîl, if your foes know to seek you here, it might be best if you kept out of sight."

"If I'm their target, the mere sight of me tells them nothing they don't already know. Besides—" He gestured broadly at their surroundings. "We are well defended inside the temple's wards. Neither spells nor spirits, blades nor—"

The crack of a rifle shot cut him off.

A flash revealed a previously unseen sphere of magickal energy surrounding the entire monastery—and in that instant the bubble *popped*.

The temple's wards were gone.

Khalîl shoved Tenzin toward the stairs. "Run!"

Another shot split the frigid morning air. Warm blood sprayed Tenzin's back and the nape of his neck. He turned to see Khalîl stagger like a drunkard and fall to his knees. A bloodstain spread across the front of the master's robe, and pink spittle foamed in his mouth as he gasped for air. Tenzin reached down to help him as a third shot rang out—

The top of Khalîl's head erupted. A bloody shrapnel of skull and brain matter struck Tenzin's face, forcing him to wince in pain, horror, and disgust. When he opened his eyes, he found himself bathed in the blood of his friend, whose body lay sprawled on the roof at his feet.

Tenzin felt trapped outside of himself as he raised the temple with his inchoate cries for help. His voice sounded distant to him, foreign, unknown. Calling for aid was pointless—there was nothing anyone could do now to save Khalîl—but he shouted as if by reflex, unable to stop himself. By the time his fellow monks found him and the slain karcist, Tenzin's voice had turned hoarse as much from grief as from the arid cold.

Sick with anger and desperation, Tenzin searched the hillsides for the killer, but there was no one to be seen, no one to pursue, no one to punish for snuffing out over half a millennium of learning and wisdom with the taking of a single life. There was only the wind howling through the world's empty spaces, giving voice to his sorrow.

The greatest privilege of luxury was privacy. As much as Niccolò Falco admired the opulence of the Tower Suites in New York's famed Waldorf-Astoria Hotel, what he respected about them was the way voices failed to carry from one room to the next when doors were closed. He had too much regard for his employer to put his ear against the wall for eavesdropping, though he doubted he would hear anything through the hotel's thick walls or doors.

Consigned to an anteroom with four other karcists—none of whom he regarded as his equal—Niccolò was loath to interrupt his employer's business. But the phone call he was about to conclude was one they both had long awaited. The gears of ambition were turning.

"Thank you for calling," Niccolò said to his operative. "The fee for your services will be wired to your account in the morning, as promised."

"It is morning now," said the gruff Pakistani assassin.

"Not here. In New York it is still Thursday night."

"Are you trying to cheat me?"

"Learn how time zones work. And if you slander me again, I'll have a demon rip out your tongue. *Ciao, verme.*" Niccolò hung up the phone and crossed the room to the double doors that segregated him and his fellow magicians from their patrons. Two quick taps on the oaken doors with his knuckles, and then he waited until a voice from the other side bade him, "Come in."

He opened the doors and entered a large parlor. Whereas the anteroom he had shared with his fellow magicians had been comfortable, this chamber was decadent—spacious, richly furnished, and adorned with art. Its broad windows looked out upon the electric splendor of midtown Manhattan—a nightscape of brightly lit high-rises and streets bustling with mad traffic.

Five men sat in the middle of the room, gathered around a circular table of lacquered mahogany resting upon a thick pedestal. All five gentlemen were fashionably dressed. The youngest of them, the Russian, looked to be in his early fifties. The white South African, the fair-haired Argentinian, and the black-bearded Arab all looked to be in their late fifties. Niccolò didn't know any of their true names. He had learned not to ask.

The eldest member of the group was Niccolò's employer. Though he knew the Old Man's name, he had learned through harsh correction not to use it in front of others, even those who, such as the other members of the Commission, seemed likely to know it.

Niccolò approached the table only after he was beckoned by his patron.

As the magician walked to the table, a well-groomed German shepherd lounging at the Old Man's feet stirred and lifted its head. The dog yawned at Niccolò and resumed its repose.

The karcist bent down near the Old Man's shoulder. "Pardon the interruption, *signore.*" The Old Man nodded for Niccolò to continue even as the other billionaires at the table glared, resenting any intrusion upon their grand designs. Averting his eyes from the table's collective reproach, Niccolò whispered, "I just heard from our asset on the subcontinent. It's done."

"Splendid," the Old Man said, his London accent uncharacteristically free of hauteur. "Thank you, Niccolò." With a look he signaled Niccolò to step back from the table but not to leave. As the magician complied, the Old Man stood and smoothed the front of his tailored three-piece suit. "Gentlemen, our plan to remake the world has been set into motion."

His peers met his declaration with looks that ranged from surprise to alarm. First to speak was the Arab, his dark eyes wide with anger. "It's too soon!"

"I agree," said the South African, in his Afrikaans accent.

The Russian, meanwhile, had recovered his composure. "There should have been a vote."

"I concur," said the Argentinian, though his mood was far less sanguine. "An undertaking of this magnitude is best effected by degrees."

The Old Man raised his hands in what he likely intended as a calming gesture. "Please, my friends, don't assume I've acted rashly. Tomorrow's regime change is a matter of necessity, one required to protect our shared investments." He downplayed the magnitude of his gambit with a shrug. "The fact that it sets the stage for an even bolder stroke—one that will advance our long-term global agenda—is a fortuitous happenstance." Behind his bone-white Vandyke beard, he smiled. "One I intend to exploit to its fullest."

The Arab made no secret of his doubts. "A foolish risk. One that could expose us all."

"I have to agree," the Russian said. "A single mistake could lead to disaster."

The South African and the Argentinian overlapped their protests, both of which were so loud and vehement that combined they became unintelligible.

Once more they were brought to silence by the Old Man's raised palm. "Friends. I've long prepared for this. I would not have moved unless I knew my assets were ready and the game tilted in our favor."

"That may well be," the South African said. "But I think it might be best if we adjourn this meeting and go our separate ways until this scheme of yours has run its course."

"I second that motion," the Arab said.

The Argentinian asked, "All in favor?" Four hands shot up—all except the Old Man's. "The motion carries. We stand adjourned."

The other four billionaires pushed back from the table and stood. The

Russian set his hand on the Old Man's shoulder, a fraternal gesture. "You've put us on a dangerous path. Need I suggest how you ought to proceed?"

"If 'twere done when 'tis done, then 'twere well it were done quickly."

The Old Man's invocation of *Macbeth* drew a nod of approval from the Russian, who walked away, followed by the others. The four oligarchs rousted their karcist retainers from the sitting room and then made their collective exit.

The Old Man took a plate of half-consumed duck-liver paté from the meeting table and set it on the floor. His German shepherd wasted no time devouring the fatty treat. The Old Man smiled and scratched the dog's head while it ate, but his voice sounded grim as he told Niccolò, "Look sharp, lad. We're on the clock now." He shot a dark glance at his senior magician. "And the sooner this bloody mess is over, the better."

Naxos wasn't paradise, but it was as close to one as Anja Kernova had ever found. The hilly, wooded Greek isle was one of many scattered across the Aegean Sea—all of them lush, beautiful, and blessed with rich volcanic soil. She and Cade Martin had made Naxos their home for over eight years, since shortly after they had married. Using aliases, they had bought a large house on the hilltop west of Apiranthos and paid for it in cash. None of the locals had ever asked them any questions—not about the sale, the source of their money, or who, exactly, they were.

"That is a good sign," Anja had said to Cade, and he'd agreed.

Transforming the house into their home had taken time. They had filled its large upstairs library with books: grimoires, codices old and new on the art of magick, ephemerides, and reference materials on anatomy, geography, history, the physical sciences, philosophy, and many other topics. At some point Cade had turned his focus to setting up their kitchen and provisioning their pantry, while Anja had seen to the critical task of equipping and securing their conjuring room in the house's basement, adjacent to its wine cellar and cheese cave.

The rest of the house had taken shape by degrees, mostly when neither of them was paying much attention. Their domestic comforts were simple but genuine, their furnishings comfortable if boring to look at. Their bedroom, the guest rooms, and the open main floor all had the feel of a rustic country home. In the afternoon its main room filled with honeyed light filtered through gauzy curtains; in the morning, the aroma of baking bread and fresh Turkish coffee wafted through the entire house, courtesy of the lamiae they had conjured as servants.

Thick woods covered most of the hill outside the house. Anja liked the privacy the trees provided. All the same, Cade had cleared enough of the property around the house to make room for a vegetable garden, a trellis for cultivating grapes, an apiary (for fresh honey as much as for beeswax, which was always needed to make ceremonial candles), and a small bellows-driven forge. Along the north side of the yard was a stand of olive trees Cade had planted a few years earlier. None of them had yet matured to the point of bearing fruit, but Cade remained hopeful; he had grand plans for pressing his own extra-virgin olive oil someday.

It was a nice dream, but Anja wasn't holding her breath waiting for it to come true.

Dawn sunlight speared through the trees as Anja stepped out of the house to check on her newest student's progress. Unlike most of her and Cade's apprentices, who hailed from various distant parts of the world, Melina Volonakis—or Mel, as the couple called her—was a local girl whose academic bona fides had attracted their attention. Though she was only nineteen years old, Mel had impressed them with her knack for ancient languages as well as modern sciences. Open-minded and detail-oriented, she had only one serious shortcoming as a student of magick: she was impatient.

Mel stood at a blade-scarred and weather-beaten wooden table, a few feet from the outdoor forge. With her was Barış Kılıç. As Cade's senior adept he had been made responsible for the early steps of Mel's tutelage. Those had included giving her a small mountain of prerequisite reading, as well as teaching her the vital labor of constructing her own set of karcist's tools. Dressed in a brown suit with a white shirt, accessorized by a bow tie and a fez in matching shades of red, Barış looked comically overdressed next to his farm-girl acolyte.

As Anja approached the pair, she saw that Mel had arranged her implements in her newly cut leather tool roll. Scents of sage, lavender, and consecrated oil lingered in the air, evidence that the young woman's tools had been fumigated and blessed in preparation for ritual work.

Noting Anja's approach, Mel beamed with pride. "I finished them!"

"I see." Anja stepped between Mel and Barış. Inspected each item in Mel's kit. Blessed it with a nod. "Very nice." Anja pushed strands of her long black hair from her face and tucked them behind one ear. To Barış she said, "Show her how to keep them safe until she is ready to strike her first pact." Barış nodded. Anja turned to head back to the house.

Mel lurched into Anja's path, her brown eyes flashing with anger. "What do you mean, *until I'm ready*? My tools are done!"

Looking down at the hotheaded young woman, it was hard for Anja not to feel a kinship with her. Mel's hair was almost identical in color and style to Anja's. A stranger might have mistaken them for cousins since, thanks to a decades-old pact with her Infernal patron ASTAROTH, Anja still looked as if she were in her twenties despite being in her early forties. And Mel's tone—righteous indignation coupled with bitter disappointment—was one that Anja recalled having used with her late mentor, Master Adair Macrae, when he had given her bad news.

Anja did her best to soften her normally brusque manner. "It takes more to be ready than making your tools."

"I've done the reading. I know it by heart, I swear." Mel sounded sincere, but when Anja looked at Barış for confirmation, he averted his eyes and fussed with his bow tie.

Ever the diplomat. Anja hardened her countenance. "What gifts might be obtained through the yoking of MARBAS?"

"The ability to cause and cure diseases, and the talent to change one's form."

So the girl had done a fair bit of reading. Anja's concerns persisted. "When drawing the Grand Kabbalistic Circle, at what point does one begin tracing the inner triangle?"

This time Mel hesitated. Furrowed her brow in concentration. "The north."

"Wrong. East. What rings the base of your candles?"

"Rings of . . . not holly. . . ."

"Crowns of vervain," Anja corrected. "In the method of Honorius, when purifying the operator, what is forbidden on the first day?"

"Red meat," Mel said with undeserved confidence.

"*All* meat and also wine." Anja shook her head. "You have learned much, but you are not ready for the circle. Barış will teach you."

The girl growled in wordless frustration as she turned her back on Anja, and then she stormed away—not toward the trail that led back to her village, but toward the wooded hillside.

Anja called after her, "Mel! Stay out of the forest!"

"To hell with you and your rules!" She quickened her pace.

It was too early in the day for Anja to fight with a petulant teenager. Instead she waited until Mel reached the edge of the tree line, and then she halted the girl by force, using the fearsome invisible hands of BAEL. Caught in midstep, Mel struggled and shouted Greek vulgarities. Anja walked over and stood beside her.

"Be quiet." Anja tightened the demon's hold. This time Mel obeyed. "The rules Cade and I set are for your protection." She pointed down at the dew-covered grass and told Melina, "Look closer. What do you see?"

Mel squinted at the ground. Morning sunlight shimmered in the dew-drops. "You mean that silvery strand?" Anja nodded. Mel continued, "Is that spider's silk?"

"A trip wire." With a wave of her hand, Anja removed the camouflage that hid a military explosive nestled against the base of a tree. "For a claymore mine. Cade put them in, all through the woods. This one would have torn you in half."

The color drained from Mel's face. "There are mines out here?"

"We hide our defenses for a reason. Make rules the same way."

Mel avoided Anja's stare of reproach. "Forgive me."

"Read more Honorius. Barış will show you which books." Anja pointed at the house.

Chastened, the teen plodded back to the house and went inside without lifting her eyes from the ground. Anja followed a few paces behind her. She paused at the back door as Barış opined, "Ah, the rash whims of youth. That might have been me, not so long ago."

She had no use for his wistful nostalgia. "Do not pity her, Barış. Push harder."

"I will. But take care you don't break her spirit. She admires you."

"Does she?" Anja went back inside the house. "Then she is a poor judge of character."

⌘

Mingled aromas of coffee and sizzling bacon roused Briet Segfrunsdóttir from a troubled sleep. She squinted at the clock on her end table. It read half past nine, which explained the golden blaze of sunlight flooding through her bedroom window. She rolled to her left, away from the light. Her head came to rest on a sprawl of her own coppery red hair, which covered her pillows and those next to hers. The rest of the king-sized bed was empty. Her lovers Alton and Hyun had gotten up an hour ago and now were downstairs, pre-paring breakfast.

Briet pushed the bedcovers from her naked body. She stood. Stretched. Yawned. Scratched her armpits—which she refused to shave, no matter how earnestly Alton pleaded with her to do so. Blinking away the last vestiges of slumber, she plodded into the master bath and donned her terry cloth bathrobe. She tried not to study her reflection while she washed her face; one of the demons she kept yoked tended to express its displeasure by afflicting her with an obsessive-compulsive desire to count her own freckles. It was the sort of thing one might dismiss as harmless until it resulted in spending an entire day trapped in front of a mirror.

Passing back through her bedroom Briet tucked her feet into a warm pair of slippers, and then she made her way downstairs. The wall beside the staircase was packed with framed photographs. A few were individual portraits of the three lovers, but most were mementos of their travels: trips to Spain, Australia, Easter Island, Stonehenge. . . . Fond memories all.

A Miles Davis record was playing on the hi-fi in the living room. Most days Briet would have protested that jazz had no place in her home until after noon, but she had risen today with a good feeling. She had wrangled the day off—a minor miracle not just because it was a Friday, but because she had already arranged to be off the entire following week for the Thanksgiving holiday. At most government jobs, such largesse was typical, but not in the Department of Defense, and it was almost unheard of within the Occult Defense Program.

For once it really is good to be queen.

She found her paramours in the kitchen, both of them still in their own bathrobes, pajamas, and slippers. Alton, tall and balding, stood at the stove and flipped eggs in the cast-iron skillet with a wide spatula and nimble turns of his wrist. A plate of cooked bacon strips was on the Formica countertop to his right, and Briet's nose told her the eggs were sizzling in the rendered bacon fat. Hyun sat at the small table in the breakfast nook, drowning a tray of fresh-baked cinnamon rolls in icing. She lit up at the sight of Briet. "Morning!"

"Good morning." Briet leaned down and gave Hyun a kiss. "Hmm." Licking her own lips, she realized Hyun had been sampling the icing. "Lemon sugar."

Hyun gave Briet's ass a playful spank.

Briet crossed the kitchen to greet Alton. She embraced him from behind, taking care not to get in the way of his cooking. "G'morning." She planted a kiss on the side of his neck. "Breakfast smells wonderful."

"I hope you brought an appetite," Alton said.

"I have. And I'm also pretty hungry." She put on a salacious smirk to help him unravel her double entendre. As soon as he mirrored her look, she let go of his waist and walked back to the table, making sure to put an extra bit of motion into her hips to hold his attention. She slid into the chair across the corner from Hyun, picked up a spoon, and started helping her dole out icing onto the cinnamon rolls. "How about you? Feel like spending the day in bed?"

The svelte Korean woman pretended to need to think it over. "Tempting. Let me check with my husband." She shot a look at Alton, who feigned a serious nod of assent. She turned back toward Briet and grinned. "He says . . . okay."

Even though Alton and Hyun had been married for several years now—and both had been romantically entwined with Briet for nearly a decade—Hyun still delighted in referring to him as her husband. The nuptials had made perfect sense to all three of them. Alton had married Hyun as much for love as to secure her citizenship after her emigration from South Korea. Because he was a natural-born American citizen, he had been able to make her an American by marriage. And though Briet had been born in Iceland, she had been granted American citizenship as one of the conditions of her recruitment after World War II, during Operation Paperclip.

For the sake of discretion, the deed to their Georgetown brownstone and its phone line were now in Alton and Hyun's names, and officially Briet was their tenant. That arrangement served to safeguard Briet's privacy while deflecting questions from the suspicious and intolerant.

Hyun swirled sugary goop on the last bare cinnamon roll, and then she scooped a dollop of leftover icing onto the tip of her pinky finger. "Seems a shame to throw it away."

Briet stroked her fingertips up Hyun's forearm, caressed the back of her hand, and then guided it to her mouth. She flicked her tongue over Hyun's icing-topped fingertip and licked it clean of the tart-sweet lemon sugar. "I wouldn't call that a waste."

They stared into each other's eyes as Hyun dipped her pinky once more into the icing, and then held it in front of Briet's lips. "Do that again."

The ghost of a smile teased the corners of Briet's mouth, and then she put Hyun's fingertip between her lips. The finger emerged bare and glistening. "Still delicious."

A mischievous twinkle in Hyun's eyes. She dipped her index finger into the icing, and then she let her hand slip under the table . . . inside her robe . . . between her thighs. . . .

The phone rang, loud and shrill.

Briet glared over her shoulder toward the living room, wherein resided their home's only telephone. "Fucking hell. It's my *day off*."

It rang again, and her frustration turned to fury. She stood.

"Don't answer it," Hyun said, but by then it was too late.

Briet left the kitchen and stormed through the living room to the phone. She plucked the handset from the cradle on the start of its fourth ring. "What?"

"Bree, is that any way to answer a phone?" As she'd both expected and feared, the voice on the other end of the line belonged to Frank Cioffi, her colleague from the ODP. His Brooklyn accent turned itself up a notch when he was annoyed, which was most of the time. *"We got a situation. I need you to come in, pronto."*

She daydreamed about choking the fat bastard with one of his own ugly ties. "What kind of situation, Frank?"

"The executive kind. One of your adepts ran a routine divination, came up with bad moons rising every which fuckin' way but loose."

"So? Log them and send them to review."

"We did. The analysts think it spells trouble for Kennedy in Dallas today. I need you to come in and double-check all of POTUS's magickal defenses."

"No. I'm on vacation."

"I don't care if you're on the fucking moon. Get your ass in here."

"No. It's a waste of time, and you know it. Between us and the Catholic Church, there are so many layers of defense around Kennedy, the Devil himself couldn't touch him. But if those jerkoffs upstairs are really that worried, call the Secret Service and tell Kennedy's protection detail to pull their thumbs from their asses and start doing their jobs. As for you? If I hear your voice again before December second, I'll make sure you spend the rest of your short, miserable life with a plague of boils on your shriveled cock. *Good-bye*, Frank."

Before he could waylay her with another retort, Briet slammed the phone's handset back onto its cradle—and then, for good measure, she yanked its black wire clean out of the wall and stuffed the whole broken mess into the bottom compartment of the hutch.

She turned to see Alton and Hyun watching her from the kitchen doorway. He lifted one eyebrow, a mild show of reproof. "Are you sure that was
wise?"

"I'll have it fixed on Monday."

"Not the phone. Spouting off to your boss."

"Frank is *not* my boss."

Hyun sounded more concerned than Alton did. "What will happen when
you go back?"

"Oh, I'm sure I'll have hell to pay. But that's a problem for *after* my vacation." She crossed the room and stood in front of the couple. "Right now, let's
go have breakfast. And then"—she smiled and slipped her left hand under
Alton's robe to rub his cock, her right inside Hyun's to cup her quim—"let's
take the rest of the day for *dessert.*"

All his life, Cade had loved libraries. When he was a child in Connecticut,
his mother had often left him at the town library on weekend afternoons
while she tended to household errands. Under the watchful eyes of the li-
brarians, Cade had passed many happy hours sequestered in the stacks, poring through illustrated books of fables and mythology. Even now, decades
later, he still took comfort and delight in the scents of leather bindings and
old paper. There were few sensations he loved better than the texture of high-
quality pages under his fingertips, and most of his favorite memories of
youth involved the words of Poe, Doyle, Wells, or Shakespeare.

His favorite cathedral of knowledge was Oxford's renowned Bodleian Library. Massive and ancient, the Bodleian possessed an endowment of books
greater than any one person could reasonably digest in a lifetime. Even now,
with the promise of seven hundred years of life from his Infernal patron Lucifuge Rofocale, Cade doubted he could make the time to read every work
in the Bodleian's ever-growing catalog. It had been years since he'd last set
foot in that library. He missed it, as well as the grounds of Exeter College and
the rest of Oxford. The days he had spent there, studying with his best friend
Miles Franklin, had been some of the happiest of his life.

Then had come the Second World War, and the murders of his parents
by Nazi sorcerers whose true target had been Cade himself. After losing his
mother and father in the sinking of the passenger ship *Athenia,* Cade had

been recruited into the study of magick with the Midnight Front and tasked with helping the Allies wage a secret war against the magicians of the Third Reich. Only now, nearly twenty years after the end of the war, was Cade starting to feel as if it were truly behind him. He credited much of his spiritual recuperation to the newest library in his life—the one he and Anja had built together, here in their house on Naxos.

It wasn't large; in fact, it was rather small, just a single room with floor-to-ceiling shelves along all the walls. In the middle of the room was a long, broad reading table of dark oak, surrounded by eight matching chairs. Though Anja had favored a more rustic style of furnishing, Cade had insisted on buying chairs with thick padding and leather upholstery on their seats, armrests, and backs. Considering all the hours he had spent in this room over the past seven years—including his current binge of uninterrupted work, which was now at the end of its second day without sleep—he was glad he had insisted upon those extra comforts.

He sat at the end of the table farthest from the room's lone door, with his back to the window, which faced north into the yard below. Indirect light through its open curtains brightened the room without throwing harsh shadows—ideal conditions for the work he was doing: transcribing the results of his latest magickal experiments and interrogations of spirits Infernal into the third volume of his new grimoire-in-progress. He had not chosen a name for the work yet, though he understood its long-term purpose well enough.

It's too early. You've only just started. Plastering some grandiose name on it would be premature. The first two volumes contained his accounts of his spiritual journey to Heaven and Hell, and his discovery that no human souls existed in either; and a documentation of the Mystery of the Dead God, which he had discovered while helping Anja steal back the Iron Codex from the Vatican's secret archives. His new volume was dedicated to recording the results of his original magickal experiments. It did not yet merit a title.

It did, however, demand vigilance and caution.

The library's door opened. Cade closed the large, leather-bound book and opened another on top of it as camouflage. He relaxed when he saw that his visitor was Anja, who had come bearing a fresh cup of tea.

She smiled as she set down the tea in front of him. "Mel finished her tools."

He was pleased to hear that. "Good. How soon can we get her a patron?"

"Spring." She intuited Cade's follow-up question. "She needs to do more reading."

"I'm guessing that's why she ran toward the trees a few hours ago?"

A soft sigh telegraphed Anja's disappointment. "She is smart, but not patient."

Cade sipped the lemon-and-honey tea. "Sounds like me at that age."

Anja flashed a knowing smile. "I remember." Her mood turned business-like as she pulled out the chair across the corner on Cade's right and sat down. "I might have a new candidate for training in Sweden. She is one year from her degree at Stockholm University."

"Another adept?" Cade signaled his reluctance with a frown. "I can barely keep track of the ones we have now. Last I counted, we were up to . . . what? Nineteen?"

"Eighteen," Anja corrected.

"Still a lot." He covered his deliberative pause by stroking his bearded chin. "Maybe more than we can handle."

"Not only do you look like Adair"—Anja flicked her index finger through Cade's shoulder-length, shaggy brown hair—"you sound like him, too." She pulled a sheet of paper from one of her back pockets, unfolded it, and spread it flat on the table. On it was written a list of names. "Some you call apprentices are ready to be karcists."

"Such as?"

"Barış. He has studied magick with you for fifteen years. He is ready."

"Maybe. He's smart but kind of twitchy. Who else?"

"All of your students with ten or more years of training. Gathii, Viên, Adelita, Garrett—"

"I know their names."

"Do you? Tell me the other five."

She had called his bluff, but he babbled on. "Um . . . Lila. And . . . Fareed?"

"Who else?"

"I give up. Bottom-line it for me. What does that get us?"

"It cuts our list of students in half." She turned the list so that Cade could read it and pushed it across the table to him. "And makes a new list—of allies."

"Okay. You might have a point: maybe I've held my students too close. And a few of them might be ready to fly solo. But it's a big step, cutting them loose."

"It is time."

"So you say. But what if—"

Her question was cut off by a muffled voice from an inside pocket of Cade's bomber jacket, which was draped over the back of the empty chair to his left. "Hold that thought." He retrieved from his jacket a palm-sized steel mirror engraved on its back with the sigil of HAEL. When Cade looked at what should have been his reflection, he saw instead the visage of Brother Tenzin, a Buddhist monk he and Anja had met nearly a decade earlier when she had trained with Master Khalîl at the Key Gompa monastery. The Tibetan man looked distraught, and his voice shook and broke with emotion. *"Cade? Is that you?"*

"Yes, Tenzin. It's me. Are you all right?"

"Master Khalîl is dead. Murdered."

Dread cast a pall over Anja's face, and Cade felt his own expression go slack with disbelief. "What happened, Tenzin? We need details."

"At dawn." Tenzin stared downward, as if he was too ashamed to look Cade or Anja in the eye. *"A sniper. One shot broke the temple's wards. The next two struck down the master."*

The notion chilled Cade's blood. He shot an anxious glance at Anja. "What could do that? I've never heard of anything like it."

"Nor have I," she said, her voice a horrified whisper.

"There is more. Our friends in other orders say this is happening all over the world. Masters and adepts of the Art are being slain by snipers. And not just Goetic karcists. Wūshī of the ancient Chinese way, Arctic shamans, doctors of the African Rites—"

"A purge," Anja said. "Just like Stalin."

"Or Hitler." Cade felt sick to his stomach. "Tenzin, who's doing this?"

"No one knows. But the murders seem to follow the sun. As the new day dawns, more blood is spilled. Take care, Brother Cade. Protect your soul and those you love. Namaste." He terminated the magickal connection between their mirrors with the command *"Velarium."*

A stunned silence reigned over Cade and Anja for several seconds.

Her anger began to rise, reddening the Y-shaped scar on her left cheek. Its branches connected her lower eyelid, the tragus of her ear, and the corner of her mouth. Inflicted by a demonic weapon when she had been barely a teen, the scar could not be healed by magick, only hidden—and Anja rarely if ever chose to conceal it. She wore it instead as a badge of honor.

When Anja's expression turned hard and cold, she was ready for war.

"Cade, our students need us. Bring them all here."

He nodded. "Safety in numbers." He tore the list of adepts in half and gave one side to her. "You find this group, I'll hail the rest. We don't stop until every one of them is safe."

A glance at his watch told Secret Service Agent Clark Warden the president's motorcade was a few minutes behind schedule. It was 12:29 P.M. as the lead car approached the intersection of Elm and North Houston streets in downtown Dallas, en route to Kennedy's speech at the Trade Mart. The joyful noise from the crowds that lined the parade route was deafening.

Jogging alongside the slow-moving vehicles, Clark stole a look at the digital clock mounted atop the corner of the Texas Book Depository, dead ahead. It displayed the current temperature as 67 degrees Fahrenheit. The moderate weather, coupled with a light breeze that fluttered onlookers' pennants and rustled the still-green leaves on their boughs, made for nearly ideal conditions: neither too hot to make it hard to keep pace with the motorcade nor so cold as to require the agents to wear cumbersome layers over their trademark dark suits.

It had rained in Dallas earlier that morning, but the storm was well past and had left the city looking as if it had just been rinsed clean in preparation for the president's arrival.

The lead car, an unmarked police vehicle driven by the city's chief of police, and which served as a rolling command center for the motorcade, crossed the intersection and headed for the Stemmons Freeway on-ramp, several car-lengths ahead of the president's black Lincoln convertible limousine. In a few moments Clark and the other agents currently on foot would need to get back inside their assigned vehicles, before they accelerated onto the highway.

In the limousine, President John F. Kennedy sat in the rear passenger seat, his dark gray suit a stark contrast to the pink dress and matching pillbox hat of his wife, Jacqueline. The First Couple's seats had been raised a few inches to make them more visible to the public as they drove past. Sitting in front of them, in the middle jump seats, were Texas governor John Connally, on the right, and his wife, Nellie, on the left.

The exposed quality of the convertible had been cited by several members of the president's protection detail as cause for concern, but President Kennedy had insisted it would be a shame to squander a day with such postcard-perfect weather. Wanting to feel the wind and the sun on his face, he had decided they would make the drive from Love Field to the Trade Mart without the car's protective Plexiglas dome. Objections overruled, the agents had complied.

The quartet of Dallas Police motorcycle officers that flanked the limo held their formation as they crossed the intersection toward the Stemmons Freeway ramp. Clark looked over his shoulder, expecting to be ushered back inside his assigned transport.

A crack echoed off of the office buildings, and Clark became a hunter seeking its source.

Untrained ears might have mistaken that sound for a firecracker or a car's backfire. But Clark and the other agents knew a rifle's report when they heard one.

A strange electricity in the air prickled the back of Clark's neck. He engaged the magickal vision of VELAR, casting the world around him into a blue monochrome. His enhanced awareness led to panic: the multiple spheres of magickal defense that should have surrounded the president's limousine had all vanished at once—a calamity he'd thought impossible.

But that would mean—

Another sharp crack of rifle fire.

Blood sprayed from the president's throat. He clutched his wound with both hands as Governor Connally slumped sideways, also hit. The First Lady reached for her husband as Connally turned toward the president. Frightened voices filled Dealey Plaza.

Roy Kellerman, the Secret Service agent in the limo's front passenger seat, looked back to see what had happened. Governor Connally leaned into his wife's arms, much as the president had come to rest in Jackie's shocked embrace.

Too late, Clark's training—from both the Secret Service and the top-secret magickal defense group based beneath the Pentagon—kicked in. He marshaled the talent of his yoked spirit XOLUS to raise a new invisible shield of protection around the president's car—

A third rifle shot exploded Clark's nascent shield as if it were a soap bubble.

Kennedy's head erupted in a crimson spray. Bone shrapnel and bloodied hunks of brain spattered the limousine's interior, freckling the First Lady as well as Governor Connally and his wife. Amid the carnage, Clark glimpsed falling bouquets of red and yellow roses as the Connallys ducked low in their seats. To his confusion and alarm, Mrs. Kennedy climbed out of her seat to crawl awkwardly onto the long trunk of the limousine.

At the same time, Secret Service Agent Clint Hill tried to clamber onto of the back of the limo. Kellerman ordered the driver, Agent Bill Greer, to rush the president to the nearest hospital. The car sped up. Hill lost his footing, but on his second attempt he climbed over the limo's trunk and guided Mrs. Kennedy back into her seat beside the president.

Feeling lost and overwhelmed, Clark looked back, scanned the crowd and all of Dealey Plaza with the Sight, hoping to flush out the assassin. There was nothing but mayhem on the ground—people running for cover, fleeing the gunfire and bloodshed—despite the best efforts of the Dallas Police Department and the Secret Service to restore calm and secure witnesses.

The shooter wouldn't have been in the crowd. He'd have sought a clear vantage—

His eyes turned upward, toward the Texas Book Depository.

An open window on the sixth floor, at the corner above the intersection.

Pushing his perception past the building's exterior, Clark spied the shooter. It was too dark for Clark to discern the man's features, but the shooter was lean of build and scrambling to abandon his sniper's nest. Within seconds, he had retreated into the building's core, out of sight.

Voices crackled over radios. The agent in the motorcade's lead car ordered Vice President Johnson's vehicle diverted off the parade route and back to Love Field, where Air Force One stood waiting. All around Clark Warden was chaos. His only chance to prevent the assassin's escape was to get to the Book Depository and order it locked down before—

Someone seized Clark's arm and whipped him around.

It was another agent, Daniel Jurow. "Hey! We need to help Dallas PD round up anyone who saw anything. That means anybody who was standing curbside."

Clark pulled his arm free and pointed at the Book Depository. "We need to lock down *that* building, *now*. I think the shooter hit us from the sixth-floor, corner window."

Jurow squinted at the Book Depository. "From all the way up there? Are you nuts?" He waved off Clark's plea. "Orders from the secretary. Witness roundup."

Frustration welled up inside Clark, like a fireball raging to burst from his chest. He couldn't explain how he knew the president's killer was still inside that building without violating operational security or exposing the existence of the U.S. Occult Defense Program. He also had no means of passing along his intel in time for anyone else to act upon it. In the interest of preserving his cover, he had to follow his orders in hand and let the assassin escape.

He purged the rage from his countenance and followed Jurow toward the nearest cluster of civilians, all of whom Clark was certain couldn't be less helpful had they all been born blind, deaf, and mute.

Less than an hour later, he heard the news over the radio.

President Kennedy was dead.

Before the day was over, someone would burn for this. Clark Warden promised himself that he would do whatever was necessary to make sure that someone was not *him*.

Outside the office's window, all was calm. The vast chasm of the Silo was empty and quiet. The sensors embedded in its five walls were dark, inactive; its large pentagonal conjuring stage stood empty at the end of a long and precariously narrow widow's walk, its braziers unlit and cold.

Hundreds of feet above the hidden black-magick laboratory and its multiple levels of command and control systems, the Pentagon was in a state of high alert, very nearly on a war footing in the aftermath of the president's assassination. Everyone had their own pet theory. Some blamed the Communists for the killing. Others pointed a finger at the Cubans, or at the Mafia. A few of the more fringe-affiliated types whispered this was all a CIA plot, long in the making and set into motion as a response to Kennedy's handling of the Cuban Missile Crisis.

Frank Cioffi didn't give a flying fuck about any of that. He had bigger problems. For starters, he was the operations supervisor of the Occult Defense Program, the most jealously guarded secret of the American intelligence community, and his principal directive, his most sacred duty, had been to protect the elected head of state of the United States government from being shot on a public street like a rabid dog. The one task with which he had been charged, above all others, and he and his team had just fucked it up. Royally.

So it didn't matter that his face wasn't shaved, that his hair was greasy and unwashed, or that his clothes smelled like he had been wearing them for three days straight. What mattered right now was that President John Fitzgerald Kennedy was dead, and a lot of very powerful people expected Frank Cioffi to explain how the fuck that was possible, after all the money they had spent on his program and all the promises he had made, guaranteeing such a tragedy could never come to pass, not on his watch. Except it had. And there was a fucking film of it. A strip of 8 mm silent footage shot by some civilian named Zapruder.

A fucking film. Jesus motherfucking Christ.

Frank had reviewed all the tapes. Reread all the transcripts. He was at a loss. None of it made sense. He and his team, led by Briet Segfrunsdóttir, had taken every precaution possible. They had warded the president not once but six times, with the sigils of each of the six great ministers of Hell. In addition, a brotherhood of White magicians working on behalf of the Roman Catholic Church had blessed Kennedy with angelic defenses, a special effort they had made in recognition of his status as America's first Catholic president.

And none of it had mattered. All those defenses, and the president's brains had ended up in the First Lady's goddamned lap. Pacing in his office, unable to make sense of it, all Frank could do was berate himself silently. *What a fucking fiasco.*

At 3:00 P.M. sharp came a knock on his office door. He faced it. "Come in."

The door swung inward. A brawny U.S. Marine sergeant and a Marine corporal escorted Briet into Frank's office, whose décor eschewed any trace of sentimentality. She looked irate and mussed, likely as a consequence of having been rousted from her home as soon as the president's murder had been confirmed by the Secret Service. To her Frank said, "Take a seat." He pointed at the marines. "Outside."

The marines left the office, and the sergeant closed the door. Briet, as usual, ignored Frank's directions and remained standing. Alone in the middle of the office, his red-haired associate in a black trench coat was like a volcanic island waiting to erupt. "Spare me the lecture, Frank, I know what happened. What are we doing about it?"

"Until we figure out how it happened? Nothing."

She began pacing in front of his desk. He had never seen her do that before. "What do we know? Do we have the bullets that hit Kennedy? The weapon that fired them?"

Frank sighed and looked out his office window, down at the fifty-foot-deep pool of black water that filled the bottom of the Silo. "You'll have to ask the FBI."

Briet pushed her hair back from her angular face. Frank could almost see the gears of her imagination turning behind her ice-blue eyes. "We need the evidence, Frank. The bullets, the weapon, all of it. And I need to see the body, as soon as possible."

"That might present more than a few hurdles."

She stopped pacing and skewered him with a look. "Why?"

"Because the president's magickal defenses were breached, and no one knows how." He felt his courage deflate as he confessed, "But right now the DOD wants to blame you."

"Oh, I'll just fucking *bet* they do."

"Can you blame them? After your little stunt this morning—"

"Be serious. If I were a part of this, I would've been here."

Frank rolled his eyes. "I can't imagine that would've helped your case."

She resumed her pacing. "I swear to you, Frank, I don't know who did this. But what bothers me more is I don't know *how* they did it."

"Well, you'd better come up with a theory, and fast." Frank tilted his head toward the door. "Before those apes outside throw your ass in Leavenworth."

Her eyes widened. "What are you saying, Frank?" She looked toward the door, then back at him. "Are you telling me they have orders to arrest me?"

"Unless you tell me something useful? Yeah."

At once her back straightened, making her look an inch taller, and her fiery stare took on a hard and icy quality. "I am *not* taking the fall for this."

"Then you'd better give the brass a better suspect right fucking now."

She seethed. "What if I can't?"

"Then you'd better get used to peeling potatoes and wearing striped pajamas."

A grin both sardonic and bitter twisted her features. "The fuck I will." She reached inside her trench coat and pulled out her wand.

"Briet!" Frank raised his hands. "You know that won't work in here!"

"Why? Because of the anti-magick defenses? I *made* them, Frank."

"Dammit, be reasonable. Once the alarm sounds, how far do you think you'll get? There are probably a hundred marines between you and the exit. You're one of the best karcists in the world, but even you can't fight those kind of odds."

"I know." She cracked a sly smile. "Good thing I didn't listen when they told me to stop yoking spirits." She flourished her wand in a dramatic spiral motion, and before Frank could call out, Briet was encircled by a vortex of pale blue flames that filled his office with a blast of freezing-cold air that reeked of sulfur and ashes.

When the flames abated, Briet was gone but the demonic stench lingered.

Just as Frank had long feared, Briet had concealed a weakness in the Silo's magickal defenses—or, as their computer engineers might have called it, a "trapdoor."

Frank sighed and slumped into his chair. Briet's latest act of defiance— just one in a long chain of such transgressions—was not going to end well, for either of them.

As for what he would tell the marines outside his door . . . ?

He opened his desk's bottom drawer, pulled out a doubles glass and a bottle of Glenlivet, and poured himself three fingers of the golden whisky.

One fucking problem at a time.

"If you can't answer my question," Cardinal Timo Moretti demanded, "who can?"

Father Bernardo D'Odorico, who had just observed his seventieth birthday with solemn gratitude, felt too old to tolerate such petulance, even from his so-called superiors within the Roman Catholic Church. He regarded Cardinal Moretti with a slack expression. "With all respect, Your Eminence, I should think the only person who could answer your query with any certainty would be the one who engineered this foul deed."

It seemed clear to him the cardinal was doing his best not to pace inside D'Odorico's cramped office at the Monte Paterno sanctuary. Consequently, Moretti turned in small circles, a behavior that only amplified his anxiety. "I was told you and your brothers were the Church's preeminent scholars of Transcendental magick."

"And so we are. But we are far from omniscient, Your Eminence."

Moretti halted in front of the director's nearest bookcase. The fiftyish cardinal let his fingertips brush across the spines of several tomes of theology, demonology, and ancient ritual. His black cassock and its scarlet accoutrements, including his eggplant-colored zucchetto, or skullcap, seemed out of place amid the rustic simplicity of D'Odorico's office, with its plain, rough-hewn wooden furniture and shelves, and its weathered floor of hand-cut planks. "No bullet should have been able to breach our defenses on Kennedy," he said at last. "He was protected by angels of the Lord Our God." There were tears of rage in his eyes. "How could this have happened, D'Odorico? Who could have done it?"

There was so much anguish loaded into that question, so much pain, so much regret. . . . In the face of it, Father D'Odorico was uncertain how to respond. He wanted to offer his friend Timo something that would sound like assurance, like comfort . . . but his superior, the appointed head of the Pauline Synod, had come to him for an explanation, not for solace.

"Forgive us, Cardinal. My brothers and I blessed President Kennedy with every defense at our command. Until today, we believed there was no power in the Goetic Art that could touch him." D'Odorico bowed his tonsured head in shame. "But the Church has tied our hands."

That admission made Moretti turn away from the shelves of books to fix D'Odorico with a stare. "Tied your hands? Explain, Father."

The cardinal's accusatory glare was too much for D'Odorico to bear. He turned toward his office's window and gazed out at the snowcapped Dolomites instead. "I'm sure you know, Eminence, better than most, the restrictions under which we conduct our research. Not only does the Covenant forbid our interference in the experiments of our dark peers, the Church itself bars us from dealing with the Fallen, even for the sake of pure research."

"I hope you aren't insinuating that Satan and his ilk should be seen as fonts of truth."

"Absolutely not, Your Eminence." D'Odorico had to choose his next words with the utmost caution. "But interrogating agents of the Adversary, when done with great care and holy guidance, can glean insights into Hell's schemes and methods—knowledge that can be used to thwart the Devil's plans against God's creation." Adopting an air of timid humility, he added, "Alas, we have been denied this insight for many decades. And so the enemy has plotted against us in the dark, beyond our perception."

Moretti clamped a pale hand over his mouth. He pulled his hand down over his bearded chin, smoothing the salt-and-pepper whiskers, and then he sighed. "Is that what you expect me to tell the Holy Father? That the blame for this tragedy rests with those who negotiated the truce that protects you and your brothers from becoming pawns of the Deceiver?"

"Of course not, Eminence. Blame for this atrocity lies with he who pulled the trigger, and with any who aided or abetted his crime. But if I and mine are to be held to account for not having foreseen this crime, or for having failed to prevent an attack unlike any other in history, then I consider it my duty to explain why such accusations are unwarranted."

The cardinal rebuffed D'Odorico with a restrained headshake. "I fear that will not be enough to stem the tide of anger currently rising inside the Holy See."

"But it's the truth."

"Since when has truth ever prevailed over emotion?" A deep frown added ravines to Moretti's well-creased forehead. "If I return to Rome without an explanation—or, better, a plan of action—the Pope will replace me with someone more inclined to produce results at any cost." His affect turned from one of rebuke to one of desperation. "Is there no one to whom you could turn for insight? Anyone who might be able to explicate this tragedy?"

D'Odorico paused. He walked to his desk and sat down. Steepled his fingers and let his face become a mask of grave contemplation. "There is one man I know of. One who knows our ways and those of the enemy. Though I doubt he had any foreknowledge of this crime, if anyone were able to unravel its workings, it would be him."

"Then why have you not already contacted him?"

"Because the Church forbade me and the brothers of my order from having any dealings with him nearly a decade ago. To be quite frank, none of us have any idea where he is or how to reach him." He cocked one silvery eyebrow and confronted the cardinal with his unflinching stare. "If you wish me to defy a papal order to seek out this man and his counsel, I shall require your personal guarantee of absolution, as well as your promise that my entire order shall enjoy the Church's patience and its utmost latitude."

Moretti narrowed his eyes. "Bring me answers and you'll enjoy every indulgence. Fail me and you'll dine on your defeat like a sinner condemned to sup on wormwood."

4

For reasons neither Cade nor Anja could explain, their marriage seemed to have evolved over the past several years for the purpose of conserving emotional chaos. This manifested itself in the phenomenon that whenever one of them was agitated, the other felt compelled to maintain a façade of calm. It was as if they understood on a cellular level that they could not survive if both of them lost their mental equilibrium at the same time. Consequently, the more the failure of their apprentices to answer Cade's mirror hails stoked his panic, the calmer Anja became.

"Where the fuck are they?" He paced beside the library table. "Why don't they answer?"

"Breathe," Anja said. "Seven are safe."

"And eleven are missing." He stopped. Pressed his hands over his face. Pushed his fingers through his long, sweat-matted brown hair. "This is taking too long."

His anxiety had long since passed being merely tiresome to Anja. "People sleep. They go places where they cannot be hailed by mirror without suspicion."

"I know, I know. It's always the middle of the night somewhere." He shot a desperate glance at the large freestanding oval mirror in the corner of the room opposite the window, to the left of the library's only door. "But what if they can't answer? Or they're hurt? Or captured?"

"Then they know what to do." She used the hand of BAEL to push a chair into place behind Cade, and to then plant Cade onto it. "As do you."

Forced to sit and be still, Cade stewed. From one pocket he pulled a flat book of rolling papers, and from another he produced a small leather pouch filled with Afghan cannabis he had acquired a few months earlier, on his most recent excursion from Naxos. "This is insane." He took out one sheet of rolling paper and cradled it in his left palm. With his right hand he filled the sheet with dried herb from the pouch. "Half our students are out there, maybe being hunted by lunatics who can shoot through magick shields, but I'm supposed to sit here and pretend to be cool." He spread the leaves on the sheet and then he rolled it, leaving a narrow edge of the paper exposed; that he moistened with the tip of his tongue before pressing it against the lumpy cigarette, to which it adhered. Then he tucked the joint between his lips and lit it with a snap of his fingers and the aid of a fire spirit. After a long drag that brightened the tip of the joint, Cade exhaled. "I don't care what anybody says." He held up the joint. "*This* isn't what's making me paranoid. I already have the rest of the world for that."

He was deep into his next toke when the library's reflection faded from the large oval mirror in the corner. The image was replaced by a churn of cobalt-blue clouds lit from within by flashes of violet light. Soft echoes of thunder rolled from somewhere far beyond the mirror's wooden frame—and then its surface rippled, like that of a pond disturbed by a thrown pebble. The image of the roiling vapors distorted and lost all cohesion.

A twist of smoke emerged from the mirror into the library. The cloud coalesced into the sun-browned form of Leyton Ferro. The young man from Rio de Janeiro was dressed in tight beige pants, beach sandals, and a pastel-peach linen shirt half open to reveal his smooth chest. Since the last time Cade had seen the man, he had shorn his head bare and shaved his mustache. He flashed a grin of white but uneven teeth at Cade and Anja. There was mischief in his eyes and a mocking lilt in his voice: "You summoned me, O great ones?"

For once, Cade didn't let himself be baited. He lifted his chin at Leyton. "I see you finally cut those long black tresses you loved so much."

"You said to cut them, Master. So I did." Leyton turned sheepish as Anja skewered him with a look of incredulity. ". . . after a beast named SALAGOG nearly pulled me out of the circle."

"We warned you," Anja said. "Never give a demon something long to grab."

"Good thing I always cover my cock." He gave Cade a curious look. "How do you and Anja manage with such long hair?"

"What, in the circle? She tucks hers up into her miter."

"And you . . . ?"

"Made such an example of the last demon that touched my hair that none has ever dared to try again since." Cade cut to business. "Did you bring your tools and grimoire?"

"They're with my porter demon." Leyton's expression shifted from surprised to concerned. "What's happening? Something's wrong, isn't it?"

Before Cade or Anja could answer, another spiral of smoke, this one lavender-colored, snaked out of the large oval mirror.

Cade taught each of his students a trick he had learned years earlier: how to transform oneself into smoke so that one could pass through a small handheld magick mirror and emerge from another. Before he had devised his workaround, mirror jaunts had depended upon the availability of man-sized (or larger) mirrors at both the origin and the destination. Now it was possible for anyone who knew the trick to transit great distances using small mirrors.

A potentially troublesome catch was that after a transit, one's mirror was left behind, which meant dispatching a porter demon to retrieve it. Most of the time that constituted only a petty annoyance. But sometimes, in a crisis, an abandoned mirror was captured or destroyed. Because it took a year for Hell to replace one handheld enchanted mirror, and seven years or more to craft larger ones, the loss of even a single looking glass could piss Cade off for days.

The misty ghost in front of the mirror solidified into Yasmin Elachi. The twentysomething woman's large brown eyes, gentle features, and curvaceous figure gave her the appearance of an innocent, but she was no naïf. Yasmin possessed a keen intellect and hard-earned magickal skills, and as a woman who had learned to survive amid the urban chaos that reigned in the contested regions of the fledgling state of Israel, she was street-savvy, as well.

Her tonsorial concession to the Goetic Art, a buzz cut of her black hair, coupled with her military-surplus fatigues, gave her the aspect of a soldier. She stepped away from the mirror. "Sorry about the delay. Took me a while to get clear." She rested her hand on the grip of her holstered semiautomatic pistol, and then she clocked the mood in the room, just as Leyton had moments earlier. "Something's fucked, right? Tell me. What's fucked?"

"Later," Cade said, "once everyone's here." To Anja he added, "Check them off the list." Then he faced Leyton and Yasmin. "Were either of you followed? Did anyone search your homes?" The apprentices shook their heads *no*. Cade let the tension ebb from his hunched shoulders. "Okay, good. But stay sharp."

The mirror's face faded once more. This time it filled with clouds of gold

and vermilion. From the luminous swirling vapors shot a jet of eerily coher-
ent and nimble green smoke. It coiled toward the floor as it exited the large
oval mirror. Upon striking the floor it rippled upward, enveloping its on-
coming stream, and then it expanded—until it fell away like a dropped curtain, revealing in one dramatic flash the figure of Zamira "Mira" Villalobos.

Cade beamed with joy: "Mira!" He dodged around the table and ran to
the striking young woman from Havana. They met in a warm embrace. Not
like lovers—Cade had never crossed that line with any of his students—but
almost like a parent and a child. They released each other. Cade held Mira by
her shoulders. "I was worried about you."

"Forgive me, Master. I came as soon as I could."

Yasmin asked, "*Now* can we know what the hell is happening?"

"Soon," Cade said. "Wait downstairs with the others. We'll be there
shortly."

There was fear in Leyton's eyes. "Are we facing the End Times?"

Anja pointed at the door. "No more stupid questions. Downstairs."

The three adepts obeyed Anja's command. As they made their way out of
the room, Mira paused long enough to share a worried look with Cade, who
reached out and gave her hand a reassuring squeeze.

The depth of affection and admiration between Cade and Mira troubled
Anja. Not because she saw the young adept in any way as a sexual or roman-
tic rival. There were few things on earth in which Anja could say she had
faith, but Cade's love was one of them. What bothered her about his bond
with Mira was the blatant favoritism he showed to her. Mira had earned his
attention by being a quicker study than her peers. She had always been dili-
gent in her research and her preparations, skillful in her practice of the Art,
and judicious in her use of magick. She was all that a master karcist might
hope for in an apprentice.

Until now, with most of their adepts being trained separately, Anja had
seen little to gain by making an issue of Cade's bias toward Mira. But now
that they had gathered all of their students together in the name of protecting
them, how long would it take before the others noticed what was so obvious to Anja? How long before resentments festered? Before someone formed a
grudge that might come back to haunt them all at the worst possible moment?

That was exactly what happened to me when Adair made Cade his favorite.
A guilty notion plagued her. *Is that why it bothers me so? Am I angry because
Cade treats Mira the way Adair treated him? Do I simply feel left out . . . again?*

Cade closed the library's door behind Mira. He faced Anja. "That's ten out of eighteen students accounted for. Let's take another half hour to find the last eight. Anybody we haven't brought in by then . . . is on their own."

Anja moved to Cade's side and took his hand. "We *will* find them."

His mask of bravado slipped, revealing his fear. "What if we're too late?"

"If they have been taken from us"—she gave his hand a firm squeeze and snared his attention with her own fearsome gaze—"we avenge them, one and all."

A knot of police blocked the doorway to the sixth floor of the Texas Book Depository. Briet had worked up a light sweat climbing the stairs, thanks to the fact someone had shut down the building's elevators within half an hour of the president's shooting and had yet to return them to service. Hard eyes full of suspicion locked on to her as she made her way up the last flight of steps. Local cops, state police, FBI agents, and men from the Secret Service were here, all of them clearly aware their every action would be scrutinized for years to come.

Briet pulled a leather ID fold from her jacket's front pocket and flipped it open for inspection as she reached the sixth-floor landing. To her surprise, a Dallas police detective seized her right arm and halted her shy of the open doorway. He squinted at her credentials. "Department of Defense?" He shifted his scrutiny to Briet herself. "*You're* from the DOD?"

"I am." She eyed his grip on her biceps. "If you ever want to use that hand again, I suggest you remove it." Noting his intransigence, she added, in a low voice imbued with a touch of demonic intimidation, "*Right. Fucking. Now.*" He let go of her. She shouldered past him and his peers. "Much obliged."

The sixth floor of the Book Depository was used mostly for storage. Cardboard boxes sealed with paper tape stood stacked in clusters, some as tall as a man, on the scuffed hardwood floor. The gaps between the cardboard mounds formed narrow lanes of passage, many of them now choked with agents from the Secret Service and the FBI, or with technicians collecting evidence and documenting the details of the brick-walled space. Rows of steel columns supported broad crossbeams beneath the high ceiling's exposed wooden joists.

Most of the activity on the floor was concentrated in its southeast corner. Briet made her way there, slipping past the various law-enforcement personnel in her path. A camera flash blinded her for half a second; when her eyes recovered, she saw the photographer set up another shot of the same subject, an open and half-empty bottle of Dr Pepper someone had left on the floor beside a two-wheeled hand truck.

Afternoon sunlight bent into the space through the south wall's row of windows, casting long, crisp shadows and illuminating every lazy mote in the air. Briet suspected this floor had likely never before seen so much human activity at once, and this sudden influx of traffic had disturbed years' or perhaps decades' worth of accumulated dust, from floor and boxes alike.

She reached the southeast corner to find a photographer snapping shots of a cluster of boxes that had been arranged to create a sniper's nest. The corner window was still propped half open. At a glance Briet saw this vantage had offered the shooter a perfect angle from which to target the president's motorcade as it passed Dealey Plaza on its way to the Stemmons Freeway on-ramp.

A masculine voice she hadn't heard in years said from behind her, "Briet?"

She turned and recognized Clark Warden, one of her former adepts from the Silo. "Clark!" She stepped forward and they shook hands. "Were you here when it happened?"

He nodded. Though he tried to keep a poker face, Briet noted the sorrow in his eyes. "I was with the motorcade. It happened so fast." He shook his head in dismay. "By the time I knew what was going on, it was too late to—" He stopped as Briet raised a hand, signaling him to be quiet.

She tilted her head toward a spot farther from possible eavesdroppers. They moved together away from the technicians and agents, and then she lowered her voice to a confidential volume. "Start at the beginning. Tell me what you know."

"The first shot was fired at twelve thirty," Clark said, his own voice now hushed. "If I hadn't been using the Sight, I might not have noticed the first shot collapsed the magickal shields around the president."

His choice of words alarmed her. "Collapsed? All of them in one shot?"

"I couldn't believe it, either. Never seen anything like it. I tried to raise a new shield for the limo, but I wasn't fast enough." He gestured with his chin at the sniper's nest. "I've picked up some lingering whiffs of demonic presence, but nothing that even *starts* to explain this."

Briet's imagination was reeling. She needed facts. "Clark, where's the evidence? There must be something. A murder weapon, spent shells, rounds recovered from the victims—"

"There is, but the Bureau has it all."

"*All* of it?"

"On a plane and headed to D.C. as we speak." He pointed at the corner: "They bagged some spent rifle cartridges there." To another area of the sixth floor: "Found the rifle over there. One round still in the magazine." Nodded sideways at the window: "Plucked a bullet out of Connally in the ER."

Suspecting she had teleported herself all the way to Dallas for nothing, Briet grew frustrated. "What about the president's body?"

"Back on Air Force One, bound for Edwards."

"*Fuck.* Is there *anything* left here to investigate?"

There was a sly gleam in his eye as he cocked one eyebrow. "You mean aside from the shooter?" He savored Briet's wide-eyed reaction. "Dallas PD picked up a guy for killing one of their uniforms a few miles from here. Turns out the guy's an employee who works right here, in the depository. Goes by the name Lee Harvey Oswald. Bureau says he has ties to the Russians, the Cubans, and who the fuck knows what else. They've got every badge within a hundred miles digging up every detail of his life."

"All right, that's more like it. We need to question him, find out what he knows about the bullets that pierced the shield. Where is he now?"

Clark frowned, telegraphing his doubt. "The lockup at Dallas Police headquarters on Commerce Street, but I wouldn't get your hopes up. Dallas PD is calling dibs on Oswald over the cop killing. Flash all the federal ID you want—they aren't letting *anyone* in there."

She dipped her chin to fix him with her best *Are you fucking kidding me?* face. "First of all, you know better than most how persuasive magick can be on the rabble. Second, I need to find out who's behind this before my bosses in Washington saddle *me* with the blame. And third, if the powers that be are ready to burn *me* at the stake, what do you think they'll do to *you*—the one karcist they know for a fact was near the motorcade when the president's shield fell?"

The tall, crew-cut magician in a black suit gave a small nod. "Don't think I haven't considered that." He produced a pair of black sunglasses from inside his jacket, put them on, and made a broad gesture toward the exit to the stairwell. "Shall we?"

She led him toward the exit. "How far a walk is it to police headquarters?"

"Don't sweat it. I'll commandeer a car once we're downstairs."

Briet couldn't help but smirk. "And they say chivalry is dead."

⚬⚬⚬

The mirror was black, but Cade stared into it, pleading with the darkness for a glimmer of hope that refused to come. *Answer, damn you. You can't be gone, you're too smart.*

"Cade." Anja laid her hand upon his shoulder. "It is time."

He shook his head, a gesture of refusal and denial. "Not yet."

Her summons broke his concentration and reminded him he had been holed up alone in the library for over two hours, lost in his obsessive search for his wayward students. Ten of them had been found and had reached Naxos safely. Seven others had not been so lucky, and one remained out of reach, to Cade's growing dismay. Now the sun was going down, and it felt as if it were taking hope with it.

Anja massaged Cade's aching shoulders. As she spoke, she softened her voice in a rare concession to empathy. "Our duty is to the living."

Despair weighed upon Cade. He looked up at Anja. "Lila's still out there. I *know* it."

For once her stern features were softened by compassion. "If she lives she will find us. But we can't wait anymore. Too many are dead already."

Cade bowed his head in exhaustion. Memories of his murdered adepts, revealed by means of a yoked demon with a powerful scrying talent, haunted him.

Elodie Thibault, lying in a Parisian alley, all but decapitated by an assassin's garrote.

Miguel Blancaflor, stabbed in the back and left to rot behind a Manila fish market.

Fareed Khalef, sprawled on the floor of a Cairo café, a teacup smashed on the tile next to him, his face a mask of fear, blue lips perfumed with the burnt-almond scent of cyanide. By the time Cade had zeroed in on the young Algerian man, he had been dead long enough for someone to have stolen his billfold, his rings, and even his shoes.

Garrett Latimer and Yong-Mi Kim, lovers since they had met in Korea during the war several years earlier, now lay tangled and bloody inside the twisted wreck of a car that without apparent cause had veered off a mountain road west of Nagano, into a deep ravine.

Fiona Keegan, one of the best magickal duelists Cade had ever trained, drowned at the bottom of Belfast Lough, chained by her neck to a cinder block.

Adelita Delgado, a sweet-natured woman from Durango who had hoped Anja could teach her to become a Pauline karcist like the monks of Monte Paterno, had been burned alive and left to die in the Sonora Desert.

Seven young lives full of promise. All cut short with an excess of cruelty. It filled Cade with a storm of rage and sorrow that made him want to burn the whole world down.

He couldn't bear to imagine finding Lila in the same condition. How could Anja stay so calm while her favorite protégée fended for herself against what had revealed itself to be an international conspiracy? "I can't give up. If Lila's in trouble—"

"She will fight. She cannot be dead. We would know."

"If I had another hour—"

"You do not."

Black clouds roiled in the ether beyond the frame of Cade's hand mirror and refused to grant him solace or cause for hope. Magick was a powerful tool, but it was one that required time and preparation in order to be its most effective. In a fast-moving crisis such as this, the optimal response was often one that no one had time to implement.

The notion of surrender filled Cade with shame and grief. He had long prided himself on being equal to every threat that life could send his way. Giving up on someone who had trusted him to put her interests ahead of his own felt like a failure of the highest order. But a cold moral calculus had to govern his actions now. He couldn't risk the safety of many out of a misplaced sense of obligation to one.

After a heavy sigh, he ended his scrying with the word "*Velarium.*" The clouds faded from view, restoring the mirror's reflective surface. Cade tucked the small looking glass into an inner pocket of his bomber jacket. Then he stood and faced Anja.

"Bring the adepts to the main room. I'll have Barış help me secure the perimeter."

"How long will that take?"

"An hour to conjure shields. Another half hour to check my wires and prep the MG."

Anja rejected his timetable with a headshake. "We may not have that long. I will load the MG and check the wires."

"The MG, yes. The wires, no. These are new, you don't know them like I—"

"They are bombs with trip wires."

Cade headed for the door. "They're called claymores, and they're a bit more complicated than that. For once in your life, believe me when I say you should leave them to me."

She scowled and suppressed a grumble. "Very well, but be quick. We are at war, and we need defenses *before* the enemy comes."

"Yes, dear. That tends to be the recommended approach."

⌁

Briet was immersed in her own schemes as Clark pulled their commandeered Buick over to the curb and parked it. He turned the key in the ignition, and the LeSabre sedan's engine rattled and stuttered its way to silence. Looking up, Briet saw a bar called Victor's Lounge across the street, just a few doors from the corner. There were few people out on the streets, but when a patron left the bar, Briet saw through its open front door that the joint was packed.

She threw a look at Clark. "Where are we?"

"Commerce Street. About a block from police headquarters." He looked over his shoulder and out the rear window. "It's the ugly pile of bricks pushed up against the back of the Municipal Building." Facing forward, he considered their situation with a creased brow. "We can't just barge in there. We have to play this smart."

She eyed the police building in her door's side mirror. "Where would Oswald be?"

"Fifth floor. Holding cells. They busted him for killing a cop, so I'm guessing he's under heavy guard."

A flash of sunlight reflected off a passing Chevy Impala, forcing Briet to wince and turn away for a second. Then the fragments of a plan started to coalesce in her mind. "Who'd be most likely to have legal access to Oswald right now?"

"Not us. At least, not with DOD badges."

"We can flash any badges we want. Who'd be able to get in?"

More pained concentration. "Forget about police IDs. All the plainclothes officers in Dallas PD know each other. Same goes for the Dallas-area state cops, Texas Rangers, and the local FBI office. Local DA's office is a wash, too. But maybe . . ." His expression brightened. "The locals don't deal much with the DOJ. We could try posing as assistant U.S. attorneys."

"That works for me. Maybe you should take point on this. You seem to have a better grasp on the local patois, and in my limited experience, the people of the American South respond better to men in authority than they do to women."

Clark reached under his jacket. "Weapons check." From a shoulder holster he drew a Smith & Wesson .38 Special revolver with a four-inch barrel. Its lacquered wooden grip looked cherry red in the afternoon sun. He released its cylinder and swung it clear of its frame with a jerk of his wrist. It was fully loaded. Another flick of his wrist slammed the cylinder back into place. He holstered the pistol.

Then he eyed Briet with confusion. "You're not armed?"

"I've never had much use for firearms."

He shrugged. "Suit yourself. Let's—"

His abrupt pause alerted Briet to the fact that four white men in gray suits, black hats, and dark sunglasses were converging upon their vehicle. Two of them—one with a mustache, the other gnawing nervously on a toothpick—hurried up to the rear of the Buick, and the other two flanked the car.

The agent on Briet's side, a hefty fellow whose face was flushed and damp with sweat, flashed a badge. "Miss Segfrunsdóttir? You and Agent Warden need to come with us, please."

As Hefty Man spoke, his skinny partner on Clark's side of the car drew a snub-nosed service revolver from a hip holster.

Briet's first reaction was fear—they knew her face and her name. That was bad. Then her impatience asserted itself. She channeled the suggestive powers of SICARIOS. "My partner and I don't have time for you right now. You'll need to speak with us *later*."

Barely had the words left her lips than she saw the man outside her window shake them off, as if her attempt at demonic mind control hadn't even occurred. "*Now*, Miss Segfrunsdóttir."

Fuck. These aren't ordinary feds. These are Hammers.

Trained about and warded against magick, the Hammers were a top-secret division within the deeply clandestine National Security Agency. Their sole function, since the founding of the NSA, had been to serve as a check against the danger of rogue karcists on U.S. soil.

And someone had just sent four of them to round up her and Clark.

She prayed it wasn't too late for diplomacy. "Gents? Let's not do anything rash."

Clark did his best to present a calm front. "Like the lady said, let's all be cool cust—"

Bang. Briet was awash in red. She blinked to find herself doused with Clark's blood and brains. Half his head had been blown into the backseat.

The Skinny Hammer outside the driver's-side window looked surprised he hadn't killed both Clark and Briet with the same shot. So did the Hefty Hammer outside Briet's door.

At the back of the car, Toothpick and Mustache looked like actors who had forgotten their cues, their lines, and maybe even what fucking play they were in.

Extending the telekinetic power of PALARA, Briet blasted the front doors off the Buick and exploded its rear window outward in a storm of glass shards. The Hammers on either side of the car were flattened by the flying doors, and the two in the back found themselves blinded, their faces flayed to expose sinew and bone.

Hammers were warded against magick; they had no defenses against collateral damage.

The car's eruption in broad daylight had drawn a crowd. The last thing Briet needed now was an audience, especially one armed with cameras that had been brought to Dallas in the hope of catching snapshots of the president's motorcade. She used her yoked spirit ROCHIEL to shift into a spectral form, an intangible state that would make her nearly transparent in sunlight. Free to move now, Briet fled from the wrecked Buick and looked for a place to hide.

She turned toward the Statler Hotel—

A crack of gunfire, a burning flash of pain in her right calf.

Briet spun and looked back. Hefty Hammer had grazed her, despite his still being pinned to the street beneath a car door. Then all she could think of were the fiery jolts of pain in her leg. She had never heard of a bullet that could hit someone in spectral form. What was going on?

Another shot, this one fired by Skinny Hammer, ricocheted off a lamppost behind Briet. The thin man had almost struggled free of the car door she had dropped onto him, and his next shot would no doubt be better aimed.

There was no time to worry about the hows and whys. It was time to run like hell.

Briet fled across the street, into Victor's Lounge—and then through the crowd, past the bar, and through its wall, into the next building, a liquor warehouse.

Try and track me now, assholes.

Out in the street, the Hammers barked orders at one another, but the two Briet had scourged with broken glass couldn't see, Hefty was still trapped because the heavy car door had broken one of his arms, and all that Skinny could do was pivot in confusion, searching in vain for anything at which to aim his pistol.

Briet passed through several shelves stocked with booze, and then she left the warehouse through its back wall into an empty lot. Still barely visible, she headed west past the Mercantile National Bank and then willed herself to drop beneath the pavement as she crossed Ervay Street toward Neiman Marcus. After a brief passage through the sewer tunnels of Dallas, she found herself in the basement of the famed department store.

The moment she was positive she was alone, she reverted to solid form— and just as quickly she felt warm blood ooze from the wound on her calf. *Fuck.*

She healed the wound with the power of MARBAS. *How the fuck did they hit me while I was spectral? Anti-magick bullets?* A disturbing notion occurred to her. *Could that have been what hit Kennedy? But if it was, does that mean there's a link between the Hammers and his killer?* Contemplating the possible scope of such a conspiracy filled her with horror. *My God, how deep does this go? What if this was an inside job? If it is . . . I am definitely fucked.*

Sounds of movement from the floor above reminded Briet the basement would not be devoid of activity forever. She had to act quickly and then make herself scarce.

She spent five minutes raiding last season's fashions from cardboard boxes and gave herself the fastest wardrobe change of her life. A flash of demonic fire disposed of her bloodied clothes and shoes. She finished her new ensemble with a pair of zip-up, calf-high leather boots. She tucked her red hair under a large hat as a temporary attempt at remaining incognito, and on her way out of the basement she swiped a long platinum-blond wig off a featureless plastic head in order to effect a more thorough disguise.

No one inside the department store noticed her emergence from the basement through a door marked EMPLOYEES ONLY, nor did they pay her any mind as she strutted out onto Main Street as if she owned it. But as she blended into downtown Dallas's late-afternoon crowd, Briet was keenly aware that she was now officially, and perhaps for the rest of her life, on the run.

Steel in his hand, bedrock underfoot—Niccolò drew confidence from their durability. He had tried to sleep on the flight from New York, but even in the relative luxury of a private aircraft he had struggled to find comfort, and the long journey at the Old Man's side had left him enervated and jet-lagged. Only now, back in this conjuring room hewn from the living rock of a mountain in the Swiss Alps, did he feel at last like himself again.

The space around him was generous. It was a nearly circular oval twenty meters across at its widest point and just under eighteen meters wide on its perpendicular axis, all beneath a six-meter-high domed ceiling equipped with several rows of recessed lights. The carved stone had been polished smooth, and a protective lacquer made its floor shine. The clear sealant also made the floor easy to clean after experiments: a pressurized spray of hot water could rinse away chalk, hematite, ashes, and blood into the perimeter drains in a matter of minutes.

Behind Niccolò, his four tanists prepared their stations inside the circle of protection. Tonight's experiment would be costly, difficult, and expensive. The grimoires said it was a ritual for an operator and two tanists. Niccolò insisted on a full contingent of four tanists; he was not one to take chances in the circle. Not with time at a premium and the stakes so high.

The tanists closest to him were Hatunde Ndufo behind his left shoulder, and Tujiro Kanaka on his right. Hatunde was a tall and muscular man from Lagos, with skin so deep a shade of brown that it looked almost like onyx. He kept his head and face shaved clean, and he lived his life in loose casual attire—the man refused to dress up for anyone.

Tujiro was shorter than Hatunde but taller than Niccolò. His features were handsome and sharp, his physique lean-and-hungry. And the man always made an impression: bespoke Armani suits, hand-cobbled Italian leather shoes, Burberry scarves, French designer sunglasses. He kept his black hair cropped short, and a pencil-thin goatee ringed his thin, cruel mouth.

Despite Hatunde and Tujiro's sartorial differences, tonight they both wore the traditional white cotton albs, paper miters inscribed with holy names of power, and leather slippers required for the Art. Hatunde's robe was cinched at the waist by a girdle of leopard's skin; Tujiro's was bound with a strip of tiger's pelt. Each man's silk-wrapped wand was tucked under his belt.

Behind the men stood twin sisters, Adara and Anorah Samuels, likewise attired in ritual garments, their wands in reserve. The thirtyish women were tall and athletic, with strong shoulders and powerful legs. They both wore their blond hair short, though they had come to favor different styles. Anorah wore hers in a severely angular bob, with pointed sideburns and a widow's peak. Adara wore her hair in a graduated bob that framed her glass-cutter cheekbones in elegant falls of golden hair. Natives of Chicago, they had learned the Goetic Art in college and then made names for themselves in New Orleans's occult community. That had brought them to Niccolò's attention, and, consequently, the Old Man's.

Less than a decade later, the serious-minded, no-nonsense twin sisters had matured into two of the most powerful Goetic magicians on earth. If tonight's experiment did not transpire as Niccolò hoped or expected, he would be grateful to have them guarding his back.

A pocket watch on Niccolò's lectern showed the hour of action drawing near. "Hatunde, light the tapers, please." He heard his colleague snap his fingers, igniting the wicks on dozens of tall candles cast with the first wax from new beehives. "Tujiro, douse the overheads, please." Seconds later, the recessed lights in the ceiling dimmed and went dark. The room's only remaining light came from the candles' weltering flames.

Niccolò clapped his hands once, igniting the flames in all of the circle's five braziers. The ones in front of his tanists danced with green flames, while tongues of blue fire twisted from the brass vessel in front of his operator's circle. He flexed his toes inside his slippers to make sure his ceremonial blade was still balanced atop his feet. Then he regarded the rectangle of steel in his hand: it was a mirror no more than half a centimeter thick, its face fifteen centimeters by nine. Its reflective surface was immaculate. On its dull metal back was inscribed a demonic sigil.

"The enchanted looking glass I hold was made by VAROZIN," Niccolò said for all to hear. "A minor marquis of Hell, bound to the service of LUCIFUGE

ROFOCALE. He serves as a messenger and courier to the Infernal Descending Hierarchy, and can be called upon to create enchanted objects such as this. His work is similar to that of HAEL, a spirit subordinate to PAIMON." A smirk tugged at Niccolò's mouth. "Similar . . . but inferior."

Niccolò reached to his lectern and opened his grimoire. He was about to draw his wand when the intercom bolted to the underside of the lectern's main surface buzzed twice. It was the Old Man calling from upstairs. Niccolò pushed a button to open a two-way channel. "*Signore*?"

"*Our scouts on Naxos have called in. Cade Martin has responded to our feint exactly as we expected. All of his apprentices we know to be still alive have gathered at his home. Are you ready to proceed?*"

"We are, *signore*. Can our hired guns on Naxos say the same?"

"*All they need is for me to give the word.*"

"Give us fifteen minutes, and we'll make sure Martin and his people can't escape."

"*Very well, Mr. Falco. In fifteen minutes I shall cry 'Havoc!' Make certain it's the* last *thing Cade Martin ever hears.*"

Pacing in the kitchen on the main floor of his villa, Cade had no idea what he was going to tell his assembled students. It didn't help that he had very few hard facts to offer them. At least seven of their number had been slain in the past few hours, but he had no idea who was to blame or how so many of them had been compromised, in spite of all the precautions he and they had taken. He felt guilty, furious, and heartsick all at once.

They'll ask me who did this. What do I tell them?

He peeked around the corner, into the main room. Anja was projecting calm to a roomful of people who had every right to be shit-scared. To the adepts' credit, they were comporting themselves respectably. Melina's attention had been captured by Yasmin, who entertained the girl by demonstrating her knife prowess with a solo game of stabberscotch. Yasmin's dagger danced back and forth, its tip landing between her spread fingers at high speed, never once nicking flesh even as it shredded the top of Cade's favorite coffee table.

Working from sly glances, Sathit Viravong, a former librarian, pencil-sketched portraits of her fellow adepts on paper scraps that she pocketed. Cade wondered if anyone other than him had seen her drawings, or if she had confided to any of the other students that he had helped her escape from forced service in a guerrilla army fighting in the civil war in her native Laos.

Yangchen Kalsang, a thirtyish fellow Cade had befriended in Tibet, paced one side of the room, taking care not to wander too close to Thi Viên, who had secluded themself in a corner behind an open book as a symbolic shield. Of all their adepts, Viên was the least sociable, and to Cade the most enigmatic. Born and raised outside Saigon, Viên had a gentle and androgynous quality to their face, a soft but low voice, and a taste for loose, colorful clothing.

But not everyone was so at ease. Viola Blair, a rough-and-tumble sort of gal Anja had met in the Australian outback, liked to play harmonica when she was a little bit nervous, and was prone to whistling when she was really scared. Yasmin had confiscated Viola's harmonica, and a warning from Anja had put an end to her whistling. Now the agitated young woman leaned against the front door, drumming her hands against her thighs without any noticeable rhythm.

Barış tried to be subtle as he moved about the room, straightening the photos and setting objects either parallel or perpendicular to one another on every surface he passed.

Leyton was passing the time by moving from one person to the next and offering to show them sleight-of-hand card tricks. He was shooed away by Gathii Kamau, who within half an hour of arriving on Naxos had somehow found a stray cat in Cade and Anja's yard and decided the animal was in need of his attention. The scraggly gray feline had since nestled in between his sinewy dark brown arm and his muscular thigh and began to purr, prompting the Kenyan-born mage to reveal his smile dotted with missing teeth.

Mira scratched the sleepy cat's head and whispered something to Gathii. He nodded, and she made a beeline toward the kitchen, prompting Cade to duck back behind the corner.

I don't want to lie to them, or to Anja. But telling them I don't know what the fuck is going on won't inspire confidence. And they need to believe in me right now. They need courage. They need hope. But how can I give it to them when I have none myself?

Footsteps coming toward him. He pulled himself together. *Mustn't look like I feel. Can't let on that I'm lost. That I have no plan.*

Mira turned the corner and cocked a thick, black eyebrow at him. "You coming?"

"In a second," he lied.

She stepped past him to take a bottle of cream from the icebox. "It's what you always said would happen, isn't it? The CIA. The KGB. All the spy agencies, moving against us."

Cade shook his head. "I don't know, Mira. Maybe."

Her fear was plain on her face. "I've never seen you like this. You or Anja. You're both acting like it's the end of the world."

"It might be. How the fuck should we know? I mean, last year, that mess in Cuba? Who knows how close we came to vanishing in fire?" Cade heaved a long sigh. "The world's hanging by a string, and our leaders are all running around like kids with scissors."

She fetched a saucer from the cupboard and poured cream onto it. "Say you're right. If the superpowers are moving against us, shouldn't we go underground? Go dark and vanish?"

"I have no idea, Mira. If I did, I—" A tremor and a muffled voice from inside his jacket's front pocket snared his attention. It was his enchanted hand mirror: someone was trying to reach him. Hoping, perhaps even praying it was Lila Matar, he pulled out the looking glass—

—leaving him to confront his disappointment at the sight of Briet Segfrunsdóttir, a former adept of Nazi master sorcerer Kein Engel during the Second World War and now the chief karcist of the United States' Occult Defense Program. The red-haired woman cut to business without the courtesy of a preamble. *"I'm in trouble."*

"Get in line."

Her normally flawless brow creased in anger. *"This is serious."*

"Like I said, take a number. Someone's killing magicians all over the world, and I—"

"Kennedy's dead."

Her declaration shut him down like a face-slap. "What?"

"You heard me. Someone put two rifle rounds straight through his magickal defenses, like they weren't even there. Shot half his fucking head off." Briet's eyes narrowed as she measured Cade's reaction. *"You didn't know?"*

Her news left Cade nauseated. "Haven't had time to follow the news. Seven of my students have been murdered since dawn." He turned a mournful look toward Mira, who returned it in kind. "I've spent the day trying to save the others."

"I'm sorry." The shift in Briet's tone told Cade her sentiment was genuine. *"But we need to regroup with Master Khalil as soon as possible, so that we—"*

"It's too late, he's already dead." A chill traveled down his spine as he added, "Shot down the same way as Kennedy."

"Fuck." Her tense demeanor turned to naked despair. *"Fucking hell."*

Cade feared to ask how grim their situation had become. "We don't know who's behind this, but someone or something with a lot of power is making a big move—and whoever or whatever it is, it seems to think we're in its way." He caught fleeting hints of worry and fear in Briet's expression. "What have *you* seen?"

Her eyes looked haunted. She managed a small nod. *"Federal agents—Hammers—came after me and a man I'd trained for the Secret Service. They killed him in cold blood. If not for a bit of luck, they'd have iced me, too."*

Her words resurrected ugly memories for Cade. He recalled being held prisoner by the Hammers years earlier, when he and Miles Franklin—his former partner-in-mischief for MI6 until about a decade ago—had tried to track down a rogue atomic threat on American soil. Cade's only reward for his patriotism had been days of incarceration, abuse, and forced sobriety—and he'd held grudges for all three slights ever since.

The more Cade heard, the more certain he became of a conspiracy aborning.

"If this isn't just a war on karcists, what is it?"

"I can't see all the angles yet. That's why I need your help, right now. You and Anja. If we can get to the witnesses and the evidence before they get killed or buried—"

"I never said I'd help you."

"Jesus, Cade. You don't get it. The Hammers who came after me had bullets that could hit me while I was ghosted. Are you listening? I was in spectral form when one of their rounds grazed my leg. I've never even heard of anything that could do that, have you?"

The more she told him, the deeper his fear became. "No."

"Exactly. So stop acting like I'm bothering you, and get your ass to Dallas. I'm in room nineteen-oh-eight at the Statler Hotel on Commerce Street. We need to start working on a plan to examine the evidence at the FBI crime lab in Washington, D.C., and to question the suspect, Lee Harvey Oswald, who's being held here at—"

The enchanted mirror exploded into dust with no warning, scorching Cade's palm and stinging his face with tiny fragments of glass and steel.

Momentarily half blind and shaking the searing pain from his hand, Cade fell to his knees.

"Fuck!" Mira scrambled to his side. "Your mirror blew up!"

"I know that." Blinking to dispel the itching and burning in his eyes, Cade saw the confusion in Mira's. "Come on. We need to ask Anja if—"

He lost his train of thought as a distant, rhythmic thudding grew louder and closer. Within moments a devil's drumbeat of helicopter rotors shook the villa and filled the air, telling Cade he and all who had trusted him enough to seek his protection had run out of time.

The enemy was here.

The war he had dreaded for two decades had begun.

Muted bangs and pops filled the villa's conjuring room. Anja felt a burst of heat and a sting of glass and steel eat into her side, under her jacket. She reached toward the pain, almost by reflex. It had come from the pocket in which she kept her enchanted mirror. Her fingertips found nothing but metallic dust and splinters of glass that lodged themselves beneath her fingernails, drawing bright red blood. She pulled back her hand in surprise—

Then she saw most of the apprentices had just suffered the same violation. All of their enchanted looking glasses, given to them by Cade, had been pulverized at the same time. Winces of pain turned into stares full of confusion and alarm. Whispers tinged with fear were traded in the flickering candlelight, a susurrus of questions for which no one had answers.

Plodding footfalls announced Barış's return from upstairs. His face and hands were bleeding as he stopped in front of Anja. "The portal mirror in the library—it just *exploded*."

Anja had no idea what to tell him. Someone or something had just compelled the demonic creator of Cade's collection of linked magick mirrors to obliterate them all, leaving her, Cade, and their apprentices cut off and cornered. She had no idea how the feat had been accomplished, and confiding her incomplete understanding of the situation would only frighten the adepts. And at that moment, they needed a reason to hope. A reason not to run.

She was on the verge of concocting such a reason when the nightmarish rhythm of rotary-wing aircraft—helicopters—shook the villa. Anja recognized their sound; she had been on the wrong side of such "choppers" in

Cambodia just a year earlier. These sounded like military aircraft, American-made. Large, well-armed, and closing fast.

She sprang into action, snapping orders as she'd heard officers do at Stalingrad, Kharkov, and Kursk during the Great Patriotic War. "Who has battle magick?" She scanned the room and noted which adepts had raised their hands. "Barış, scout the woods. Leyton, check the cliffs on the south side. Viola, Yasmin, give us overlapping shields inside this room." As the battle mages carried out her orders, she asked the other students, "How many of you are trained to shoot?" Only two hands. "Sathit, Viên! To the rear bedroom on this floor. Sathit, grab all the rifles and ammo you can carry, bring them here. Viên, grab the shotgun for yourself, and bring me my rifle, the Mosin-Nagant." The shooters scrambled out of the room. Anja faced Gathii, Yangchen, and Melina. "Get the go bags and meet back here. Move!"

The last three adepts hurried from the room to gather the duffels of essential supplies that had long ago been set aside by Cade and Anja in case this day ever came. In the middle of the conjuring room, Yasmin and Viola worked on coordinating their magickal shields to create nested spheres of protection. The house and property had their own defensive enchantments, but adding to them was always a wise precaution.

Anja reached out with the Sight to assess the tactical situation outside the villa. She had just spotted three Hueys and a platoon of heavily armed infantry approaching from the north when Mira and Cade entered the main room. Cade's right hand was blackened and bloody.

"We need to go," Cade said. "*Now.*"

"We won't stand a chance out there!"

"If I'm right, we don't have a chance *in here.* We need to save the—"

"Stop. What are you saying?"

Cade looked vexed at being cut off, but he regrouped quickly. "I was talking to Briet when someone dusted my"—he noted the glittering debris on the floor—"*our* mirrors. Someone killed President Kennedy today. Shot him *right through* his magickal shields."

The shock of recognition left Anja feeling hollowed-out. "Just like Khalîl."

"Exactly. And if the troops and choppers coming at us have the same kind of magick-piercing rounds—"

Anja raised her palm to stop him. "Absurd. They would cost a fortune to make. Arming snipers is one thing, but choppers? Soldiers?"

He moved closer and lowered his voice. "Anja, it takes only *one* of those rounds to break a shield. Briet said one of them hit her while she was ghosted. The troops outside have automatic rifles, and the choppers have machine guns. If even *one* round in a thousand of their load-out is a bullet like the ones that hit Kennedy and Khalîl, our magickal defenses won't be worth shit."

Her empty feeling was filled with a sick tide of dread. "It would be a slaughter." She turned toward the shield-makers. "Yasmin, Vi: Forget shields, get Barış and Leyton. Mira, round up everyone else, get them—"

Cade cut in, "We need to save my work from the library upstairs."

Anja put herself between Cade and the stairs. "Leave it!" The thundering of the Hueys' rotors quaked the house. "Let's go!"

"Not without my work!"

Melina returned and dropped a go bag between Cade and Anja. "I'll get it!"

He pressed his palms to her cheeks, leaving the left side of her face smeared with his blood. "Library. Three books. Cherry case, top shelf. Then get to the basement. Go!"

Mel didn't look to Anja for confirmation of the order, she just sprinted upstairs.

Aghast that Cade would risk the girl's life, Anja glared at him. "If your books are so important, get them yourself. Or send a demon."

"Demons can't touch them, and neither can angels—not without protections I don't have time to make." He walked to the front door. "Get everyone downstairs, as fast as you can."

She shouted at his back, "And where are *you* going?"

"To buy you time." Cade drew his wand from under his jacket. As he left the house, he looked back at Anja with fear in his eyes. "Leave a light on for me."

The demons inside Cade's head were laughing. They taunted him as one: CAN YOU TASTE IT ON THE WIND, EVE-SPAWN? YOU DIE TONIGHT.

Not fucking likely. His foes were coming; nothing could stop that now. But he could at least force them to do it while blind. He flourished his wand over his head in great arcs and marshaled the powers of ANEMOS to choke the sky with storm clouds and flood the woods with fog. As he marched toward the tree line, he heard the thundering percussion of incoming choppers, which slowed as they were swallowed by fast-moving walls of vapor.

He surrounded himself with AZAEL's shield and engaged the Sight, his yoked gift from RAUM. The magickal vision pierced the drifting veils of fog and smoke and revealed the dozens of armed soldiers advancing in the dark toward the villa, as well as the Hueys hovering above the trees. Cade had faced worse odds, but that didn't lessen his dread—there were no guarantees in combat. He would never forget his brothers-in-arms being cut down at his side on D-day by bullets none of them had heard coming. He invoked GADREEL's gift of insubstantiality to metal and non-magickal projectiles and continued his march toward the enemy.

Flashes of golden fire lit up the mist-filled woods with roars of detonation and screams of pain: the soldiers' point men had set off the outer ring of claymores. The ground was still trembling under Cade's feet and the mines' projectiles were still in the air when the enemy opened fire. They filled the night with bullets flying in every direction. Cade guessed most of them were shooting at nothing, returning fire out of reflex at the first sign of enemy contact.

Beneath the din of explosions, a man shouted orders.

Soldiers bellowed and charged toward the villa.

The helicopters advanced, tails up, noses down.

Cade hurled XAPHAN's fire into the woods. Storms of green flame ignited men, trees, and brush. Magazines loaded with ammo exploded on soldiers' uniform belts, tearing chunks from their torsos. Grenades detonated, engulfing squads of men in smoke and shrapnel. Bodies fell, blackened and torn, as the next rank of troops surged past, pressing the charge. Even from a distance, Cade felt the firestorm's brutal heat and smelled its foul carnage.

Bullets caromed off his invisible shield of magickal energy, deflected into the night. Overhead, the Hueys broke free of the swirling black clouds he'd conjured.

He hurled one of ZOCAR's lightning bolts at the lead helicopter. Its crackling tendrils enveloped the buglike military aircraft but didn't seem to do it any real damage.

The Huey's pilot fired a rocket at Cade.

Cade put all of his strength and focus into his spherical shield. His world went white as the rocket detonated a few meters ahead of him. The force of the blast hurled him backward. He slammed against the wall of a storage shed. Robbed of his balance, he struggled to get up. He was felled by a stabbing sensation inside his skull, as if his brain had been skewered like a kebab. He stood again, only to stagger and flail like a drunkard.

Two choppers strafed the house as they raced past overhead. The third bore down on Cade and hectored him with machine-gun fire. He weaved and stumbled to cover behind his shed, dived flat, and put his face in the cold dirt.

The shed disintegrated under the Huey's high-caliber barrage.

As smoky splinters rained down upon Cade, one round in the Huey's flurry of thousands popped his sphere of magickal shielding as if it were a soap bubble.

Cade felt AZAEL being knocked free of his yoke.

His shield-demon was gone.

The helicopter sped south, halted, and made a fast pivot into its next attack run. Its two wingmen had banked off to the east and west, and now were starting second passes at the villa. Cade peeked over the pile of debris that had once been a shed. More soldiers moved through the woods and closed on the tree line, firing every step of the way.

Coming out here might've been a bad idea.

Cade sprang from the splinters and zigzagged across the wide yard, not out of tactical savvy but because he was too dizzy to hold a straight line. Autocannon rounds ripped up turf on either side of him. With each dodge he made, the bullets got closer. The Huey was going to gun Cade down long before he reached cover. The demons in his head chortled with evil glee—

Cade stopped and turned to face the chopper at his back.

And with the mighty hands of JEPHISTO, he tore off its rotors.

The broken rotors spun off into the night. The rest of the chopper fell like a stone and vanished into the rocky gully far below the cliff on which the villa stood.

Stutters and burps of automatic rifle fire split the air, driving Cade toward cover. Without a magickal shield, he couldn't risk being in the open. Most rounds would still pass through him without harm, thanks to the gift of GADREEL, but if another magick-piercing round like the one that had collapsed his shield found him . . .

That was a risk he couldn't take.

Charging headlong into gunfire, Cade sent a mental warning to the yoked demon he needed now more than ever: *Stand fast, GADREEL. 'Cause if you ditch me now and I survive, I'll use you to redefine the meaning of "eternal motherfucking pain." You get me?*

A burst of gunfire passed through him—no magick-killers in the bunch, but Cade's breath caught in his throat until he was sure his immunity to metal was intact. Then he skewered the half dozen soldiers who had fired at him with arcing forks of lightning as he ran.

I SERVE AT THY COMMAND, replied GADREEL.

Goddamned right you do. And don't you fucking forget it.

———※———

Anja stood at a window in the villa's second-floor hallway, loading a five-round magazine into her Mosin-Nagant rifle. In the library, Melina scrambled to gather Cade's manuscripts for travel. The adept fought to bundle the trio of large leather-bound, handwritten tomes with thick twine, first along one axis and then the other. Each time she tried to change the direction with a twist of the rough string, she fumbled it and lost the tension, and each bungled knot led to frustrated swearing in rapid-fire Greek.

"Tear down the curtain," Anja said, loud enough for Mel to hear over the rumbling of the helicopters above the villa. "Use it to wrap the books and go!"

Mel acknowledged the order with a nod, scrambled to the library's window, and tore down its left curtain, pulling the rod from the wall in the process. She spread the curtain across the library's reading table. Then she grabbed the books from the shelf and laid them in the middle of the flattened curtain.

Anja winced and shrank in terror as a wild buzz of large-caliber bullets disintegrated part of the villa's roof and the ceiling above her head. She and Mel dived to the floor—Mel beneath the reading table, Anja against the wall under the window. Bullets chewed the rest of the ceiling into dust and splinters. When at last Anja dared to look up, she saw open sky through a tattered veil of smoke, and the last few timbers of the roof's frame, broken and smoldering.

She shouted into what remained of the library, "Mel! Are you hit?"

"I'm okay!" Mel scrambled out from under the table, hurriedly folded the curtain over the three books, and tied the bundle shut with twine. She hefted it over her shoulder and bounded past Anja, toward the stairs. "C'mon!"

"Go! I will be there soon."

"But the helicopters—"

Anja got up on one knee and balanced her rifle on the windowsill. "Cade needs me. Go." Mel darted down the stairs. Anja leaned into her weapon. Scoped out the battlefield. Soldiers were charging out of the woods toward Cade, and he was running toward them. Anja targeted the enemy's point man as he emerged from the trees. Then she fired.

A sharp report, the acrid tang of gunpowder—and in the distance a scarlet mist erupted from the back of the point man's head, taking off his helmet with it.

Anja ejected the spent cartridge with a pull of her rifle's well-oiled bolt. The brass pinged across the debris-strewn hallway floor as she lined up her next shot and fired.

Fifty-five meters away, a man in camouflage fatigues dropped his automatic rifle as Anja's second shot ripped out his throat. His body struck the ground at the same time as the brass from the killing round hit the floor at Anja's side.

Her third shot took out a soldier's knee. She cursed herself; she had been aiming for his groin. She ejected the cartridge and aimed again.

Cade had almost reached his destination. He threw lightning at the troops in the forest, and had knocked one of the Hueys out of the sky, but there were still two more helicopters, and both were starting new attack runs at the villa. Anja had time for just one more shot before she'd have to abandon this position and flee downstairs.

Using the Sight granted to her by MEVAKOS, she spied the approaching infantry and found a man equipped with a flamethrower. She lined up her sights on the nozzle for the twin tanks on his back and put a bullet through the hose connected to it.

Flaming jellied gasoline shot from the severed hose and turned the forest into a hellscape. Within seconds half a dozen troops around Mr. Flamethrower were baptized with liquid fire.

Then his tank exploded.

The blast flattened his already burning squadmates. His orphaned limbs flew from his charred torso. Then there was nothing left but a spreading wall of fire.

Anja moved in a crouch, surrounded by her magickal shield of AMYNA as she scrambled downstairs. Above her, the whine of a .50-caliber autocannon cut through the pounding beat of the Hueys' rotors. Anja gave up her crouch and sprinted down the stairs. The choppers' fusillade shredded the second floor and blew apart the staircase half a second after she'd leaped clear of it, on her way to the basement door, at the east end of the house.

Smoking wreckage of the roof and upper floor fell in, driven downward by a merciless wind from the hovering Hueys' rotors. Everywhere Anja looked, she saw either smoke or the violence of large-caliber guns grinding her home into splinters. All of the villa's magickal defenses had been obliterated, over-powered in a matter of moments. A safehold she had believed invincible was being blown away like a house of straw.

Seeing her adepts huddled in terror in the main room, Anja felt sick with shame. *I did not bring them to safety. I led them into a trap.*

She pointed toward the east end of the house. "Basement! Go!"

Anja wanted to wait for Cade, but there was no time. If she was going to save their students' lives, they had to run now—even if that meant leaving her husband behind.

------~~------

One of the first things Adair Macrae ever taught Cade about magick was never to use it for any task that could be accomplished with less effort or expense by non-magickal means.

That lesson echoed in Cade's memory as he dispelled the illusion camou-flaging his home's chief instrument of non-magickal defense.

Situated near the tree line on the north side of the property, the gun em-placement was double-ringed by low berms of concrete slabs with iron cores. A pitched gable formed from two welded plates of inch-thick steel served as its rear and overhead cover. Its interior consisted of a meter-wide, horseshoe-shaped trench of reinforced concrete around a gun platform set at Cade's chest height. It afforded him a one-hundred-eighty-degree field of fire for its tripod-mounted, German-made MG42 machine gun. The belt-fed weapon was already loaded, and six boxes of ammunition were stacked between a pair of spare fast-swap barrels—a necessary precaution, as sustained firing caused the MG42's barrel to overheat after a hundred and fifty rounds.

Gotta save the magick for the heavy shit.

Cade primed the MG42 and swung it toward the advancing troops in the woods as he communed with his demon of burden. *Look sharp, KERIGOS. Keep feeding fresh belts into the gun.* He put his shoulder against the gun's stock, raised its targeting sight, and widened his stance. *Here we go.*

The weapon shrieked like a bone saw as it spat lead and belched out smoke and brass. Its wild jackhammer kickback numbed Cade's hands and made his elbows and shoulders ache.

In the woods, skinny trees fell as 7.92-millimeter rounds chewed their trunks into pulp.

Men dropped in clusters—some from direct hits, others from ricochets. The wild ripping buzz of the MG42 drowned out the staccato cracks and pops of incoming small-arms fire, which kicked up dust and sparks as dozens of rounds peppered the concrete blocks in front of Cade.

He counted emptied ammo belts as they hit the ground at his feet. After the third belt of fifty was spent, he snapped at KERIGOS, "Swap the barrel!"

It was a perfect job for a demon: a creature tempered in the fires of Hell was impervious to the searing heat of the gun's barrel. While KERIGOS opened the gun's side hatch and expertly traded the overheated barrel for a cool one, Cade pulled a fresh belt of ammo from the green metal box at his feet. KERIGOS closed the side hatch and set down the hot barrel.

Cade tossed the demon the fresh belt. "Load!"

Two seconds later, faster than any human could have done the job, the weapon was ready to fire. Cade braced its stock against his shoulder, sighted the moving shadows in the woods, and let the buzz saw chew into them. The gun's brutal juddering rattled the fillings in his teeth and let him feel every organ in his body vibrating against its neighbors.

The charging troops spread out. Cade pivoted to one side, then the other, widening his field of fire. Out in the trees, more claymores went off in quick succession, blinding flashes of white paired with booms that rocked the ground under his feet, even at a distance. Visibility in the woods dropped to zero as men and trees were swallowed by rolling walls of black smoke.

Cade engaged the Sight and was about to keep picking off enemy troops in the woods—then he heard the whine of the Hueys' autocannons behind him. Using the Sight to peer through the metal plates at the rear of his emplacement, he saw the Hueys' rotary cannons obliterate the roof and upper floor of the villa. Anguish and terror seized him as the top of the house caved in.

Anja! He reined in his fear and sharpened his focus. *Time to bug out.*

He detached the MG42 from its tripod.

"KERIGOS! Grab the ammo and the barrels. Stay close and keep me loaded."

He tossed the machine gun over the inner berm and climbed out after it.

Hefting it with both hands, he unleashed a spray of bullets into the woods, sweeping from west to east as he stepped over the emplacement's outer berm. He had expected it to have more kick free of the tripod, but the weapon's own weight absorbed a great deal of its recoil, so long as he fired in short bursts. The moment he finished the belt, KERIGOS fed another into the weapon.

Cade turned south, toward the crumbling, burning remains of his home.

He raised the MG42 and let it rip at the nearer of the two helicopters. Sparks danced across the chopper's main fuselage, and then a plume of smoke shot from its tail.

Both helicopters broke off their assault, turned south, and dived below the cliff behind the house. For a moment Cade felt a sensation akin to victory.

Then the thundering of rotors grew louder, and the choppers reappeared in unison, rising straight upward—both of them facing Cade's position.

Ignition sparks flashed inside their rocket launchers.

Fuck.

Cade dropped the MG42 and sprang toward the concrete shelter.

He made it almost two and a half steps before his world turned to fire.

～

The villa was imploding. Walls crumbled as if they had been made of sand. Furnishings fell to pieces, scattered in hails of gunfire Anja heard but couldn't see. Thick smoke stung her eyes, dust choked her every breath. She tried to move, only to find her legs pinned by a fallen ceiling joist. She had no memory of becoming trapped. *Please don't let it be a concussion.*

Her first instinct was to free herself, but then she remembered the others who had been with her. What if removing the joist from her leg endangered one of them? She looked around. Several of the students lay in the hallway behind her. Some were trapped, others were dazed or unconscious. Groans of pain and confusion were barely audible through the cacophony of gunfire and explosions from outside.

No one else seemed threatened by the beam on Anja's legs, so she focused the telekinetic power of BAEL to lift it while she crawled free. She was still on all fours as a spray of bullets ripped past above her. She let the beam fall and threw herself flat on the soot-covered floor.

When she lifted her head, she counted the wounded. Seven she could see.

Scrambling on her hands and knees, she moved to the nearest of the fallen. It was Yangchen. His eyes fluttered as she touched his chest. "Yangchen?

Can you hear me?" He nodded, so Anja continued. "Are you hurt? Can you move?"

"Dizzy." His speech was slurred.

Anja pressed her right palm to his forehead and invoked the healing gifts of BUER. In seconds she felt the youth's life force surge back to normal. "You will live. Get up."

A blast rocked the house as she crawled to Viola. Her face was bloody, and she didn't stir when Anja shook her, but she was alive. Anja called out, "Yangchen! Get Vi to the basement!"

As Yangchen dragged Viola down the smoky hallway, Anja scrambled to the next adept, who was lying facedown. "Gathii?" She rolled him over and saw the bullet wounds in his chest and gut. He was gone. There was no time now to mourn, so she moved on.

A meter past him was Leyton. The bald young man looked as still as a cadaver, but he bolted upright at the touch of Anja's hand. "What—? Where are—?"

"Calm down," Anja said. "Are you hurt?"

He took a second to assess himself. "Don't think so."

"Then help me!" She pulled him along as she moved to a trio of bodies near the wreckage of the former staircase—Barış, Viên, and Sathit. She pointed Leyton at Barış. "Check his pulse." She pressed her fingertips to Viên's jugular, but found no pulse. Viên was gone.

Leyton cradled Barış's head. "He's alive but weak."

Anja checked Sathit. "Her, too." She pointed at Barış. "You take him." She pulled Sathit across her shoulders into a fireman's carry. It was hard to stay upright under such a burden.

Watching with concern, Leyton started to ask, "What about—?"

He let his question trail off. Anja looked past him through the smoke to see Melina, her young body mangled by machine-gun fire. In her outstretched hands, Cade's bundled books.

"Leave them," she told Leyton. "People first."

"I'll get them," said Mira, who emerged like a phantom from the veils of smoke at the east end of the hallway. She darted past Anja, hefted the swaddled tomes from the floor, and toted them over her shoulder. "Let's go!"

The trio trudged down the hall with their burdens. Masking her worry with anger, Anja said to Mira, "What are you doing up here? You should be in the basement!"

"Yangchen said there were wounded. I came to help."

"Next time follow orders," Anja said, her tone sharper than she'd intended.

Leyton and Barış were the first ones through the open basement door, followed by Mira, with Anja and Sathit bringing up the rear.

Anja was halfway down the rickety flight of wooden steps when a blast of light and heat swept away the walls of the villa's first floor, partially exposing the basement and stinging them all with flying splinters of wood, bits of shattered stone, and fiery motes—

Before a second blast buried her and the apprentices in a maelstrom of ash and fire.

The only sound was a distant echo of wind, and there was nothing to see but the faint outlines of a world gone gray. No odors, no tastes, not a single tangible object—the entire world was a collection of mists to Cade while he existed in the smoke form of PHENEX.

He rode the wind in the middle of the killing field he'd once called his front yard, his vaporous shape mingling with the smoke from half a dozen fires ignited by the choppers' rockets. The last five enemy soldiers stalked past him—and partly through him—as they advanced toward the collapsing villa. They looked to Cade like clouds in the shapes of men, the outlines of their rifles vague and indistinct. When they spoke, he had to strain to make out what they said; it was like trying to eavesdrop on beachgoers from underwater.

They all had passed him when the leader raised his fist, signaling the others to stop. Using hand signals, he directed the two men closest to him to fan out to either side, and he motioned for the two men in the rear to crouch and hold position.

They're scouting for survivors.

Cade had no intention of letting them reach the villa.

A breath of wind was the only announcement of Cade's shift back into solid form. He savored the sharp smell of cordite while he eased his knife from its sheath, gripping it for battle as the Rangers had taught him to do. Then he struck with speed, stealth, and commitment.

His first target was the kneeling soldier to his left, the one farthest to the squad's rear. Cade covered the man's mouth with his hand and plunged his knife into the man's throat, severing his jugular. The man's body went slack in Cade's grip.

The soldier ahead of him to his right turned toward Cade, who freed his blade from the dead man and stabbed it deep into the second man's throat, cutting off his shout of alarm.

Cade caught the dead second man and moved behind him.

The soldier sent to the right flank glanced back, saw Cade, and raised his battle rifle as he pivoted toward him. Cade drew the sidearm from the holster of the dead man he was using as a shield and put a .45-caliber round through the flanker's face.

Bullets from the squad leader and the man on the left flank slammed into Cade's meat shield. A few rounds blasted all the way through the corpse, only to pass through Cade without harm thanks to the protection of GADREEL. He put three rounds into the squad leader's center mass before a rifle round fired by the last soldier exploded through Cade's shield corpse, tore a bloody chunk off of Cade's left rib cage, and knocked him onto his back.

A magick-piercing round had forced GADREEL from Cade's control.

So much for immunity to metal.

The last soldier rushed at Cade, his rifle braced against his shoulder as he fired. Bullets kicked up sod and rocks all around Cade, who raised his borrowed Colt. The pistol in his hand *clack*ed empty. Cade dropped it and conjured a flurry of VAELBOR's blades, which dismembered and disemboweled the soldier in a flurry of blood and steel.

Cade pushed away the dead body on top of him and struggled to his feet. It hurt to stand, to walk, to move at all, but he had to reach whatever was left of the villa.

He clamped his right hand over the bleeding wound in his side and staggered toward the villa. The two Hueys hovered while facing the house, unleashing a storm of lead into the collapsing heap of timbers. How long could Anja and the others survive in the face of that?

His strength was failing as blood sheeted down his side, soaking his shirt and trouser leg. A quick mental inventory confirmed his worst fears. Along with GADREEL and AZAEL, who had been dispelled by the enemy's magick-piercing rounds, Cade had lost his yokes on ANEMOS, JEPHISTO, and XAPHAN, the sources of three of his strongest combat talents. Worse, he felt ZOCAR and VAELBOR straining against their psychic bonds, struggling to free themselves at Cade's next signs of weakness. He would soon be defenseless; the time for him to strike was now.

He was several paces from the house, short of breath and soaked in sweat, when one of the choppers' side gunners spotted him. The gunner swiveled his .50-caliber toward Cade, who skewered the man from afar with VAELBOR's barbed spear.

Cade plodded onward as the dead gunner's Huey pivoted toward him, no doubt hoping to puree him with its autocannon. Cade wrapped the Huey in ZOCAR's lightning, as much as he had the strength to conjure. A single bolt hadn't been enough to knock one of these birds down, but a steady surge of demonic lightning turned it into a sparking, smoking brick.

As it started to spin and wobble, Cade hurled VAELBOR's sword into its tail rotors.

A crimson flash was followed by a shower of white sparks—and then the chopper came down hard. Cade lurched away from the villa as the Huey crashed down beside it.

The burning aircraft rolled like a Catherine wheel. Then it exploded.

Its blast wave slammed Cade face-first into the dirt and sheared away the last remnants of the villa's first floor. Blazing hunks of wood scattered into the darkness as the other chopper peeled off, diving southward to escape the rising bloom of fire and smoke.

No time to lose.

Cade stumbled and then dragged himself through walls of flame to reach the exposed foundation of the villa. What had been a basement with a wine cellar and cheese cave had become a heap of smoking debris. Even as he clambered over the low concrete wall and dropped into the mess, he saw heaps being shifted and displaced by unseen forces—signs of magick being put to work. Through tattered veils of dust and smoke, he found Anja. Her face was smeared with soot, and gray ash clung to her black hair. He staggered to her. "Are you okay?"

"For now." She looked back at the handful of surviving adepts clawing their way out of the wreckage. Her eyes narrowed in anger. "Many are not."

A shift in the wind hit Cade with a stench of blood and excrement, mingled with petrol fumes and the bite of gunpowder. These odors had haunted him on D-day, and again after the bombing of Dresden. It was the smell of death in battle. The reek of carnage. And it was all that remained of what seemed like at least half of his students.

Above them, the sound of the last Huey's rotors grew louder.

Anja pointed toward the heavy wooden door in the southwest corner of the foundation. "Everyone move! Get to the door!"

Desperate bodies climbed and scurried over heaps of shredded furniture, broken beams, splintered flooring, and obstacles of twisted pipe from the villa's antiquated plumbing. Blinded by the dusty haze and fighting to keep up in the rush to the door, Cade couldn't tell who was who. The survivors all had been rendered anonymous by thick coatings of gray ash.

The roar of the rotors became deafening. Cade turned back to see the last Huey hovering with its nose angled toward him and the others, its pilot targeting them with the autocannon.

Cade tried to hurl lightning at the chopper, only to find that ZOCAR had capitalized on his weakened state and slipped its yoke.

He hurled VAELBOR's black scimitar, which struck the Huey's windshield hard enough to shatter it. As soon as the blade was airborne, though, Cade felt VAELBOR desert him, as well. He was now without offensive talents, and his few remaining defenses wouldn't last much longer.

"Keep moving," he snapped at Yasmin, who had paused to gawk at his fight with the chopper. He drew his wand and invoked MERSOS's talent for concealment, to shroud the villa's shattered foundation in distorting illusions to foul the Huey pilot's aim. Then he turned—

And fell on his face as he tried to hurdle a mound of mangled chairs.

The pilot fired blind into Cade's illusion. At point-blank range the autocannon's drone was the sound of terror incarnate.

Cade caught sight of sweet Mira as she fumbled his sack of books—

A random burst from the autocannon vaporized her head and sprayed Cade's face with blood, tattered flesh, and shards of bone from a woman he had loved like his own child.

His mind went blank with horror and disbelief.

All he could do was tremble and scream in rage.

He was still screaming when the whine of the cannon ceased.

Sathit grabbed the books Mira had dropped and ran toward Anja, whose voice rose above the weeping and howls of the wounded. "Cade! Move!"

Hot tears stung his eyes. He couldn't see where he was going. The wound in his left side burned, but he threw himself forward in clumsy lunges, forcing himself over obstacles, toward Anja's voice. He was light-headed but his vision cleared just enough for him to see Anja standing with her wand raised in front of the door, her voice strong and certain: *"Aperiri libertatis!"*

A blue flash shot from Anja's wand and set the door aglow.

She opened it with a single push. It swung away from her, and at first all

Cade saw on the other side was darkness. Then a flash of lightning revealed a rain-scoured lakefront.

"Move!" Anja yelled at him and the remaining adepts.

First through the doorway was Sathit, clutching Cade's bundle of books. Half a step behind her, Yasmin dived through like someone who had spent her whole life dodging bullets.

Anja pulled Barış from the chaos.

Then the Huey opened fire again.

Hot metal raked the villa's foundation. Cade watched in horror as a hail of lead struck Leyton in the back. The youth jerked and fell to his knees before he and Viola, cradled in his arms, were shredded into pulp just a few meters shy of the escape portal.

A hot burst of pain slammed into Cade's thigh. It struck with enough force to throw him forward and leave him stunned in the muddled pool of muck and blood.

Yangchen rushed toward Cade, a portrait in courage.

A hellish whine filled the air as an autocannon pulverized him into a red stain.

Barış and Anja reached Cade's side. "Grab him!" she yelled.

Cade felt his strength fade as blood poured from his flank. His control of his last few yoked spirits slipped away, along with his hold on consciousness.

As he was dragged off the field of battle, the last thing he saw with his dimming vision was the mass grave of good people who had trusted him, only to be led to a slaughter.

My demons were wrong. I won't die here today.

But I deserved to.

Gunfire chased Anja and Barış as they dragged Cade through the magickal doorway. Holding him, they dived as one toward the rain-soaked lakeshore and sank into a shallow marsh as autocannon rounds screamed past above their heads. The barrage ceased as Sathit kicked shut the door, which vanished with a thunderclap as soon as its latch struck its lock.

Anja and Barış dragged Cade ashore. Barış inspected Cade's leg wound while Anja tied a tourniquet above it. "Looks like ground beef," Barış said.

A flash of lightning lit up the landscape for miles around. They were on the shore of a large lake in a sparsely populated region of the island territory of Tasmania, southeast of Australia. Several dozen meters from where Anja and her handful of survivors now lay, there stood a long and modest-looking lodge. Its lights were off, which was not surprising. By Anja's best estimate, the local time in Tasmania was somewhere around four in the morning.

She had not had time to take a head count during the desperate bid for escape from Naxos. Looking around and piercing the darkness with the aid of the Sight, she discovered that aside from herself, Barış, and Cade, the only other survivors were Sathit and Yasmin.

Whoever did this will pay for it in blood.

The adepts gathered around Cade, who remained unconscious while raindrops pelted his face. Sathit's voice shook with fear. "Will he live?"

"He will." Anja placed her right palm on his torso wound and channeled BUER's healing gift. Within seconds the bleeding stopped, the wound closed, and she saw from the change in Cade's aura that his vigor was returning. She repeated the process for the injury to his leg.

His eyes fluttered open. He blinked into the rain, and then he sat up. First he looked at Anja, and then at their last three adepts. He didn't try to hide the sorrow in his voice. "Is this all of us?" Anja nodded in grim confirmation. Cade nodded, but his eyes looked haunted. "We need a plan. I have to yoke more spirits. As soon as possible."

Barış looked worried. "Maybe we should lie low for a while."

Weary and unsteady, Cade stood. "No. Whoever did this to us went after Briet in Dallas. She needs our help—and we're gonna need hers."

Confused, Sathit asked, "To do what, Master?"

He squinted as lightning arced across the sky. "Hunt down every last fucker who had a hand in this."

Anja cupped Cade's face in her hands and touched her forehead to his. "We will."

Yasmin said with a note of mild concern, "Someone's coming."

Anja and the others followed Yasmin's eyeline. As lightning flashed once more, Anja saw a barefoot figure in a hooded robe walking toward them from the house. It had been many years since last she had seen him, but she recognized his gait. "It is all right," she said.

"He's a friend," Cade added, and the adepts relaxed.

Moments later, the man who lived in the lodge stood before Anja and company. He pulled back his hood to let the rain dance atop his tonsured head. He smiled. "Cade. Anja."

"Father Pérez," Anja said.

Cade nodded. "Luis. Good to see you."

The defrocked Brazilian Jesuit priest and Gray magician frowned at the group. "Judging from your haggard state, I presume this is not a social call."

"Afraid not," Cade said.

A sympathetic nod, and then Luis gestured toward the house. "Very well. Come along, then. Let's get you all out of the rain."

SATURDAY, NOVEMBER 23

The hotel room was clean and tastefully furnished, but to Briet it felt like a prison cell. She paced in front of the large window that faced Commerce Street in downtown Dallas. Morning sun poured in, hot and blinding, barely mitigated by the gauzy curtain she had left closed.

It was almost 10:00 A.M. She had been holed up in this trap for hours. Using an alias and paying cash, she had checked in the day before, ordered room service for dinner and breakfast, cursed at the sloth of the service and its outrageous prices, and spent a restless night tossing and turning in between stolen moments of troubled sleep.

That morning's weak and tepid shower had not improved her mood. Nor had the long and ominous silence from Cade and Anja after the abrupt end of their conversation, which had disintegrated Briet's mirror and left her palm full of sparkling dust and freshly drawn blood. Something terrible had been set in motion. Something too large for her to face alone.

She had tried turning on the television to banish the crushing silence. Every channel had been packed that morning with news shows talking about the murder of President Kennedy. Hearing the details rehashed three times every hour had eroded what little remained of Briet's composure. The radio had offered a better distraction. She had set it to a station that played innocuous schmaltz. It wasn't her kind of music, but she couldn't find a radio broadcast in Dallas that played jazz, so she made do with what was available.

Anxiety started to get the better of her. *What if help never comes? What if I'm on my own now?* It was a chilling notion, but one she had long feared was coming her way. During the night she had sent her porter demon to fetch her a pistol and several boxes of ammunition, as well as a brick of cash. During one of her bouts of insomnia she had left the room and gone just far enough to scout all the exits, including the hotel staff's service passages, the freight elevator, and which doors to the roof were unlocked. She had at least five exit strategies that didn't require the use of magick. Someone who could shatter one of Cade's mirrors might be capable of anything.

A soft knocking at her door. Something about that sound in that setting had always made Briet think of illicit encounters; a discreet summons to something tawdry.

But not this time. Now it was cause for both hope and fear.

Treading softly, she moved to the left of the door. Put the muzzle of her Luger P08 semiautomatic pistol in front of the peephole and used the Sight to peer through the locked portal. If she didn't recognize the person on the other side, and he or she wasn't wearing a hotel uniform, Briet was going to put a bullet in her visitor's head.

Her magickal vision pierced the door and saw Cade standing outside. He was disheveled, bruised, and had the glum affect of a man who had not slept in far too long.

Briet opened the door but kept her pistol ready behind her hip, just in case. "Where have you been?"

"Reliving the fucking Alamo." Cade shouldered past her without an invitation. For once his rudeness came as a relief to Briet. Had he tried to be nice to her, she might have considered him a threat. But an asshole? That was the entitled American with whom she had been at odds for most of the last two decades.

She shut the door and followed him. "Nice of you to join me."

He stopped in the middle of the room. Looked around. "Got anything to drink?"

"Just tap water that smells like rust."

"Only the best at the Statler Hilton." He shook off his bomber jacket and draped it over the back of the chair in front of the room's small desk. "Don't suppose you have a minibar? I've been up all night yoking demons, and tele-portation while sober is a major fucking drag."

"If this room had a minibar, I'd have emptied it already."

"Don't try to match shitty days with me, Red."

His taunt made her tighten her grip on the Luger. "You want to compare? I had a man's brains shot into my lap yesterday. A man I trained. Murdered right in front of me."

Cade turned and confronted Briet at point-blank range. "I watched *seven* of my students get murdered last night. Blown to fucking pieces by mercs with magick-piercing rounds. That's on top of the seven I lost *before* the massacre started. If it weren't for Anja, I'd be dead right now. And adding insult to injury? They blew up my fucking house! So you want to tell me again what a shitty fucking day *you* had?"

Briet shut her eyes and bowed her head, ceding the rhetorical point to Cade. She took a breath and purged herself of her selfish anger. "Is Anja all right?"

"She's fine." Cade backed up half a step and relaxed. "She's heading to D.C. while Luis patches up the last of my apprentices."

The mention of the former White magician jogged Briet's memory. "I haven't seen Luis since the battle on Shemya Island. How is he?"

"Older, but he assures me he's also wiser, so no regrets."

"That sounds like Luis." She set her Luger on the desk. "Shall we get to work?"

"I didn't come all this way just for the barbecue." Cade leaned against the wall between the desk and the large window. "By now all the evidence from the shooting has been sent to the FBI's crime lab in D.C. Anja's on her way there to see what she can dig up."

Briet nodded. "That's a good start. Can you get a message to her?"

"It's hard without the mirrors. But we can use astral messengers, or flamescrying if we need to. What should I tell her?"

"To focus her search on Oswald's rifle and spent cartridges. If the people behind this haven't swapped them out yet, it might give us a clue to who's behind the conspiracy."

Cade arched a single eyebrow. "Which conspiracy? The one that's hunting down the world's magicians, or the one that killed the president?"

"I'm pretty sure they're the same thing." Briet stepped toward the window. "But that's only our first objective. Second, and equally important, is Oswald himself. And he's still in Dallas." She pulled aside the sheer curtain and looked down at the street. "Right down there, a block away, in the police headquarters on Commerce Street."

Cade moved to Briet's side and looked out the window. "The big building with the fancy columns?"

"No, that's the Municipal Building on South Harwood. Police HQ is the glorified brick shithouse behind it."

He nodded. "Ah. Okay. That looks more like a police station." He pulled a pack of Lucky Strikes from inside his jacket, lipped one free, and lit it with a snap of his fingers. After taking his first puff, he said in a gray plume, "Call me crazy, but Oswald's got to be the most heavily guarded man in America right now. Why risk our asses trying to get to him?"

"Because he fired magick-piercing rounds at Kennedy. Anything he can tell us about them—Who did he get them from? Who manufactured them? How many did he receive?—could be vital in tracking them to their source."

Cade took a long drag. His features turned hard and mean as he exhaled. "Gotta be honest: I'd like to have a word with the motherfucker who made those bullets." He threw a side-eye at Briet. "So how do we get in? I presume you have a plan."

"Walk in the front door. As long as you look the part, no one will stop you."

"Just me? What about you?"

"The local Hammers know my face, and Dallas PD has to be looking for me by now. I can't risk getting anywhere near Oswald."

The weary karcist sighed. "I knew I'd regret coming here."

"That makes two of us. I need you to reach Oswald while he's in his cell on the fifth floor and find out everything he knows." Briet appraised Cade's attire and grooming with a disapproving look. "But first you need a shave and a shower, and then you'll need a new suit. Luckily for you, Neiman Marcus is only a block away."

Cade frowned. "Wait—you want me to cut off my beard?"

"And they say vanity is a woman's sin." She put her Luger into her purse, and then she pushed a twenty-dollar bill into Cade's hand. "There's a barber in the hotel lobby. Get a shave and a haircut. I'll buy you a suit and meet you back here in twenty minutes."

As she walked to the door, Cade pocketed the twenty. "Get me a Zegna in a forty-two regular, dark gray Merino wool, with a red silk tie and black Oxfords—not brogues."

Briet fixed him with a glare. "You'll get what's on sale."

◆◇◆

It was just after eleven thirty in the morning when Cade walked into the headquarters of the Dallas Police Department feeling as if a rabid howler monkey were clutching his balls. Projecting confidence was proving more difficult than he'd expected because Briet had somehow—he suspected deliberately—gotten every detail of his suit fitting wrong.

His trouser legs rode a quarter of an inch too high on his ankles, around which his too-loose socks lay in wrinkles. The waistband was too generous, so that even with a belt he felt as if his pants might fall at any moment. His shoes were a shade too narrow and pinched his toes. His jacket fit fine, but the shirt underneath it was a cruel joke: the sleeves ended an inch shy of his wrists, and the neck was half an inch smaller than he'd asked for, making him feel like a fisherman's half-throttled cormorant. The final insult atop Cade's heap of sartorial injuries? Briet had bought him a necktie of lavender paisley.

Cade climbed a tall flight of granite steps to the building's Commerce Street entrance. At the top he caught his reflection on the station's glass door and cursed under his breath. The barber in the Statler hotel had given him a ridiculous schoolboy's haircut and nicked his chin three times while removing his beard with a straight razor. *Between getting sheared by an idiot and dressed by a sadist, I look like a stunt double for the Three Stooges.*

The ground-floor corridor was packed with reporters, most of them bearing newspaper or magazine credentials. The line at each pay phone was six people deep, and a knot composed of dozens of sweaty bodies blocked the path to the elevators. Leading with his shoulder, Cade bladed through a cluster of fact-starved journalists and turned right toward the building's main stairwell.

The weather outside that morning was mild, but the air in the switchback stairway was hot and thick. Holding up his trousers with one hand, Cade climbed the steps two at a time, working up a sweat on his way to the third floor. When he reached the third floor, he found his passage through an intersection of corridors impeded by an even larger contingent of newsmen than he had evaded in the lobby. Up here it was mostly television crews. Technicians had run cables every which way, blanketing the floor with black electrical spaghetti. Producers argued with Dallas cops while their on-air talent took deep breaths and struggled not to mar their tailored outfits and made-up faces with perspiration. Any space not occupied by TV people was filled by federal agents, lawyers, and Dallas County sheriff's deputies.

Elbowing and gently shoving his way through the scrum, Cade reached the Robbery-Homicide offices. Seated just inside the door was a uniformed sergeant. Cade looked the cop in the eye as he invoked the suggestive powers of ESIAS in a confident, steady timbre. "I'm Assistant U.S. Attorney Robert Kaufmann. I need to see suspect Lee Harvey Oswald right now."

Half mesmerized, the sergeant blinked. Then he murmured, as if by rote, "I'll need to see some ID, sir."

From inside his suit coat, Cade pulled out a billfold and flipped it open on the desk. "Here are my credentials." One interior face of the billfold was covered by a blank piece of paper. Taped to the opposite face was a circle of aluminum foil. Neither looked like anything of note—not until the demon's power of suggestion kicked in. "If we're done dotting i's and crossing t's, Sergeant, I'd like an answer. Where is Oswald?"

"In his cell. Fifth floor." He gestured with his chin over his shoulder. "It's lunch break."

"I see. And how do I get to the fifth floor?"

"Take the jail elevator, next door." He checked the prisoner log on his desk. "Oswald's in F Block." He picked up his phone's receiver. "I'll tell 'em you're coming, Mr. . . . ?"

"Kaufmann, with two 'n's. Assistant U.S. Attorney Robert Kaufmann."

"Got it."

Cade closed his billfold but kept it handy as he left the Robbery-Homicide office and evaded the media circus on his way to the small jail elevator lobby at the northeast corner of the intersection. A burly uniformed officer stood in front of it, his body language sending a clear message: *None shall pass.* His partner stood at the nearby desk, receiving orders over the phone.

Cade prayed for his pants to stay on as he approached them. With his free hand he raised his billfold and let it drop open. "Robert Kaufmann, assistant U.S. attorney," he said, once again projecting the demon's power to influence minds. "I have permission to question Oswald."

The guard on the phone nodded to the one blocking the way. "He's cleared."

The big man moved aside. Cade hit the call button, and the elevator opened at once. He stepped in and pressed the button for the fifth floor.

Its climb was slow and creaky. A violent tremor shook the elevator car as it stopped on the fifth floor, making Cade wonder if it was about to plunge into the basement with him trapped inside. After a few more seconds the elevator ceased its hydraulic seizures, and its doors opened.

Cade stepped out onto the fifth floor. It was dimly lit. A reek of stale sweat, fresh puke, and urine pervaded the place. From darkened corners and segregated cell blocks came the groans and ramblings of the pitiful and the deranged.

Directly ahead of the elevator was a small office behind a window. A uniformed officer sat on the other side of the glass. He hung up a phone when he saw Cade. "Kaufmann?"

"That's me."

"ID?"

Cade showed the billfold again, marshaling the power of ESIAS as he did so. The man behind the glass nodded. "Fine." He pointed past Cade. "Block F is out the door, that way, first door on your right. Cell two."

"Thank you." Cade put away his billfold and left the receiving area. As promised, Cell Block F was only a few steps down the corridor. He entered and approached the armed guard stationed in front of the middle of three cells along the wall on his left. He focused the demon's power on the guard as he smiled and said with as much courtesy as he could feign, "If you don't mind, Officer, I need a few minutes alone with Mr. Oswald."

It took a second for the demonic suggestion to overcome the guard's aversion to leaving his post, but he did. Once he was gone, Cade stepped in front of cell two and faced the skinny, drab-looking young white man seated on a steel bunk. His short brown hair was greasy and mussed. He wore dark pants, black loafers, and a dirty white T-shirt. His belt was absent, possibly confiscated by the police as a safeguard against a suicide attempt.

"Lee Harvey Oswald, I presume."

"Who wants to know?"

Cade pulled out his pack of Luckies, popped one into his mouth, and lit it with his Zippo. "Who I am doesn't matter. I need to ask you some questions, and unless you like pain, I suggest you tell me the truth."

Lee reclined onto his pancake-flat mattress and folded his hands behind his head. "I haven't played ball with the cops. I sure as hell ain't singin' for you."

"You don't want to play the hard case with me, kid. I'll fuck you up."

His threat made Lee smirk. "Yeah, sure you—" The assassin let out a sound that was somewhere between a gasp and a gag as Cade used the hands of GŌGOTHIEL to strangle him.

"If I tell the demon to hand me your spleen, it will. So knock off the bullshit." He released Lee from the demon's grip and took a puff of his Lucky. "Ready to talk?"

Lee sat up and massaged his throat. There was terror in his eyes. "You gotta believe me: I'm just a patsy, I swear."

It was time for Cade to switch to the big guns. He invoked the truth-compelling powers of EVAKIEL. "Are you telling me you didn't shoot the president?"

"No, it was me. I fired the shots. But I had no choice."

Cade moved closer to the bars. "What do you mean you *had no choice*?"

Naked desperation took hold of the killer. "From the second I touched that rifle, I've felt like a puppet. Like someone else was using me, and I couldn't say no."

"Where'd you get the rifle?"

"Mail-order. From a catalog."

Cade recalled newspaper articles he had read that morning about the assassination. "It was a Mannlicher-Carcano, right?" Lee nodded. "Pretty obscure choice. Why that one?"

"It was cheap. And it's the one the man told me to get."

Now Cade's interest sharpened. "What man?"

"Isidro Rocha. Same guy who gave me the cartridges. Just one clip with five rounds in it. He told me not to waste any of them on practice, 'cause that's all there was." A fleeting look of shame crossed Lee's face. "But I had to test the rifle. I had to *know*. So I used one for practice." He cracked a wan smile at a memory. "Made the best target shot of my life."

Cade maintained a poker face while he smoked, but in his mind, gears were turning. *An enchanted rifle with magick-piercing rounds. Makes sense.* Cade needed more, but his mind trick on the guard would wear off soon. "Who's Isidro Rocha? Where do I find him?"

"He's a Cuban. A diplomat. I met him through the embassy in Mexico City. I think he lives there, but I don't know for sure."

"Good enough. Thank you for your cooperation, Mr. Oswald." Cade released the man from EVAKIEL's control and turned to leave.

Lee stood and moved to the bars, as if he were desperate not to see Cade go. "Wait!"

Cade looked back and made no effort to hide his contempt. "What?"

"When I fired my first shot . . . I saw a pulse of light around the limo. I was sure I'd lined up the shot perfectly, but nothing happened except the flash. I've been losing my mind trying to figure out what happened. I asked the cops, but they won't tell me."

"Tell you what?"

"Whether my first shot really missed."

Cade took a final drag off his Lucky, and then he flicked it at Lee. The stub erupted into sparks as it bounced off the assassin's chest and rolled away from the cell on the stained concrete floor. Exhaling disgust along with a lungful of smoke, Cade answered as he left the cell block, "Trust me, asshole: You didn't miss."

Delegate, the Old Man always said, *delegate.* It was practically his cardinal rule, the defining characteristic of his management style. Niccolò could not remember the last time he had seen the Old Man handle a pen. The reclusive tycoon had long since insulated himself from the need to set his signature to paper. He had built shells of incorporation around himself, one within another like Russian nesting dolls, so that the tedium of paperwork was never his to endure.

He applied the same philosophy to communications with the world beyond his sanctums: Avoid taking meetings whenever possible; send proxies to negotiate, intimidate, or acquire; and never, *ever,* speak to anyone on the phone. Those tasks were the purview of underlings.

So it was that Niccolò found himself hunched over a speakerphone on the Old Man's mahogany desk, in the top-floor study of his Swiss mountainside retreat, which Niccolò had nicknamed the Alps Haus. The desk, like those of many other wealthy souls, was all but bare, adorned only by a glass-shaded Tiffany lamp, a leather blotter, and the speakerphone—a modern innovation that looked out of place amid the rustic luxury of the room's hardwood floors, natural stone walls, and exposed-beam ceilings.

The Old Man sat in a leather-upholstered chair on the other side of the desk. He had turned to the side, and his profile was backlit with moonglow reflected off the snow-covered slopes beyond the broad window behind him. In his left hand he held a plate piled with cooked bacon and chunks of rare prime rib. He leaned forward and hand-fed a slice of the bacon to his faithful German shepherd, which lounged at his feet. He feigned disinterest in the conversation Niccolò was conducting on his behalf, but the matter at hand was grave.

"My patron and I are well aware of the current tensions in Dallas,"

Niccolò said. "That does not excuse your operatives' failure to neutralize Miss Segfrunsdóttir when they had the chance, or your tardiness in reporting this error."

Over the telephone, Ben Dobyns, a deputy director at the United States' National Security Agency, sounded shaken. *"Our Hammers did the best they could. They got Warden—"*

"Which is why we are still talking, Mr. Dobyns. Had they both escaped, my patron would have directed me to make his displeasure known in a more *direct* manner." Niccolò took note of a quick sidelong glance by the Old Man, a subtle cue to move matters forward with haste. "The fact remains, *signore,* that the job for which you were paid remains only half done. How do you propose to finish it?"

"There's nothing more we can do. At least not in Dallas." It was not the answer the Old Man wanted, and his glare expressed his displeasure to Niccolò.

"Why not?" the magician asked.

"The botched hit happened in broad daylight on a city street. There were witnesses. That kind of fallout is hard to cover up." Dobyns's voice grew tense. *"The Pentagon wants this buried. They never want Briet showing off her unique skill set in public again, and they want you and the rest of the Old Man's dogs on a leash, as well."*

The Old Man cocked one eyebrow. Niccolò held up a finger to beg the boss's indulgence, and then he said to Dobyns, "Ben, my old pal. Maybe we could agree on a compromise?"

The NSA spook replied with obvious suspicion, *"I'm listening."*

"We respect your desire to keep order in your streets, and we share your preference for discretion where the Art is concerned. We can even empathize with your community's reluctance to engage in wetwork against one of your own."

"How noble of you. Get to the point."

"If you cannot neutralize Miss Segfrunsdóttir, and you will not permit us to complete the sanction, allow me to suggest that you disavow her. Revoke her credentials."

"What will that accomplish?"

"There are foreign agencies who have their own reasons for wanting her out of the picture. One in particular has a reputation for efficiency and discretion. My employer and I would make certain that news of her disavowal reaches that agency in a timely fashion. Result: A foreign actor eliminates our shared liability, while you, your agency, and your government retain full plausible deniability."

Across the desk, the corner of the Old Man's mouth betrayed the curl of smirk.

On the other end of the international phone call, a pensive silence.

Then Dobyns replied, *"Okay. She'll be disavowed in precisely thirty minutes."*

"Splendid, Benjamin. Leave the rest to us. *Ciao.*" Niccolò pressed a button and ended the call without waiting for Dobyns to finish his own farewell. The magician stood tall and waited for some acknowledgment from his patron.

The Old Man fed a hunk of steak to his dog. The canine gnawed on the rare meat, blood spilling from between its teeth. The Old Man kept his gaze averted from the magician. "What are you waiting for, Niccolò? A curtain call? A dozen roses? I'm not paying you to take a bow."

"Of course not, *signore*. With your permission, I will continue." Clocking a dismissive nod and a wave from the Old Man, Niccolò opened a new line on the speakerphone and dialed.

A bemused look from the Old Man. "You have their number memorized?"

"But of course." Niccolò smiled as the call started to ring. "One never knows when one might need to get in touch with the Mossad."

⌇⌇⌇

The sixth floor of the U.S. Department of Justice Building in Washington, D.C., should have been all but deserted at midafternoon on a Saturday, but because it was home to the FBI's forensic laboratory two days after President Kennedy's assassination, it was busier than the Roma Termini station at rush hour.

On any other day, braving such a crowded setting would have left Anja paralyzed with anxiety—she preferred to live in isolation whenever possible. Today, however, the fact that the FBI Laboratory had called in every forensic specialist it could find to assist in the processing of evidence from the shooting in Dallas provided her with excellent cover. She had used an illusion to hide the Y-shaped scar on her left cheek, since that was her most recognizable feature. For her disguise she had gathered her black hair in a tight bun, put on a fake pair of angular tortoiseshell eyeglasses, and donned a long white lab coat over her white blouse, gray skirt, and gray flats.

Walking the corridors of the sixth floor, Anja felt the energies that defended the place from most forms of scrying or intrusion. Like many federal build-ings, it secretly had been warded by Briet and her karcists in the Occult De-fense Program.

Thanks to a message from Briet, sent via Cade, Anja had been able to embark upon this mission with the intel she needed to bypass most of the building's defenses. Much to her chagrin, though, even Briet could not defeat her own safeguards against teleportation into or out of the building. Conse-quently, Anja had been forced to portal onto its roof and pick the lock on its door the old-fashioned way, and only from the roof could she safely make her eventual exit.

Walking the long corridor, she stole glances into each laboratory she passed. Everywhere she looked there were technicians and assistants running tests, peering into microscopes, taking measurements, drafting or dictating reports, and logging in new items.

When she extended her perceptions using the Sight, she saw her environ-ment in a bluish monochrome, within which anything magickal blazed white. At once she saw the hidden glyphs concealed inside the walls, floors, and ceil-ings. Taking care not to blunder into any devil's traps or angel's snares, she did her best to avoid making eye contact with the people she passed in the hallway. The last thing she needed was to be engaged in a conversation that would re-veal her Russian accent—another distinguishing characteristic that would be certain to attract unwelcome attention in America's capital.

Beyond the pale blue ghost-shapes and fiery white sigils that surrounded her, Anja saw the telltale glow of enchantment. It emanated from a room ahead of her, one located in a short transverse passage around the corner from the next intersection. She turned toward it without hesitation. *Some-times the best part of a disguise is confidence.*

She arrived at a locked door marked EVIDENCE STORAGE. Focusing the Sight, she peered through the door to make certain there was no one on the other side—no loitering scientists, no one manning a desk, no armed guards. Seeing the room was unoccupied, she summoned the lock-opening gifts of QAFIL and opened the locked door with one turn of its knob. She slipped inside, eased the door closed, and then she flipped the wall switch for the lights.

Overhead, fluorescent tubes flickered to life and cast a sickly glow on rows of metal shelving, which reached from the floor to the drop-tile ceiling. The shelves all were packed from end to end with orderly rows of evidence. Each item was sealed inside a paper bag, to which was affixed a paper tag with handwritten information concerning its contents and their provenance. Almost every bagged exhibit Anja saw as she moved through the room was connected to the Kennedy assassination, and nearly all of them related in some way to the case's chief suspect, Lee Harvey Oswald.

In the back of the room, shining like beacons, were the only pieces of evidence in which Anja had the least interest: the Mannlicher-Carcano 6.5 mm bolt-action rifle, three spent cartridges, a fired bullet and some fragments, and one unfired cartridge recovered by the FBI.

The rifle lay flat, taking up most of a shelf section by itself. On the shelf beneath it was the ammunition. She opened the paper bags with care, one at a time.

Bagged together were the three spent cartridges found in the sniper's nest on the sixth floor of the Texas Book Depository. In another bag were the single unfired cartridge recovered from inside the rifle, which had been found discarded behind some boxes near the sniper's nest; some fragments recovered from the interior of Kennedy's limousine; and a curiously intact bullet that had been found on the stretcher of the wounded Governor John Connally, after he was taken into surgery at Parkland Memorial Hospital.

Traces of magick lingered on the spent cartridges, fragments, and fired round. White-hot auras surrounded the rifle and the unfired cartridge. Anja picked up the cartridge. It shone like the sun in her hand. She attuned herself to MEVAKOS, the spirit from which she had yoked her magickal vision. *Look past its power. I need to see the truth within it.*

The glow abated, and her spectrum of vision shifted until she perceived the cartridge as if it were flesh penetrated by an X-ray. Symbols too small for her to discern ringed the inner surface of the cartridge case. *Clever. The magick hides inside the brass.* Again she directed her will toward the demon. *Magnify my vision. I need to see those symbols clearly.*

The ghostly, see-through image of the cartridge enlarged as Anja concentrated upon it, until the symbols on the inside of its case became legible. They were a series of invocations, not unlike defensive wards tattooed upon important persons to keep them safe from Infernal harassment. But these were configured in a most peculiar manner, one that Anja had never seen before.

I will need demonic counsel to make sense of this. Anja had foreseen such a possibility before jaunting to Washington, and had yoked a new spirit suited to the task.

Lend me your wisdom, PSEMAEL. The spirit writhed inside of her, full of rebellion. *See what I see and reveal to me its purpose and the details of its function.*

Even among the prehistoric multitudes of Hell, PSEMAEL was considered ancient. The spirit's knowledge of hidden truths, the origins of things, and secrets of magick was said to be without equal under Heaven. For her sake as well as others', Anja hoped that was true.

The spirit's mind moved like a cold shadow behind hers.

SHOW ME. Its voice inside her mind was the scratch of a skeleton dragged across stone.

Anja trained her piercing vision on the cartridge.

A POWERFUL ENCHANTMENT. IT BEARS THE MARKS OF FIVE OF THE SIX MINISTERS OF HELL. NO ONE MAGICIAN COULD HAVE MADE THIS. IT WOULD TAKE FIVE KARCISTS WORKING IN TANDEM.

"Are those what enable it to destroy magickal shields? Or hit a ghosted karcist?"

YES. SUCH A ROUND COULD EVEN STRIKE A SPIRIT. The spirit compelled Anja to look up at the rifle. BUT ONLY WHEN FIRED FROM A WEAPON CONSECRATED WITH THE SEAL OF HELL'S PRIME MINISTER.

She looked more closely at the Mannlicher-Carcano. Hidden inside its trigger assembly was a tiny engraving of the seal of LUCIFUGE ROFOCALE:

She reasoned out the puzzle. "Combining the cartridge with the weapon gives it the power of all six ministers of Hell."

CORRECT, EVE-SPAWN.

She picked up the bag of three spent cartridges. When she searched their inner surfaces, she found no sigils of any kind. "Why don't these have the marks?"

THEIR WARDS ARE CONSUMED BY HELLFIRE WHEN THEIR MAGICK IS INVOKED.

"Convenient." She reached into her lab coat's pocket and fished out a handful of spent brass and a spare rifle cartridge she had brought along. Unlike the enchanted cartridge and brass collected in Dallas by the FBI, these were ordinary rounds procured by her demonic porter DANOCHAR from a bulk U.S. government order fulfilled by the Western Cartridge Corporation.

She cleaned her fingerprints from the ones she'd touched and set them on the shelf next to their bagged cousins. "DANOCHAR, exchange the three brass cases inside the bag for the three I have put beside it, and swap the whole cartridge for the one in the bag."

The transfer was an easy one for the demon. It took less time than the blink of an eye, and the spirit left no fingerprints or other detectable signatures on the bags or the stolen evidence. Anja swept the brass and the cartridge into fresh evidence bags, which she pinched shut and tucked into her coat's deep front pocket. *Cade will want to see these.*

She considered stealing the rifle by entrusting it to DANOCHAR, but without a dummy to take its place it was too great a risk. Someone would need it for further tests at any moment, and she couldn't risk triggering a state of heightened alarm by having it go missing. The same risk applied to the bullet fragments, whose shapes must have been documented by now.

She shut off the lights, moved to the door, and peered beyond it with the Sight. It took nearly half a minute for several people to pass by, some alone, others in pairs, before the transverse passage had a moment free of traffic. Anja opened the door swiftly, slipped past it into the corridor, and did her best to shut it with both speed and stealth. As soon as its lock clicked into place, she was on the move, her hands in her coat pockets, her eyes on the floor.

In the wider and longer outer hallway she blended back into the flow of bodies. As she passed the elevator, its doors opened, and out stepped a pair of tall, broad-shouldered men wearing dark suits and black sunglasses. They looked conspicuous amid the forensic experts in their white lab coats. One of the big guys, a square-jawed brute, cornered the first person he saw, a short and nervous man with white hair. "You. Where's the evidence lockup?"

Dr. White Hair trembled as the two larger men loomed over him. "I'm not sure I can—"

Square Jaw flashed NSA credentials at Dr. White Hair. Anja did her best to seem small and insignificant while she slipped past behind them. "This is a matter of national security," said Square Jaw. "Direct me to your evidence room. Now."

The scientist pointed down the long passageway with a shaking hand. "That way. Take your second right. It's in the transverse."

Without a word of thanks, Square Jaw and his partner marched away down the hall, no doubt on a mission to whitewash or disappear the very same evidence Anja had just stolen.

There was nothing to be gained by confronting them, no value in slowing them down. All that mattered to Anja now was escape.

She walked in short, meek-looking steps to the end of the corridor. Slipped through the emergency exit door into the stairwell.

And then she ran for the roof like the Devil himself was at her heels.

———

The three young magicians were everything Luis had ever expected of adepts recruited and trained by Cade and Anja: secretive, sullen, and intense. Of course, all of those qualities could be ascribed to the fact they had just survived a brutal slaughter and had no idea who he was, aside from being told by Cade that Luis was "an old friend."

It had fallen to him to tend to their injuries. Most of Anja's healing strength had gone into making herself and Cade ready to return to action. Both of them had stayed awake through the night and into the morning, yoking new spirits to replenish their arsenals. That had left their students in Luis's care. Fortunately for the young trio, Luis had learned more than his share about first aid living alone in a Tasmanian cottage, and he had in recent years taken to keeping an angel with healing talents yoked to his bidding whenever the Divine allowed.

He had used conventional medicine to treat their minor wounds. Magick he saved for bullets lodged beyond easy extraction, or for major wounds or blood loss.

Now, several hours later, in one of the lodge's guest rooms, Luis breathed easier knowing the adepts were out of medical danger. Barış, a handsome man in his mid-thirties, had been the most seriously injured. While Luis had attended him, Sathit had magickally cleaned and restored the man's suit, fez, and bow tie. Now she sat at his bedside while he lay unconscious.

The sleeves of her shirt were rolled up past her elbows, revealing the colorful tattoos that wrapped around both her arms, down to the wrists. With her thumb she stroked Barış's brow, betraying her anxiety for her friend's recovery. As Luis passed by, Sathit reached out and halted him. "Father? Are you sure he's all right?"

Luis rested a comforting hand on Sathit's shoulder. "Divine healing magick sometimes takes a toll upon the patient. Let him rest. He will awaken whole." Sathit accepted Luis's assurance with a small nod and a sadly wistful expression.

Leaving the kind-eyed young woman to watch over Barış like a guardian angel, Luis continued to the bedside of Yasmin, who lay awake and restless with her back to the rest of the room. Luis sat at the foot of her bed. "You've been through quite an ordeal."

"I'm fine," the young woman with a crew cut said through nearly gritted teeth, as if she were willing her own truth into existence. "Preach your scripture someplace else."

Her defiance was not entirely unexpected. In recent centuries the Catholic Church had done much to aggrieve the Arabic peoples, especially those of Islamic faith. That made it feel imperative to Luis to convey to Yasmin that he came in peace. "I am not here to preach."

She regarded him with dark brown eyes full of anger and suspicion. "Then why *are* you here? To banish my demons?"

"Hardly." He touched the crucifix he wore around his neck. "Don't let this mislead you. I might have started my career in the Pauline tradition, but I've practiced my share of the Goetic Art, as well. Just like your masters, I'm what one might call a Gray magician."

Yasmin hunkered into a curl. "Good for you."

Luis lifted the sheets to steal a look at Yasmin's feet, ankles, calves, and shins. As he had expected, they were crosshatched with scabs and fresh scratches. None of the wounds on the young woman's legs had been inflicted by bullets or blades—they were too shallow and ragged. He recognized the wounds because he had seen their like many times before.

"You scratch at your legs. Sometimes with your fingernails." He looked closer and dared to handle Yasmin's foot, to steal a look at her toenails. Several were chipped and untrimmed with dried blood caked underneath. "But most often with the sharp nails on your toes."

She yanked away her feet and pulled the blanket over herself. "That's not your business."

"Which demon makes you do that? ARAMAEL? Or is it MALTHUS?"

Her tone grew more strident. "Leave me *alone*."

He folded his hands together. "I won't try to compel you to speak with me, but some of those cuts on your legs need to be disinfected." Luis stood. "I'll get a washcloth, some iodine, and some bandages."

Yasmin looked up from her pillow. "Bandages?"

"To cover the wounds. So they can heal." He saw the desperation in her eyes, the confusion, the pleading: *How will I scratch that itch if you bandage it?*

He took pity on her. "Haven't your masters taught you the art of self-medication? It can spare you pains such as this."

"Islam forbids the consumption of alcohol or narcotics."

"It also forbids the practice of magick, and any form of consort with demons." As soon as Luis had said the words, he saw that he had struck a nerve. "And that's the root of your anxiety, isn't it, Miss Elachi? Hence, the scratching."

A guilty nod, then she looked at him. "I won't compound one sin with another."

"Keep practicing the Goetic Art and you'll commit far greater sins than imbibing alcohol or injecting opiates to quiet your mind. I don't profess to be an expert in Islamic law, but I have read the Quran. I think Allah will forgive you a few drinks if they keep you from going insane."

He turned away but stopped as she asked, "Are the bandages really necessary?"

"Yes. I cannot permit you to contract gangrene while under my care. I promised your teachers I would see you restored to health."

"Then can you show me some way to resist the urge?"

He cast his memory back nearly thirty years, to his first missionary posting in Japan. "Are you familiar with the art of transcendental meditation?"

"No."

"Then I suspect we have an interesting day ahead of us." Noting the brightening of her mood, he added, "Just as soon as I clean your wounds. With your permission."

"Of course." Yasmin winced as if she were fighting the compulsion to scratch even then. "I'd do damned near anything to be rid of this."

"Then I shall endeavor to be quick. If there is one blessing we people of the cloth live to dispense, it is *deliverance*."

<p style="text-align:center">~~~</p>

"What do you mean they're gone?" Niccolò tightened his grip on the phone receiver to the point that he feared it might splinter in his fist. "Where are they?"

"No idea," said Agent Curtis, one of the Hammers the Old Man had sent to the FBI Laboratory to retrieve the enchanted Mannlicher-Carcano 6.5 mm rifle cartridges before they fell into the hands of the Americans' Occult Defense Program—or anyone else. *"All we found in the evidence lockup was regular ammo. The brass and the unfired cartridge you told us to bring back weren't there."*

Niccolò paced in the Old Man's office, looking out the broad window at the predawn stars on the western horizon. "Which means someone else took them."

"If you say so. I'm just telling you what we found. Or to be precise, didn't find."

Niccolò felt his pulse quicken as his breaths grew shallow. None of the architects or agents of this conspiracy could risk those rounds being subjected to a full magickal forensic examination. There was no risk to leaving the fragments, but examination of the full unfired cartridge from the rifle could reveal the magickal glyphs inscribed inside of it. The theft of those key pieces of evidence represented a grave violation of the plan's operational security. Feigning calm, he asked, "Did anyone at the lab see anything unusual?"

"Nothing that got their attention. But it's not like we could put the place on lockdown. After all, we couldn't tell them what was missing, could we?"

"No, you most certainly could not. Discretion was the wiser course of action."

"I'm glad you think so. Now, when do we get paid?"

"For what? Our agreement was a reward for the cartridges. Which you do not have."

"Don't split hairs with me, fuckball. We risked our badges going in there."

"And you want a reward in kind? Fine. I'll send you a tasteful floral arrangement. But if you say another word before I hang up, those flowers will be lilies—for your *funeral.* Good-bye, Mr. Curtis. You've been most useless." Niccolò set the phone's receiver back in its cradle, and then he fumed at the Americans' incompetence. *It was a simple mission.*

The only saving grace in which he could find comfort was the fact that the Old Man had already retired for the night when the call came in. For now, there was no need for him to know that a simple but crucial step in the plan had gone haywire, all because their opponents had proved harder to kill and quicker to respond than Niccolò had expected.

No, this was an error to be kept quiet.

I will fix this bungled detail myself. There is no reason the Old Man ever needs to know.

All he had to do was find the stolen cartridges.

Of course, there were only three people in the world who likely knew of the cartridges' existence and had the requisite magickal talent to have stolen them so quickly.

Cade Martin, Anja Kernova, and Briet Segfrunsdóttir.

If the thief was either Martin or Kernova, then the attack on Naxos had not been anywhere near as successful as Niccolò had hoped, or as complete as he had promised the Old Man it would be. If it had been Segfrunsdóttir, then the woman was even more resourceful and resilient than he had feared.

No matter which of them had taken the cartridges, the Old Man was going to be vexed.

In which case, it would be best to have the bullets back in our custody before he finds out they were ever gone. And if accomplishing that happens to involve eliminating the last enemies standing in the way of our new order . . . so mote it be.

8

"I think it's time to admit we've hit a dead end." Cade snuffed the stub of his Lucky in an ashtray crowded with the rest of its pack. "We've tested that bullet every which way we can without leaving this room, and we still don't know who made it or how the fuck they did it."

He looked out the window of Briet's room in the Statler Hilton. Sunset painted the high-rise towers of downtown Dallas in shades of pink and orange. Cade struggled not to fixate upon the neon allure of Victor's Lounge, located across Commerce Street from the hotel's front door. Briet had run out of vodka an hour earlier, and Cade felt the threat of incipient sobriety creep closer with the passage of every dry minute.

Anja sat on the bed, camped beside the end table's phone with a notepad and a pen. Dark circles had gathered beneath her gray eyes. "Your lead from Oswald has not helped. I have phoned all the Cuban embassies and consulates in America, Mexico, and Canada. They all deny any knowledge of a man named Isidro Rocha."

Cade's grousing and Anja's impatience flustered Briet. "What did you expect? Did you think the Cubans would just roll over and confirm that one of their assets is active on U.S. soil?"

"I think he is a ghost," Anja said. "No one by his name in any phone book. Not in Dallas, New Orleans, or anywhere else."

Cade respected Anja's insistence on being thorough. It was fortunate that the Statler Hilton and the new Dallas Public Library had been built side by side. Anja had slipped unnoticed out of the hotel shortly after her arrival via thunder jaunt onto its rooftop helipad. A ten-second walk later she had been inside the library, poring through its public information section.

If only her expedition had been as informative as it was discreet.

Briet pulled a gold-foil pack of Benson & Hedges cigarettes from her hand-bag. "If we've exhausted the easy solutions, maybe it's time to call in favors."

That earned a derisive *hmpf* from Anja. "No one owes me favors but him." She lifted her chin to indicate Cade.

Lighting one of her oversized, imported British cigarettes, Briet turned toward Cade. "What about your old partner? Isn't he some kind of big shot at MI6 now?"

Cade shrugged, played it cool. "He's a spymaster on permanent assign-ment at HQ. But he's a long way from the top of the layer cake."

Smoke spilled from Briet's mouth as she spoke. "Still, he'd have access to resources we don't. Classified files, Interpol dispatches, that kind of thing."

"True. But the first rule of the spy trade is that our own people are always watching and always listening. If we reach out to him, they'll know—and they'll tell the NSA."

Briet took another drag off her extra-long coffin nail, radiating incredulity the whole time. "Are you really telling me you two don't have a back channel? For emergencies?"

She wasn't wrong, but for Cade that wasn't relevant. "If I need to, yes, I can reach Miles. But asking him for help puts *him* in the crosshairs, and that's not a risk I want to take."

"Fine, tough guy. Tell me what other choices we have." A puff through pursed lips, followed by a rich plume of white smoke. "You want to put the question to Hell? Because I'm betting a guy who traffics in magick-piercing ammo is probably warded. My own government put a price on my head, so I don't think we're getting any tips from the CIA or the FBI." Briet aimed her icy blue glare at Anja. "How 'bout you, comrade? Anybody in the spook trade you *haven't* pissed off in the last ten years?"

Anja's reply was droll but freighted with implied violence. "I don't keep count."

The last thing Cade needed was for his two strongest allies to declare war on each other. "All right. Let's say I reach out to Miles. What do I ask him to help with? Finding Rocha? Or tracking the bullets to their source?"

Briet and Anja replied in unrehearsed but perfect unison, "Both."

"I think I like it better when you two aren't on the same side." Cade lit a fresh Lucky. "Fine, I'll ring Miles and see what he can do to get us unstuck. But it's after midnight in London, and tomorrow's Sunday, so it might be a while before he gets the message."

Once more Briet's impatience flared. "And what're we supposed to do until then?"

Anja stood and stretched. "I must return to our students. They will be worried." A notion darkened her countenance. She looked at Briet. "If your government marked you for death, they might attack your family."

Briet tensed, seized by competing tides of fear, alarm, and anger. "That's what the Nazis would have done. Or the Stalinists. This is America."

Now it was Cade's turn to look at Briet as if she had lost her mind. "Whoever's gunning for us doesn't act like they give a shit about collateral damage. If you've got loved ones, I'd get on the phone right now and tell 'em to make a fucking run for it. While they still can."

Briet, normally so composed, began to pace and didn't seem to know what to do with her hands. "No, I can't. Can't call them."

Anja's voice was sharp. "Why not?"

"Because I broke our only phone yesterday. Ripped out the wire." She stopped and covered her face with both hands while she took deep, calming breaths. When she lowered her hands she still looked petrified, but her breathing was steady and her eyes were clear. She picked up her wand and her Luger from the bed. "I have to go home, *now*. I need to get them out."

"Wait," Cade said, "your house—"

Briet made a balletic turn as she flourished her wand, surrounding herself in a tight vortex of green fire that flared to white—and then she was gone, leaving nothing behind but a stink of sulfur and a scorch on the carpet.

Cade sighed, and then he finished his sentence under his breath: "Your house might be under surveillance." He shot a glum look at Anja. "What do we do now?"

Anja walked over to stand with Cade. Wrapped one arm around his waist. Stole his Lucky from his hand. Took a slow drag and exhaled. "Hope her luck is better than ours."

Cars lined the streets, dark and empty. Night had settled upon the D.C. neighborhood of Georgetown, bringing with it a grave silence. This was not a typical Saturday evening before a holiday. The United States was in mourning, and a somber mood infused the capital's public spaces. Awash in grief, all of its monuments had, for tonight, been transformed into cenotaphs.

It was still early by Washington's standards, just after 8:30 P.M. Most of the houses on the block were dark. Its narrow sidewalks stood desolate, and a cold wind rustled the bare branches of trees already resigned to the coming of winter. Overhead, dark clouds pushed eastward, blotting out the moon and stars.

Sheltered in the darkness between houses, It waited. Its gaze was unblinking. Cold and unfeeling, It thought of nothing but Its task, constrained only by Its master's commands.

Rain drizzled on Its hat and shoulders. A faint mist gathered into a fog. Soon the street was shrouded in gray vapor illuminated by the dull orange glow of streetlamps. The shroud spread into every crack and crevice, moved beneath, between, and behind every house and car, wrapped itself around the lampposts, crept into the grates of sewers . . . all without a sound.

Tendrils of mist snaked inside and under Its knee-length trench coat. It paid the fog no mind. Such details did not matter. Immobile but alert, It waited.

Headlights speared through the mist as a car turned onto the residential street. As the sedan passed the house It had been sent to watch, the car's headlamps illuminated a woman walking alone on the sidewalk, her head down. When she looked up, It saw her face.

She was the Target.

The car rolled past her and paused at the intersection. Brake lights bathed the Target in red light as she hurried up the steps of a brownstone. While the Target unlocked the building's front door, the car disappeared into the foggy night. The Target opened the front door, slipped inside, and then closed it behind her. From across the street, It heard the door's locks being turned and its bolts being pushed into place.

It emerged from Its hiding place and crossed the street. Its steps were ponderous, but though Its progress toward the Target was slow, this encounter's conclusion was inevitable.

Moving with inexorable resolve toward the brownstone's rough-hewn front steps, It set Its mind upon the singular objective imparted by Its master:

The Target known as Briet Segfrunsdóttir must die.

～

The closing of the front door resounded through the brownstone. By the time Briet had secured its lock, deadbolt, and chain, her lovers Alton and

Hyun had come from the dining room to meet her. He approached her with open arms as Hyun declared with joy, "You're home!"

To Alton's surprise and dismay, Briet rejected his embrace with arms straight and stiff. "I'm not here to stay, and neither are you." She pushed past her lovers, who followed her as she darted into the living room. "You both need to get out of here, as fast as you can."

Alton's voice pitched upward with desperation and alarm. "Sweetheart, what are you on about?" He caught her by her shoulders. "Slow down and talk to us!"

She shook free of his grip. "There's no time! You're in danger, both of you." She turned away and walked toward the far wall. "It's because of me, and for that I'm truly sorry."

Hyun's wide-eyed shock betrayed her relative innocence. "Did you do something wrong? Are the police after you?"

"Worse." Briet pulled out her switchblade. "Much worse."

A push on the weapon's spring trigger released its blade with a *snikt*. She pulled from the wall a framed artwork—an expensive print of Monet's 1899 masterpiece *The Water Lily Pond*—and flipped it over to reveal its paper-covered back. "Hyun, go upstairs, pack a bag for each of you. Essentials only. Two changes of clothes, toiletries, bare necessities."

"Not until you tell us what is going on."

"Goddammit, there's no time." *Fuck, I've got to get them out of here.*

Briet's pulse raced as she sliced through the paper backing, following the edges of the wooden frame. When she had enough to pull on, she tore away the paper to reveal the hollow frame was packed with bricks of paper currency and a trio of passports. She took the new passport she'd had made for herself, and handed the others to Hyun and Alton.

"Take these, learn the details. Names, date of birth, city of birth." Before either of them was able to process why they had been handed fake passports containing their photos, Briet slapped wads of cash into their hands, in bundles of twenty- and fifty-dollar bills. "And as much cash as you can carry. Hide it in your clothes, in your luggage, anywhere you can."

Alton stared at the money in his left hand and the new passport in his right. "Bree, I know you're more than a secretary at the DOD, but I've never asked what you *really* do there." When he looked at Briet, his gaze was unyielding. "I'm asking now."

"And you've every right to." She jammed money into her coat's pockets.

"If we're all still alive in a few weeks, I'll tell you. But for now, you've got to fucking *listen*. Don't travel together. Call different cab companies. Have their drivers meet you someplace other than here. One of you go to the airport, the other to the train station. Go to different—"

A monstrous *bang* of impact on their front door cut her off.

No! Panic made Briet forget her intricate plan. *I have to get them out! Have to—*

Another *bang*.

This was no knocking fist—it was the thunder of a battering ram.

Something large and powerful was forcing its way into their home.

Briet faced the doorway and used the Sight to peer through the door. Where she expected to see the fierce glow of a demon attacking her wards, she saw nothing but an inky shadow—no sign of life or will, just a rock-solid form bashing her front door to pieces.

Her blood ran cold. Whatever it was, it was neither spirit nor human.

She reached under her coat, and for the first time in all the years that she had known and loved Alton and Hyun, she drew her wand in front of them.

"Both of you upstairs. *Now.*"

Alton bristled. "To hell with that!" He ran toward the closet under the stairs.

Briet shouted, "No, don't—!"

Chunks of the front door exploded inward.

In came a gloved fist larger than Briet's head.

Another blow broke the door in half down the middle.

Alton opened the stair-closet door and pulled out his twelve-gauge pump-action shotgun.

Briet wanted to attack, but Hyun was in the way.

A shoulder like a side of beef in a gray overcoat bashed through the remains of the door. It was followed by an anvil of a head beneath a charcoal fedora, and a barrel torso on top of tree-stump legs in black trousers that looked ready to split their seams.

The intruder stomped into the foyer on booted feet the size of cinder blocks.

Beneath the hat's low brim blazed two red eyes full of hate.

Hyun screamed. Briet shoved her aside and raised her wand.

But not before Alton fired his shotgun.

The shell exploded against the goliath's chest, to no effect. The giant plodded toward Alton, who pumped another ineffectual shot into its gut.

The hulking brute raised a gloved fist with which to pummel Alton, who froze.

Briet used the hands of PALARA to push Alton backward, out of the goon's reach. Then she torched the big fucker with a cone of fire from her wand. Its overcoat burst into flames, but instead of panicking or trying to quash the blaze, the silent colossus tore off its coat.

It flung the burning rags into the corner—where they set the curtains on fire.

Hyun's screams turned to high-pitched shrieks.

"Run!" Briet screamed at her lovers. "Go!"

The monster advanced on Briet. She wreathed it in lightning. Scoured it with envenomed needles. Shouted a jet of killing frost into its shadowed face—anything to keep it focused on her.

It pushed ahead, its pace slow but inexorable as it backed her toward a corner.

Her foot caught on something—a chair leg—and she stumbled backward before landing on her ass. The man-shaped mountain lifted its foot and stomped it down with fearsome speed. She barely had time to invoke HOZIKIEL's protection of stoneskin before the boulderlike foot slammed against her chest, knocking all the air from her lungs.

The fire on the curtains spread to the furniture and raced across the living room.

Lying on her back, Briet gasped for air and prayed her lovers had fled.

Please tell me you ran. Let this be the one time you listened—

She heard the *ker-clack* of the shotgun's pump action being primed.

Alton did the noble thing. The courageous thing. The stupid thing.

The monster pivoted to face Alton—who fired point-blank into its face. The blast scattered the intruder's fedora like ashen confetti, revealing its huge, hairless head.

Then it backhanded Alton with terrifying speed and power. A single blow caved in Alton's skull and knocked his limp body out of the living room, back to the foyer.

No! Hot tears stung Briet's eyes, but she had no breath for a scream. She stared at Alton's lifeless form and prayed for the impossible. *Please get up! Goddammit, Alton, please. Get up!*

His body remained motionless. The monster turned back toward Briet.

She fought to draw one good breath but failed. Her head swam as she struggled to get up to face the creature—

And then Hyun's wails of terror became growls of fury.

Oh, no. No, my love—please run. . . .

Hyun grabbed the coatrack with both hands. With a fierce twist she broke its pole free of its base. Gripping it like a spear, she spun toward the goliath.

The monster reached toward the desperately gasping Briet, who saw its inhuman face for the first time: a viselike closed slit for a mouth, barely a hint of a nasal cavity, deep sockets filled with fire instead of eyes—and, across its broad blocky forehead, Hebrew characters scribed in Kabbalistic pact ink:

A golem!

Hyun let out a battle cry, charged, and tried to skewer the golem.

Her improvised spear deflected off the golem's stony hide.

The creature turned and seized the weapon. Tore it from Hyun's hands.

Hyun froze just as Alton had, staring up at the soulless killing machine.

With one thrust the golem impaled Hyun and staked her to the floor.

Briet recoiled as if the monster had driven a stake through her own heart.

She got up, gulped in a breath of hot, smoky air—and let out a battle cry, a song of mad sorrow and a declaration of war fused into one raw-throated bellow.

The golem turned toward her.

"That's right, you bastard. Come get me."

The fire had spread to the ceiling. The living room burned like a crucible around Briet and the golem. Within minutes the house would be a funeral pyre.

Briet conjured KUSHIEL's demonic whip. With a snap of her wrist she coiled it around the golem, pinning its arms. The monster fought its captivity, but the snare held as Briet used the hand of PALARA to erase the *aleph* character from the letters on the golem's forehead, transforming *emet*—"truth"—to *met*: "death."

The monster ceased its struggling; the fires in its eye sockets dimmed and went out.

By then the entire house was burning. Windowpanes shattered, and gusts of wind fueled the conflagration. Immune to the blaze thanks to the talent of PYRGOS, Briet stood and watched the flames consume the last vestiges of her life as it used to be. As it never would be again.

Vacation photos shriveled and blackened in their frames.

Alton's precious jazz records melted. Hyun's meticulously chosen furniture turned to cinders. All of their books, all of Briet's mementos, the photos of her with her late beloved familiar Trixim . . . all gone. Dead and gone.

Tears fell from her eyes and evaporated in the searing heat.

Numb with shock, mute with grief, Briet staggered out of the blaze. Stumbled down the front steps to the sidewalk. Neighbors gathered as approaching sirens wailed. She ignored their questions. Tuned out their hollow condolences. Alone and bereft, she vanished like a ghost into the night. She was blocks away before she stopped and looked back through a prism of bitter tears.

Flashing lights surrounded the inferno she had left behind. The fire consumed her home of the last seventeen years—and with it, the only people she had ever loved. The only thing that had given her life meaning and joy since the end of the Second World War was gone forever.

Hot tears of rage and sorrow stung her eyes, and a knife of guilt twisted inside of her.

My fault. If I hadn't come back . . . hadn't broken the phone . . . if I'd realized sooner it was a golem. . . . One recrimination after another spun through her tempest of grief. *They died because of me. They trusted me . . . and I got them killed.*

I've lost everything.

Staring into the heart of the fire, she discovered within herself a shadow that she had hoped she had left behind in Germany almost two decades earlier.

If I've nowhere left to run, then it's time to stop running. She walked away from the blaze. *Someone gave the order that led to this. And whoever that someone is . . . I'm going to make them wish they'd never been born.*

SUNDAY, NOVEMBER 24

There were no such things as weekends for those who worked in one of the United Kingdom's vaunted special services. An occasional day off, possibly. A tentative holiday once in a blue moon. But the business of espionage and counterintelligence had never been one to respect the hours or the arbitrary divisions of a calendar. When duty called, one answered.

So it was that Miles Franklin had been roused this fine Sunday morning, not long after daybreak, by a phone call from his office. An asset using a verified check-in code had left an urgent message for him, the GCHQ operator had said.

"Which asset?" Miles had asked.

The answer had sent a chill down his back: *"Prospero."*

That was Cade's handle, one of a handful of code names Miles had been careful never to identify to MI6 for fear that the organization might seek retribution against Cade for his abrupt resignation from their ranks nearly a decade earlier. To the best of Miles's recollection, this was the first time Cade had ever used the code name to reach out to him directly.

That alone had been enough to roust Miles from bed.

He'd thanked the operator and hung up the phone. As Miles had donned his slippers, his beloved Dez stirred from his sleep and blinked at him with tired eyes. "Off to save the world?"

"Nothing so dramatic." A quick kiss from Miles on Dez's forehead had been enough to forestall further questions. "Back to sleep. I'll be home for brunch, I promise."

Dez had wrapped his pale hand around Miles's dark brown forearm for just a moment before letting him go do whatever was demanded of him by crown and country.

Now, an hour later, Miles sat ensconced behind the closed door of his office on an upper floor of 54 Broadway in London's Westminster borough, just over a block from St. James's Park. The established protocol for Miles to contact Cade was to use the enchanted mirror that Cade had gifted him years earlier, by way of an interlocutor named Khalîl el-Sahir. When Miles had gone to retrieve the mirror that morning, he had found it reduced to dust. Consequently, he had been compelled to reach out to Cade through the only phone number he had on file for him.

Miles listened to the call ring over the long-distance connection. *I hope this number is current. If not, this will be the most expensive wrong number ever dialed.*

From the other end of the line came the sound of a receiver being lifted. A man with a Portuguese-sounding accent answered, "*Estou?*"

It had been years since Miles had so much as ordered Portuguese food, never mind tried to speak the language. He hoped the party on the other side of the call understood English. "Hello, this is Miles Franklin. I'm trying to reach Cade Martin."

"*Sim,*" said the man. "*He has been expecting your call.* Um momento por favor."

Muffled sounds attended the handoff of the call. The next voice on the line was Cade's. "*Miles? Is that you?*"

"Yeah, mate, it's me."

A deep sigh of relief. "*Thank fucking God. After the mirrors got fragged, I was worried you might've lost this number.*"

"Not a chance, old boy. But since you mentioned it, what happened to the mirrors?"

"*Long story. Did your people find what we needed?*"

"They did." Miles flipped open the folder in front of him on his desk. "I checked the archives myself. The fewer people who know about this, the better." He set aside the top sheet to reveal the dossier beneath it. "Isidro Rocha. Cuban national. Part of Castro's revolution before he got transferred to G2. Fluent in English, so DGI uses him quite a bit in the States."

"*What about magick?*" Cade's question had a ring of desperation to it. "*Any sign he's been trained in the Art?*"

Miles flipped ahead to peruse Rocha's MI6-documented timeline. "Doubtful. No gaps in his history. Nothing to suggest he'd have the chops for it. Plus, he was a fairly devout Catholic before Castro denounced the Church." He could almost feel Cade's frustration over the phone. "Do I even want to know why you asked?"

"You'll sleep better if you don't."

"I haven't slept right in years. But suit yourself, mate."

"Where can we find Rocha now?"

"Not in the mood for small talk, eh? All right, then." Miles skipped to the end of Rocha's timeline. "Our last travel records for Rocha have him in Mexico City as of three days ago."

"Got an address?"

"A bachelor pad in the Polanco district. Have a pen handy?"

"I'm ready. Give it to me."

Miles read out the address. Cade read it back, to confirm he had taken it down correctly. "Right, then. I'll send a copy of his photo and top sheet to your Mexico City dead drop."

"Thanks, Miles. And I know I don't need to say this, but be careful. Anja, Briet, and I are all in some serious shit right now. I'd never forgive myself if any of this blew back on you."

"Don't sweat it, old boy. If anyone asks, I'll say I was running down leads on Oswald for the CIA. Being a good 'team player,' as the Yanks like to say."

"As long as your ass is covered, buddy."

"Always, old friend. Always."

"Thanks again. I'll be in touch. 'Til then, watch your back."

"And you as well."

Cade hung up, and Miles returned his phone's handset to its cradle.

Bloody hell. What has the old boy gotten himself into now?

<hr />

There was no time. No telling how many people had grilled the gunman already, never mind what they had wheedled out of him. He had to be silenced. Neutralized.

The Old Man's plan had called for Lee Harvey Oswald's nearly immediate elimination after President Kennedy's death was confirmed, but something had gone wrong. Instead of going into hiding as Niccolò had instructed him, Oswald had changed clothes and taken to the streets. Less than an hour after killing Kennedy with the enchanted rifle and ammunition that Niccolò had put into his hands via the Cuban cutout Rocha, Oswald had used a revolver to gun down a Dallas police officer in the street, after which he'd forced his way inside a movie theater in search of cover. Then, most vexing of all, he had let himself be taken alive. Some part of the magickal compulsion with which

Niccolò had tasked him clearly had failed to take hold, because Oswald had landed himself in police custody a mere ninety minutes after the president was shot.

He was supposed to go down shooting. How did he get taken alive?

Now the expendable gunman, who was supposed to have perished in a hail of police and Secret Service bullets inside the Texas Book Depository, was the most publicly visible person on the face of the earth. He was surrounded by police guards, interrogating detectives, state and federal prosecutors, and a public defender—not to mention a Roman legion's worth of representatives of the Fourth Estate, better known as the press.

Niccolò lamented his paucity of options as he approached the entrance to the Dallas Municipal Building. To prevent Oswald's assassination attempt from being predicted by the U.S. Occult Defense Program by means of a divination ritual, Niccolò had been forced by the Old Man to ward Oswald against scrying and demonic interference. To make sure his wards could withstand the strongest scrutiny America's militarized karcists might bring to bear, it had been necessary to employ charms that once invoked could not be rescinded remotely. Consequently, there was no clean or easy way for Niccolò to dispose of the assassin. He had to confront him in person.

That, of course, had come with its own delay. After recently hopping all over the globe in the service of the Old Man, Niccolò had exhausted the patience of the yoked spirit he had been using for teleportation. Despite his best efforts, it had slipped his yoke the day before and returned to its repose in the Flame Everlasting. Consequently, Niccolò had lost a good portion of the previous afternoon and night preparing and then executing a yoking ritual to bind a new spirit that could keep him magickally mobile for at least the next few days.

The media circus inside the Municipal Building was worse than Niccolò had expected. Reporters trailed by cameramen choked the first-floor lobby, along with a drove of newspaper and magazine reporters. Dozens of portable lights had combined to make the lobby brighter than the sunny day outside. *Fortunate, then, that I have come dressed for battle.*

Unlike many of the clods who packed the lobby around him, Niccolò knew how to choose a quality suit, and how to wear one. Coiffed and tailored with expert precision, he moved through the lobby projecting power and confidence. The crowd parted to make way for this man who wore a cold smirk and angular black Italian sunglasses like badges of honor.

Past the knot of bodies, Niccolò eschewed the elevators down the corridor to his left. Instead he bounded with speed and grace up the broad staircase at the end of the hall on his right.

As he passed the third floor, he noticed it was quiet. Everything he had seen on the news had led him to expect that floor to be a madhouse. Instead it looked nearly deserted.

Good. If he's not there, I'll bet he's in his cell. A perfect place for him to die.

Niccolò reached the top of the stairs—the fourth floor, one level beneath the jail complex, where that morning a television-news talking head had reported Oswald was being held. Niccolò checked his watch. It was 11:18 A.M. Central Standard Time.

He invoked several yoked spirits at once, rendering himself invisible and intangible as he ascended through the fourth-floor ceiling and fifth-level floorboards, and then through a wall into the jail complex. Just like the third floor, it was quiet. He shed his invisibility and resumed solid form. The intel provided by the Old Man's contacts said Oswald had been placed in Block F, Cell 2. Following the signs on the walls, Niccolò walked right, past the floor's small office and elevator lobby, and then turned right again into Cell Block F. He was surprised to find no guard there, as he had been warned to expect.

Cell 2 was empty. On the ground, in the corner, was a cigarette stub. Niccolò squatted, picked it up. It was a Lucky Strike. Cade Martin's preferred brand.

No. . . . No! Niccolò hurried to the office, abandoning discretion and subtlety. He faced the sergeant behind the window and seized his mind with the truth-compelling power of OREXAS. "Where is Lee Harvey Oswald?"

Wide-eyed, the uniformed officer behind the window said, "Transferred."

"Where?"

The cop looked bewildered. "To County. Through the basement."

"Fanculo!" Niccolò snapped his fingers at the cop, invoking the memory-erasing powers of DEDISCOS: "I was never here, and we never spoke." He hurried toward the jail elevator, leaving the cop behind him dazed and befuddled. Again he rendered himself invisible and intangible, and he stepped through the elevator doors into the shaft beyond. He drifted downward faster than a falling feather but far more slowly than a solid man succumbing to gravity.

Near the bottom of the shaft he passed inside the elevator car, which was parked at the basement level. He resumed solid form and slipped out of the elevator, into the scrum of bodies that had crowded the building's basement-level exit to the underground garage. Beyond its glass walls and open door, flashbulbs popped nonstop and shouting voices merged into a sonic fog.

Niccolò pushed his way out of the jail's basement lobby into the hallway.

A single loud *pop* of gunfire from the direction of the garage, followed by screams.

Niccolò tried to move closer, but a wall of people resisted him. The harder he tried to move forward, the more resolute the barrier became. When the crowd dispersed, he saw Oswald lying on the ground. The man's dark sweater made it hard to see his injury, but a quick look with the Sight confirmed for Niccolò that Oswald's life force was fading. Several other men had tackled and restrained a squat, dark-haired man. A nearby plainclothes police detective used a handkerchief to pick up a revolver from the garage driveway and collect it as evidence.

A frenzy of reporters hovered around the new captive and the unconscious and bleeding Oswald. Beyond that bloodthirsty circle of professional voyeurs, pandemonium reigned among the civilians. Standing in the basement doorway of the Dallas Police headquarters, all Niccolò could think about was how he could possibly spin this sequence of events to the Old Man as anything other than a grotesque blunder and a deviation from his plan.

No version of this catastrophe plays to my advantage. The Old Man will gut me for this.

"*Sono fottuto,*" he muttered.

10

Packing a ruck for a covert op was, for Cade, like trying to predict the future. What would he need? What would be dead weight? He tried to imagine all the most likely scenarios he and Anja might face in Mexico City during their hunt for Isidro Rocha. This was supposed to be a recon. Identify and investigate. No combat. But he had learned the hard way that no plan ever survived contact with the enemy. In the field, anything could happen.

One change of lightweight clothing seemed more than adequate for a short excursion. He had no idea what people were wearing these days in Mexico City, so he had erred on the side of bland and nondescript to match his fresh buzz cut—a drastic but necessary remedy to the atrocious haircut he had suffered in Dallas. If dull clothes proved to be a misstep, he and the others would buy new duds there, to better blend in with the locals. He tucked two bricks of demonically acquired high-denomination Mexican paper currency into the bottom of his leather ruck. *That ought to cover a group wardrobe update. Plus a few bribes.*

Next into the bag: a Beretta semiautomatic pistol, a spare magazine, and a small box of hollow-point rounds. He had come to appreciate the hollow-points for their superior stopping power as well as their reduced likelihood of overpenetration against hard targets, such as the fragile hulls of small boats or aircraft. If he was going to sink a ship or knock a plane out of the air, he would do it on purpose with magick, not by accident with a wild shot.

He tossed in his combat knife, a multi-tool, and a carton of Lucky Strikes.

Last into the bag were his shower kit and a couple of fake passports.

So much for the essentials.

The rest of his load-out he planned to entrust to his demonic porter, KERI-GOS. The demon would haul his leather roll-up of karcist's tools, his grimoire, and some heavier weapons and ordnance that he might not need but would be glad to have available if the operation turned ugly.

Satisfied with his preparations, he was shrugging into his bomber jacket when Anja knocked on his door and leaned her head inside. "Briet is here."

"Did she get things sorted in D.C.?" As soon as Cade had asked the question, he noted the unease in Anja's demeanor. "How bad?"

Anja slipped inside and closed the door behind her. "Bad."

"So she's on the warpath. Great, just what we needed." He checked his coat's pockets to confirm he had an open pack of Luckies, his steel Zippo, and his sunglasses. "You packed?"

She nodded. "*Da*. Briet needs a few minutes. So do the adepts."

He tensed. "We talked about this. They aren't coming."

"I think they should."

Cade shook his head. "They'll be safer here with Luis."

"I think we are safer together."

He wondered if his growing headache was the result of her stubborn refusal to take no for an answer or a consequence of the throng of demons he was holding in his spiritual yoke. "That's a bad idea. You know how fast shit can go wrong in the field. And none of them has any training in tradecraft. I'll bet they can't tell the difference between a dead drop and a honey pot."

Anja crossed her arms, a signal that she was getting angry with him. "So what?"

"So? They might botch the hunt for Rocha before it gets started. One wrong word on the street, one look at the wrong person, and they could blow the whole op."

"They can be lookouts. Backups. Decoys."

"All of which sound like easy jobs, but aren't." Why was she so adamant about exposing three novices to danger? "Look, if we were talking about filling a circle, that'd be one thing. Barış and Sathit are perfectly good karcists. But neither of them is suited to spycraft."

Anja cocked one eyebrow. "What about Yasmin? Is she not a good magician?"

"Sure, but she's only just started her third year. She's barely mastered yoking, never mind magickal combat. I'm not putting her into a cross fire."

"The enemy already has." She plucked the cigarette from Cade's hand. Took a drag. Exhaled as she continued. "They are in this whether you like it or not. Let them do their part."

"Their part is whatever we fucking say it is. And I say they stay here."

"I disagree." Her next cone of smoke enveloped Cade and circled him like a serpent. "Mexico City is a big place. Lots of ground to cover. We will need them to watch our backs."

"And who's gonna watch *theirs*?"

She rejected his point with a roll of her eyes. "If Rocha has magick, or if he is protected or watched by someone who does, he will be too dangerous for us to capture. We will need to split up. One team to watch him, the other to search his home or office."

"Are you kidding? He's a professional spook. He'll spot amateur shadows a mile away."

"They can stay with me. I will search his home. You and Briet watch Rocha, warn me if he heads my way."

The more he heard of this plan, the less he liked it. "How the fuck did I end up paired with Briet?"

"I thought you would be happy. She is a master karcist and a trained spy."

"She's also a walking time bomb. You didn't see her in Santa Fe nine years ago. She practically leveled a house after a demon killed her rat familiar. What kind of mayhem do you think she'll cause when she's mourning *both* of her lovers?"

"I know what she has lost. It means she is motivated to get results."

"No, it means she's motivated to get *revenge*. She's a wild card right now, and that's the last thing we need."

"Too bad." Anja finished the Lucky and snuffed its stub under her heel. "We don't have many friends left in the world. Like it or not, she is one of them. The same is true of our students." She shut Cade's rucksack and shoved it into his arms. "This is war. No whining. No excuses. Everybody on the front line, *right now*. Fight. Or die."

He was too tired to keep arguing, and too proud to admit she was right.

"Fine. I'm opening the portal in thirty minutes. Anybody not there on time gets left here." He caught Anja's hint of a smirk as she walked to the door—she had won the debate, as usual. As she opened the door to leave, he added in his sternest tone, "And make sure they *all* remember to bring their toothbrushes. I am *not* fucking sharing again."

Over the phone the Old Man sounded more curious than upset, which perplexed Niccolò. *"What makes you so certain it was Cade Martin who questioned Mr. Oswald?"*

"As I said: the cigarette stub. A Lucky Strike." Standing in a phone booth on Pacific Avenue in downtown Dallas, Niccolò felt exposed and out of place—and not just because he was overdressed. His accent was drawing stares from passersby, and it was stoking his paranoia.

"Lucky Strike is a popular brand. Anyone could have left it outside his cell."

"Sì. But this is Dallas. The police here all smoke Marlboros."

"An interesting observation, Mr. Falco."

"Sì, signore." Niccolò was at a loss to parse the Old Man's subtext. Was he saying he believed Niccolò was right about the possible breach in their operation's secrecy? *I must proceed with care.* "Going forward, I suggest we assume Cade and his allies have acquired intelligence that might lead them to our distributor." A shady-looking man—maybe a pimp, or a gambler—gave Niccolò the evil eye as he passed the phone booth. Turning away from the accusatory stare, Niccolò added, "And if Martin finds our man, we should consider our source to be compromised, as well."

"I concur." The Old Man *tsk*ed softly. *"A shame you didn't arrive soon enough to put these questions directly to Mr. Oswald. His perspective might have been most valuable."*

"I came to Dallas as soon as I was able, *signore*." He covered his free ear with his hand as a truck rumbled by. "I missed Mr. Oswald by a matter of minutes, and for that I apologize. But who could have predicted he would be shot by such an unlikely actor as Jack Ruby?"

"I could have. I hired him."

That revelation sharpened Niccolò's focus with a sting of betrayal. "You what?"

"Don't sound so surprised. Even my contingency plans have backups."

Niccolò massaged his temples and did his best to expunge any trace of anger from his voice. "Such intelligence would have been useful to me a few hours ago, *signore*."

"It's called compartmentalization. Oswald was your mission. Ruby was Tujiro's. Had you reached Oswald in time, Ruby would have gone on with his life, none the wiser. Even now, if Tujiro followed instructions, Ruby should have no idea he's just a pawn in a larger game."

"I see." Niccolò's tone was civil, but inside he seethed. He was the senior karcist in the Old Man's circle. A scheme of this kind should never have been put into motion without his knowledge and approval. But he knew better than to protest to the Old Man.

"*Your questions do illuminate a valid concern,*" the Old Man said. "*Loose ends are an error we can't risk—not when our objective is so close to being secured.*"

On this, at least, he and the Old Man agreed. "How do you wish me to proceed?"

"*If you have reason to think Cade or his allies know anything that could lead them to me or the Commission, their knowledge must be suppressed with extreme prejudice.*" A thoughtful pause. "*On the other hand, if Oswald told Martin about our man Rocha, this could present a unique opportunity to set a new trap and finish what we started on Naxos.*"

"Do you want me to go to Mexico City?"

"*No. Let Hatunde handle it. I need you here.*"

"Understood, *signore.*"

A soft *click* on the line informed Niccolò the Old Man had hung up. He set the phone back in its place and stepped out of the booth. The crowd on the sidewalk parted to either side of Niccolò, coursing around him like a river would flow past a stone. He looked at the gaudy neon signs that lined Pacific Avenue, and he felt a profound relief that he would soon put an ocean between it and himself.

Gliding with grace and aplomb through the rough tide of humanity, Niccolò smiled. *Insects and vermin never notice the presence of gods—until they get stepped on.*

11

After dark, the narrow tree-lined streets of Mexico City's Zona Rosa over-flowed with revelry. Rum, laughter, and music brimming with bright horns all spilled from the open fronts of swank nightclubs. The air was rich with the tantalizing aromas of meats searing over charcoal fires. Groups of young men cruised in open convertibles, whistling at whichever pedestrians caught their fancy, men and women alike. Crowds gathered around and beneath tables with umbrellas clustered on a triangle of concrete where two roads met. To either side of the intersection, eager crowds packed into bars and small restaurants lit by paper lanterns.

Cade moved through the cheerful chaos with Briet by his side. Though they were *gringos* in an area of the city not yet well known to *turistas,* no one paid them much mind. After Cade had picked up Rocha's MI6 file from his local dead drop, he and Briet had bought new clothes that fit the setting: for him, a sharp, cream-colored suit of tropical-weight linen with matching dress shoes and a burgundy-hued shirt; for her, a loose but still flattering floral-print dress in vivid hues, and leather sandals. Neither of them sported any jewelry, and Cade was careful not to make a show of how much cash was wedged into his money clip. Their natural instinct toward discretion, coupled with the fact that they both were, for tonight, magickally fluent in Spanish, helped them blend in among the festive masses.

Briet took his elbow, as if they were a couple. She used a gentle tug and a nod to direct his attention across the street. "Eleven o'clock. Sky-blue suit and hat. Looks like our man."

The crowd gave Cade and Briet plenty of cover, but he still exercised caution. He noted the pale blue suit at the edge of his vision, and then he stole a quick look at the man wearing it. He recognized Isidro Rocha from the photo Miles had sent with the man's dossier.

He pulled a thousand-peso note from his money clip and passed it to Briet, settling their recent wager. "Okay, so the dossier was right for a change." He put away his cash and fished his Luckies from inside his blazer. Not wanting to draw attention by lighting his smoke with magick, he used his Zippo. He exhaled as he tucked away the steel lighter. "Any sign of a bodyguard?"

"None that I can see." She stole a look over her shoulder. "No tails, either."

Cade saw Rocha cut the twenty-person line outside a dance club with a nod and a subtle pass of cash to the bouncer. "Looks like he found his party for the night."

He steered Briet to a halt in front of a tapas restaurant with a window and an outdoor menu across the street from the dance club. They pretended to review the bill of fare while watching Rocha's reflection in the window. Cade said, "He's heading for the bar."

Briet noted Rocha squeezing a much younger man's ass. "And making new friends."

"Or greeting an old one." Cade feigned interest in the menu for a moment, and then he clocked Rocha ordering and paying for a round of drinks across the street. "Either way, I think he's staying put for at least ten minutes."

"Depends how smooth his game is." Briet shrugged at Cade. "I've taken debutantes from drinks to a hotel room in under five."

"Well, it'll take him ten minutes to get to his place from here, so even if he beats your record we should be okay. Keep an eye on him. I'll give the others the green light."

He slipped away from Briet, ducked into the lobby of the Hotel Geneve, and walked to a row of oaken phone booths. The nearest one was empty, so he stepped in, shut the door, picked up the handset, and pushed a few coins into the phone. When he heard the dial tone, he dialed the number of the commandeered local flat where Anja was lying low with the adepts.

It rang only once before Anja picked up. *"¿Hola?"*

"It's me. Rocha's bartering with a rent boy down at the Copa."

"Keep him there. I can be at his place in three minutes."

"He can be home in ten, so get a move on. And don't forget the signal when you leave. We're at the bar in the El Trompito."

"Okay." Anja hung up.

Cade left the booth and crossed the lobby on his way back to Briet—hoping that Anja finished her illicit plunder before Isidro Rocha returned home to begin his.

———～～———

Time was a factor, so Anja acted without hesitation. She opened the locked front door of the luxury apartment building with the power of QAFIL, proceeded to the elevator, and pressed the button for the top floor, the location of Isidro Rocha's "bachelor pad," as Miles had described it.

Outside the front door she had left Barış, the oldest and best-trained of her and Cade's adepts. He had no experience in espionage tradecraft, so his instructions were simple, as were those for Sathit, whom Anja had set to guard the building's rear. If somehow Rocha eluded Cade and Briet and returned before Anja left the building, Barış and Sathit were to use magick to jam the lock of the door they guarded and retreat to the building across the street.

There, in a fifth-floor apartment with a view of the front of Rocha's building, Yasmin was stationed next to a phone. If Cade or Briet called to say Rocha was on his way back, or that they had lost track of him, or if either Barış or Sathit returned after spotting Rocha, Yasmin was to ring the phone in Rocha's apartment, twice and then once, to signal Anja to get out.

As tradecraft went, it was fairly rudimentary. But there was no way Anja or Cade would risk any of their last three pupils by letting them try to engage an experienced field operative such as Rocha in person. Observe, evade, and report—that was enough to keep them occupied.

A semi-musical tone preceded the opening of the elevator's doors. As Anja stepped out, she slipped her hand into the leather satchel at her side. She hesitated for a moment, uncertain whether to clutch her wand or her Browning Hi-Power. She chose her wand.

The interior of Rocha's building was as posh as its exterior. The Polanco district of Mexico City was known for its prime real estate and upper-class residents. *Apparently, that translates into tasteful art prints and real potted plants in the hallways,* Anja noted as she walked to Rocha's door.

Before she touched the knob, she studied the door using the magickal perception of MEVAKOS. There were no hexes or wards on the door, and there was nothing special about its lock. Neither its chain nor its deadbolt were in place. She channeled the power of QAFIL to release its lock, opened the door, and slipped inside.

Anja left the lights off. If Rocha's pad was being watched, turning on the lights would attract unwanted attention. Marshaling the Sight to pierce the darkness, she surveyed the front room. Viewed through magick's lens, reality turned monochromatic.

The furnishings were few but expensive. A long sofa with a matching otto- man. A large television. An expensive hi-fi stereo system with tall speakers. In the corner stood a small but well-equipped and lavishly stocked wet bar. This was the home of a man who liked to entertain.

Nothing in the front room had a magickal aura, so Anja moved on. The kitchen was immaculate: its counters uncluttered and spotless, its sink empty, its cupboards and icebox bare, and all of it free of sorcery's telltale shimmering. Rocha was a man who preferred to dine out.

Past the kitchen she found the bedroom. The king-sized bed was made, its goose-down pillows fluffed. A peek inside the end table's drawer revealed silk ropes, a sleep mask, and a jar of lubricant. Then Anja turned and saw the closet. Behind its slatted doors, her enhanced vision detected the golden radiance of magickal energy.

She opened the doors, which slid on tracks and folded at hinge points like an accordion. The inside of Rocha's closet was as tidy as the rest of his home. He clearly was a man with an orderly disposition, an attention to detail. He had discipline.

Anja pulled out the items stacked inside the closet. She was careful to keep track of where each one belonged. Buried under several boxed pairs of shoes and some collections of memorabilia, she found a small steel safe. To her surprise, there were no magickal protections on any part of the safe, even though it shone with the radiance of something powerful.

Maybe Rocha really is just a middleman. If he does not practice the Art, he might not understand what he is trafficking. Which would also mean he does not realize special means are needed to hide it.

QAFIL's talents made short work of the safe's combination lock. Inside the safe, Anja found several boxes of ammunition. Most of them were fairly mundane. Reloads for various small-caliber revolvers or semiautomatic pis- tols. A single box of twelve-gauge shotgun shells.

Then she found the one box that blazed brightly with magick.

She had to squint to make out the writing on the side of the box: 6.5 MM MANNLICHER-CARCANO.

Rifle cartridges. The same ones Oswald had used in Dallas two days earlier. Anja opened the box and pulled out one of the long rounds. In her hand, viewed with the Sight, the cartridge glowed like a flare. Digging deep with the talents of PSEMAEL, Anja confirmed the rounds in this box bore the same enchantment as the one she had found at the FBI Laboratory.

Printed on the end of the box was a manufacturer's logo, but nothing else. It was not a symbol she recognized. None of the other ammo boxes in the safe bore the logo, leaving her at a loss. *I will have to take it. Perhaps Miles can identify the maker.*

She slipped the box of rifle cartridges into her satchel and closed the safe.

One by one, she put Rocha's things back inside his closet. Once everything was returned to its rightful place, she shut the closet's doors.

Crossing the front room, she half expected the phone to ring with bad news. It remained silent. Even once she reached the hallway outside the apartment she listened for it, but the building was quiet. It was a Sunday night, after all. People had jobs to go to in the morning.

Anja's hand gripped her wand inside her satchel as she left the elevator and crossed the lobby. A glance over her shoulder caught the eye of Sathit at the rear entrance. With one nod she cued the younger woman to head back to the rendezvous site across the street.

She walked out the front door of the building projecting calm even though she was alert to every sound and movement on the block. Noting the absence of traffic, she cut across the street, assured by the sound of Barış's footsteps that he was only a few seconds behind her.

So far, all had gone to plan. She had breached Rocha's apartment and found evidence that, she hoped, would lead them closer to their enemy in the shadows. Now all they had to do was regroup and escape from Mexico City before their mysterious foes found out they were here.

Unfortunately, that meant that responsibility for the safe completion of this op was on Cade's shoulders—and in Anja's experience, her husband's knack for finding trouble had sent more than a few of their missions completely fucking sideways.

She wanted to believe tonight would not be one of those times.

Half a minute later she reached their commandeered apartment. Barış caught up to Anja as she opened the door, and he followed her inside.

It was a bland but tastefully appointed box, its decorations a tad heavy on religious iconography. Its décor and odors suggested its normal occupant was very likely an old woman who enjoyed cooking with lethal amounts of garlic.

Yasmin, dressed like a Cuban revolutionary with a knife fetish, met them in the front room. "Sathit's right behind you. I watched her cross the street, like you said. She wasn't followed."

"Good. Lock the door after you let her in." Anja stepped past Yasmin and walked to the bedroom, where she picked up the phone. Next to it, on a slip of paper, was the callback number Sathit had jotted down for contacting Cade and Briet. She dialed it.

It rang twice before a man answered. "Buenas noches, El Trompito."

"*Buenas noches, señor. ¿Puedo hablar con el señor Macrae, por favor?*"

"Por supuesto. Un momento por favor."

She waited for the maître d' to get Cade, who had established himself at the bar under the alias "Mr. Macrae," as an homage to their beloved late master.

Cade sounded only halfway trashed on tequila when he picked up the phone. *"What's the word, hummingbird?"*

"The word is 'fly.' As in, back to the nest. We have what we came for."

"Shit. And I was just starting to enjoy myself." A sigh. *"Hang tight, we're on our way."*

"Cade?"

"Yeah?"

"Maybe you should have a *café con leche* before you come back."

"No need. Bree scored some snow from a guy at the bar. We'll see you in ten."

He hung up before Anja could tell him what a bad idea cocaine would be in their current predicament. She took a deep breath and prepared herself for the worst.

It was going to be one of *those* nights.

———⚬⚬⚬———

It paid to be invisible. Not magickally invisible—though such a feat was well within Hatunde Ndufo's capabilities—but socially invisible. Most places he had traveled treated him as if he were no one of consequence. All they ever saw was his ebony skin, deep brown eyes, broad shoulders, and shaved head. It never occurred to most people he met that he was the lone scion of a Nigerian oil dynasty, or that he had attended boarding schools in England before completing his education in ancient history at the Sorbonne. He could blend in as easily amid the crowds on the streets of Zona Rosa as he could at a black-tie affair in Zurich.

I am Ralph Ellison's "Invisible Man" come to life.

Mexico City's youth cavorted around him. He leaned against the corner of an alleyway, his black trousers and midnight-blue silk shirt helping him become all but inseparable from the shadows.

His gaze fixed upon the couple at the bar inside the El Trompito club. A white man in a cream-colored linen suit, and a pale woman with fiery red hair in a floral dress. Her body language was reserved, her movements small and designed to deflect scrutiny. The man leaned back against the bar, resting on his elbows. Everything about his posture telegraphed overconfidence. Hatunde had seen his kind before. *I would bet real money he's an American.*

Neither of them seemed to have noticed his presence. That was for the best.

He paid close attention to what the couple found interesting. Their focus was not on each other. They weren't in El Trompito for the band. And though their glasses were empty, neither seemed in a hurry to summon a bartender. Instead, they took turns staring at a reflection in the mirror behind the bar— at an angle that would give them a clear look through the club's open front and into the club across the street, where far raunchier celebrations were in progress.

And in the middle of the bombastic debauchery across the street? The man whose safety and privacy Hatunde had been ordered to guarantee.

The man in the linen suit lit a cigarette, his third since arriving at El Trompito. Hatunde had never understood why so many people insisted on poisoning their bodies. Alcohol, tobacco, narcotics, amphetamines—he had no use for any of them. His one concession to hypocrisy was that he had become fond of Turkish coffee during the years he spent studying magick on the island of Cyprus.

Other karcists coped with the strains of yoking spirits by dulling their minds with liquor and opiates. Hatunde preferred to sharpen his wits with caffeine so that he could master his demons on his own terms.

Inside the El Trompito, a bartender brought a phone to the overconfident man.

If someone knows where to find them, they must be working with partners. I should apprise Mr. Falco. He backpedaled into the alley and ducked to cover behind a small mountain of garbage that reeked of rotting meat and spoiled seafood. Hidden from the view of passersby on the street, he kneeled beside a broad puddle, which he converted into a scrying glass by invoking the combined talents of HAEL and ALITUREX.

The oily pool shimmered with color, and rippled from the center outward as Hatunde intoned, *"Audi vocem meam, Niccolò. Ostende te."*

Within seconds the distorted bands of color in the pool coalesced into the familiar visage of Niccolò Falco, the Old Man's senior karcist. His voice sounded distant, as if he and Hatunde were conversing through a wall. *"What news, Hatunde?"*

"Your hunch was correct. Oswald must have talked about Rocha, because there are two people following him in the Zona Rosa right now."

"Who?"

"A cocky young white man, and a tall woman with red hair."

Niccolò sucked air through his teeth. *"Be careful. That would be Cade Martin and Briet Segfrunsdóttir, two of the most dangerous magicians on earth."*

"I will take appropriate precautions."

"Have they tried to question Rocha?"

"No, they just watch him. But Cade received a phone call a minute ago. He and Briet must be working with someone."

The concerned expression on Niccolò's face twisted into one of anger and frustration. *"Anja Kernova must be with them. If they're watching him, she's probably tossing his flat."*

"If so, she might already have found the spare cartridges Rocha kept for himself." A bottle broke nearby. Hatunde poked his head up and confirmed he was still alone in the alley. "What should I do if Cade and Briet move to take Rocha?"

"Kill Rocha. He's a soft target, and he must not be allowed to talk."

"And if they continue to tail him?"

"Follow them, but do not engage. Most important, if they abandon their surveillance, it means their partners found what they were looking for. In that case, forget Rocha and follow Cade and Briet. If I am right, they will lead you to the rest of their comrades."

"If so, what then?"

Niccolò shrugged. *"If you have a clear shot? Kill them all."*

12

Most of the time the difference between Black magick and Gray magick was little more than a matter of semantics. That had been Father Luis Pérez's experience, at any rate. In his mind, the chief distinction resided in the purpose of one's experiments. He could rationalize dealing with Infernal spirits for the sake of divination so long as he never crossed the line into using them or their abilities for acts of violence. Within that fine line of separation he had found the twilight realm between the Left- and Right-hand paths, between White and Black magick.

The Roman Catholic Church, of course, did not share his ethical flexibility with regard to the Art. It was the official stance of the Holy See that any invocation, conjuration, or interaction with demons was an abomination, a practice of Black magick regardless of one's intentions.

Mortals also were not supposed to seek dealings with angels, though the Church's reasoning on that point was less clear. When pressed, the elders of the faith most often resorted to an argument predicated on the prevention of the worship of false idols. They seemed to think that a White magician, confronted by the supernatural powers of angels, might choose to worship them instead of the Lord. Luis found that logic specious, but it had been years since he had enjoyed the privilege of debating his point of view with other men of the cloth.

Other men of the cloth, he chided himself as he stepped inside his operator's circle. *As if you were still one of them.* It still stung him to recall he had been excommunicated from the Roman Catholic Church and expelled from his monastic order at Monte Paterno. Nine years had passed since he was cast out for lending magickal aid to Anja Kernova, who had come within a fraction of a second of being vaporized by an atomic blast at Bikini Atoll. Only a timely rescue by an angelically assisted Luis had saved her from a fiery end.

She saved the world. I saved her life. And the Church calls us both villains.

That was what passed for justice in the postwar world.

He gave his conjuring room a final inspection. Years of warnings from his former peers at Monte Paterno, as well as from Cade and Anja, had made him hypercautious whenever he conducted Goetic experiments, no matter how benign their purpose might be.

All of the circles and glyphs of warding were correct. The totems were in their proper places, and all had been prepared according to the *Grimorium Verum*. His grimoire stood open on the lectern next to his circle. He had crafted all of the tapers himself from the first wax of a new hive, the vessels of camphor and brandy on either side of him were full, and the brazier was fueled with consecrated charcoal, freshly made from the wood of an apple tree.

Luis sighed. *Why must demons be so particular?*

Still concerned he had overlooked some picayune detail, he inspected his garments. His white robe, whose hem and cuffs were embroidered with Divine names of power, was tied at his waist with a girdle of leopard skin. Wrapped in crimson silk, his wand was tucked under the girdle near his left hip. A silver medallion of protection, scribed with the demon's sigil, hung around his neck under his robe. He squatted to straighten his ceremonial sword so that it lay balanced atop the toes of his white leather slippers. As he stood, he adjusted his white paper miter, upon which had been written several of the holy names, with EL prominent in the front.

The Gray magician struck together a flint and steel to ignite the charcoal.

Turquoise flames danced from the coals, and sparks jetted upward from the brazier. Its fountain of blue-white motes bounded off the ceiling and then scattered across the floor.

The room and the operator were ready. It was time to begin.

Luis drew his wand, unwrapped it, and draped the silk around his neck. He raised his hands and imbued his voice with the gravity of command: "*Veritas. Veritas. Veritas.*"

He reached inside a small pouch concealed inside a pocket of his robe, removed a pinch of powdered rose petal mixed with the dust of a crushed diamond, and cast it into the brazier. The blue-green flames turned white and surged upward in violent twists.

With regret, but knowing that demons never appeared without at least a token gesture of coercion, Luis thrust his wand into the burning coals. Monstrous wails and howls of suffering filled the darkened room, and rolling waves of noxious fog swirled just beyond the safety of the grand circle. Lights flickered inside the foul mists, and as the cries grew louder, the flames brightened. If for nothing else, Hell was always good for a bit of theater.

Luis raised his voice above the clamor. "I adjure thee, AMON, as the faithful servant of BELIAL, who is thy master as well as my patron, to appear instanter! I command it by the power of the pact I have with thee, and by the names ADONAY, ELOHIM, JEHOVAM, TAGLA, MATHON, ALMOUZIN, ARIOS, PITHONA, SYLPHAE, SALAMANDRAE, GNOMUS, TERRAE, COELUS, GODENS, AQUA, and by the whole hierarchy of superior intelligences who shall constrain thee against thy will, *venité, venité, submirillitor* AMON!"

A waterfall of fire spilled from the ceiling above the bounding circle to the southwest. Burning liquid struck the floor and pooled within the confines of the magickal boundary. As the demon took shape inside the flaming shower, the conjuring room filled with mingled odors of ammonia, sulfur, and burning rust. A cloud of urine-smelling mist erupted inside the bounding circle, extinguishing the firefall. The revolting vapors dissipated to reveal the demon AMON, a marquis of great power in the Pit. For once, perhaps having remembered Luis's past mercies, it had appeared in its true form, that of a brown-skinned man with a raven's head.

Its voice was the hiss of lava striking the sea. AVE, MAGICIAN.

"*Ave,* Great AMON. Please accept my thanks for thy prompt and true appearance." Even after years of practice, it still turned Luis's stomach to converse with demons. The only reason he had been willing to risk signing an Infernal compact with BELIAL had been Cade's sworn assurance that the entire premise of selling one's soul was nothing but pantomime.

The demon radiated contempt. WHY HAST THOU SUMMONED ME?

"I seek visions of things past, and things to come. Powerful forces have moved against my allies, and I would know the mind of our adversary."

MY TRIBUTE FIRST.

From the left pocket of his robe, Luis removed a silken pouch filled with precious stones, a medley of sapphires, rubies, and emeralds. He lobbed the pouch to AMON, who snapped it from the air with its great black beak and swallowed it whole.

MOST GENEROUS, EVE-SPAWN. The beast cocked its head and regarded him with cold black eyes. WHAT DO YOU WISH TO SEE?

"The future. Divulge to me any foreknowledge you possess, for good or for ill, of imminent threats to me and those I consider mine."

Your demand is too broad, and the future too uncertain.

Luis stabbed his wand into the burning coals and brought the demon low with torments of a kind he only barely understood. The demon dropped to its knees and then curled into a fetal position. Still not satisfied his point had been fully understood, Luis gave his wand a few twists in the fiery brazier, and he tried not to betray his pity as he watched the fallen angel writhe in agony inside the bounding circle. After a full minute of corporal punishment, Luis removed his wand from the coals. "Do not lie to me again. Show me what I have commanded you to reveal."

The formerly pliant spirit struggled back to its feet, staggering and trembling as it did so. No longer were its birdlike eyes cold—hatred blazed behind those black orbs. The beast's antipathy, its barely restrained violence, hit Luis like a putrid breeze.

Lowering its head in a mockery of self-subjugation, the demon said, Gaze into the flames, Eve-spawn, and there will I show you your future.

Luis squatted and looked into his brazier. The fire changed from blue to bloodred, and its dancing tongues of flame came to resemble the facets of a great and ever-changing jewel, one forever turning and casting distorted reflections of the past, the present, and the future. . . .

Then he saw it.

A sneak attack. A merciless slaughter. Fire and thunder, ashes falling like snow. The screams of the wounded, the groans of the dying—and the laughter of the victors. Then . . . the snap and pop of burning timbers, the shrieks of bending metal . . . and when the din of battle faded away, nothing but the hollow benedictions of wind against blood-soaked stone.

Luis recoiled from the vision and nearly lost his balance.

Inside the bounding circle, Amon's beak parted in a saw-toothed smirk.

Luis stood and gripped his lectern to steady himself. "Begone, foul spirit! You are dismissed. Go in peace, doing harm to none, and return to thy repose, returning when, and only when, I shall call for thee!"

The demon held its ground and widened its grin.

I shall settle with thee another time, Eve-spawn.

"By the holy names Adonai, Elohim, and Jehovam, I banish thee!"

A pillar of hellfire screamed up from the floor and consumed Amon in a green flash.

Stunned and alone once more in the conjuring room, Luis fell to his knees.

Accursed spirit! Why show me that? That, of all things? He pounded his fists on the parquet floor. *Spiteful fiend!*

The longer Luis reflected on AMON's vision, the more he blamed himself. *I was not specific in my request, nor in my definition of terms.* The demon had complied with the letter of Luis's demand—but in the process it had burdened Luis with a foreknowledge he could either accept to his great sorrow, or act upon, to his peril.

I know what Anja would do. She would walk away. I can even hear her voice: "Why risk my life for people who call me their enemy?" But just as clearly, Luis heard the rebuttal that was demanded of him by his faith: *Because it is the teaching of Our Lord Jesus Christ that we forgive those who trespass against us.*

As fervently as Luis tried to deny it to himself, he knew what had to be done.

He got up. Put away his sword and wand. Walked around the circle, snuffing tapers as he went. When at last the room was dark, he closed his grimoire and tucked it under one arm, then gathered up his roll of karcist's tools under the other. He left the door open as he made his exit. *The conjuring room will have to be cleaned and exorcised another day.*

Luis had no time to waste on such frivolities as packing a bag. Lives were at stake, and whether they lived or died depended entirely upon him. He could only hope Cade would be able to forgive him when the mayhem was past.

He strode out of the house into the open air.

And in a stroke of heavenly lightning and a crash of thunder, he was gone.

≈

The outskirts of Mexico City were quiet at a quarter to midnight. Hatunde was thankful for the sparse traffic this far from the city's center. He was driving with his car's headlights off and relying on the Sight to navigate in the dark. A hundred meters or so ahead of him, Cade and Briet were in their own vehicle, a gold Chevrolet Impala convertible. They had stolen it from a side street shortly after abandoning their surveillance of Isidro Rocha.

Not willing to be left behind, and in no mood to explain himself to a taxi driver, Hatunde had stolen a car, as well, a boxy Ford 200. Though his crime had been necessary in the moment, it nagged at him while he drove in silence. He had taken lives, but only in the name of war. Made unholy pacts, but only at his own expense. Never had he thought of himself as a thief. It was too lowly, too base a sin for a man born to a noble lineage. Worst of all, the car he had taken had all the hallmarks of belonging to working-class people, and the variety of toys in the backseat suggested they probably had at least two children to support.

A passenger jet on a landing approach to Mexico City Central Airport roared past, so close overhead that Hatunde feared its jetwash might blow his car off the road. He white-knuckled his steering wheel and kept his eyes on Cade and Briet's car in the distance. Soon the airport was behind him, and they were speeding down unlit streets lined with squat, dilapidated buildings. It wasn't long before the journey crossed a railroad junction, and the cliché of being "on the wrong side of the tracks" came to life around Hatunde.

Pavement gave way to dirt roads with no signage. Cinder-block hovels roofed with rusted sheets of corrugated steel told him he had followed his prey past Xochiaca, all the way into the hillside slums of Chimalhuacan. Even for an armed karcist, this was not a good place to venture alone after dark. Here the streets belonged to the gangs, and outsiders were not welcome.

The blocks in the slum were short, providing many opportunities for Cade and Briet to lose Hatunde. He closed the gap and struggled to keep an eye on their car, or at least on the dust clouds its tires kicked up from the dry, unpaved roads.

Then he made a turn onto a long straightaway. He saw their Impala parked several dozen meters ahead, off the road in an empty lot, next to a shack of pale bricks topped with dry-rotted planks and scattered straw masquerading as a roof. There was no sign of Cade or Briet outside. Hatunde pulled over, stopped his car, and turned off the engine. He got out and skulked toward the small house. As he drew closer, he noted a faint glow of electric light inside the brick hovel, slipping through the narrow gaps between its windows' closed shutters.

Invoking the power of AQUIEL, Hatunde cloaked himself in silence as he neared the tiny house. Even as he stepped over broken glass and loose gravel, his passage made no sound. He crouched as he approached the building's rearmost window and ducked into place beneath it. Then he cocked his head to listen to what was happening inside. There were several voices—some masculine, some feminine, all of them conversing in English.

"We can learn nothing more here," said a woman with Russian accent: *Anja.*

An American-sounding man added, "She's right, we should go." *Cade.*

Another woman, whose accent Hatunde couldn't place: "Back into hiding?"

"There's no shame in regrouping," Cade said.

A different man's voice: "Master Cade is correct. Best not to engage the enemy until we know what they want—and how to beat them."

Curious to see his foes, Hatunde rendered himself invisible with the talent of BALAM, and then he lifted his head to peek through the gap in the shutters. At a quick glance he counted six people inside the brick hut. With the Sight he confirmed all six had yoked spirits.

Cade and Briet he recognized from the Zona Rosa. Anja, the Russian, he knew by her scar and her gray eyes. The other three were strangers to him: a lean, mustached man with light brown skin, black hair, and dark eyes; a Southeast Asian woman with sleeve tattoos on both arms who looked to be in her early twenties; and a young woman with a military crew cut, a golden tan, an innocent face, and six knives Hatunde could see.

Those must be the surviving apprentices.

He ducked beneath the window while he pondered his options. *I am outnumbered. And I have strict orders from Niccolò and the Old Man not to be careless with magick in front of possible witnesses. Especially not in North America, Europe, Australia, Russia, or Japan.* He strained to eavesdrop on the group, whose discussion had submerged into whispers. As hard as he tried, he was unable to pick out what they were saying now. *They will not wait here for me to bring back reinforcements. Even if the apprentices are pushovers, I would still have to face three of the most dangerous karcists on earth if I go through that door alone. The element of surprise by itself will not be enough. I need to hit them with overwhelming force.*

As he pondered what he might achieve through unorthodox combinations of his yoked magickal talents, his roaming gaze fell upon the propane tanks behind the house. He crawled over to them. One at a time, he put his ear to the metal tanks and tapped them with his fingernail to see if they sounded empty. He was elated to find both were nearly full.

A gas explosion. A plausible accident. And good cover in case they survive and I want to finish them with more fire. He smirked. *Yes, this will do.*

Muting his footfalls with the silence of AQUIEL, Hatunde retreated from his foes' hovel and took cover behind the corner of the next building on the mostly empty block.

He focused his will on his demon of burden: *AKROTH, go and slightly nick the hoses on those propane tanks. Not enough to sever them, just enough to create a leak.*

As THOU COMMANDS, the demon responded inside his mind. A few seconds later, the demon informed him, IT IS DONE.

Time to light this fuse. He filled his palm with blue flames courtesy of RAGERION, and hurled the burning orb at the sabotaged propane tanks.

The explosion nearly shook the fillings from Hatunde's back teeth.

Its detonation pulsed blue-white, followed by a cloud of fire that pulverized the brick hovel next to the propane tanks. As the firestorm expanded it cooled from blue to orange, and then it belched a black mushroom of smoke into the night sky.

Nothing moved within the hovel's scorched pile of debris, but a pale shimmer of silvery light weltered within the smoke and fumes. Perplexed, Hatunde emerged from cover and approached the blackened heap of shattered bricks and broken furniture. As he moved closer, burning bits of debris rained down on him from above. He swatted away the flaming motes as if they were mere nuisances, like the city's omnipresent mosquitoes.

When he reached the edge of the blast zone, a curtain of smoke parted to reveal, in the center of what had been the brick hut, an almond-shaped rip in space-time. It was as tall as a large man, and its edges crackled with an unnatural-looking black energy. Bits of debris falling from above the blast site crackled and disintegrated as they drifted into the rip's threshold.

On the other side of the threshold were Cade, Briet, and Anja—all confronting Hatunde with stern and unforgiving glares, despite the fact he was still invisible. Cade held an athamé with a glowing blade in his right hand. With his left he flipped his middle digit at Hatunde—and then he snapped his fingers, and the portal zippered shut and vanished in a blue-black flash that left Hatunde seeing spots.

Hatunde would have to take responsibility for this failure, though the truth would anger the Old Man. *I was not supposed to be seen. Now the enemy knows my face.* He sighed and let go of his fear and his disappointment. *Now we must go forward.*

Locals crowded around the fire and the mess. Hatunde did not think less of them for it. It was just human nature. *Everyone loves a tragedy when it's not theirs.*

Still shrouded in invisibility and silence, he resolved to make his way back to his hotel on foot, to give himself time to think about what had gone wrong, and how he would need to prepare himself for his next meeting with the ones the Old Man so desperately wanted dead.

In the meantime, Hatunde saw no reason not to task his demon of burden with making his amends for him. *AKROTH, take the car I stole tonight and return it intact and with discretion to its owner, along with a few thousand pesos of cash from the reserve I left in your care.*

As you command, the spirit replied. Moments later the stolen Ford 200 vanished, ported away by the demon—along with Hatunde's lingering pangs of shame over having stolen it in the first place. *Honor is a funny thing. Take a man's car and I feel unclean. But take his life while his back is turned and I call it my duty.* He chortled at the strangeness of his moral code. *I can only imagine what delights Hell has in store for me after I die. . . .*

———✦———

"That was close," Yasmin said. Cade watched her unburden herself of several hidden blades: a Swiss Army knife, a box cutter, a hunting dagger whose spine had a row of saw teeth, a spring-action switchblade, a stiletto she'd hidden up her sleeve, a tiny matte-black push knife disguised as a belt buckle, and her athamé. She also was still wearing six throwing knives—one in each boot, one on each hip, one across her chest, and one on her back between her shoulders.

Cade regarded his pupil with a cocked eyebrow. "That all? No cleaver in your bra? No machete down your pants?"

She was in no mood for ribbing, gentle or otherwise. "Pray you never find out."

On the other side of the Tasmanian lodge's conjuring room, Barış meditated in a corner. Sathit stood at the window and stared into the bright haze of the afternoon. It was summer in the southern hemisphere, a fact hammered home by the heat and humidity that assailed the lodge. Luis's home was warm but bearable thanks to its array of ceiling fans. There was at least one in each room to keep the air moving. Combined with the blinds and curtains that blocked out the daylight, the interior of the large lakeside house was at least comfortable rather than stifling.

Briet sat on the floor near Cade. When he turned his head toward her, she seemed lost in her own thoughts. He was reluctant to disturb her, but he did anyway. "Thank you."

"For what?" Her eyes remained fixed on some imaginary point a million miles away.

"For spotting our tail back there."

She shrugged one shoulder. "If I hadn't seen him at the airport, you'd have picked him up when we hit the slums."

"Maybe. But I'm glad I didn't have to."

"It wasn't—"

"Would you just take the fucking compliment?"

She slid her eyes toward him. They stared at each other for half a second, the air electric with the promise of conflict. Then she smiled, and her lips parted into a grin as she snorted out a laugh. Cade laughed, too, though he wasn't sure what they were laughing about. Their instinct to pick fights with each other? The absurdity of their new alliance? Or just their shared sense of overinflated self-worth? Whatever the reason, he figured it probably didn't matter as much as the fact that they had broken the tension.

She shook her head. "Thank you."

"You're fucking welcome."

Anja returned to the conjuring room looking bewildered. She squatted between Cade and Briet and lowered her voice. "I searched the house. Luis is not here."

"Don't suppose he left a note?" Cade asked.

"Nothing. But his tools are gone. And his grimoire."

Briet considered that. "Not making a run to town for supplies, then." She looked at Cade. "His wards should hold even if he's away. This is still our best bet for safe ground."

"Agreed. But we can't stay here long." As Anja settled onto the floor in a cross-legged pose facing him and Briet, Cade continued, "We need to figure out our next move, and fast."

In response, Anja planted a box of ammunition on the floor between them. "This is the only clue I found in Rocha's apartment. I would have preferred we question him, but . . ."

"Sorry," Cade said, "wasn't an option. We were lucky to get out of Mexico with our skins." He nodded at the box of rifle cartridges. "So what does that tell us?"

"Not much we did not already know." Anja picked up the box, turned it over to inspect its various sides. "No name for the maker. No city or country." She tapped one of the box's narrow end panels with her index finger. "Just a name and a logo."

Cade looked closer at the image, which resembled a coat of arms with a ram's head and a serpent on opposing sides of a bend sinister, over a name printed in block letters: TKAM. "That's gotta be the most obscure fucking thing I've ever seen."

"True," Briet said. "But it can't be a coincidence it features a serpent and a ram. I mean, c'mon—two of the most widespread animal representations in the Goetic Art?"

He nodded in agreement. "It certainly seems to merit further investigation. But without more to go on—a city, a country, or anything specific—I'm not sure what this gets us."

Anja frowned. "We must impose again on Miles."

"No." Cade raised his hand to preempt debate. "He's done enough for us."

"She's right," Briet said. "Without his access, it could take us weeks or even months to find out who made these bullets." She leaned closer to Cade. "This is specialized intel, not the kind of thing you can get from your local library's reference desk."

Cade felt a headache coming on. "You don't know what you're asking. If we're really dealing with some kind of an elite global conspiracy, just *asking* these kinds of questions could put a bull's-eye on Miles." Anja's and Briet's stares showed no sign of relenting. Cade's tone became more insistent. "He's the closest thing I have to a brother. I can't do that to him."

"Time is against us," Anja said. "Contact him."

"Making too many inquiries in too short a time? It sends up red flags. At the very least we might cost him his job."

Briet slumped against the wall behind her. "Then tell us a better option. Do you want to send a demon to find a factory that makes magick-killing bullets? Or do you think that somebody might've put wards on it to hide it from people like us? Tell us your master plan, Cade."

"Please. Consider the risk to Miles."

Anja regarded Cade through narrowed eyes. "All my brothers died for less than this."

"Everyone I've ever loved is rotting in the ground right now," Briet said. "But sure, Cade, tell me more about *your* fucking problems."

This is clearly not a debate I'm going to win. Cade sighed. "Fine. But it's the middle of the night in London. I'll call him in a few hours and see what he can do for us, okay?"

Briet cocked her head. "Why the fuck is it always the middle of the night for Miles when we need something from him?"

Cade's patience was exhausted. "For starters, because the earth is an oblate sphere, only half of it is illuminated by the sun at any given time. Humanity coped with this phenomenon by creating arbitrary temporal divisions known as 'time zones,' and those—"

"Fuck you," Briet said, conceding the point with an eye-roll.

Cade stood and yawned. "I'm gonna crash. I suggest you all do the same. We have hard days ahead of us, and I can't promise when we'll get to rest again. Especially since, without our mirrors, long-range travel is gonna be a major pain in the ass." He plodded out of the conjuring room. "If any of you wakes me up for anything short of the Apocalypse, I swear to God I will feed you to the Devil himself."

"Sweet dreams," Briet called out with a mocking lilt.

"Fuck you. Fuck you very much."

MONDAY, NOVEMBER 25

Cursing under his breath about the morning's traffic, Frank Cioffi shambled toward the elevator to the Pentagon's top-secret sublevels. The briefcase in his left hand was too heavy; in his right, the paper cup holding his morning coffee had already gone cold. His shoes pinched the arches of his feet, his trousers rode low on his hips, and his shirt bulged in front of his gut. In his younger days he might have hidden his fashion blunders by buttoning his suit jacket, but the time when that was possible was long behind him. Bald but for the graying tufts above his ears, and knowing his age was betrayed by the crow's-feet extending from his bloodshot eyes, Frank had resigned himself to the truth he was no longer anyone's idea of an Adonis.

A point Jeanne drove home all too well during the divorce.

It was just a few days until Thanksgiving. He was still angry he wouldn't be seeing his son and daughter on Turkey Day this year. Jeanne and her new Wall Street investment banker husband would be hosting a gala dinner at their estate in Connecticut.

I wonder if I'll get to see the kids on Christmas. He pressed the elevator's call button. Then he remembered how soon Christmas would come, and that he hadn't even started shopping yet for presents. *I have to get them something. But what do they want? Joey's nine. I can probably get away with more baseball gear for him. But Lina's fourteen. What do I know about buying gifts for a teenaged girl?* He dreaded having to ask Jeanne for advice.

The elevator doors opened. Frank stepped inside and pressed the button for sublevel fifteen. The doors closed and the car began its descent.

Should I give Lina clothes? I don't even know her size. And forget accessories. I don't know from handbags and all that shit. He wanted to give his daughter something extravagant. Something luxurious. Something that would rekindle her appreciation for her old man. He pictured himself holding up a mink coat as she shimmied into it, and then basking in her smile. *Then she'd be my little girl again.* He smiled at the idea, until reality turned his fantasy of joy into a prophecy of sorrow. *Like I have the money to buy real fur.*

Frank sighed. His middle age was a daily exercise in coping with disappointment and loss. He wanted to believe there was still some way for him to turn things around, to correct the course of his life, but he just couldn't see a better way forward.

The elevator doors opened. Frank was surprised to see two men in dark suits and sunglasses facing him as he stepped out onto sublevel fifteen. The taller of the men, an Asian-looking fellow with hair silvered by age, put his hand to Frank's chest and stopped him cold. His voice had a flat, midwestern affect. "Director Frank Cioffi?"

"Yeah, that's me. Who the fuck are you?"

The other stranger, a brown-skinned fireplug of a man, had the face and personality of an anvil. "We have orders to escort you to the Silo auditorium for an emergency briefing."

"Orders from who?"

Fireplug locked a hand on Frank's upper arm, hard enough that Frank was sure it would leave a bruise. "Come with us, sir. Time is a factor." The goon started walking and gave Frank a shove toward the hallway on his left. He was not accepting refusal as an option.

Silverhair fell in behind Frank and his strong-arm escort. They marched him past several computer bays and research laboratories housed on the command sublevel. Frank stole glances into the rooms he passed. All were deserted—an odd state of affairs.

"Can one of you tell me what's goin' on?"

"All your questions will be addressed at the meeting, sir," said Fireplug.

They arrived at the auditorium. It was a drab space, just large enough to hold the Silo's research and command teams, which comprised a few hundred people. Tiers of seats radiated up from its stage, the rows widening toward the back of the room, where Frank was ushered through the main entrance with a hard shove. As he regained his balance, the men in suits closed the doors behind him. Then they stood guard outside, watching through the doors' narrow windows.

Subtle, guys. Not suspicious at all. Frank set down his briefcase and cold coffee. Shrugged off his overcoat. Took a quick head count. He saw department heads and senior researchers from every unit in the Silo. Even Briet's three most recently transferred adepts had been summoned to this briefing, though the ODP's master karcist was nowhere to be seen.

Frank felt his sphincter tighten. *I got a bad fuckin' feeling about this.*

The paranoid part of his brain told him they were being watched. He kept his body language loose and open as he strolled down the center aisle, and then he veered left to climb one set of stairs to the stage. A few of those waiting in the auditorium looked up expectantly, as if he might be the one who had commandeered their attendance that morning.

The stage was a narrow platform, just large enough to host a lectern to one side of the projection screen built into the wall. Frank ducked left, behind a curtain into one of the shallow wings that flanked the stage. To his relief he saw no one outside the auditorium's rear exit.

He peered through its slender window and confirmed there was no one in the corridor beyond. *No guards back here? Is that a mistake? Or did I just get lucky?* He applied gentle pressure to the door's crash bar, opened it quietly, and slipped into the corridor. He closed the door behind him as softly as he could.

Now to find out what the fuck is— He heard voices approaching from beyond the corner at the end of the passage ahead of him. *Fuck me.*

There was no time for clever. He darted to the nearest door, a janitor's closet, and prayed to God it was unlocked. It was. He slipped inside and eased the door shut. Then he peeked through the door's upper ventilation slats to see what was happening in the corridor.

Two men in dark suits passed his hiding place. One was fair-haired and sported a golden mustache. The other had a classic military crew cut and a chin full of stubble.

Golden Mustache carried a thick steel door brace with a rubber foot, which he wedged into place against the rear exit door's handle. "That ought to hold."

Captain Stubble raised a bulky military-grade walkie-talkie and pressed its talk switch. "Leda, this is Castor. You're clear to proceed. Over." He released the switch.

A man's voice crackled back in reply: *"Roger, Castor. Delivering package now. Over."*

From the other side of the auditorium's rear door came several muffled thumps, followed by cries of alarm, and then a chorus of hacking coughs. As the symphony of pain grew louder and uglier, the two men guarding the rear door seemed to pay it no heed.

Golden Mustache leaned against the wall. "Any plans for the holiday?"

Captain Stubble shook his head. "Just the Lions-Packers game. You?"

"My wife's parents are coming over. Maybe a few aunts and uncles, some cousins."

"Sounds like a fuckin' nightmare."

"You have no idea."

Golden Mustache pulled out a pack of Camel cigarettes. Offered one to Captain Stubble, who accepted it with a nod. Golden Mustache struck a match. Lit both smokes. Snuffed the match with a wrist-shake. "I swear to Christ, if her Uncle Louie tries to sell me life insurance one more time, I'm gonna kill him in front of his kids."

"You should. 'Let the punishment fit the crime,' that's what I always say."

"Goddamned right."

A crash of collision resounded through the rear door. Its brace held steady as desperate but weakened people threw themselves against it. Frank stared in mute horror at the faces of people he knew, visible through the door's narrow window, as they coughed up blood and gasped for air, their fingers clawing in vain for purchase—while the men in suits ignored them.

They puffed their cigarettes until the cacophony of terror on the other side of the door faded to silence. Stubble raised his walkie-talkie again. "Leda, Castor. All quiet at the back door. How're things lookin' out front? Over."

"*Castor, Leda. Not a soul is stirring, not even a mouse. I think we're done here. Over.*"

"Roger that. Meet you back at Ops in five. Castor, out." Stubble nudged Mustache with his elbow. "Fun's over. Nothin' left now but boxin' up and buggin' out. Let's roll."

The pair retreated back the way they had come. Frank listened at the closet's door for several seconds after their footsteps faded away. Confident he was alone, he left the closet, went to the auditorium's rear door, and looked through its narrow window.

A thick haze lingered in the air on the other side. Beneath the door and throughout the auditorium, scores of bodies lay draped over seats or sprawled in the aisles. Moving amid and around the dead were a half dozen persons in hazmat suits, full-body gear designed for working in areas compromised by toxic chemicals or radioactivity.

One of the hazmat-suited team members noted movement by a survivor on the stage. Without delay he skewered the woman's carotid with a large hypodermic needle and injected her with a large dose from a syringe full of blue fluid. The woman on the floor was racked by spasms, and then she coughed up a pink foam of blood and spittle. Seconds later she went still, her lifeless eyes staring, it seemed to Frank, directly into his soul.

Fuck. Fuck! Fucking goddamned cocksucking fucking motherfuck bastard fuck . . .

He struggled to control his panic. *Keep it together, moron. You panic, you die. Get your shit straight, now!* He took several deep breaths to slow his heart rate. *Better. Now think!*

The facts on the ground were grim. He was outnumbered. There was no way for him to be sure how many opponents he might have to evade or confront on this level alone in order to escape. *For all I know, this is an official burn. I could be a marked man.*

He pushed that notion away. *Don't assume. You don't know that. Stay calm.* He moved in light steps to the end of the corridor and checked the corner before he continued onward. *You'll have a better chance of getting out if you're armed. Get to your office, get your Colt.*

Frank crouched as he neared the next intersection. He heard lots of people moving about the sublevel. Something large was going on, and no one involved seemed concerned about subtlety. The closer he got to the main command area, which was located just outside of his glass-walled office, the louder the commotion became.

Great. I'll have to sneak through a damned circus to get my Colt, and probably have to dodge a fucking parade of elephants and a clown car to reach the emergency stairwell.

He paused short of the command area and considered his chances. Recovering his pistol would give him more confidence, but was it worth the risk? Based on where he heard activity, he saw a better chance of skirting the perimeter to the stairs instead of going to his office. From the stairwell he could escape into one of the Silo's "doomsday" tunnels, which would enable him to flee the Pentagon, exit through a hatch by the Potomac River, and then decide whether to return with reinforcements or run for his fucking life.

Time to get the fuck outta here.

He started toward the stairwell door—and then more men in dark suits entered from a connecting passage at the far end of the corridor, blocking his way out.

Frank had only a moment in which to act. He veered away from the stairwell door, ducked between banks of computers, and snuck behind an intruder's back into his own dark office. *So much for making a run for it.* He crawled behind his desk, opened the bottom drawer with his key, and retrieved his Colt 1911 semiautomatic pistol.

A quick check of its magazine confirmed it was fully loaded. *Seven rounds of .45-caliber hollow-point,* Frank told himself, hoping it would assuage his fear. It didn't. *There's a lot more than seven people here.*

He poked his head up over his desk to see what was happening out in the brightly lit command center. Through the half-open venetian blinds covering his office's glass walls, he saw men in coveralls and high-tech "clean suits" take reels of magnetic tape off the computer drives and pack them into boxes. They worked in three-man teams. One man packed, another labeled the boxes, and a third loaded the boxes into large crates designed for shipping.

Visible beyond a sea of drab workstations, men in suits emptied file cabinets of years' worth of legal analysis of demonic pacts and contracts. Others sealed up the physicists' research into the effects of magickal conjurations on the presence of high-energy particles and exotic forms of radiation. A few boxed up the center's library of rare grimoires and magickal reference works, which included a unique, complete and unabridged copy of the *Grimorium Verum.*

In the center of it all was a woman Frank had never seen before. She looked young, early twenties. Her features were as striking in their beauty as in their darkness. Her umber skin had cool jewel undertones, and her straight hair, as black as a moonless night, was tied in a loose tail that hung between her shoulder blades. She wore a navy blue suit with an A-line skirt over knee-high black leather boots with low, strong heels. In her right hand was a gnarled length of blond wood decorated with elaborate carvings—a karcist's wand.

"The Old Man wants the grimoires loaded first," she told one of the dark-suited men. "After that, the legal analyses and then the scientific data." As that man nodded and moved away to carry out her orders, she snagged another as he passed near to her. "You. How long until the charges are set on the conjuring stage?"

"Thirty minutes."

"Tell your people they have ten. I want to be out of here in twenty. Go."

Another obedient nod. The man hurried away from the woman. She casually waved her wand at the sealed shipping boxes as if she were a conductor guiding a symphony.

Clutching his pistol, Frank stole from his desk to his office's doorway. *Briet needs to hear about this. Which means I need to get out of here, now.* When the path seemed clear, he dashed from the control center to the nearest stairwell entrance.

His hand was on the doorknob.

White heat flared in his gut as he heard the gunshot.

The strength left his hands, and his legs turned to jelly.

He tried to turn, slumped against the door, and then he collapsed onto his back in front of it. Lying on the cool concrete, he shivered with deep chills even as sweat soaked his brow.

He tried to lift his Colt. It was too heavy. He could barely shift his gaze far enough to see the bleeding exit wound in his gut. *Fuck. I'm going into shock. Fuck.* Frightened and desperate, Frank pictured the faces of his children. *Hold it together. For them. Hold it together. . . .*

Hostile strangers gathered above him. Men in suits . . . and the dark woman.

Captain Stubble joined her. In his hand was a pistol, smoke curling from its muzzle.

The weapon that just ended me.

Golden Mustache moved up behind Captain Stubble, looked over his partner's shoulder at Frank, and then he frowned. "Nice one, Mitch." To the dark woman, he continued, "What now, Lila? We can't blame a gunshot wound on a gas leak."

Lila's gaze was cold, her voice condescending. "We're standing next to a pit filled with fifty feet of black water. Do the math, genius." As she turned away from Frank, he was certain, if only for a moment, that a shadow of remorse betrayed itself in her eyes.

Then came another gunshot—the one that ended all Frank Cioffi had ever been, ever done, or ever hoped to be.

⟊

There was nothing like starting the day at a deficit. Miles Franklin had for years prided himself on clearing his inbox before leaving his office each evening. His policy had consigned him to many a late night at MI6 headquarters, but he had always slept better knowing he had done all he could every day. He also had learned to relish his first few minutes of peace on workday mornings, when he could read the news and sip some tea before the next round of crises began.

Today would not be such a day.

He had arrived to find a brief message on his desk. It was from Cade, using his code name Prospero. A request for information about an ammunition manufacturer with a distinctive coat of arms, one that featured a ram in the upper dexter opposing a serpent beneath its bend sinister, and a cryptic logo: TKAM.

Miles's imagination had wheeled. *What are you into* this *time, old boy?*

It had taken MI6's research division less than an hour to generate a file about the company behind TKAM. It was a producer of ammunition for various types and calibers of small arms, including handguns, rifles, and machine guns. Based in Adana, Turkey, TKAM had no clear owner. The research team's preliminary inquiry had uncovered no fewer than three shell companies layered around it, each one little more than a mask for some other corporation.

That detail had so intrigued Miles that it had compelled him to ring Clarence, the lead researcher, and ask, "Is this sort of obfuscation typical for this kind of business?"

"Not at all," Clarence had said while chewing a mouthful of roasted pistachios. *"Shell games like this are what big conglomerates use to hide their money from the tax man. I've never seen a small factory set up like this."*

"Can you get me a deeper look into TKAM's finances? Unravel its web of phony owners to see who's really behind it?"

"Might take a day or three. Got time to wait?"

"No. Expedite it."

"On whose account?"

"Soviet desk. Their budget can take it."

"Righto. Ring you back when we know more."

Most of the day had bled away since that exchange, and Miles had passed the hours clearing other items from his agenda. He wanted to be ready to move as soon as—

His phone rang.

About bloody time. He lifted the receiver, his mood hopeful. "Franklin."

The voice on the other end was decidedly not that of Clarence. It was older, coarser, and freighted with a lifetime of unspoken secrets. *"Mr. Franklin. This is Nigel Maxwell."*

Miles froze for half a second. He had heard of the upper-level MI6 director, though he had never met the man in person. He adopted a reserved but genial tone. "Good afternoon, Sir Nigel. How can I be of service?"

"I'm looking over a research order you fast-tracked this morning. It seems our boys and the team at GCHQ have dug up something interesting. I should very much like to review it with you"—his manner took a grave turn—*"in person, Mr. Franklin."*

Sir Nigel had phrased the summons as an invitation, but it had been meant as an order, one that Miles did not have the luxury of refusing or postponing. "Of course, Sir Nigel. Are you prepared to receive me at your office directly?"

"This conversation requires a tad more discretion, I think. I'm in the Regent's Suite at the St. Ermin's Hotel. It's a quarter to four now. I trust I'll see you at the top of the hour?"

"Without a doubt, Sir Nigel."

The director hung up without the courtesy of a valediction. Miles set his phone back on its cradle and felt his stomach fall away, as if his insides had just gone hollow. *Bloody hell.*

He had never conducted official business in the St. Ermin's Hotel, but the establishment's reputation was well known within MI6. Because of its proximity to headquarters, it frequently was used for clandestine meetings between top-level directors and members of Her Majesty's Government, as well as with important foreign contacts. But it also was used to arrange for the disappearances of those who the service or the Crown had deemed "problematic."

No matter how many times Miles urged himself to be calm, he couldn't shake the sickening dread worming its way into him. This bizarre summons had come within hours of his requesting a financial profile on something Cade was investigating. *That can't be a bloody coincidence.* He paced behind his desk. *I tripped somebody's alarm, that's for certain.* He considered picking up the phone and calling Cade to warn him, but then he stopped himself. *No, if they suspect me of anything, my phone's already tapped. If I call him now, I'll just be painting a target on him.* He lamented the recent sudden loss of the magick mirror. *That would be a really useful widget right about now.*

The hands of the clock crept onward, pushing him closer to his fateful meeting. Whatever he was going to do, he had very little time in which to act.

Time for Plan C. He gathered all the documentation he had so far on TKAM and stuffed it into an envelope for secure posting. The address he filled in from memory; for security reasons, Cade had asked him to memorize it and never write it down. It was for a nondescript residential address somewhere in Wales. In order to avoid putting it on the radar of MI6 or any other intelligence service, Miles had never gone there. He hoped the address was still a valid one, and that he wasn't consigning valuable intelligence to the hands of an unsuspecting civilian.

The clock read ten to four as he left his office with the envelope tucked under his arm. As he neared the lobby, he saw the mail cart stopped in front of a colleague's office. Miles stopped, pulled out his pen, appended his peer's secure postal authorization code to his envelope, and tucked it into the bottom of the outgoing stack of letters and parcels.

By the time the mail clerk returned, Miles had made his exit to the lobby and was waiting for the lift. No one seemed to have noticed his surreptitious addition to that day's post.

The ride to the ground floor was brief and quiet. Outside, Miles moved through the crowded sidewalks of Westminster at a fast clip. *Even if I am walking into a trap, it would be rude to be tardy.* Less than a block from MI6 headquarters he got the feeling he was being followed. He tried to steal glimpses of his shadows, but it had been years since he had served in the field, and his tradecraft was more than a little rusty.

The closer he got to the St. Ermin's Hotel, the more certain he became that he was being tailed, and that he was unlikely to return from this meeting alive.

He detoured across the street into a public telephone box. He pulled the door shut with one hand and fished for spare coins with the other. For a second he considered trying to call Cade, but he had barely enough change to place a local call, never mind ring someone on the far side of the world. Trying to make the call collect would require the help of an international operator. GCHQ monitored all such calls. It was too dangerous.

After feeding the box's coin-eating maw what few pence he had, he dialed the number for the law office of his beloved Dez. They had always been careful to speak in euphemism and artful omissions whenever one or both of them was at work or in public, because in Miles's experience, one never knew who might be eavesdropping.

This time he would be forced to employ euphemisms for an entirely different reason.

The phone rang twice. As usual, Dez's secretary answered his phone. *"Good afternoon—Hawkins, Barrow, and Spencer."*

"Lydia, this is Miles Franklin. Is Desmond in?"

"Yes. I'll put you right through, Mr. Franklin."

A few seconds of silence followed while Miles waited on hold. Then Dez picked up the line. *"Miles? To what do I owe the pleasure?"*

It was hard for Miles to keep the fear out of his voice. "Bad news, I'm afraid."

"Oh?" Dez picked up on Miles's tone at once.

"Yes. I know I'd promised you a chance to reclaim your honor in darts one of these days . . . but it looks as if something has come up."

The silence between them was freighted with their mutual understanding. Over the line, Miles heard Dez's stiff upper lip trembling as he said, *"Something important, I presume?"*

"Terribly important."

"No way out of it?"

Miles's throat felt as tight as a tourniquet, and his eyes stung with tears he couldn't risk letting free. "Sorry, old boy. Not this time."

"I see." On the other end of the phone, Dez fought to recover his composure. *"Well. Nothing for it, then. . . . Until we meet again."*

"Until we meet again. Cheery-bye, Dez."

There was nothing cheerful in Dez's voice as he replied, *"Cheery-bye."*

Miles hung up the phone. Straightened his tie. Lifted his chin with pride.

He opened the door of the phone booth and rejoined the madding throng that coursed along the walks of Westminster. He was running late but determined to keep his appointment with whatever Fate he had tempted for asking the wrong question one time too many.

14

A sheet of ice covered the path leading to the monastery's door. This high up in the Dolomites at this time of year, it was to be expected. Bladelike towers of black stone rose from the earth to form this imposing mountain range in northeastern Italy. Their ragged edges were dusted with fresh, immaculate snow that glowed in dusk's salmon light. That same pink radiance landed gently, like the grace of the Virgin, upon the walls of Monte Paterno—the last great redoubt of White magick sanctioned by the Roman Catholic Church.

Enervated from the angelic labor that had been required to teleport to the mountainside, Luis paused his slow, barefooted climb up the icy trail. Though he had been excommunicated from the Church nearly a decade earlier for his role in assisting Cade, Anja, and Briet in their mission to save the world from an Infernal catastrophe, he had never borne any grudge against his peers in the monastic order. They, like him, were merely students of magick. Unlike him, they all still adhered strictly to the tenets of the Pauline Art, commonly known as White magick.

Luis did not think less of the monks for their refusal to explore the Goetic Art, as he had done, nor did he think himself in any way superior because he had embraced a middle path between the White and Black traditions. He had, nonetheless, accepted with humility his exile from those he had once considered his mentors, peers, and friends. The path he had chosen had come at a price, as he had known it would. He had never questioned the justice of that fact.

Now those who had shunned him needed his help, though they didn't know it yet. Worse, they might not believe his warning when they heard it. But he still loved them all, in the unconditional manner known as *agape,* and he could not turn his back on them when they had just become the prey in danger's crosshairs.

The soles of his bare feet felt numb as he walked the last few meters to the door. Cold winds groaned and whipped up snow devils that spun down the steep slopes on either side of him. As he reached the door and gathered his courage to knock, he hesitated out of fear.

What will they do when they recognize me? Send me away? Arrest me for the Cardinal Inquisitor? Luis tried not to fixate upon worst-case scenarios, but optimism eluded him. *Even if they hear me out, will they believe me? Can they possibly trust me, after all that's happened?*

He took in the crisp alpine air, and with it he stoked the fires of hope. *The Lord is my shepherd. I shall not fear.* He knocked on the door.

After several seconds Luis heard dull scuffles of motion behind the dark oaken portal. Then came the scrape of its iron viewing hatch being slid aside. A pair of bright hazel-green eyes looked out at Luis, and a youthful-sounding male voice said, "*Sì?*"

Luis responded to the man in Italian, which he recalled was the most common shared language inside Monte Paterno. "Hello. My name is Father Luis Roderigo Pérez. I have come to speak with your director. It is a matter of great urgency."

The young monk on the other side of the door was openly suspicious. "I will let Father D'Odorico know that you are here." He started to close the viewing hatch.

"Wait!" When the young monk halted with the hatch half shut, Luis added, "Could I please wait inside? It's rather cold out here."

"I'm sorry, Father. Your reputation precedes you. I could be expelled from the order, maybe even excommunicated, if I let you inside without permission." A note of regret crept into his voice. "Forgive me, Gray Master."

That was not a title Luis had ever heard anyone use before, with respect to him or to anyone else. Before he could ask about or comment upon it, the young monk closed the hatch.

Minutes passed while Luis waited in reverent silence. Cold winds wailed around him. Downy flakes of snow fell in endless battalions.

Luis did not know what answer to expect from Father D'Odorico, his former master in the Pauline Art. *Bernardo would be perfectly justified in sending me away. He owes me no favors. And he has every right to resent the way I left.*

Years of meditation and reflection upon Eastern philosophical teachings had given Luis a deeper sense of patience and perspective than he had enjoyed during the years he had studied here at the monastery. He had learned not to expect any outcome, either good or ill, nor to hope for either one, but merely to exist in the moment and accept what he found. There was a peacefulness of mind that grew out of freeing oneself from the cycle of expectation and disappointment. Learning to live in the moment, and to understand that the ever-present *now* was all a human being was likely ever to know of eternity, enabled one to let go of the past and escape the futility of trying to define the unwritten future.

So it was that he had no sense of how many minutes had passed when, at last, the door opened. He turned and was overjoyed to see a smile on the familiar, aquiline features of Father Bernardo D'Odorico, the director of the Monte Paterno sanctuary. Barefoot just like Luis, he stepped out into the icy cold and embraced his former adept.

"Luis, my brother," he said in his Calabrian-accented Italian. "So good to see you."

"I've missed you, too, Master." He leaned back and noted his master's ring of silvered hair was absent. "You've shaved your head."

A good-natured frown. "I wish. Nature made this choice for me, sad to say." He kept one arm across Luis's shoulders and ushered him inside. "Come. Let's get you out of the cold."

"Thank you." It was a relief to Luis to step inside the warmth of the monastery, and to feel the icy mountain winds blocked out as the door was closed.

Father D'Odorico gestured down the corridor that Luis remembered led to the dining hall. "Can we offer you something to eat?"

"Not right now." Luis cast off the nostalgia that had gripped him and set his mind to the mission that had brought him here. "We have urgent business to attend."

His declaration put creases of concern onto Father D'Odorico's brow. "What sort of business?"

"The existential sort." Luis stepped closer to his old master and lowered his voice. "A new darkness rises. Its principal aim appears to be the slaughter of any and all karcists not under its exclusive control. If I've understood the vision granted to me this morning . . . you and all the other members of this sanctuary are the next ones it means to kill."

His abduction had been fast and professional: pushed inside a van, a hood pulled over his head, a hard sap across the back of his noggin. For that, at least, Miles was grateful. During his years as a field operative for MI6, he'd endured his share of amateur kidnappings, most of which had been made uglier than necessary by the clumsiness of his captors. The inept often resorted to violence and volume when things went wrong. Professionals tended to distinguish themselves with the expression, "Just stay quiet and follow directions, and no one needs to get hurt."

Of course, "hurt" was a relative term. Miles understood full well the people who had taken him off a Westminster street in broad daylight intended to kill him after they finished his interrogation. He could only hope they intended to make his death clean and relatively painless. A double-tap to the chest followed by a shot to the forehead. Smooth and by the numbers. His body wouldn't be fit for an open casket, but at least his final exit would be swift.

He tried taking a deep breath. His left nostril was caked with dried blood and snot. As his chest expanded, he felt no pain in his ribs or spine. *I haven't been beaten. That's good.* He ran his tongue over his teeth. *None loose. No taste of blood. All good signs.* His wrists were bound to the arms of his chair, and his ankles were tied to its legs.

He heard footsteps. Someone was approaching him from behind.

The hood was pulled off his head. Footfalls retreated behind him as he blinked and let his eyes adjust. His surroundings were dim, the light sources few. Everywhere he looked he saw old stone. There was nothing modern about the place; it looked quasi-medieval.

I'm underground. An old tunnel. Maybe a dungeon.

A sly glance left spied a man in a full-head mask standing beside a rolling cart, atop which was a tray filled with implements of torture. Most of them looked as if they had been inspired by surgical tools, but some had a more culinary pedigree, and a few resembled home-gardening equipment.

It would appear I'm to be the evening's entertainment.

As his vision acclimated to the deep shadows and far-off lights, Miles discerned the shadows of two people standing behind him, beyond the range of his peripheral vision. "Nice to know someone respects me enough to send two of you. If they'd sent only one, I'd feel slighted."

Neither of the guards behind him replied. Miles aimed his next quip at the man next to the torture gear. "Pardon? You with the mask. I'm a 'man of the world,' as they say. And I can see you're the kind who likes toys. But I think we should set a safe word, don't you?"

Masked Man said nothing. He was expressionless and as patient as a statue.

A flash of green fire lit up a pitch-dark corner. Spots of darkness between the flames fused into a human shape. A beautiful woman with rich brown skin and flowing ebony hair emerged from the dwindling pillar of fire. She was smartly dressed, in a skirt and matching jacket of navy blue with an off-white blouse. Her knee-high black leather boots tapped out a crisp rhythm on the stone floor as she walked toward Miles.

She stopped next to the cart of torture toys. From it she took a folder, which she opened. Perused its contents with aplomb. After she had finished, she closed the folder and held it close as she moved to stand in front of Miles. "Mr. Franklin?" Her accent sounded either Algerian or Moroccan to his ear. "My name is Lila Matar. Perhaps you've heard of me?"

Miles shook his head. "Can't say as I have."

He read a small measure of disappointment in her face, but it quickly vanished. She held up the folder. "My employer knows you made several official inquiries, to both GCHQ and MI5, about a Turkish ammunition factory. Would you care to tell me why?"

"I wouldn't, no."

Lila sighed. "Please, Mr. Franklin. We both know how this game is played. In the end, you *will* break and tell me what I want to know. Why not spare yourself the pain and possible lifelong consequences of resistance, and just cooperate instead?"

Despite the gravity of his predicament, Miles smiled at her. "You know why."

"I had so hoped you might be reasonable."

"Where would be the sport in that?"

She looked at the Masked Man. "Break him."

The man in the mask picked up a hammer and a spike, and then he moved behind Miles. Hoping to buy time, Miles asked Lila, "Why let this punter do your dirty work? Can't you force the truth out of me with magick?"

Her poker face remained steady. "My master taught me never to waste magick on any task that can be done effectively without it."

There was no preamble to the pain. Just the sudden white agony of a spike being hammered between two of Miles's lower vertebrae into his spinal column.

His body tensed at the moment of impact, and that only made the pain worse.

His spine seized upon the spike—and then he couldn't feel any part of his body beneath that. His hips, his groin, his legs—it was as if they had suddenly vanished.

"That should keep you from running off," the Masked Man said with a Germanic accent. "Now I'm going to show you something special I learned in Cambodia."

He lifted a pair of pliers from his tray, and with his other hand, he seized Miles's right index finger. "We always take things for granted until they are gone. Things like . . . fingernails."

"No, wait, you—"

The pliers gripped the nail on Miles's right index finger.

Masked Man pulled off the nail in one sharp jerk that took tender flesh with it.

"Fuck!" Miles screamed. Spittle fell from his mouth, which suddenly overflowed with saliva in response to his injury. His body and mind were overcome with nausea, panic, and pain. "Stop! Ask me whatever you—"

The pliers tore the nail from his right thumb.

"God!" Miles wailed, tears pouring from his eyes, his whole body shaking.

He had been years behind a desk. He was no hard case, no superagent, no hero. The worst he had ever suffered had been a few ordinary beatings. Nothing in his life had prepared him for this. "Stop!"

The Masked Man didn't listen.

He took the nails from every finger on Miles's right hand in under a minute. Agony like hot needles traveling up his wrist into his elbow left the MI6 veteran a broken, bleeding, gibbering mess lashed to a chair. He was sobbing himself hoarse, drooling down his chest, his entire lifetime of pride stolen in a matter of seconds by a monster with no conscience.

He wept like a child. "Please . . . ask me anything."

Lila waved off the torturer and squatted in front of Miles. When he looked into her eyes, they were hard and cold. "Where are Cade and Anja now?"

"I don't know. They didn't tell me. Safer that way."

She stared for several seconds into Miles's tear-filled eyes. "He's telling the truth. He doesn't know."

The Masked Man elbowed her aside. "I don't believe him."

Lila raised her voice: "I told you, he *doesn't know.*"

"So *you* say." The torturer grabbed the back of Miles's chair and dragged him across the floor. "Give me three minutes and we will *know.*"

Miles felt as if he were falling backward. His chair was tilted until its back rested atop the edge of a basin filled with water. "Wait, what are you—?"

A wet towel was slapped over his face.

Then came the deluge.

Torrents of ice-cold water slammed down onto his face and poured up his nose and into his mouth. His fear response kicked in, filled him with panic, sent all his muscles into spasms.

He tried to exhale in short bursts, to push some of the water out of his upper respiratory tract, but it was as hopeless as he had feared it would be. With his head tilted back, there was nothing to stop the water from entering his sinus passages and pharynx. He ran out of breath, and every cough provoked by the sensation of choking drew more water into his lungs.

Terror clouded his thoughts, and he thrashed in vain against his bonds.

More water splashed onto the towel and into his mouth.

Miles wished he had intel he could give up to make it stop, but he had already told them all he knew. Even if he hadn't, this would have broken him. MI6 trained its field agents to expect this barbaric torture if they were captured by the Chinese or the Russians. No one could hold out against it for long. Being water-boarded felt like drowning without the release of death.

It was a quasi-execution, carried out over and over again.

The Masked Man brought Miles up for air. Standing at his side, Lila asked again, "Where are Cade and Anja? Tell me and this can stop."

"I'd tell you if I knew! Please, don't—!"

The wet towel was slapped back onto Miles's face, and the torrents resumed.

Time became elastic, stretched by pain and fear, until Miles had no idea how long he had been dying, or how he had gotten here. His whole body hurt, he couldn't think, he was consumed by the desperation of drowning, the terror of seeing the last glimmer of light fade from view—

Muffled gunshots. Muted submachine gun fire.

The torrent stopped flowing. Miles's chair was knocked over, and he landed on his side, coughing out water, gasping for air as the dank pit around him echoed with gunfire. Muzzle flashes were blinding in the darkness, and ricochets danced off the stone walls.

"Everyone down!" shouted angry masculine voices with British accents.

Each command brought another burst of automatic gunfire.

"SAS! Drop your weapons! . . . On the floor! Now! . . . Drop it!"

A burp of fire from a submachine gun was followed by the Masked Man collapsing to the floor next to Miles. The left side of the torturer's head had been blown off, leaving exposed meat and skull, from which poured a wash of blood.

Miles twisted his head and searched the shadows for Lila Matar—just in time to see her retreat to a distant corner and vanish inside another pillar of emerald smoke and flames.

The gunfire ceased, and Miles heard running steps reverberate in the darkness around him. An SAS sergeant kneeled at his side and shouted back to his comrades in a Mancusian accent, "He's here! And he's alive! Get a candy car!" The sergeant placed a comforting gloved hand on Miles's shoulder. "Hang on, sir. Medics are on the way."

Miles coughed up water and blood, and then he asked, "How did you find me?"

The answer came as Miles lost consciousness: "Anonymous tip, sir."

<hr />

Every part of the director's office was just as Luis had remembered it. Nearly a decade had gone by since he had last visited Father D'Odorico's sanctum within the monastery, but he could swear the room was exactly the same, a shrine to austerity. Unremarkable tomes filled the pine bookshelves, and his simple desk was devoid of clutter. The only unchanged detail that didn't surprise Luis was the view outside the window behind the director's chair; in a world awash in constant change, the Dolomites possessed that rarest of auras: permanence.

Father D'Odorico settled into his chair and motioned for Luis to sit in one of the guest chairs. The older man still wore a look of elation when he regarded Luis. "I still can't believe it's really you, and now of all times. It's quite a coincidence."

"Why? What's so special about today?"

The director raised his eyebrows. "Three days ago the Synod asked me to find you. I told them I had no idea where you were, nor did I have any idea how to contact you. But they were quite insistent." He planted his elbows on his desktop and steepled his fingers. "I was still looking for some way past your wards when all of a sudden—*there you were.*" He let out half a chuckle. "Your arrival has all the hallmarks of Divine Providence."

Luis had no desire to rob Father D'Odorico of his good mood, but he saw no benefit to feeding the man's illusions. "I'm not sure Providence deserves the credit for my visit. I was brought here by a vision, one I received from the powers Below." He drew a deep breath. "I had a premonition, Father. One of fire and blood, death and mayhem. I saw the destruction of this sanctuary, and the murders of those who call it home." He leaned forward, against the desk. "And I have reason to believe this catastrophe is imminent."

His warning made the director recline from his desk and set his hands in his lap. "I would take care not to trust a prophecy delivered from Hell without confirmation from Above."

"I had the same thought. Which is why I verified the prophecy with Celestial sources." That was a lie, but a necessary one, in Luis's opinion. He waited for the director to process that. After a few seconds without a response, he could see Father D'Odorico was in denial. "Father, you need to evacuate the sanctuary. Get your people to safety before it's too late."

The director refused with the waggle of a bony index finger. "No, I won't abandon our last patch of warded ground. If anything, I'll redouble its defenses." He shifted forward again, back toward Luis. "And while that's being done, you and I should go to Rome."

"Rome?" It took effort for Luis not to bolt toward the door. "Are you mad?"

"The Synod wants a word with you, and it sounds to me as if you have much to say."

"No, absolutely not. If I get within a kilometer of Vatican City, I'll be arrested. Put in the dungeon. Fed to the Cardinal Inquisitor's menagerie of torture devices."

Father D'Odorico frowned. "I think you exaggerate. Yes, you were excommunicated. But that doesn't mean the Church put a bounty on—"

"I assaulted the Cardinal Inquisitor, freed two Goetic karcists who had broken into the vault of the Pope's private archives, and helped them abscond with the Iron Codex."

From across the table, a steely gaze of appraisal, followed by a pained grimace. "You're right. For you, Rome would be a death sentence." He covered his mouth with the side of his fist while he pondered his options. Then he lowered his hand to speak. "What if I could persuade Cardinal Moretti, the head of the Pauline Synod, to meet with you here? I could grant you amnesty and sanctuary for the duration of your visit."

"What's to stop him from bringing in a company of the Swiss Guard?"

The director tilted his head toward the view outside the window. "We'd see them coming from dozens of kilometers away. There's no way they could make it up the road from Misurina without being spotted. You could be long gone before they got here."

That made sense to Luis. "All right. Do you think Moretti will accept those terms?"

"Only one way to find out." Father D'Odorico picked up his phone's receiver, flipped open his address book, and dialed. Then he held the receiver to his ear and waited.

Luis tried to affect a casual air while the director navigated the formalities of greetings and salutations, the tedium of plumbing the Vatican's benthic depths of bureaucracy in order to speak directly with a cardinal. Was someone in the Vatican stonewalling them? Perhaps being overzealous in his or her role as gatekeeper?

Then the director's face blanched and his jaw slackened.

All Luis heard from the phone was a tinny squawk of chatter. He gauged the news solely by Father D'Odorico's reactions.

"Are you sure?" The director's eyes filled with horror. "In that case, I need to speak with Cardinal Kovacs, as soon as—" More urgent chatter transformed the director's expression to one of despair. "When? . . . And this was confirmed? . . . I see. Would it be possible to—?" More news led the director to cover his eyes with his free hand. "I see. Thank you. *Ciao*."

He hung up the phone. For a few seconds he was silent, in shock.

"Cardinal Moretti is dead. A fire in his home, late last night."

The news left Luis feeling as if his veins had just been flushed with ice water. He dreaded to ask after the next-most-senior member of the Synod. "What of Cardinal Kovacs?"

"Hospitalized this morning, just before dawn. His doctors are calling it a stroke."

Luis's mind reeled at the implications of two members of the Synod both being lost in a single night. "That leaves only Cardinal O'Meara."

"Who just renounced his holy orders, ninety minutes ago."

"Are you telling me there's currently no Synod?"

"I wish that were what I was telling you. The truth, I fear, is far worse." He looked Luis in the eye. "Until a new Synod is appointed by the Pope, operational control over the Church's practice of White magick falls to . . . Umberto Lombardi. The Cardinal Inquisitor."

A sick feeling swelled in Luis's gut. "Do you believe me *now*, Father? The

Synod's gone, and your order's been put under the thumb of a man who hates everything you stand for. I'd say the fall of your sanctuary isn't just imminent—*it's already begun.*"

⌁

A scooter puttered down a quiet residential street in Swansea, Wales, a few hours after dark. Its driver, an MI6 courier, did her best to appear nondescript: gray trousers, a dark blue windbreaker, and a matching helmet with a mirrored visor. On the back of her jacket was printed the name and logo of a real courier service, one long used by the British intelligence services as a cover for domestic deliveries of top-secret documents.

The graveled street had a steep uphill grade. On the left stood a clustered row of squat duplexes that looked as if they'd been pressed from an industrial cookie cutter loaded with cheap drywall and matching doors. The other side of the road was lined with a dense hedgerow whose branches boasted spikes large enough to skewer small mammals.

At the terminus of the dead-end road, the courier halted her scooter, turned off its engine, and dismounted. A cold wind rustled leaves long dry yet too stubborn to quit their boughs.

The courier opened her satchel and removed the parcel. The thick, heavy envelope was bound with orange tape—an MI6 convention that indicated it was for "eyes only"—i.e., to be opened only by its named recipient.

She carried it to the front door of the last house. Lifted the door's mail gate and forced the parcel through it. It landed on the floor inside the house with a *fwump.*

The courier got back on her motorbike, marked the parcel as "delivered" in her log, and began the long ride back to her dispatch point in Cardiff. As far as she was concerned, the parcel's journey was complete.

In truth, it had only just begun.

Lying beneath the mail slot, the parcel lay alone inside a miniaturized version of a magickal circle. Within seconds of its arrival, QERGAEL, the demon tasked with minding that circle, used its powers to open a portal beneath the envelope, which tumbled through the gap into the rainbow fogs of the ethereal plane. QERGAEL took hold of the parcel to keep it safe. As per its master's meticulous instructions, the demon took care to make sure its talons did not pierce or tear the parcel in any way. It understood the penalty for damaging the master's property in transit would be cruel and everlasting.

Moving through the ever-changing realms of the ethereal plane, QER-GAEL sought the unique aura of its summoner. In a flash, the demon knew its master was somewhere on earth. Somewhere far from the parcel's drop point. Almost on the far side of the planet.

The aura of the *nikraim* came into focus. QERGAEL sped toward it. The sooner the demon delivered this item, the sooner its duty would be discharged and it would be free to return to the Pit until summoned again.

Not too soon, it hoped. *Better to burn Below than to serve a human.*

QERGAEL's talons split the intangible barrier that separated the ethereal realm from the physical one, and the spirit was all but overcome by the brilliance of the *nikraim*'s radiance. Bad enough human souls all shone like tiny suns; those bonded before birth with angels blazed like the Empyrean flames of the Divine. For a demon, it was too bright a pain to bear.

Almost as quickly as the fabric of reality had been pierced, it began to heal. QERGAEL forced the parcel through the interdimensional wound. Several anxiety-producing seconds later, it heard the package slap against a hard surface on the other side. Delivery had been made.

My task is done. The demon felt profound relief. *I return to my rest. To the perfect solitude of Hell. . . . Until a human orders me forth once more.*

A spark of hatred flickered deep inside QERGAEL's essence.

When I answer some future summons to earth, I will slay and eat every last one of these talking monkeys SATAN loves so much.

"I'm not saying I want to go back to Mexico City," Cade said. "My point is, we might have no choice. Miles went dark hours ago, and right now the only lead we have to the enemy is the karcist who tried to frag us. If we question Rocha, he might know who that guy was."

Anja and Briet stood at either end of the dining table in the kitchen of Luis's fishing lodge. Cade sat at the middle of the table with his back to the stove, facing the entranceway and preserving a clear line of sight to the back door—because old habits died hard.

"Going after Rocha is a fool's errand," Anja said. "The enemy has killed him by now. Scrubbed his name from their files."

Briet looked dismayed. "She's right. It's what I would've done if he were my asset." She lit one of her Benson & Hedges cigarettes. Exhaled smoke through her nose as she spoke. "I want these pricks to bleed as much as you do, but right now our leads are weak as shit."

"We should go underground," Anja said.

Cade shook his head. "No. Not until we've dealt with this."

His refusal stirred Anja's temper. She rounded the table and loomed over him. "This has gone far enough. Too many have died. No more." She poked his chest to drive her next points home. "Our enemy knows us, but we do not know them. We are *exposed*. Vulnerable. Until we have a name for the enemy, it is time to hide. We can work from the shadows."

He was about to concede the argument when a thick envelope sealed with orange tape materialized from nowhere and landed in the center of the table with a loud *fwump*. Its appearance and subsequent impact made the women leap back from the table. Briet was the first to ask what they all were likely thinking: "What the hell is that?"

Cade cocked an eyebrow. "Judging from the orange tape and the Swansea address, I'd guess it's a special delivery from our friend inside MI6." He pulled out his combat knife and cut the tape and broke the seals on the thick envelope. From it he pulled out a massive sheaf of papers and sifted through them.

Briet came closer and looked over his shoulder. "Looks like Miles hit the mother lode."

"*Da.*" Anja's tone was laced with suspicion. "But why did he not call?"

Cade paged through the file. "He must've thought he was being watched. I set up a magickal dead drop a few years ago—Miles was the only one who had the address. I told him to use it only if he had no other safe way to contact me."

Anja took the end seat on Cade's left. Briet sat at the other end of the table. Both leaned in, their curiosity evident in their faces. Briet arched one eyebrow. "So? What did he send us?"

"The first stack of pages is about that ammo maker." Cade passed a handful of the papers to each woman. "I've got factory sites, supplier lists, client rosters. And . . . stuff."

Now it was Anja's turn to shoot a quizzical look at him. "Stuff?"

"Well, what do you call it? Pages of numbers in grids, weird graphs . . ."

"Those are financial reports," Briet said. "And I'll bet most of what your friend Miles sent us is corporate ownership documents." She reached across the table and grabbed up more papers, which she reviewed by the handful.

"Look! TKAM is owned by another corporation, which is a wholly owned subsidiary of some big international conglomerate." She tapped her stack of papers on the table to neaten them into an even pile. "It's a Matryoshka doll."

Cade held out his open hands. "A what?"

Anja replied, "Russian nesting dolls. Biggest outside, smaller inside, smallest in center." She eyed Briet. "How is the business like the dolls?"

"It's a scam. A shell game played with different types of corporations to conceal ownership, hide profits, and launder money."

Cade asked, "For whose benefit?"

"The man at the core. That's who's calling the shots. The one making the magick-piercing rounds, the one who wants us dead. But he hides by surrounding himself with phony companies, which are owned by more of the same. And it just keeps on getting bigger all the time. But in the end, it doesn't matter how many masks our enemy wears. Dig deep enough and you'll always find one person. One name."

Briet gathered the papers Cade had liberated from the package. He put his hand down to halt her efforts. "What do you think you're doing?"

"Making use of the only clue we have." She looked around. "Is there a free room I can use to spread all this out?"

Anja pointed toward the main room. "In there?"

"Yes, that'll do." Briet pulled her hands and the papers free of Cade's grip and carried them away. Shocked but also impressed by her defiance, Cade followed her, and Anja was close behind him. When they entered the main room, Briet was already hard at work spreading the pages from the envelope across the floor. She separated the documents into different clusters. After the fourth cluster she ran out of room and looked back at Cade. "Be a dear and start moving the furniture out of the way, would you?"

What was he supposed to do? Tell her to move the heavy chairs and end tables herself? Delegate the grunt work to Anja? He sighed and set to work, using the telekinetic powers of GŌGOTHIEL to empty the room of furniture. The demon's talent was strong but lacked finesse, and within a few minutes his loud, clumsy labors had attracted the attention of Barış, Yasmin, and Sathit, who stood in the far doorway and watched Briet continue segregating the file's pages.

Cade watched Briet work, but he remained skeptical. "I presume there's a logic to this?"

"I'm organizing it based on the corporate relationships. Once I've grouped it all, I'll use colored yarn to chart the connections between data points and people."

"And where do you plan to get colored yarn?"

"There's basketsful outside the laundry room. Apparently, our friend Luis likes to knit." She glanced up at the wall, which had been decorated with a crucifix and a few pieces of devotional art. "Could we clear that shit away? I need space to lay out a timeline."

Anja waved her hand and swept the wall clean of ornaments, all of which smashed to the floor in the next room.

Cade shot his beloved a weary look of reproach. "You get to explain that to Luis."

From the other side of the room, Yasmin asked, "What will this be when you're done?"

"I'm building a picture of the enemy's corporate web," Briet said. "Once we're able to see its big picture, and how it all fits together, we'll be able to find its center—and that's where we'll find the spider who made it."

"And then?" Barış asked, adjusting his fez.

"Then," Cade said, "we stomp the fucker."

15

The night's business promised to be bloody, but that had become de rigueur for Tujiro Kanaka. He had stumbled upon the mysteries of the Art in the 1920s, during his studies at Cambridge University. From his first brush with the Goetic Art he had sensed its potential, just as he had understood the cost it exacted from those who dared to unlock its secrets. Since then he had chosen his own Infernal patron and ensured himself centuries of longevity—boons he had safeguarded by not returning to his native Japan for nearly thirty years.

That is no longer my home. My place now is at the Old Man's side.

The violence of the Goetic Art, both implicit and explicit, had never bothered Tujiro. Even as a child he had been able to read between the lines of his schooling to see that not only had history been written by the victors but it had been scribed in blood. Violence was just the hard edge of change.

Tonight he would set that edge against the Monte Paterno sanctuary.

The journey up the mountain road from the village of Misurina had been steep and difficult. Winter had descended upon the Dolomites and the rest of northern Italy, erasing the horizon with gray clouds. Dense curtains of snow fell beneath the sky's leaden dome, blotting out the moon, the stars, and anything else more than a few meters out of reach.

Each labored breath Tujiro took burned his throat with cold air; every exhalation fogged his vision with condensed vapor. Already the snow on the road was higher than his knees. If it kept falling like this, it would be up to his hips by morning.

He had every intention of being long gone by then.

A Sno-Cat, a vehicle with four treads optimized for traversing snow, would have made for a faster and more comfortable trip, but even in the storm its piercing blue headlights would have been visible from miles away. The growl of its engine would have been heard by the monks inside Monte Paterno far in advance of the vehicle's arrival.

Tujiro needed the element of surprise tonight.

On foot, he had been able to hide himself and his companions with magick. RALIOTH had cloaked them with its gift of invisibility, while NEZKAEL had obscured any evidence of their passage through the snow. Now, as they reached the top of the road and the monastery came into view, Tujiro felt the pushback of resistance from its defensive magickal wards. He stopped.

The rest of his team spread out and halted alongside him. To his left were Anorah and Adara Samuels. The blond twin sisters both looked positively miserable in the cold, despite being garbed in matching fur-lined parkas and insulated ski boots.

Flanking Tujiro on his right was a trio of the Old Man's mercenaries, who had been sent along by Niccolò to "assist" Tujiro and the twins with this mission. Before the mission, Tujiro had had no idea why. He had doubted they could do anything with their firearms and explosives that he and the sisters couldn't do with magick. Now that he stood in front of Monte Paterno, out of breath and with his legs trembling from the effort of cutting a path through snow up the long and winding road, he discovered a grudging respect for Niccolò's foresight in sending the mercs.

A galaxy of snowflakes swirled around Tujiro and his colleagues. The scene on the hilltop was serene. He took a moment to drink in the beauty, and then he sighed in resignation.

"All right, men. Light it up."

The boss merc raised a grenade launcher and fired a shell at one of the monastery's windows with a low *foomp*. The grenade shattered a pane of stained glass, which fell apart with an almost musical noise.

The grenade detonated, shaking the ground as it blasted out several adjacent windows and filled a corridor of the sanctuary with orange flames and black smoke.

That was the cue for the other two mercs to strafe the monastery's stained-glass windows with automatic rifle fire. As they blasted in the windows, lights flickered on inside, only to be snuffed out as the lead mercenary shot more grenades inside the eleventh-century stone building.

From inside came the shouts of men trying to rally others into action.

The Samuels sisters looked at Tujiro, who nodded his permission for them to join the assault. The two young women joined the mercs' firing line.

Adara filled her hands with lightning, and Anorah wreathed hers in flame. They took turns hurling devastating magickal attacks through the sanctuary's crumbling outer walls, until the passageways of Monte Paterno became a crucible.

Even from a distance, the heat of the blaze stung Tujiro's face.

No more hoarse orders issued from inside the burning sanctum. The roar of the bonfire was punctuated by the wails of the maimed and the dying, throaty cries of agony and terror.

Using the Sight, Tujiro peered through the flames to see monks, their robes aflame, stagger and collapse atop one another. Greasy black smoke belched from the mounded corpses. After a few hideous minutes, the screaming and groaning faded away.

The stench of seared flesh fouled the frigid air.

Support columns and massive joists snapped with sounds like gunfire as the inferno split them into pieces. Several sections of the monastery's roof fell in, permitting towers of flame to reach into the darkness, evaporating the flurries of snow above.

Tujiro drew a deep breath and focused the power of MOLOCH . . . with which he called down a single thunderbolt. It slammed into the burning shambles of the monastery and caused the fiery mess to collapse in upon itself.

He stepped back to appreciate the full scope of the destruction he and his associates had wrought. Great spires of red and yellow flame danced on the ruins of Monte Paterno like Kagu-tsuchi, the mythical *kami* of fire whose birth had consumed its mother.

Tujiro reached inside his coat, pulled out and opened his flask, and took a swig of Yamazaki whiskey. Savoring the sweet burn in his throat, he admired the blaze on the hilltop.

The Samuels sisters returned to his side. Anorah asked, "Is that it? Are we done?"

Another pull of whiskey, then a slow nod. "Yes. This will do."

"Good," Adara said. "I'm fucking freezing out here."

Anorah held out a hand to her sister. "This'll warm you up." She handed Adara a small vial of cocaine, which the younger twin eagerly uncapped and inhaled.

The mercs passed Tujiro as they started down the mountain road. The boss merc said on his way by, "We're heading back. You want to watch the cinders go out, you're on your own."

"I will be right behind you." Tujiro let the mercs and the twins start back while he stood and let the weight of the night's slaughter settle upon him. It was best not to become too blasé about such things. That was how monsters were made: through indifference.

He put away his flask. Zipping up his parka, he saw the snow on the front of his coat smear beneath his glove. Then he saw it wasn't snow that had smeared, but cremated human remains that were falling amid the snow, the pure and the profane side by side.

He banished his disgust and followed his colleagues back down the mountain road.

No time for regrets. You knew what this job was when you took it.

Ahead of him, he heard the twins and the mercs laughing.

With his head bowed to hide his somber mood, Tujiro took a fleeting refuge in silence while the heavens crowned him with ashes.

———

"Excellent," Niccolò said over the phone to his contact inside the Kremlin. "I will inform him at once. *Spasibo. Do svidaniya.*" He hung up the phone and pivoted away from the desk to see the Old Man standing in front of the wide bay window, admiring the beauty of snowflakes tumbling through shafts of light that illuminated the slope south of the mountainside chalet. His dog sat by his side, dutiful and quiet. "Good news, *signore.*"

The Old Man angled his head just enough to regard Niccolò. The note of anticipation in his voice was muted by his natural British tendency toward stoicism. "Do tell."

"Your counterpart in Moscow has confirmed the last remnants of the Red Star have been disbanded, and the few survivors of the purge have been absorbed into local or regional branches of the Bratva." It had taken effort for Niccolò not to wince as he'd delivered the first part of his report. Though he had known it was vital to dismantle the Soviets' state-run magickal defense program, he remained skeptical of the Commission's decision to let nearly a dozen karcists be covertly recruited by the Russian mafia. Behind a mask of dispassion, he continued his update. "In addition, the scattered cells of the Black Sun that were still operating in South America have been neutralized, and, at your behest, the Americans' Occult Defense Program has been shut down, its personnel liquidated, and its considerable research assets acquired for our private archives."

That was good enough to elicit small nods of approval from the Old Man. "Splendid. Despite a few setbacks, we remain close to our projected schedule." Like most Britons, the Old Man insisted on pronouncing the first half of the word "shed" rather than "sked" as Americans were wont to do. "Any word from Tujiro?"

"*Sì, signore*. He reports Monte Paterno has been leveled. No survivors."

"Brilliant." The Old Man turned his back on the slow grace of falling snow outside his window and returned to his desk. His German shepherd followed half a step behind him. The Old Man pulled back his chair, sat, and then pulled himself forward. He rested his elbows atop his desk and steepled his fingers. "That leaves our handful of renegades as the last fly in the ointment. What are we doing about them?"

"Closing the net, *signore*. Slowly but certainly."

"Do we even know how many people Martin has left?"

"*Sì*. Based on the intel we gathered before our attack, the bodies we found on Naxos, the information shared by our defector Lila, and the people Hatunde saw in Mexico City, we know Martin and Kernova are being aided by Briet Segfrunsdóttir of the American ODP, and that three of their adepts survived and fled Naxos with them."

The Old Man's eyes narrowed as he concentrated. "Which adepts?"

"Barış Kılıç of Ankara, Sathit Viravong of Vientiane, and Yasmin Elachi of Jerusalem. Kılıç is the most educated, but Viravong and Elachi both have combat training."

The Old Man reclined, pulled a bag of tobacco and an ivory Meerschaum pipe from his jacket pocket, and packed the pipe's bowl. "Do you have a plan for containing this threat?"

"Of course. The good news is they've gone to ground, which gives us time to regroup and—"

"They haven't gone to ground, you fool. They've simply withdrawn to prepare their next assault. My people in London tell me they have a friend inside MI6—out of our reach now, alas—who sent Cade critical intelligence about our Turkish concern." The Old Man picked up a lamb shank and lobbed the mostly meat-free bone to his dog, who caught it in his fangs and gnawed it greedily. "We need to leverage this knowledge to get ahead of our enemies."

Niccolò dreaded to ask, "And what might that entail, *signore*?"

"For starters, you need to be in Turkey no later than tomorrow afternoon."

The karcist sighed. "If you are counting on me to teleport there, I should warn you: My spirit for such jaunts is denied to me for the next three days, by the terms of its compact."

The Old Man struck a match on his desktop, filling the air with the bite of sulfur. He lit his pipe. "I plan to send you by plane. It's a short hop from Bern to Rome, and you can catch a flight from there to Adana." He waved the match to extinguish its flame, and then he puffed on his pipe. "Will any of your peers be back in time to join you?"

"Hatunde, I think."

"Yes, good. Make sure Cade and his friends find what they've come for—then get rid of them. But try to make it look like an accident, or a crime gone wrong. I'd much prefer to avoid any entanglements with the Turkish authorities. They can be quite . . . *opportunistic*."

"I understand, *signore*. But might I sound a note of caution?"

Niccolò's query drew a suspicious look from the Old Man. "Losing your nerve?"

"Not at all, *signore*. But Martin and his allies seem to be moving as a single unit. That gives them strength. If we know for certain they are going to Turkey—"

"We don't know that," the Old Man said, "or anything else. But the evidence in hand suggests that's their most likely next target."

"All the same, *signore*: If our enemies move in strength, perhaps we should, as well."

There was disappointment in the Old Man's voice. "Really, Niccolò? Even with the element of surprise, are you *that* daunted by Martin and his band of fugitives?"

"I prefer to think of it as a healthy respect for his skills." He watched the Old Man feed another bone to his dog, as if he were trying to ignore Niccolò's warning. "The global community for my art is extremely small—"

"And shrinking further all the time."

"—so rumors and gossip travel quickly. Cade, Anja, and Briet are the most powerful karcists on earth. Only a moron would face all of them alone." He planted his palms on the Old Man's desktop and leaned forward. "Those three have taken more lives in battle than some army regiments. We've tried twice to ambush them, and have failed both times. Perhaps this would be a good time to consider negotiating a truce."

The Old Man looked at Niccolò as if the karcist had just shit in his soup.

"I don't pay you to *craft* policy, Mr. Falco, I pay you to carry it out. We are well past the point of parlay. Martin, Kernova, and Segfrunsdóttir were *never* going to consider a truce. These are not reasonable people, Mr. Falco. They aren't like Ware or Ballard—those two are as much businessmen as they are magicians. No, this last trio of the old guard represent something far more dangerous: They're idealists. Purists. Which means they all must die."

Niccolò tried and failed to conceal his frown. "And you think this ambush is the way?"

Two puffs on the pipe left the Old Man ringed in sweet-smelling smoke.

"My dear boy, in addition to all of Cade Martin's other flaws, he's an obsessive with an overdeveloped sense of vengeance. That makes him *predictable*. . . . And *that* will be the death of him."

The lodge's main room had become an obstacle course for contortionists. All the furniture had been removed, but now the room was filled with vividly colored lengths of yarn and string, all pulled taut and held steady by tacks driven deep into the walls, ceiling, and floor. They crisscrossed at various angles, making it a challenge for Cade to navigate the room without becoming entangled or pulling half the mess down in a wild flurry of scrap paper.

Pages from the MI6 file festooned the walls, and some Briet had spread out on the floor. Where she lacked documents, she had resorted to scribbling names on the walls and ceiling.

Cade stood in the kitchen doorway and watched Briet expand her art project. He half expected to see her trip at any moment, but she ducked and snaked through the peculiar maze like smoke flowing through the branches of a tree. She worked with a keen focus, her eyes always on the hunt for new connections, especially when she tacked up a new page or inscribed a new name onto the wall.

Footsteps in the kitchen turned Cade's head. He watched Anja approach. Her black hair was bound in a loose ponytail. She held on to a mug and handed him a green tumbler. "Whiskey, the way you like it: lots, in a glass."

He sipped the warm booze. It was harsh like turpentine but he drank it anyway, to muzzle the demonic voices nagging him from within. "What're you having?"

"Tea."

"Any good?"

"No."

If there was one thing Cade envied about Anja, it was that her nature as a true *nikraim*—one of "Heaven's chosen," as opposed to himself, a *nikraim* created by a magickal ceremony conducted before he was born—meant that the natural bond she enjoyed with her angelic partner made her better able to withstand the agonies of holding demons in yoked thrall. Unlike Cade and so many other karcists, Anja had less need to resort to alcohol or opiates to maintain her peace of mind, even when she had as many as a dozen spirits in her service. He hoped that might mean she could avoid the pains of addiction that he had struggled with since the Second World War.

There's nothing worse than going cold turkey.

Anja shouldered into the doorway beside Cade and eyed Briet's handiwork. "Four hours now. She is starting to worry me."

Cade was reluctant to criticize. "She seems to know what she's doing."

"Would you be able to tell if she did not?" She fixed him with a keen stare. When Cade found himself without a reply, Anja added, "As I thought."

Briet twisted and sidestepped her way to the center of the room, stopped, and looked up at the empty spot above her head. As she planted her hands on her hips, Cade noted that this was the first time he had seen her hands empty since she had started.

He raised his voice so Briet would know he was talking to her. "How's it going?"

"I've found places for it all." She pivoted slowly to take in her creation. "And I've tracked all the connections I think we can prove based on the file."

Anja crossed her arms. "Very pretty. What does it tell us?"

"Not a fucking thing." Briet's hopeful mien turned grim. "Whoever set this up is an evil genius. Every time I think I've hit the center, I find new layers." She gently twanged various lengths of yarn as she continued. "It's an endless shell game. Corporations, partnerships, trusts, conglomerates—all of them international, and if you follow any one trail far enough, you wind up back where you started. It's a goddamned financial ourobouros."

Cade reached inside his jacket and pulled a Lucky from his pack. "Does any of this shit tell us who owns these things?" He put the cigarette between his lips and lit it with a snap of his fingers. "Or did I risk Miles's life for nothing?"

"All the documents in the MI6 dossier were from public filings. The only way we'll find the owners is if we dig into the private financial records of these companies."

Anja entered the yarn maze with cautious steps. "You both think too far ahead." She made her way to a patch of the floor that was outlined with chalk. Inside the crudely drawn circle was the unfired rifle cartridge she had confiscated from the FBI Laboratory in Washington. "You talk of finding names. Laying blame." She squatted, grabbed the cartridge, and held it up in front of her as she stood to face Briet. "But someone is making bullets that kill magick. That kill *us*. Blame is for later. Today we deal with *this*." She waved the bullet at the mad array of documents that surrounded them. "Do any of these papers tell you where this was made?"

Her request left Briet searching the walls and ceiling until she zeroed in on a single page. She moved through her labyrinth with leonine grace and plucked the sheet of paper off the wall. Holding it on her palm, she gave a huff of breath that made the paper flap into motion, like a weird flat bird or a manta ray undulating through the sea. It navigated the string maze with ease and landed in Anja's hands.

As Anja read the paper, Briet said, "A small factory outside Adana, Turkey."

"Good." Anja turned, slapped the page against Cade's chest, and walked past him on her way into the kitchen. "Wake the students. Time for a fact-finding mission."

~∞~

The snow falling upon Monte Paterno was no longer mixed with ash. Where the monastery had stood only an hour before, its ruins lay cold and dark, its final cinders snuffed out by the winter damp. Brisk winds had swept away the twisted spires of smoke, and a gale passed over the sanctuary's broken remains with a mournful sound. Not a soul stirred for miles.

Then came signs of movement, from the base of the great tower of dark rock in front of which the sanctuary had been built. The stone rippled like water, disturbed from within by forces far older than earth or its sun. Flakes of snow riding the wind passed inside the rock and vanished, rather than accumulate upon it. Nature's laws were being overruled.

A foot emerged from the stone, followed by the leg behind it, and then the rest of Luis. The last part of him to slip free of the mountain was his right hand, which clasped that of another man—Father D'Odorico, who followed Luis out of hiding, into the bitter night. One by one, more of the sanctuary's brothers appeared, each holding the hand of the man ahead of him. The ones who were already free of the mountain continued to hold hands, their chain unbroken, until the last of their order stepped free of the stone, whole and unharmed. They carried their karcist's tools on their backs, and the lucky ones wore their grimoires on chains around their necks.

The surviving monks looked with varying degrees of sorrow and anger at the wreckage of their home, the desecration of what had been holy ground. Father Pantelis fell to his knees and pawed at the ashes; tears of rage streaked the face of the portly Greek cleric.

Father Malko staggered into the middle of the ruins and then stopped, his expression blank. Tall and pale, he resembled a ghost rising from the blackened debris. His longtime research partner, Father Hakkila, drifted slowly along the edges of the field of destruction, his stoic countenance unreadable.

Standing at Luis's side, ignoring the bite of the cold and the flakes of snow gathering in his beard, was Father D'Odorico. The elderly priest looked forlorn. "You were right, Luis. You told us what they would do. But I didn't believe it until I saw it with my own eyes."

"To be honest, Father, this was one time I had hoped to be wrong."

The director forced a sad smile. "And I know how much you hate being wrong." His attention was diverted for a moment by the sight of several younger monks chanting Latin prayers while feverishly trying to cleanse themselves with handfuls of snow—only to recoil when they found they had fouled themselves with a hidden layer of ash. "It seems a few of the novices are having trouble accepting their salvation at the hands of the Goetic Art."

Luis remembered the profound aversion to Black magick he had been forced to overcome nearly a decade earlier, when he'd embarked upon his study of "Gray" magick. "You can't blame them, really. If all they've ever known of magick is the Pauline Art, I imagine consenting to the touch of POVATHRAEL must have felt like shaking hands with a fouled commode."

"If only it had been that pleasant." Father D'Odorico sampled the air with a few deep sniffs. "I can still smell the reek of the Fallen. Though how much of that came from our foes' attack and how much from your illusion of our deaths, I can't really say." He turned a suspicious look at Luis. "I had no idea you were so skilled at symphonies of carnage."

Luis waved off the comment as if it had been a compliment and not a slight. "I can't take the credit. SCURRIOS is the composer and conductor. I merely call the tunes." He did a quick count of the survivors—twelve in all, counting the director. "I just hope I have enough strength to jaunt you all to safety with me."

"As generous an offer as I'm sure you think that is, the only place they and I are going now is Rome."

Luis recoiled from his former master's stubborn foolishness. "Are you mad? After what happened to the cardinals of the Synod? You know the enemy is watching Vatican City."

Father D'Odorico waggled an index finger at Luis. "No, I know they *were*. But if our foes think we're dead and the Synod's fallen, they might well have moved on from Rome."

"That's quite a gamble when the stakes are all of your lives."

"Call it an act of faith."

"I'll call it an act of stupidity, Father, because that's what it is. The Lord helps those who first help themselves. He also commands us not to test Him, especially not by putting ourselves in peril and then counting on His intercession to protect us." Not wanting to agitate the other monks any further than circumstances already had, Luis moved a step closer to the director and lowered his voice. "Please trust me when I tell you that going to Rome would be a mistake."

Father D'Odorico looked down his long nose at Luis. "No, it would be a mistake for *you*. That's one of the consequences of making an enemy of the Vatican's cardinal inquisitor. But your dilemma does not absolve me of my responsibility to the Church. A heinous crime has been committed here. One that must be brought to the attention of the Holy See."

It was maddening for Luis to argue with someone so entrenched in his ways. "Please, I'm begging you, Father. There's no time for the Vatican's bureaucracy, not now. And you know as well as I do Cardinal Lombardi won't protect you or the other members of the order. He's wanted to see us extinguished for as long as he's known we existed. He is *not* our ally."

"But he *is* our superior in the Church hierarchy. And despite his obvious, long-standing animosity toward the Pauline Art in general, and us in particular, I am required by my vows and by ecclesiastical law to respect his temporal and spiritual authority." The director took a deep breath and calmed himself. "Come with us to Rome. You don't have to enter Vatican City. I'll go in alone to speak to Cardinal Lombardi, and I'll make sure he knows we owe our lives to your timely intervention."

Luis suppressed a rueful laugh. "I doubt he'll consider that penance suffi-cient to forgive my theft of the Iron Codex, or my role in the escape of Martin and Kernova."

"Probably not. Forgiveness has never been one of the cardinal's virtues. But I'm counting on his vengeful nature to serve our needs in one regard." Father D'Odorico surveyed the charred plateau and the smoldering remains of his sanctuary. "This attack was a blatant violation of the ancient truce guaranteed by the Covenant between White and Black." He looked back at Luis with hard eyes and a sharp edge in his voice. "This means *war.*"

16

Teleportation via water was far less painful than anything Briet had experienced when jaunting by way of fire or lightning, but something about the experience still did not sit well with her. It made her think of being born, and then of baptism by immersion. *Childbirth and religious indoctrination. Two of my least favorite subjects.*

Anja led the group—which consisted of herself, Cade, Briet, Barış, Sathit, and Yasmin—through a water jaunt between two deep shoreline eddies, the first in the river that fed Arthurs Lake outside Luis's lodge in Tasmania, the other in the Seyhan River on the outskirts of Adana, Turkey. The magickal journey went smoothly enough. The group surfaced in the water just a meter from the west bank of the river, as planned.

Close above their heads, jutting some seven meters from the shore and perched on two rows of concrete pilings sunk into the riverbed, was the floor of the eastern end of the factory. On the far side of the river there was nothing but trees and dense ground-covering foliage.

Everyone continued to hold hands as they waded ashore and climbed from the river one by one. Maintaining their daisy-chain connection to Anja meant that, in spite of their mode of travel, none of them were wet, thanks to the protections of one of her yoked demons.

Sathit, at the end of the chain, was the last person out of the water. As soon as she found her footing, the other members of the group let go of one another's hands and huddled for cover behind a line of thickly grown shrubs close to the rear corner of the factory.

Crouched beside Briet, Barış squinted at the three-quarter moon, which lay low in the west beyond the fenced compound ahead of them, and then he fiddled with his watch. "It was just after five A.M. when we left Tasmania. Do any of you know the time here?"

Briet arched an eyebrow. "Why? Are we synchronizing watches?"

"I just wish to know how long we have until daylight."

"We've got all night," Cade said. "It's nine minutes past ten."

"Not to mention it's yesterday again," Yasmin said. "It's Tuesday morning in Taz, but here it's still Monday night." She cracked a quirky smile. "Almost like we time-traveled."

"It is *nothing* like that," Anja said, apparently irked by the least hint of frivolity.

A wave of Cade's hand opened a wide slash in the chain-link fence at the top of the riverbank. He addressed the adepts. "I'll go in with Briet and Anja, have a look around. You three stay here, spread out, and stay under cover. You'll be our lookouts."

Sathit rolled her eyes. "I am starting to see a pattern here."

Her complaint drew an insincere smile from Cade. "It's called 'keeping you alive.' You see or hear anything, come in and let us know. If you get split up, or cut off from us, or outnumbered, you fucking *run*. Got it?" All three apprentices nodded. "Good. See you soon." He drew his Beretta pistol and slipped through the gap he had cut in the fence.

Anja drew her Browning. Briet unholstered her Luger. They followed Cade inside the compound. As soon as they were past the fence, Briet looked back. From the inside, she saw it was topped with coils of barbed wire, which the trees' thick foliage had obscured.

The lot around the factory was empty but large enough for several vehicles. As Briet followed Cade and Anja to the front of the building, she saw three loading platforms, but no trucks parked at any of them. Their large roll-up doors were closed and locked. Anja climbed the steps at the near end of the dock. Cade was right behind her. The duo moved quickly, and Briet quickened her pace to keep up. They paused only briefly at the employee door while Anja magickally released its locks. Then they were inside the factory.

Acting on instinct, Briet engaged the Sight to pierce the darkness. The factory's interior was revealed in cool green monotones and deep shadows. Behind the loading dock's large roll-up doors stretched a storage bay. Boxes stood stacked on wooden pallets and wrapped under heavy plastic. A pair of forklifts were parked at the far southern end of the bay. Along the bay's long back wall were two large entrances blocked by thick, overlapping strips of translucent plastic. Briet had seen similar setups many times. The plastic

strips muffled noise and impeded the flow of dust and other airborne con-
taminants to and from the production floor.

Cade stood and peered intently at all the loaded pallets in the storage bay.
"No signs of magick ammo." He looked at Briet. "You sure this is the place?"

"As sure as I can be." She tilted her head toward the production floor.
"Let's head inside. Even if the magick bullets are gone, we might find the assembly lines that made them."

Cade motioned for Anja and Briet to go ahead of him. "Ladies first."

Anja shoved him forward. "I am no lady. Besides—age before beauty."

"Beauty? Someone's got a high opinion of herself."

"Cade? I am behind you with a pistol."

He faced the plastic curtain. "Yes, dear."

Cade held his pistol at eye level with both hands as he pushed through the
plastic curtains. Briet kept her Luger low and ready as she followed him, with
Anja bringing up the rear.

The production area looked like many others Briet had seen. Concrete
floor. A ten-meter-high ceiling of corrugated metal with several grimy sky-
lights. Large, insectlike assembly machines stood in straight lines beside
stacked conveyor belts loaded with empty brass casings. At the far end of
each line were long tables crowded with precision tools, measuring equipment, and magnifying lenses mounted on adjustable pivot arms.

Anja said in a hushed voice, "You two check the floor. I will check the office." She split off from Briet and Cade, toward a suite of offices that had been
elevated above the production floor along the north side of the building.

Moving down a broad aisle between two production lines, Cade and Briet
poked their heads into each station they passed, to examine the factory's
products.

"Definitely a small-arms specialist," Cade said. "Lots of pistol rounds and
small-caliber cartridges. Nothing much bigger than nine-millimeter over
here."

"This line is turning out Soviet-compatible rounds." She pointed toward
the machines flanking the next aisle to the left. "But if you ask me, those look
like fifty-caliber shells." She aimed a grim look at Cade. "Sniper rounds."

"Makes sense." He nodded in the same direction. "The line along the far
wall's cranking out larger shells and belt loads. Probably for air- and truck-
mounted guns."

As they passed a gap in one of the production lines, a flash of magickal illumination caught Briet's eye. "There." She pointed. "In the back, on the left. A line of machines all showing residual demonic auras."

"I see it." Cade fell into step beside her. They hurried to the farthest part of the factory, the eastern end, which had been built to extend several meters out above the river. Circles on the floor indicated the locations of the concrete pilings rising from the river below.

Against the rear wall of the production floor were several machines bright with the touch of magick. Stacked on a pallet beside the last machine were cases of ammunition that also radiated magick with feverish intensity. Cade looked pleased. "Bingo."

Briet squatted beside the pallet and examined the markings on the ammo boxes. "Quite a variety. Six-point-five-millimeter Mannlicher-Carcano. Nine-millimeter hollow-points. Seven-six-two rifle cartridges. Fifty-caliber sniper rounds. Thirty-eights and three-fifty-sevens, twenty-twos and forty-five ACP by the case. Thirty-millimeter belt rounds. Fucking hell. They've got magick-piercing rounds for every occasion."

"Look on the bright side," Cade said. "At least we know we're in the right place. Which means we know exactly what to do next." He turned toward the cluster of enchanted machines and with a few dramatic gestures, directed one of his yoked spirits to mangle the entire line into iron origami. Then he set the pretzeled mess aglow with a barrage of lightning that fused any moving parts he hadn't already destroyed and melted the last traces of magick out of it all.

When he turned back toward Briet, he looked like he had just enjoyed some exercise. "Now we need to know who built this. They did it once. That means they could do it again—unless we make sure this knowledge dies with them."

"What about all the magick-piercing ammo that's already loose in the world?"

Cade shrugged. "Best we can do is turn it into a finite resource and then keep our heads down." He pointed at the stacked pallet of enchanted ammo. "How 'bout this? Should we boost it? A little sauce for the gander, as they say?"

"You heard Anja—the magick ammo is useless without an enchanted rifle to match it." Briet looked over the cache of demonically infused bullets. "Safer to get rid of it."

Cade conjured a handful of hellfire. "So, torch it, then?"

Briet held her poker face as she stared him down. "Sure. Light a fire inside an ammunition factory, in a heavily wooded area. What could possibly go wrong?"

He snuffed his fireball by closing his fist. His mood soured. "Or I could have my porter demon take the whole kaboodle and dump it in the Mediterranean."

"Whatever. You're in charge."

Glum-faced, he took out his cigarettes and lit one. "I hate you sometimes."

"Only sometimes?" She stole the Lucky from his hand, savored his look of chagrin, and took a drag. "I *knew* you'd warm up to me."

Old wooden stairs creaked with each step Anja took. She hurried down to the factory floor, her arms loaded with folders and loose papers she had pilfered from the office. Whoever ran the place apparently operated under the misconception that their cheap knockoff safe constituted secure storage. Anja had absconded from the office with nearly a ream of documents detailing the factory's recent acquisition by its new corporate owners, among other key financial details, such as where it kept its money and to whom it sold its wares.

Following the music of voices in conflict, she found Cade and Briet at the eastern end of the factory, at the farthest point from the floor's main entrance. Twisted heaps of metal smoldered around them, tainting the air with the fumes of hot oiled steel while they argued beside a pallet loaded with boxes of ammunition.

Cade strained to keep his voice down as he protested to Briet, "I was only kidding about tossing it in the sea. You don't really want to throw this out, do you?"

"The sooner it's all destroyed, the safer we'll all be."

Anja's magickally enhanced vision detected the aura of enchantment emanating from the ammo boxes. It was bright enough to be distracting. "She is right," she said as she joined Cade and Briet beside the pallet. "Get rid of it."

Her declaration put a desperate look on Cade's face. "Hang on, honey. Hear me out. One of the jobs of an ammo plant is quality control. To test this stuff, they'd need to keep enchanted weapons on site somewhere. If we can find them and match them to their ammo—"

"There are none here," Anja said. "We would have found them."

He looked pained. "Why not just hold the ammo until we find match-ing guns?" Anja reacted to his question by looking at him as if he had just said the dumbest thing in history. After taking a second to think about it, he groaned with embarrassment. "Because the magician who made it can find even one of these bullets with a simple spell—and us with it."

"Just like that idol you stole in Peru." Anja gave Cade's cheek a playful pat, coaxing a grin from him. "So you *do* learn from your mistakes." She pointed at the ammo. "*Sink it all.*" She held up the documents she had taken from the office. "But smile: I have something better."

Briet snatched a handful of the loose papers from Anja's hands. Her eyes widened as she looked through them. "Corporate financials. Merger con-tracts." She looked at Anja wearing a smile tinged with a hint of madness. "Tell me you found purchase orders."

A nod from Anja. "And client lists. With real names and addresses. Not just shell companies and postal boxes."

Cade pulled out his combat knife and kneeled beside the ammunition pal-let. "Maybe I'll take just one box of rounds for my Beretta, in case we can find a way to enchant our own guns."

Briet shook her head. "So much for learning from mistakes."

Watching Cade, Anja saw something tiny fall between them, moving fast, as if it had been dropped from a great height.

The blast was blinding and hit her like a kick in the gut.

Magickal light blinded her, Cade, and Briet. The glare subsided but a thick purple fog shrouded them all. Anja felt the smothering sensation of being cut off from the powers of her yoked spirits. When she tried to run, it was like slamming into a brick wall.

On the concrete floor between her and Cade lay the dust of a shattered en-chanted pearl, a technique that had been a favorite of their late master, Adair. Its breaking had spawned a magickal circle around them: a devil's trap. Karcists with yoked demons caught in such a snare would be unable to leave it, release any spirits from their yokes, or use any of their powers.

And now Cade, Briet, and Anja were its prisoners.

"Welcome to Adana," a man declared from somewhere above them.

The trio looked up in unison.

Two people floated down from an open skylight. Without the benefit of magickally enhanced vision, Anja strained to see any kind of detail; they were barely shadows against the darkness. Then lightning crackled around the enemy karcists' wands, illuminating their faces.

The man she had never seen before. The young woman she knew all too well.

Lila Matar. Their best student. Anja's most beloved protégée. One of the most gifted karcists she or Cade had ever seen, barring those gifted with angelic or demonic bonding. She loomed above them, attired all in black, her raven hair tied back tight. Hovered at the right hand of a thirtyish man with a fair complexion, a pencil-thin mustache, and a well-tailored suit.

Cade glared up at her. "If it isn't the traitor."

Lila shrugged. "You taught me 'the nature of all things is change.' But Master Niccolò taught me what you were afraid to: that controlling magick means we get to *direct* the change."

With a few flicks and flourishes of her wand, Lila pulled the wands, blades, and firearms off of Anja, Cade, and Briet and cast them away, just beyond reach outside the devil's trap.

Lila smiled, but there was evil in her eyes.

"He also taught me students exist to surpass their masters."

Cade was trying and failing to think his way out of the devil's trap when the fluorescent lights above the assembly lines snapped on, bathing the production floor in greenish light.

The clamor of armed men running filled the cavernous space. Cade, Anja, and Briet turned to see a platoon of mercenaries charging up the aisles, all of them brandishing combat rifles, shotguns, or submachine guns.

Following them at a more leisurely pace was the well-dressed, muscular black man Cade and the others had seen in Mexico City. His bearing was proud, like a conqueror's. Unhurried, unconcerned. Cade felt a grudging respect for the man, in spite of the fact he likely had come here to murder him, his wife, and Briet.

"Time for a chat," said the skinny white magician hovering above the trap. His phony smile radiated smugness. "My name is Niccolò Falco." He gestured toward the mage walking up the center aisle. "I believe you have met my associate, Signor Hatunde Ndufo."

"*Doctor* Ndufo," the other mage said, mildly offended. "I hold a doctorate in theology."

Niccolò bowed his head to his colleague. "My apologies. *Doctor.*" To Cade he continued, "I should thank you, Signor Martin, for being so utterly predictable. We fed you one clue, and true to your dossier, you just can't stop running it down. I've wondered more than once whether you were born this obsessive, or if it's the result of the decades you have spent yoking demons."

Cade's stare became a mask of anger. "A bit of both, I guess." He shifted his attention to his ex-student. "Lila, do you know what you've done? Did they tell you the other apprentices are dead?" She met his continuing accusation with defiance. "Mira. Viên. Leyton. Even Melina. All dead because of *you,* Lila. Is that what you wanted?"

Her anger was pure, her confidence steady. "Better them than my sisters. Or my mother."

Niccolò heaved a sigh thick with contempt. "Are you finished? This kind of naïve appeal to shame might pass for entertainment on American daytime television, but I find it tedious."

"That's pretty rich coming from the poster child for Tedious Asshole Syndrome." Cade looked with scorn at his former apprentice. "Goddammit, I thought you were loyal. Were a few threats really all it took to break you? Tell the truth, Lila: Why'd you turn? The *real* reason."

Niccolò answered for her. "The same reason every sane person turns, Signor Martin. The same reason she gave us her enchanted mirror so that we could sabotage all of yours. Every soul has its price, and my employer is more than willing to pay it, and then some."

Anja spat at the hovering Niccolò, but was unable to launch her spittle high enough to hit him. "Honor has no price."

"And therein lies the crux of our problem," he said. "Only a fool, a madman, or a zealot puts principle ahead of survival. Alas, I have it on good authority that principles bring no comfort when one is dead." A fiendish grin. "As the three of you are about to discover."

———

Yasmin stumble-sprinted through the dark woods alongside the factory, running face-first into low branches with every other step. Everything had gone tits-up. Her heart slammed inside her chest like a trip-hammer. *What are we supposed to do now?*

She was half a step from a nosedive into the river when two pairs of hands caught her. Sathit sat her down as Barış shushed her. "Are you all right?" he asked in a whisper.

"I'm fine." Yasmin looked back at the factory. "What happened? Where did those guys come from?"

"The roof," Sathit said. "I think they were there the whole time, waiting for us."

Barış's face scrunched like a fist. "The masters walked into a trap." He looked at the part of the factory that stood over the middle of the river. "Can either of you see through the walls?"

"I can," Yasmin said. She concentrated on her yoked gift of the Sight, which she gleaned from the spirit DEMOGORGON, one of Hell's more powerful minor nobles. Depending upon the spirit that granted the Sight, some karcists gained nothing more than the ability to see in the dark. Others became capable of seeing people's auras, the shines of enchantment, and the shadows of hexing. Many variants of the Sight could also penetrate solid barriers.

Her vision pushed past the factory's outer walls, then through its inner walls, to find Cade, Anja, and Briet surrounded by their enemies.

"I see them," Yasmin whispered. "They're stuck in a devil's trap."

"Which means they can't run, shed their spirits, or use magick," Sathit said.

Barış asked, "How many foes?"

"Thirty-odd men with guns, three karcists. The guy we ran from in Mexico City, a skinny white guy in a fancy suit, and—" Her voice caught in her throat. "It . . . looks like . . . *Lila*."

Sathit sounded incredulous. "It can't be. Are you sure?"

Yasmin looked closer. "It's definitely her. And she's with the enemy."

"*Bok.*" Barış pulled off his fez in dismay.

Sathit cracked her knuckles. "Three of us. Three of them. Even odds."

Barış sleeved the sweat from his cheeks and forehead. "They have hostages and a lot of guns. If we go in there with wands blazing, our masters are as good as dead."

Still peering into the factory by means of the Sight, Yasmin was alarmed by a new wave of activity. "Whatever we're going to do, we'd better do it fast. The mercs are using one forklift to haul out a pallet full of enchanted ammo, and another to bring in a pallet loaded with barrels."

Her news made Barış and Sathit tense. He asked, "Barrels? What kind?"

"Petrol. Two hundred liters per." Watching the mercs, Yasmin felt a sickening sense of foreboding. "They're pulling off the lids . . . and dumping fuel on the floor."

"They're being set up," Sathit said. "Framed as arsonists who got caught in their own blaze." She turned toward Barış. "No bullets inside the corpses, and no bindings on them? The police won't even think of calling it murder."

"We've got a minute to figure this out," Yasmin said, "maybe two. Depends how much the boss man likes to hear himself talk." She felt the seconds slipping away. "Well? C'mon! Think! What're we gonna do?"

Barış clenched his fists while he pondered their options under his breath. "Charge into a stand-up fight, we all die. Do nothing, the masters die. Try to lure the enemy mages out? They'd send their goons. No—they'd burn the masters, *then* come after us. Split them up? Why bother? They die, we die, *everybody* dies." He buried his face in his fez. "God help me, we're fucked."

Sathit drew her wand and glared at Barış. "Not helping."

Yasmin tried to concentrate. "Do we have any yoked spirits who can quench a fire?"

Sathit shook her head. "If we snuff the blaze, the bad guys will see it and come back."

"Shit." Yasmin's mind was a storm of ideas. "What if we just keep the fire away from the masters? Make a ring of safety?"

"We could block the flames," Barış said, "and maybe even the heat, but not the smoke. They'll suffocate in less than a minute."

Yasmin saw the pilings under the factory's eastern end, the portion that extended into the middle of the river. Compared the pilings' locations to the masters' positions inside the factory.

Then she, too, drew her wand and looked at Barış and Sathit.

"I have an idea," she said, "and you're both going to hate it."

———

A trio of mercenaries prowled around the devil's trap, splashing gasoline from buckets onto Cade, Briet, and Anja. It was the first time Cade had ever tasted petrol, and it was just as disgusting as its odor had always led him to expect it would be. It wasn't the horrid, chemical flavors that most repulsed him but the texture—slick and viscous, it coated his tongue and clung to his lips, no matter how many times he coughed or tried to spit it away.

Lila and Niccolò continued to hover a few meters above Cade and his companions. Hatunde moved through the factory with a squad of mercs, directing the dispensation of gasoline between the machines and into the nooks and crevices of the factory's walls.

Cade did his best to hide his mounting fear of being torched alive. *If the adepts followed directions, they're miles away by now. Please don't let them do anything stupid.*

He aimed a hate-filled look at Niccolò. "You haven't thought this through, have you?"

The fashion-conscious magician looked confused. "In what respect?"

"Why are you enabling the genocide of other karcists? Whatever government you work for, sooner or later it'll turn on you. You get that, right?"

The question seemed to amuse Niccolò. "Who says we serve a government?"

His flippant reply vexed fuel-soaked Briet. "If you're not government, why did NSA Hammers try to kill me in Dallas? Why did a Mossad golem murder my family?"

"*I* told the Mossad to send that golem, just as I had the Hammers kill your friends Clark and Frank"—he looked at Cade—"and forced MI6 to betray your old chum Miles." Niccolò let those revelations sink in. "I never said the governments of the world were *not involved*. I merely said *we* do not serve *them*—because they exist to serve my employer."

Cade wiped petrol from his eyes. "And who's that?"

"No one you will ever meet." To the goons doing the sloshing, he said, "Are you nearly finished? I am ready to light the candles on this cake."

The mercs hurled the last of their fuel onto the trio inside the devil's trap and then walked away. Shaking off the fresh coat of gasoline, Cade said to Niccolò, "You still haven't answered my question. Why do the bidding of some kook who clearly wants us all dead?"

Niccolò laughed. "What do you think this is? Some kind of mad jihad? A vendetta run amok?" He shook his head. "This is just *business*, Signor Martin."

"Business! Drenching us in gas is just *business*? Who do you work for, the Mob?"

Lila faced Niccolò. "Tell them the real reason why. They deserve at least that much."

"Fine." Arms spread in a gesture of surrender, he said to the trio inside the trap, "The Old Man marked you and your students for death because he knows you have too much pride to let yourselves be bought." An evil smirk. "Your reputations preceded you—and condemned you."

Cade felt as if he had skipped a chapter in a book and now was lost. "Wait—*bought*? The fuck are you talking about?"

Niccolò looked exasperated, so Lila answered for him. "The Old Man isn't trying to purge the world of magick. He just wants to control the supply. He wants a *monopoly*."

Contempt manifested as rolling eyes and groans of disbelief from the captive trio. Shaking her head, Briet muttered, "You've got to be fucking kidding me."

Looking up at Niccolò, Cade wished he could lock his hands around the man's throat. "You and your boss really thought I'd rather see all of my students *murdered* than take a bribe? What kind of boy scout do you think I am?"

"The kind who refused Kein Engel's offer of alliance in June 1942, despite facing death by ritual sacrifice. The kind who willingly threw himself into a hellmouth in February 1945"—he shot a meaningful look at Anja—"to correct another's mistake." Looking back at Cade he added, "The kind who in 1954 refused an invitation to take over the United States' Occult Defense Program, and then in 1959 turned down a half-million-dollar bounty from the Chinese government and risked public execution to help the Dalai Lama escape Tibet. Need I go on?"

Briet shouldered her way in front of Cade. "What about me? I could use the money."

Niccolò furrowed his brow. "You? You've been hunting my employer and his peers for nearly a decade. And judging from the havoc you've caused during your time at the ODP, I would have to say you're every bit as dangerous as Signor Martin."

When Niccolò's gaze fell upon Anja, she said with flat hostility, "I do not beg. I just want to kill you."

"As your dossier predicted. This is why we knew there would be no bargaining with any of you. You are too old-fashioned about the Art. You refuse to see its *commercial* potential."

At the far end of the factory floor from the captive trio, the last of the mercs slipped out the exits to the storage bay and loading dock. In front of the plastic-curtained entranceways to the production floor, heavy doors descended and sealed off the only route of escape. The air inside the factory was so thick with petrol fumes that it made Cade dizzy, and the stink of it filled him with the urge to retch. *Fuck. This is gonna be a shitty way to die.*

Inside his head, more than a dozen demons clamored for escape, only to find themselves constrained by the devil's trap. Though none of them would perish in the flames as Cade and his friends would, for as long as they remained yoked, they would share his every pain—and his death. The agony of the Reaper's scythe was one no spirit was eager to face.

Niccolò and Lila ascended to just beneath the open skylight. He smiled. "Before we end this conversation—and your lives—I want you to know I am not an unreasonable man. My patron wants you dead, so you must die. But if you give me what I want, without further strife, I will grant you quick, merciful deaths—neck-breaks so swift you will hardly feel them—rather than letting you be cooked alive."

Cade had no intention of cooperating in good faith, but any chance to delay the inevitable was worth taking. "We're listening."

Niccolò eyed Anja. "First, hand over the Iron Codex to me."

Anja was antipathy incarnate. "I will gag you with your own shriveled manhood."

Pointing his wand at Cade, Niccolò continued, "I also want your manuscript, all your research into the Mystery of the Dead God."

"I've barely started writing it. Why would you want that?"

"To burn it, of course." A sinister gleam. "As a favor to Cardinal Lombardi."

"Naturally."

"So! What is it to be? The easy way? Or the hard way?"

Everyone looked at Cade, as if this decision were his to make.

He took a deep breath, weighed his options, and frowned.

"You don't really leave us much choice." He looked up at the pair in the skylight. "I think I speak for all of us when I say, 'Choke on my big hairy balls.' Also, go fuck yourself."

Any semblance of patience that had lingered on Niccolò's face vanished. Now his dark eyes burned with rage. "Perhaps I failed to make myself clear."

He thrust his wand downward.

Knifing pain tore into Cade's gut and dropped him to his knees.

Briet and Anja collapsed beside him. Both women clutched at their own stomachs as they curled in upon themselves.

The burning fury in Cade's abdomen traveled inside of him, like a marauder laying waste to organs and tissue on its march toward his heart. Cade clutched at his chest, growling as he fought to master the pain, but as it grew worse spittle poured through his gritted teeth. Down on all fours, he could barely lift his head to glare at the bastard responsible.

Niccolò hovered just beneath the skylight, twisting his wand to and fro. "Give me what I want, and the pain will cease. Defy me, and I *promise* it will double."

Cade's body shook violently. He spat out a mouthful of blood. "What part of 'fuck yourself' wasn't clear?"

Niccolò shook his head, clearly disappointed.

Then he gave his wand a turn and kept his promise.

Anja writhed in agony beside Cade and Briet. Bound inside the devil's trap, her yoked spirits were worse than useless; they were just more voices of panic drowning out her own inner pleas for calm. *Be silent,* she berated her demonic entourage. *I need to focus.*

Sensory overload made it hard to concentrate. The sensation of barbed wire being pulled through her guts, the stings of a million needles on her skin, Cade's growls, Briet's screams, Niccolò's shouted demands for information, the reek of gasoline mixing with the demonic perfume of sulfur—it took all of Anja's training to block it all out, even for a second.

She reached out with her innate *nikraim* talent, the one granted to her by virtue of her soul having been bonded before birth with the spirit of an angel. She had learned years earlier that the binding charms of a devil's trap had no effect on the natural powers of *nikraim*.

During her captivity in India, she had summoned a mongoose to chew through her bonds and set her free. Now she hoped there was any kind of wildlife in the immediate area she could call to her aid before the matter became moot. A bear, or maybe a tiger to maul her foes. She would have settled for a badger, a beaver, or any kind of weasel to smudge the glyphs of the devil's trap and give her, Cade, and Briet a fighting chance. But she sensed no animals for miles—at least, none that could plausibly be of any help.

Niccolò ceased his tortures, ostensibly out of frustration. "Hand them over, damn you! They're just books!"

Cade sprawled on the floor, coated in sweat and fighting for breath. He glared at his new nemesis. "If they were *just books,* you wouldn't be torturing us to find them."

"The Old Man is right. There really is no bargaining with fanatics. So vexing."

He delivered a final jolt of demonic power, and Cade's back arched upward from the floor as if he had been impaled on a spike. A moment later, Cade collapsed in a heap.

Anja kneeled at his side, fearing the worst. "Cade? Can you hear me?"

His eyes were dim, and frothy blood spilled from his mouth. "Anja . . . ?"

"*Da?*"

His voice grew weak. "If you make it out . . . leave a light on for me."

Niccolò tucked his wand inside his jacket. When his hand emerged, it held a pack of cigarettes. He took out two and offered one to Lila. "Signorina Matar?"

She accepted it, and they put the cigarettes between their lips. Niccolò lit both with a snap of his fingers. Puffing lazily, they both levitated toward the open skylight above them. He passed through it first and said to Lila as he went, "Please do the honors."

Lila hesitated. She held her cigarette between her thumb and forefinger, and she kept her back to Niccolò. His order seemed to have stirred up some residue of her conscience.

Briet regarded the young woman with a baleful look.

Lila flicked away her cigarette and flew through the skylight, into the darkness.

The falling cigarette danced and tumbled through the dark.

It struck the edge of a machine. Launched a hundred sparks.

Each found its own lake of fuel. A hundred flash points ignited at once.

Blue-and-orange flames raced through the factory with a hellish roar.

A wall of heat struck Anja's face, crisping her brows and lashes.

Fighting for air, the trio in the trap fell to their hands and knees.

They stole a few thin, hot breaths before towers of flame rose around them. Within seconds the factory became a hellscape—and then the flames found the trails of fuel that led across the trap's indelible lines, straight to the gasoline-soaked trio.

Fear paralyzed Anja as fire raced toward them from multiple directions. She wished a cache of bullets or a box of gunpowder would explode and spare them this ugly death.

Flames sped across the trap's outer boundary.

Anja wrapped her arms around Cade. *If we die, we die together.*

Thunder rocked the building from below—and launched the snared trio up from the concrete floor, which bulged upward and fractured violently beneath them, destroying the circles and glyphs of the devil's trap, whose hold on them vanished.

Briet dived toward the weapons Lila had taken and dropped just outside the now-ruined trap. As she scooped up all three of their wands, the burning floor collapsed beneath them.

They plunged into the frigid water of the Seyhan River, along with a few tons of broken concrete and shattered iron rebar, followed by several tons of assembly-line machines.

"Shields!" Briet cried as they fell, conjuring her own.

Anja had already cocooned the three of them in magickal protection. Concrete slabs and wooden beams bounced off her shield as she and Cade sank into the middle of the river.

She surfaced holding the barely conscious Cade, her shield at full strength. A quick look with the Sight confirmed Briet and the adepts—who had arranged this rescue from below—also had their shields up. But even their united strength wouldn't be enough.

Because the ammo factory's oil-powered generators were about to explode.

"Dive!" Anja snapped. She shut her eyes and invoked a stoneskin talent to sink herself and Cade to the river's bottom. She hoped the others did the same in time.

Then the factory exploded, its blast searing hot and painfully bright, even through murky water and Anja's closed eyelids. The detonation trembled her guts against her skeleton and tore Cade from her arms as it blew away the river.

Protected by her shield, Anja went into a fetal curl and let the detonation roll her and the others like a dice on a burning craps table.

Her entire world was reduced to motion, chaos, flames, and darkness.

And then—impact. Anja struck something harder and less forgiving than herself. It was like being crushed in a giant's fist for seconds that felt like forever.

The glow and heat of the conflagration faded, and she opened her eyes.

She and her friends had been hurled beyond the opposite riverbank, into the woods.

The air was thick with smoke that stank of gasoline and gunpowder. Burning timbers and chunks of brick from the factory's exterior had been scattered for half a mile in every direction. Close-knit stands of trees—those that hadn't been leveled—had caught fire.

Where the factory had stood, there remained only the blackened metallic skeletons of the largest, heaviest machines. A pillar of smoke climbed into the night sky, blotting out the stars. Through the haze, the moon vanishing into the west had turned an ominous dull crimson.

After several seconds, the interrupted river surged back to its former strength, refilling its basin as it coursed southward toward the sea.

Searching high and low with the Sight, Anja found no sign of Niccolò, Lila, or Hatunde. She found Cade in a patch of tall grass, barely conscious, moaning, and clutching his gut.

Anja noted the approach of Briet and the adepts, who all looked as beaten-down as she felt. She tried to sound calm and in charge. "We need to leave. Now."

Briet nodded. "I'll second that. Let's get the fuck out of here."

Briet helped Barış carry Cade back to the river. The three of them entered the water first, and then the others joined them. The group once more linked hands to form a chain.

This time Yasmin was the closest to Anja. She held Briet's free hand but looked at Anja as she asked, "Will Master Cade be all right?"

"Ask me after we get back to the lodge."

Uncertain which of Cade's wounds she would be able to heal and which ones she wouldn't, Anja focused her will for the water jaunt and took her friends and husband home.

TUESDAY, NOVEMBER 26

There was never any hiding from the pain. Not here. Inside the conjuring circle, alone with his courage and whatever spirits he conjured from Hell, Cade would stand exposed. Faced with a demon, his entire being became a raw nerve.

Because the truth always hurt.

He had wanted to come here directly after his return from Turkey, but Anja had made him sit and let her heal his wounds before letting him undertake a magickal experiment. Now the sun was climbing high above Tasmania, which meant Cade's learned response was to take shelter indoors. More than twenty years of immersion in the Art had left him averse to direct sunlight. He thought it fitting that the Latinate term for one who flees from sunlight is a "lucifuge"—the first half of the name of his Infernal patron, LUCIFUGE ROFOCALE.

Hell's petulant prime minister stood before Cade, its forked tail twitching, cloven hooves stamping, yellow eyes blazing with unbridled hatred. Conjured outside of the time prescribed for its service, the demon radiated murderous intent as its inhuman voice thundered around Cade and shook the fishing lodge to its foundations. IT IS NEITHER MY HOUR NOR MY DAY. WHY DOST THOU TROUBLE MY REPOSE, EVE-SPAWN?

"I need your skills of divination." Weary from the ordeal outside Adana, it took all of Cade's focus to keep his balance and not let the ceremonial sword slip from its perch atop his slippered toes. "My enemies have been kicking my ass, and I fear one of my friends is hurt or dead. I need you to tell me the whereabouts and condition of Miles Disraeli Franklin."

The demon sucked air through a grin of jagged teeth. YOUR FRIEND CLINGS TO HIS LIFE IN A LONDON HOSPITAL, BUT HIS HOLD ON THIS WORLD FALTERS.

"How did he come to this state?"

Struck down by agents of thy new foe, as directed by thy former pupil Lila Matar. A sinister grin of fangs. Paid for thy sins, he has.

"How grave are his wounds?"

His spinal cord is severed. He will not walk again.

Cade's heart sank. In ages past, he might have worked a healing charm to give Miles back his legs, but the days of such miracles were past. Now there would be X-rays, photographic documents of the damage to Miles's bones and spinal cord. Any sudden restoration or repair of his injuries would invite inquiries that neither Miles nor Cade could afford.

If only there had been some way to heal him before the X-rays were taken. . . .

It was a futile wish, as pointless as hoping for time itself to reverse its direction. Too many people had seen Miles's X-rays by now for Cade to redact all their memories. There could be copies of the X-ray film hidden in any of a thousand different secret spaces inside MI6 headquarters in London. That was too much evidence to overcome. Too great a risk to take for one man, even one whom Cade loved as much as Miles. That level of scrutiny would be more than dangerous—it would be fatal. It wounded Cade deeply to realize he had to accept that Miles was broken and maimed. *He's been like a brother to me my entire adult life. Leaving him paralyzed when I know I could heal him . . . it makes me sick.*

But if I make him whole again, none of us will be able to explain it.

They'll hunt us all down. They'll have no choice.

The demon regarded Cade's prolonged melancholy with disdain. Dost thou have any further need of me? Or might I be permitted to return to the shadow?

Cade was too tired and too heartbroken to be bothered with Hell's endless formalities. "Yeah, we're done for tonight. Fuck off, and don't hurt anybody or break anything on your way back to Hell, or I'll turn you inside-out through your asshole. You hear me, fuckface?"

Thy commands are understood, and thy terms acceptable.

"Great. Don't call me, I'll call you." An impudent wave of his hand. "Get lost."

The floor beneath the demon vanished for a few seconds, revealing a black and starless void. Lucifuge Rofocale plunged into nothingness, splitting the air with its plangent howl of terror as it fell. The tip of the demon's tail was the last part to pass through the opening. As soon as it was on the other side, the floor reappeared, the howling stopped, and the putrid yellow-green vapors that attended any summons of the prime minister dissipated.

Cade kicked away the sword atop his feet. He pulled the paper miter from his head, crushing it in his grip as he fell to his knees and wept in near silence. His tears cut warm trails through the soot that had coated his face during the fire in the factory. He wanted to lash out, to hit someone or shoot something or see something explode and vanish in a column of fire . . . but there was no simple balm for his pain. No easy salve for his guilt.

I never should've brought him into this. He was out. Free and clear. The events of the last few days haunted Cade. *I should've let it go. Walked away.*

His eyes burned as his grief and shame took over. *They maimed him. Crippled him. Because I put him in danger.* He remembered their youthful days at Oxford. How much he had admired Miles, perhaps even envied him. Taller than Cade, and stronger, not to mention more handsome, with a voice born for theater . . . Miles had embodied everything Cade had ever wanted to be— and everything he had given up to tread a path less traveled.

Now Miles would never tread another path again. At best he would spend the rest of his days in a wheelchair, cut down for no good reason, and all because he had made the terrible error of choosing to help Cade at a moment when anyone with a lick of sense would have told him to go pound sand. *He loved me enough to risk his life for me.* Cade's self-contempt deepened by the moment. *And there's nothing I can do to help him.*

"Did you hear what I *said,* Eminence? They *burned our sanctuary to the ground.*"

Impelled by wrath, Father D'Odorico was half out of his guest chair. He leaned upon the desk of Cardinal Umberto Lombardi—a stance he had taken in the hope of provoking the Vatican's cardinal inquisitor and pro tem voice of the Pauline Synod into answering him.

Behind the desk, Lombardi sat slightly reclined, his fingers steepled atop the curve of his belly, his demeanor placid. "I heard you the first time, Father." He avoided eye contact with Father D'Odorico by putting on a contemplative air and letting his gaze drift about his spacious Vatican City office. Like the cardinal himself, the room lacked humility. Its shelves and furniture had been crafted from precious woods, and the upholstery on the chairs seemed to match the bindings on Lombardi's collection of rare books. Shafts of late-afternoon sunlight bent through the window behind the desk and fell upon a wall of paintings and a shelf of priceless curios. The room even *smelled* rich:

three varieties of incense mingled with the scent of lemon oil on freshly polished wood and the earthy perfume of well-conditioned leather.

Father D'Odorico tried to be patient. Tried to wait for the cardinal to
make eye contact and offer him some cue that it was once again his turn to
speak. Instead his anger got the best of him. "Since you admit you heard me,
I want to know what you intend to do about this."

The seventyish cardinal mustered an exaggerated frown. "Nothing."

"I beg your pardon, Eminence? How can you let this go unanswered?"

Lombardi sighed, ceased his evasions, and looked at Father D'Odorico. "Tell
me, *signore* director: Aside from reporting the incident to the local authorities
as an act of arson, and filing an insurance claim for the lost property . . . what,
precisely, do you expect the Church to do?"

"Are you being willfully obtuse? This was a clear abrogation of the Covenant!"

The cardinal's manner was subdued. "Indubitably. I can't imagine a more
blatant violation than a direct assault on consecrated ground and an occupied sanctuary."

The weariness of Lombardi's reply made Father D'Odorico wonder if his calamity was boring the man. *Almost as if he's been* expecting *this conversation.*

Lombardi parted his hands and spread them wide. "But I ask you again,
Father: What would you have the Church do in response to the attack on
your monastery?"

"My first request is that we declare the Covenant dissolved."

"Absolutely not."

"Why? The enemy has declared *war.*"

"We don't know that. There's been no formal declaration."

"My sanctuary lying in cinders *is* the declaration."

The cardinal stood. His arrogance engulfed D'Odorico. "Is that so? Did
the arsonists perchance leave behind a written confession? Or maybe they
introduced themselves before they lit your monastery on fire." Reading the
answers on D'Odorico's reddening face, the cardinal came out from behind
his desk as he continued, "Did they at least leave a calling card? Or announce
their allegiance before they demolished the sanctuary you were meant to
defend?" He finished his tirade while looming over the still seated White
magician. "Or would it be more correct to say that you don't actually have
the slightest idea who to blame for this disaster?" He nodded at D'Odorico's
sullen but unspoken confirmation. "I thought as much."

Lombardi walked behind his desk and returned to his chair. Now he sat with his back straight, his aspect proud. "If the Church had torn up the Covenant after every act of aggression by dark magicians, it wouldn't have lasted a year, never mind six centuries." He shook his head. "I will not ask the Holy Father to vitiate the truce between two entire schools of the Art just because a handful of dark magicians broke the law. If you or any member of your order could identify your attackers by name, perhaps I could recommend that they personally be stripped of the Covenant's protections. But for the good of the many, we must act with care."

"From where I sit, it looks as if you mean not to act at all."

"I choose not to act recklessly. Do not mistake caution for indifference."

Frustrated but desperate to preserve a calm bearing, Father D'Odorico switched topics. "There's one other reason for my visit today, Eminence."

Lombardi motioned for him to go on. "Quickly, please. I have other business to attend."

"The only reason my monks and I are still alive is because we were warned of the attack by our former brother—Father Luis Roderigo Pérez."

The mention of Father Pérez's name made the cardinal bristle. His shoulders hunched and the lines of his face furrowed. "I made it clear I never wanted to hear that name again, and that contact with him by any member of the Church is forbidden. Nor is he to be addressed as 'father,' or with any other title of holy respect."

"We haven't forgotten, Eminence."

Father D'Odorico left unsaid that he and many of the other karcists at Monte Paterno considered the Church's excommunication of Father Pérez to be unjust, even in light of his assault on Lombardi, his role in the escape of Goetic karcists from the dungeon of the Apostolic Palace, and his theft of the Iron Codex. It was clear the cardinal felt differently.

"However," the director continued, "you should know that Cardinal Moretti, before he passed, came to me at Monte Paterno and directed me to seek out Fath—" He caught himself just in time. "To seek out Signor Pérez in order to solicit his counsel and assistance with investigating the assassination of the American president."

Lombardi's glare was scathing and filled with doubt. "How unfortunate for you both that Cardinal Moretti left behind no official record of his request."

"Be that as it may, I would implore you to lift the order of banishment from Signor Pérez. In this troubling hour, my order and I have need of his expertise."

"I don't possess the authority to rescind that sanction. Only the Holy Father can do that."

"But he does so—or refuses to do so—on your counsel, does he not?"

A nod. "He does." Lombardi's scowl deepened. "But I will not be Signor Pérez's intercessor with the Holy Father. Not today. Not ever." He gestured toward the door. "You can go now, Father."

"Go where?" D'Odorico stood but then held his ground. "My sanctuary lies in ashes, and my order was bound by vows of poverty. You've made it clear we aren't welcome within the walls of Vatican City, but we cannot simply check ourselves into the Hilton, now can we?"

The demand prompted a raised eyebrow from Lombardi. "Shelter awaits you with the monks of Monte Albano. Your order will reside there until our present discord runs its course. After peace and order return, Monte Paterno will be rebuilt and its grounds consecrated anew. But until that day, I don't want to hear a word about you, your monks, or the outcast."

Father D'Odorico walked to the door and stopped to claim his hat and coat from the rack. He draped the coat over one arm and held the hat as he looked back at Cardinal Lombardi. "With all respect, Eminence, shutting out Luis is a mistake. He just wants to help."

"I don't care *what* he wants. He knew the cost of his crimes and committed them anyway." Lombardi feigned being lost in his paperwork. "He belongs to the enemy now."

⁓

Everyone in the lodge had seen it, but no one seemed willing to talk about it. Briet had been adding new pieces to her evidence web when Cade had emerged from the conjuring room, his eyes bloodshot and his gaze hollow. Briet had seen Anja try to stop Cade as he marched toward the lodge's front door, but he'd been in no mood to talk or be delayed. He'd pushed his way out the door with enough force to bang it off the exterior wall of the lodge, and he'd left it half open behind him as he stalked over a grassy marsh thick with scrub brush, on a direct path toward Arthurs Lake, which shimmered crimson in the fading dusk.

The adepts gathered behind Anja, who stood between them and the door. Sathit, the shortest of the trio, stood on tiptoes to look past Anja's shoulder. "Where is he going?"

"Out," Anja said.

The group watched Cade walk without pause into the lake.

Yasmin sounded more curious than concerned: "Y'think he'll try to drown himself?" Her question got no answer from Anja and a pointed look from Barış.

Briet stuck another sheet of evidence into its proper place on the wall. "If he wanted to drown himself, he'd have brought his karcist's tools for ballast." She chose a length of salmon-colored yarn to link the new information to a related piece of content on the ceiling above it. "The bigger question is: Did he take a pistol?"

Anja stared out the door. "*Nyet.*"

"Then odds are he's coming back."

Sathit did not sound reassured. "I don't know. He's pretty far from shore. . . ."

"I've seen anglers out there in the mornings," Barış said. "Arthurs Lake has wide shallows. Master Cade will be all right."

A snort from Yasmin. "Wanna bet? He's still going."

Unable to ignore the idle chatter, Briet put down the stack of papers Anja had stolen from the ammunition factory, and then she ducked and weaved her way out of the main room to stand behind Anja and her students. Framed inside the doorway was a vertical slice of the lake painted red by the sunset. Lost in its midst was the top half of a blurry silhouette: Cade, thigh-deep and continuing to wade farther from shore.

Barış frowned. "This is not a good sign."

Yasmin crossed her arms. "Whatever happened in the conjuring room, it sounds like it broke him."

Briet shouldered past the adepts and walked toward the door, only to be stopped by Anja. She confronted Briet. "What are you doing?"

"Let me talk to him." She looked out at the lonely figure trying to disappear himself in the lake. "I know what he's feeling right now."

Her simple statement angered Anja. "Are you saying I do not? He is mine, not yours."

"I'm not trying to poach your husband. I think I can help him." Briet sensed Anja's reluctance. "If I fail, you can always kill me later."

"Already my plan." Anja signaled Briet to go. "Good luck."

Briet left the lodge and crossed the grassy marsh to the water's edge. The ground beneath her feet was spongy and damp. Each step landed with a faint squish of displaced water and pulled free of the mud with a muted squelch.

Cade had a long head start, but as Briet took her first step into the lake she saw he had stopped moving. He was more than a hundred meters from shore, standing in water up to his waist. Muddy water filled Briet's shoes. Its bracing cold stung her skin, then numbed it.

This is going to suck. Her next several steps confirmed her fear. It was difficult to move quickly, because overcoming her body's reaction to the frigid water was harder than she expected. But she knew not to let herself stop advancing, because the moment she did she might be unable to resume going forward. Her hands shook, and steady shivers traveled up her spine. By the time the water was above her knees, her teeth chattered so fiercely she was certain the lake had cooled her blood to match its brutal chill.

It took her only a few minutes to reach Cade, but each one had felt like an hour. She came to a halt beside him, her arms clutching her torso to conserve what little body warmth she had left. Then she turned her head and saw in the day's dying light that Cade's face was streaked with tears. He stared into the distance, despondent, all but paralyzed in his grief. Briet wondered if he had even registered her presence. Then he said in a trembling voice, "Go away."

"No." Clocking his angry reaction, she added, "Not trying to goad you. It's just that I went through way too much pain and trouble to stand here, so I plan to make the trip worth it."

"Then you came for nothing."

"I don't believe that." She studied his face for any fleeting secrets it might betray. "What happened in the conjuring room? You were fine when you went in."

"No I wasn't." Cade shook his head, his sorrow deepening. "I haven't been 'fine' since Naxos. I'm up against someone who's clearly been stalking me for years, and all I've been able to do is flail around like a boxer in the dark." His grief transformed into rage. "They murdered my students in front of me! Slaughtered them like animals!" More tears fell from his eyes, and his fury melted into guilt. "I told them I'd protect them. Keep them safe. . . . I never knew the meaning of the word." He stared into the dying sun. "I'm a fucking fraud. A failure."

"You are *not* a failure, Cade."

"Really? An enemy I wasn't ready for killed over a dozen of my pupils."

"I know how you feel. Believe me."

Doubts deepened the creases in his forehead. "Oh, do you?"

She wanted to slap the shit out of him. "How short *is* your memory, Martin? Niccolò and his people wiped out over a dozen of *my* adepts, too. Turned at least one of them against me that I know of. Or have you already forgotten about Dragan Dalca?"

"The lunatic who wanted to open the gates of Hell with an atomic bomb."

"That's the one."

Cade palmed tears from his face. "Bree . . . they crippled Miles. Damned near killed him, all because he tried to help us." He looked down at the water, which sparkled in the sunset like a fortune in rubies. "I never should've brought him into this. I've ruined his life."

"You want to talk collateral damage? Alton was an accountant by day and a poet by night. Hyun was an artist and a pastry chef. I loved them both more than I've ever loved anyone. More than I've ever loved myself. And four days ago I had to watch a fucking golem murder them in front of me and burn down my house. My career, my family, my whole life as I knew it—it's all gone." She stepped in front of him to make sure he saw her own tears, as well as the fury in her eyes. "Do you get what I'm saying? You're not the only one suffering here. You aren't the only one in pain." She let go of some of her anger, in the hope of reaching him with a gentler tone. "I know what it's like to want to just lie down and die. To pretend it'll all go away if you just give in. But it won't. We're at war, Cade. People are counting on us. On you and me. We don't have time right now to fall apart." She offered him a faltering smile. "So let's go back to shore, get dry, and figure out our next move."

His eyes remained downcast as he considered her offer. He looked weary. More than just bruised and worse for wear. As twilight turned to shadow, Cade Martin looked humbled.

"How are we supposed to fight something this big?"

"As long as you watch my back, I'll watch yours. Agreed?"

There was disbelief in his voice. "We're watching each other's backs?" He let slip a rueful laugh. "Twenty years ago we'd have put knives into them."

"And we might yet." She dismissed the idea with a tilt of her head. "But that's a problem for tomorrow. So . . . are you with me or not?"

He gave in with a nod, and together they started the long walk to shore.

She threw him a sly sidelong look. "Your balls shrink and retract yet?"

"I think they're hiding behind my spleen."

"Serves you right. Oh, and the next time you decide to take leave of your senses? Have the courtesy to do it on dry land."

Flanked by rows of towering angels carved from white marble, the monks of Monte Paterno huddled in the middle of the Ponte Sant'Angelo. Tourist traffic on the footbridge over the River Tiber steered a wide berth around the tight cluster of barefoot, cassock-garbed Catholic ascetics, who spoke in the kind of cautious whispers reserved for confessionals and conspiracies.

Luis stood in the center of the group and absorbed the bad news being delivered by Father D'Odorico, who was holding court to his left. "There was nothing I could say to make Cardinal Lombardi see reason," the director said. "He would rather lose the war than let us defend ourselves. At this point, I'd wager the enemy could present itself on his doorstep, confess its crimes, and he would still refuse to act." Grim nods of agreement surrounded him.

"What now, then?" asked Father Hakkila, the only member of the group who seemed not to mind the cold wind gusting off the river and whistling through trees stripped bare by the coming winter. "If the Church won't support us, should we just surrender?"

"His Eminence would prefer to see us in exile, hidden away and silenced. He has arranged lodging for us with the monks of Monte Albano."

A feeling that resembled hope kindled inside Luis. "That might serve us better than he thinks. Monte Albano used to be a sanctuary of the Pauline Art, as Monte Paterno was."

The director seemed dubious. "That was more than fifty years ago, Luis. The last brother of Monte Albano who knew anything of the Art is probably long gone."

"True. But the physical spaces of Monte Albano might yet serve our needs. I'd wager the conjuring room, though no doubt converted to some mundane purpose, is still there."

Father Pantelis opened his eyes wide with surprise, giving his strangely round face and head a comical affect. "Are you proposing we practice magick inside Monte Albano?"

Murmurs of dissent traveled among the monks. Father Malko eyed Luis. "Our hosts will not consent to that."

"Forgiveness is granted more readily than permission, which is why we won't be asking." Luis raised his voice just enough to cut through the whispered side-talk in the huddle. "I won't force anyone to join my experiment at Monte Albano. But I fear I've been away from my own sanctuary for too long, and my friends may be in danger without me." To the director he added, "And I worry the longer I stay, the greater the risk I pose to all of you. Once I've left, it'll be up to you to persuade the monks of Monte Albano to reinforce their own defenses. We can't afford to let the enemy catch us unprepared again."

"I agree," said Father D'Odorico. "Which is why I plan to go with you." His declaration focused the group's attention upon his next words. "As I told the cardinal, we're at war. He and the Church refuse to accept it, but those of us gathered here don't have that luxury." He took Luis's hand in a strong grip. "You risked your life to save all of ours. I, for one, won't forget it." Still grasping Luis's hand, Father D'Odorico kneeled in front of him. "Your fight is my fight."

The other monks in the circle emulated the director's example—just a few of them at first, and then the entire group, until Luis was the last one left standing, encircled by a dozen monks young and old looking up at him like disciples.

"Please, Brothers," Luis said, as much out of humility as from a desire not to attract attention from passersby on the bridge, "rise and stand with me as friends and equals." When all the monks were once more on their feet, he continued. "Tonight we'll travel to Monte Albano. In the name of discretion, I'll employ an alias when we make our introductions."

"We'll call you Father Domenico," said Father D'Odorico. "After my late mentor."

"*Muito bom.*" To the rest of the group, Luis added, "Tonight, after the monks of Albano retire, we'll find the old conjuring room and conduct the necessary rituals to facilitate tomorrow's journey to my lodge on the far side of the world. And from there"—he paused for breath and for dramatic effect—"we shall ready ourselves to make war."

18

"My web of the enemy's conspiracy is complete. At least, as finished as it can be with the evidence in hand." Briet regarded the bewildered expressions of Cade, Anja, and their adepts. "The trick now, apparently, will be explaining it so all of you can understand it."

Her guests sat in a circle at her feet. They looked up at her hundreds of crisscrossed pieces of colored yarn, which linked documents, names, and photos on the walls and ceiling of the lodge's main room. Cade looked amazed by her creation; Barış, Anja, and Sathit vacillated between confusion and suspicion. Yasmin played stabberscotch on the floor with a knife.

Briet pivoted in a tight circle so as not to tread accidentally upon her audience or disturb the three-dimensional web of relationships she had obsessively midwifed into being. "The papers Anja took from the ammo factory filled in a lot of gaps. Not all of them. But we definitely know more now than we did this morning." She pointed at parts of the outer periphery of her creation. "I've identified several holding companies that are public-facing. Behind them, I've uncovered a number of shell corporations, limited liability partnerships, and other types of corporate entities that are used to move money around and conceal its source."

Sathit asked, "Why do they do that?"

Barış answered, "Mainly, to avoid taxation." He noted everyone's curious looks in his direction. "My principal vocation is in banking. I see this sort of thing all the time."

Briet nodded, and then she pointed at other parts of her web's outermost ring. "He's right. It's also done to take the profits from criminal enterprises and make them look like legal income, whether taxed or not." She pointed some out, one by one. "Guns. Drugs. Slaves. Blackmail. Stolen goods. Each of these represents a huge source of profit for the criminal underworld. But if they spend their riches too lavishly, the government asks where the cash came from. And therein lies the criminals' greatest problem: laundering their dirty money."

Yasmin pointed her knife at the next ring of the web. "What happens then?"

"The shell game." Briet noted a lack of comprehension by Sathit and Yasmin. "Have you ever seen a magician use three cups to make an audience guess which one hides a ball or marble? Or seen a street hustler shuffle three cards and make someone guess which is the queen?" She was encouraged by their nods of asset. "That's what this is. Money earned from criminal activity gets deposited into the accounts of dummy companies with no clear owners. Then it gets moved from one offshore account to another. The money is used to buy bearer bonds and securities. Those get sold to shell companies, which resell them and then disburse the cash to front men and agents, who deposit the cash into nonprofit entities, charities, and other tax-exempt foundations. Then it gets moved into a trust."

A cocked eyebrow from Yasmin. "And that's what, exactly?"

"When a third party holds assets on behalf of a beneficiary," Barış said, stepping on Briet's explanation. "In most cases, the beneficiary is another shell company—often two or three steps removed from the person who actually controls the money."

"Is that it?" asked Sathit. "Then the money's clean?"

Briet shook her head. "Not quite." She pointed at the innermost rings of the web. "The laundered cash is used to buy high-value assets. Mostly real estate, but also stock in legitimate corporations, and sometimes commodities such as oil, gold, or other precious metals. It can also be invested in new clean businesses." Looking up at her web, she added, "At this scale, it's sometimes used to create new offshore banks with mysteriously large cash reserves in spite of having no publicly acknowledged clients. These tend to crop up in countries with strict financial privacy laws, such as Switzerland, Cyprus, or the Cayman Islands."

"Great," Cade said. "Do the pieces of your web have any banks in common?"

"A few. But at the center of the web, most of the activity moves through a single bank in Geneva."

Cade studied the web. "Then that's where we'll find out who he really is."

Sathit sounded horrified. "You cannot be serious."

Barış's eyes opened wide. "Tell us you aren't suggesting a heist on a Swiss bank."

Cade shrugged as if he had no choice in the matter. "If that's where the intel is—"

"Then that is where it stays," Anja cut in. "Swiss banks have lethal magick defenses. We would not survive the attempt."

"The Swiss use deadly magick only on their *vaults*," Cade said. "We aren't after their cash. We just need a look at their client records." He eyed Barış. "Banks don't tend to keep that kind of information in their vaults, do they?"

Barış cocked an eyebrow and frowned. "Not in my experience, no."

Briet looked displeased. "Even so, the enemy has been ahead of us at every stage. They came to your house on Naxos with overwhelming force. They had a golem waiting for me in case I returned home. They anticipated our move on the ammo factory. And I'm betting they already know we made it out of there with a fair bit of paperwork." She glanced at her web. "Which means they might know what we've learned. If I were them, I'd be regrouping, setting a trap in that Geneva bank. And the moment we blunder into it"—she clapped her hands loudly, startling the group—"I'd crush us like bugs."

Yasmin nodded in anxious agreement. "That's right. Every fight we've had with these guys has happened on their terms. At times and places of their choosing."

Cade shook his head. "It might seem that way, but our enemies aren't tactical geniuses. They just have deeper resources than we do."

Anja leaned forward. "Explain."

"It's like a game of roulette, and we're the ball. For the enemy to win, it has to know where we'll land before we do. But if you're a billionaire with a global empire, you don't have to gamble—you just cover every possible bet. To us, it looks like these assholes are always a step ahead. But the fact is, they just have enough money and people to cover all their open targets at the same time."

Anja's eyes roamed the colorful web of collusion. "A rigged game. Typical."

"Just once," Cade said, "I wanna play offense instead of defense. I wanna catch these assholes off balance." He shot a hopeful look at Barış. "With the intel we have in hand, if we can get inside that bank—"

"Lloyds Bank," Briet offered.

Cade continued to Barış, "Could we identify the owner of the account number behind the ammo factory?"

"Yes," Barış said. "But it will not be easy. Swiss banks guard the privacy of their clients with a passion. Perhaps not as jealously as they defend their gold, but close."

Before Cade could continue, Anja frowned in disapproval. "Most Swiss banks are warded against the use of magick inside their premises. Most will know if you have yoked spirits from the moment you cross their threshold. So what is your plan if you get inside?"

A shrug from Cade. "We'll do it the old-fashioned way. Smoke and mirrors."

"Misdirection?" Yasmin said. "That's all we have against a Swiss bank?"

"It should be all we need. Barış, once you're inside, how long would it take you to dig up the client file?"

Barış pondered that. "Depends on their security. But if I can get a few minutes of unobserved access to their files, that should do it. In and out, no trouble."

Cade smiled. "Call me crazy, but that sounds like a plan. Pack your bags, kids: We're going to Geneva . . . to pull the weirdest bank job in history."

⁘

Outside the wall of windows, snowflakes did mad dances in the moonlight, prisoners of a howling wind. Inside, the Old Man sat cloaked in his own wrath as he confronted his chief karcist. "Last night you told me they were dead. What are you telling me now?"

Shame flushed Niccolò's face with warmth. "We watched the factory burn, *signore.* Hatunde and I." He felt the Old Man's contempt from across the desk. It stirred a profound discomfort within him. "No one came out, we were sure of it."

The Old Man lifted a thin file from his desk. "And yet"—he let the manila folder drop—"when firefighters searched the building and dredged the river this morning, they found no bodies. Not a single one." He drummed his fingertips on the desktop. "What conclusion should I draw from this troubling absence of evidence, Mr. Falco?"

There was no point in lying to the Old Man. All Niccolò could do was confront the truth and swallow it like a bitter pill. "Clearly, the enemy escaped our trap."

"*Your* trap." The Old Man's emphasis clearly was meant as a rebuke. "The one you designed. Whose bread crumbs you so carefully set out for Martin and the others to find, and which you promised would lead them to their doom."

Niccolò hung his head, less out of embarrassment than out of a desire to avoid provoking the Old Man's temper with eye contact. "*Sì, signore.*"

The Old Man rotated his chair away from Niccolò. He faced the wall of windows behind his desk and looked out on the wooded alpine slopes beyond the chalet. He rested his hands upon his chest. "Perhaps it's time I gave Hatunde or Tujiro a chance to prove themselves as my chief karcist."

"No, you will not," Niccolò said, with perhaps a bit too much confidence.

The Old Man barely turned; he swiveled just enough to catch Niccolò on the edge of his vision. "Really? Why won't I?"

"Because neither of them is capable of syncretizing my research with Martin's, and then fusing that knowledge with the arcana of the Iron Codex. If you want the kind of power that comes from breaking the rules of Hell itself, you are going to need *me*."

Niccolò caught the hint of a smirk on the Old Man's face as the ancient tycoon turned away once more. "That would be a far more compelling argument if you had acquired either the Iron Codex or Mr. Martin's new research. But as you so far have neither—"

"I *will* find them. I promise."

"So you've said. But empires are built on deeds, Mr. Falco, not promises."

He had to win back the Old Man's trust. "*Signore,* I know that Martin and his friends could be just about anywhere on earth. But I think we could narrow the search by—"

"Never mind that," the Old Man said, cutting off Niccolò's plan for self-redemption. "If Martin and his allies have gone to ground, it could take years to find them. And while they lie low, they'll be studying the records they stole from the factory."

"Records, *signore*?"

"The factory's safe was fireproofed. Its contents were pretty much all that survived that blaze. And based on a list of which files were missing, we have a good idea of what Cade's people learned."

Niccolò felt a sickening twist in his gut, the dread he had missed something vital, some detail for which the Old Man was about to make him pay in dearest blood. "What did they take?"

"Financial records. Indecipherable to most people—but, as we've learned, Cade and his ilk are not 'most people.'" With a push off one foot, the Old Man set his chair into a slow turn. He halted it when he once again faced Niccolò. "I'm concerned they might have obtained banking information that could compromise my privacy, and therefore my security. Specifically, records that link my account at Lloyds' Geneva branch to the factory."

"I understand. What should I do to fix this?"

"At the very least, we need to close the account. But that will mean extracting my rather sizable holdings from their vault. Including—"

"I am aware of what you keep in their vault, *signore.*"

"Then you understand why I can't risk letting it be captured by the enemy. I want you and Tujiro to take some of our hired guns. Go to Geneva. Get my gold, my cash, and the artifact. Put the money in a private armored truck and move it to the main Credit Suisse office in Zurich. I'll have a new account set up by the time you arrive, under a suitable *nom de travail.* As for the artifact: I want that returned to me here. We'll store it in my personal vault from now on."

"Of course. Though it will take a day to acquire the truck and plan a safe route—"

"Yes, yes, get it done. My lawyers in Geneva have signed letters on file for this occasion. I'll have them contact Lloyds Bank so that everything is arranged for Wednesday morning."

"Very good, *signore.*" Niccolò backed out of the Old Man's office, grateful both for clear marching orders and an excuse to put some distance between himself and his patron. As humbling as it might be to find himself engaged in a mop-up job after a glaring failure, it was far preferable to remaining at the chalet and suffering regular torrents of ice-cold scorn.

He was almost out of the room, pulling its double doors closed in front of him, when the Old Man's voice cut once more through the empty chalet's eerie hush.

"Just in case I wasn't clear, Mr. Falco? If, by some cruel turn of Fate, you return to me *without* my artifact . . . you had best come ready to tender your *resignation.*"

19

An icy breeze off the Rhône sent a chill up Anja's back and left her teeth chattering. She flipped up her coat's collar to protect the back of her neck, and then she resumed holding her paper cup of café au lait with both hands to keep them warm. The unseasonable cold of this late-autumn morning in Geneva reminded Anja of Russian winters from her youth.

Cade stood beside her, leaning against a waist-height wrought-iron railing. He smoked a cigarette as he looked east, past the Pont de la Machine and the Île Rousseau. Even behind his sunglasses he had to squint as he confronted the sun, which burned bright in a sky as clear and blue as the alpine waters of Lac Léman beneath it.

From the west, Briet approached the couple. She strolled at a languid pace along the Quai Bezanson-Hugues, a promenade barely three meters wide on the Rhône's left bank. Her gloved hands were stuffed deep inside the pockets of her dove-gray trench coat, and the heels of her boots snapped out a crisp rhythm on the cobblestone walkway. Like Cade, she had donned sunglasses, though the lenses of hers were much larger. She also had pulled her coppery hair into a compact beehive—a feat far beyond the patience of Anja, who had tucked her loose mane of black hair inside her coat to keep the wind from whipping it into her face.

A meter shy of Anja and Cade, Briet stopped and mirrored Cade's pose against the railing. Once she had settled into place, Yasmin, Barış, and Sathit emerged from the *rive gauche* café a few paces up the quai, and moved in the trio's direction. Barış settled into a chair at the last of the café's outdoor tables and flipped open that morning's edition of *Tribune de Genève*, a local French-language newspaper. A few paces from him, Sathit and Yasmin set themselves in front of Cade and Anja, took turns lighting each other's Gauloises, and then turned their backs on the sun.

Anja looked west, toward their target at the end of the quai: the Geneva office of Lloyds Bank, at Place de Bel-Air. Then she said to her compatriots, "What did we find?"

Yasmin spoke first. "At least two armed guards in the main lobby at all times."

Sathit added, "All doors leading out of the lobby look reinforced. And there is no direct customer access to the upper floors, or to the basement vault."

A frown darkened Briet's features. "It's a fortress. Steel bars set in concrete on all the ground-floor windows. And that's nothing compared to the magickal defenses inside."

Her comment drew Cade's attention. "How strong are the wards?"

Briet shook her head. "Not that simple. The bank isn't set up to bar entry to people with yoked spirits. I was able to walk inside without a problem. But there's no using yoked talents once you're inside. Using magick in there is like trying to strike a match underwater."

Cade flicked the stub of his Lucky into the river. "That's promising, actually. A setup like that means the bank is probably set up to hold magickal artifacts."

Concerned, Anja narrowed her stare at Cade. "I thought we came for information."

"We did, but the fact we can do this job without having to shed our yoked spirits is a definite plus. We just need to be careful while we're inside."

Still pretending to read the day's news, Barış said from behind his broadsheet, "That is for the best. Showing off talents such as ours in public would not serve our need for discretion."

That earned a nod from Anja. "Correct."

Cade seemed not to share her conviction. "Though it would be nice to have options." He clocked her reproachful side-eye. "But yeah—let's all play this as straight as possible."

Sathit took a long drag off her cigarette. Smoke spilled from her mouth as she spoke. "So, we've cased the bank. What's our next step?"

All eyes turned to Anja. She sipped her coffee. "We need to know more about the people who run it. The top-floor executives."

Her instructions drew an incredulous response from Yasmin. "And how are we supposed to know which ones they are? One old Swiss guy in a suit looks pretty much like another."

"Because while the rest of you scouted *inside* the bank, I had a few of my feathered friends perch outside its fifth-floor windows. I will point out the boss men. The rest of you will follow them. Learn their names. Go where they live. Get me details about their families."

A sly smile tugged at Briet's lips. "Is extortion part of the plan now?"

Anja scowled at Briet. "Until we know more, there *is* no plan." She moderated her tone to avoid provoking her ally of necessity. "Get me facts. I will make a plan to fit them."

Cade reached into a pocket of his gray wool longcoat, pulled out a thick roll of Swiss francs, and started doling out cash to Briet, Sathit, and Yasmin. "You three have been seen by the bank's guards, so you should all buy wigs and new outfits before tomorrow's job." He sized up Barış, peeled several more bills off his roll, and pressed them into Barış's hand. "You need to stay out of sight today and look sharp tomorrow."

"Why? Anja said there is no plan."

"There's a germ of a plan." Cade waved off further questions by Barış and the others. "We're still working out the details, but I wouldn't have brought us here if I didn't have some idea for how to get what we need." He returned his full attention to Barış. "Do you trust me?"

"Of course, Master."

"Good. Listen up, these are your instructions for today: Get your hair cut by the best barber in Geneva. Then, find a tailor who can make a bespoke suit by tomorrow morning and pay him double whatever he asks to make you look like you fucking *own* the Lloyds Bank. Then buy yourself a new briefcase, a new pair of shoes, and some silk socks. And a new hat. And while you're at it, find a printer who can make you some fake business cards and the sharpest-looking résumé in the history of curricula vitae."

Barış stood, folded his newspaper, and tucked it under his arm. "I dread to ask for what role you are having me prepare."

Cade grinned. "Oh, it's a *classic*."

Before Barış could ask, Anja spelled it out for him:

"You will be a Trojan horse."

———

Nothing, in Cade's experience, ever unlocked a tendency toward excess with quite the same ferocity as the certainty that one's death was imminent. That was the only explanation he could imagine for Anja's decision to house them and their band of magickal malcontents in a top-floor suite in the Hotel des Bergues, the oldest and most luxurious hotel in Geneva. Located on the shore of Lac Léman near the egress point of the Rhône, the nineteenth-century Victorian building had the best views, softest beds, and finest food in the city. And every indulgence it offered cost nothing less than a king's ransom.

Of course, that hadn't stopped the adepts—to say nothing of Briet and Anja—from ordering damned near every item on the room-service menu. The debris of their grand repast littered the table in the suite's dining room. Plates crowded with gutted lobster shells left in pools of *jus* spilled from rare beef filets surrounded half-emptied bowls of vegetables and one of potatoes au gratin. Empty bottles of wine—including a few drawn from the best vintages in the hotel's well-stocked cellar—perched on windowsills in every direction Cade looked. Trails of powdered confectioner's sugar led away from a tray that had arrived stacked with fresh pastries and now lay bare atop an end table.

Cade suppressed a smile as he shook his head. *If I didn't know we were skipping out on the bill tomorrow morning after the heist, I'd think this was our last supper.*

The others had left the dining area and gathered in the suite's spacious main room. Briet had set herself up in the largest armchair, a red upholstered number with a high back. Legs crossed and chin lifted, she projected a haughty air. The others seemed to pay her no mind.

Barış, Sathit, and Yasmin occupied the long sofa. Barış, whose new haircut flattered his lean face, poked at a dessert pastry with a small fork. As always, he was the only one in the group who had not spilled any of his meal on himself. His dark brown suit, white dress shirt, and red bow tie all remained immaculate. Sathit nursed her night's third cup of French roast, while Yasmin sank into the far corner, holding a deep pour of dark purple cabernet in a wide-bodied glass in her left hand and balancing a slender dagger on the tip of her right index finger.

All of them watched Anja. She busied herself laying out the elements of the next day's scheme in neat clusters on the floor in front of them. Sathit had penned a diagram of the bank's interior on a bed linen, and around it Anja created a diorama of the surrounding streets, the tram bridge outside the bank's entrance at Place de Bel-Air, and, to its north, the Rhône.

Around these she set down scribbled notes and blurry black-and-white photos—all of them taken that day, and then developed and printed with great speed thanks to a very generous bribe to a local professional photographer with his own darkroom. The photos showed the bank's senior executives, whom Anja had identified thanks to a few avian spies.

Cade leaned against the wall opposite the sofa and lit a Lucky.

Anja looked up at him. "Ready?"

"You start."

She swept a spill of her black hair behind one ear. "It is almost all bad news."

Briet rolled her eyes. "What else is new?" Noting everyone's dirty looks in her direction, she refused to relent. "As if you weren't all thinking it."

Exhaling as he spoke, Cade stepped forward. "It's worse than you think. There's no way we can beat the bank's wards against magick use on the premises. Plus, we dug into the bank's top men and found out *none* of them are vulnerable to blackmail."

Disgust curled Anja's mouth into a frown. "I have never seen bank executives so honest."

Cade took another drag off his Lucky. "At any rate, since none of us knows shit about robbing banks"—he paused to see if anyone wanted to contradict him, but got only silence—"and because hiring a team of pros to do this for us would take months and cost millions of dollars we don't have, we're going to proceed as Anja and I suspected we would from the start: with a high-speed short con."

Yasmin downed half her wine in a long tilt and then sleeved her lips dry, all without disturbing the dagger perched on her fingertip. "I knew I should have poured whiskey. What are you getting us into now?"

Anja stood. "Barış, you will enter the bank and say you have an appointment with its president. Tell them you are there to fill an open vice presidency."

Sathit arched one slender eyebrow. "Does the bank *have* an open vice presidency?"

"*Da.* There is an empty office for a senior vice president on its fifth floor."

Barış squirmed, if just a little. "What if it's already promised to someone else?"

"Then this'll cause anger and controversy," Cade said. "Both work in our favor." He looked at Yasmin. "You'll watch my back inside the bank." A nod at Sathit. "You'll stand lookout near the entrance. Watch me and Anja. If we need you to do something, we'll cue you."

Before Barış could protest, Anja continued. "Barış, bluff your way up-stairs, to the executive suites. On your way, break a ballpoint pen inside your pocket. Let the ink dirty your fingers. Use that as a reason to stop and use a washroom before you meet the boss."

Wide-eyed, Barış asked with obvious alarm, "Then what?"

Cade smiled. "Ninety seconds after you go upstairs, I'll start a small fire in the lobby and pull the alarm, triggering an evacuation. When you hear the alarm, hide inside a toilet stall." To Yasmin and Sathit he added, "We'll walk out with the employees and other civilians."

Anja picked up the narrative. "Barış, once the upper floors are clear, locate the depositor records. Find the one that matches the enemy's account number and get us all the information you can about the person behind it. Name, address, holdings, business partners. We need it all."

"Understood."

Sathit shifted her gaze between Anja and Briet. "And what will you two be doing?"

"I am escape," Anja said. She gestured toward Briet. "She is defense."

Yasmin flicked her wrist—and bull's-eyed the bank's first-floor schematic with her dagger. "Care to elaborate?"

Cade resisted the impulse to flick his Lucky into Yasmin's lap. "Anja's gonna be ready to water-jaunt us out of Geneva as soon as we have the records. We'll meet on the tram bridge and jump as a group into the Rhône. Once we're in the water, Anja will take us back to Arthurs Lake in Tasmania."

Barış asked Briet directly, "And what 'defense' will you be providing?"

"I'll tangle all the vehicle and pedestrian traffic between Lloyds Bank and the fire brigade on Rue du Bains, the municipal police on Rue du Stand, and the cantonal police on Rue de Berne, across the river." She shot a dubious look at Barış. "Assuming you can find the records and get out of the bank in under five minutes, we should all be back in Taz before the local authorities even reach the scene."

"Even with Briet running interference," Cade added, "local police on pa-trol might get there faster, so when you leave the building, don't use the front door on Place de Bel-Air. Slip out the side door onto Rue du Rhône." Ad-dressing the rest of the group, he asked, "You all have your new outfits and wigs for tomorrow, right?" He was answered with weary nods from one and all. "Okay, then. Any questions?" No one met his stare. "Let's call it a night, then."

Everyone stood to leave. Barış paused and turned toward Cade. "Do you really think we can do this?"

"I think our chances are as good as they've ever been."

Barış frowned. "So you think we're doomed."

Cade took a final drag off his Lucky and then snuffed it on one of the dinner plates. "Maybe. I was trying to be nice."

"That scares me even more."

"Try to get some sleep. First thing tomorrow—we've got a bank to rob."

WEDNESDAY, NOVEMBER 27

Whiskey frothed with backwash sloshed in the bottom of the Jameson's bottle as Cade passed it to Anja, who handed him his still-smoldering vintage opium pipe. They had been going back and forth for the better part of an hour, neither of them able to sleep on the eve of such a risky scheme as their ill-conceived assault on the Lloyds Bank. Seated in front of an open window, they reveled in the exquisite contrast of sweet warm smoke and crisp night air.

Few things in Cade's life had ever deserved to be considered "religious experiences." In the years since his discovery of the Mystery of the Dead God, and the realization the entire universe was nothing more than the infinitely expanding remains of God, who had committed self-sacrifice to bring about the creation of the cosmos, true moments of spiritual epiphany had become even rarer still. But there was one corporeal manifestation of the Divine upon which he could always rely, and in which he could forever invest his faith: the opium poppy.

Half drunk as Cade was, the hardest thing about smoking opium was keeping the bowl of his pipe steady above the glass chimney of a small lamp burning coconut oil. Precision mattered here. The goal was to soften the *chandoo,* or purified opium, but not to burn it. As it lingered in its semi-liquefied state it released its precious vapors, filling the air with the scent of roasting hazelnut—but only so long as one maintained a strong inhalation on the pipe's mouthpiece.

Every pull on the century-old Chinese pipe—which was as long as Cade's forearm, a cylinder of bamboo with a damper saddle of silver and a bowl of red terra-cotta—filled his lungs with the drug's numinous breath. Reeling in a haze of its floral perfume, he reflected on the long, strange union of opium and humanity, a marriage that stretched back for millennia, perhaps longer.

Holding the transformative mist in his chest, he imagined Adam receiving the kiss of life from JEHOVAH—and awakening to the smell of opium on the lips of the Almighty.

It was a joy to smoke. To taste the wind of Paradise. To revel in God's own medicine. No better friend could any battle karcist have than a well-crafted opium pipe, a generous supply of quality opium and jasmine joss sticks, and a safe place in which to indulge. Properly engaged, it could erase the cares of the day and the worries of a lifetime in less than an hour, leaving nothing but the relaxing splendor of recumbent intoxicated bliss.

Unlike refined morphine or heroin, which beckoned the desperate with promises of oblivion, classic opium offered an experience of ethereality, an invitation to visit an otherwise inaccessible realm of dreams and delusions. It tantalized the jaded with the possibility of real transcendence and a slow drift into serenity, not just self-erasure and a swift plunge into the void.

So soft and gentle was the smoke. The only word that did it justice was "ambrosia."

Sooner or later, alas, either he or Anja would ruin the moment by speaking.

It was her turn this time. "You really think they can do this?"

He exhaled smoke and feigned ignorance. "Can who do what?"

"Don't play stupid. The adepts. The bank." She took a swig of whiskey. A bit dribbled down her chin. She palmed it away with a clumsy swipe, and her eyelids drooped almost shut. Then she drew a deep sharp breath, her nostrils flaring as her eyes opened wide, and she poked Cade's shoulder. "They could be hurt. Jailed. Killed."

"They won't be." Cade spoke with a confidence he didn't feel. "We'll keep them safe. We have to." He offered Anja the pipe, and she took it, handing him the whiskey in return.

Her hands were steady as she conjured a narrow flame from one of her fingertips. The lick of green fire danced beneath the terra-cotta bowl. The opium smoldered, rich and fragrant.

Cade took a pull of the Jameson's. Savored its burn in the back of his throat. Then he leaned against his side of the window's frame and watched vapors snake from Anja's nostrils for half a second before she exhaled in earnest, cloaking herself in a pale narcotic fog.

She let the pipe come to rest in her lap. "How many have died for us? For our mistakes?"

Such a simple question, but it conjured up complex feelings. Cade looked out at the moonlight shimmering on the lake. "I stopped counting a long time ago."

Anja absentmindedly touched the scar on her left cheek. "We need to remember."

"We need to keep living." Cade set down the whiskey between them. "If we owe the dead anything, it's to finish what they started." He picked up the opium pipe. "To carry on."

She nodded while watching him smoke. "Yes, we keep fighting. But we must not be careless. We have lost enough already."

"Agreed." Cade inhaled from the pipe. The smoke tasted like an English garden blended with toasted nuts and tropical sunlight. Holding it inside his lungs, he felt its heat suffuse his flesh and burn away his cares. Then he exhaled and felt purged of sorrow, if only for a moment. He looked up at Anja. "Too many lives have been lost because of me. Lost to a war I don't want to fight. But I don't get to make that choice. Neither of us does."

Anja drank some more Jameson's, and then she cradled the bottle against her chest. "Do we really need to use Yasmin? Or Sathit? Why not let them sit this out?"

It was a ludicrous proposition. "If we try to shut them out, they'll force their way in. And fuck only knows what they'll do if left on their own." Cade shook his head. "No. We gotta keep 'em where we can see them, and where Briet can *protect* them."

Anja tensed at the mention of Briet's name. "Tell me again why we trust her."

"Because we don't have any choice."

"She used to serve the Nazis, and until a few days ago she served the Americans. And what do those two have in common?"

Raised eyebrows from Cade. "More than you'd expect."

"They both want us dead."

"Well, they can take a number and get in line." He passed the pipe to Anja. "Look, I know Briet's not your favorite. But she's not a monster. Remember Shemya? And Bikini Atoll? We never would've beaten Kein and his goons if not for her. She stood with us when it really mattered. Now, if you still hate her anyway? Fine. You don't have to *like* your allies. You just need to know that when shit goes down, they'll be shooting at the same enemy as you."

"Then I guess we need to break into that bank and find out who our enemy *is*."

"Best plan I've heard all week."

Anja set aside the pipe. "If you like *that* plan"—she held his hand and led him away from the window, toward their bed—"you will *love* this one."

She pulled him on top of her, and they tumbled into the sheets, laughing like teenagers.

An hour later, Cade lay on the edge of slumber, with Anja asleep on top of his right arm. He studied the graceful lines of her face, limned in moonlight. He noted the flutter of her eyes beneath their lids. *She must be dreaming.* He exhaled a deep breath. Tried to let himself sink into oblivion. Anja stirred and rolled onto her side, freeing his arm. Cade propped himself up, kissed the slope between her shoulder and her neck, and whispered to her in the dark: "Love you."

He didn't suspect for even a moment that he would never get to say those words to her again.

21

The salesperson at the boutique had insisted to Yasmin that the current fashion—especially for athletically toned young women such as herself—favored tighter skirts and close-cut jackets. She couldn't deny the suit and its matching calf-high red leather boots looked good on her. She just wished the ensemble had afforded her more places to conceal her arsenal of knives. In the name of "not ruining the line" of her outfit, she had been forced to embark upon this hastily conceived bank scam with only four blades on her person instead of her usual nine.

It will just have to do.

Briet had been the first one out of the suite that morning, because she had the most work to do, setting up magickal traffic snares at multiple locations around the center of the city. The rest of the team had convened at 9:25 on the tram bridge over the Rhône. It linked Place de Bel-Air and Quai de l'Île, a promenade on the south bank of a sliver-thin river islet piled high with towers of stone, steel, glass, and brick.

It was a beautiful morning, just after nine thirty. A cool breeze nearly stole the crimson beret from atop Yasmin's blond wig. She held both in place and squinted into the glare of a blue sky reflected in Lac Léman. Smartly dressed people hurried past her. Thousands filled Geneva's pristine sidewalks, rode its trams with their faces hidden behind morning newspapers, or lingered in its cafés. From somewhere nearby echoed an accordion's rustic waltzing tune.

Cade walked with Yasmin toward the bank. Clean-shaven and dressed in a charcoal three-piece suit, he looked like he might really be worth a million dollars.

Sathit had deployed ahead of them. Dressed like a socialite with more money than sense, she had set herself up in front of a leather shop across Rue du Rhône from the bank entrance.

Yasmin nudged Cade and gestured toward Sathit. "She calls that window-shopping?"

Her mentor stifled a chortle. "No shit. She looks ready to burn the place down."

"Remind me to teach her to play poker. She'll be terrible at it."

Cade opened the bank's door and stepped aside to let Yasmin pass. "After you, miss."

She answered his courtesy with a nod. "*Merci.*" A quick look over her shoulder confirmed Anja was still in position on the tram bridge. Then Yasmin entered the bank.

As soon as she passed its threshold she sensed the difference. It felt as if her yoked spirits had been wrapped in a robe of lead and throttled with choking collars. They had not been forced out of her, but they were contained. Scouting the bank the previous day she had misinterpreted those sensations as anxiety. Now she knew they were a warning: Whatever magickal talents she harbored would be suppressed for as long as she remained inside the bank.

Cade tried to conceal his discomfort, but Yasmin noticed his grimace. He clearly disliked the bank's magick-damping wards as intensely as she did. Perhaps more, since he had become accustomed to traveling with a higher number of yoked spirits than she could handle.

They stuck to the plan and moved away from the entrance. Less than half a minute later they were on either side of a narrow courtesy table, which had been provided for customers who needed to complete paperwork prior to approaching the tellers at their barred windows.

Yasmin acclimated to the bank's wards by slowing her breathing, but across from her, Cade continued to wince. She made sure no one was close enough to eavesdrop before she whispered, "Master? Are you all right?"

"I'm fine."

She suspected he was lying, but this was not the time or place for a debate. She plucked a deposit slip from a stack inside a holding frame on the table and filled its spaces with gibberish and random numbers. "Maybe I should open an account while we're here."

"If you've got a spare million burning a hole in your pocket, go ahead."

The front door opened. Barış strode in, clothed in the sharpest-looking gray suit ever tailored in a single night. The wind that followed him through the door made his long black jacket flutter and rise dramatically behind him. His eyes were hidden behind an expensive pair of glasses whose silvered lenses seemed intended to echo his brushed-aluminum Zero Halliburton briefcase. On his head was a dark blue fez, and at his throat a matching blue bow tie.

From the other side of the courtesy table, Cade muttered to Yasmin, "Here we go."

Barış wasted no time seeking out a junior manager, a thirtyish man seated at a desk in the back corner, away from the commotion of the rest of the lobby. Affecting his most imperious stance and tenor, Barış loomed over the pasty, slender young executive. "Good morning. My name is Çelik Enver. I am here to meet with Mr. Wainwright."

Struck dumb with surprise, the junior man looked up at Barış, jaw agape. Like any good Briton would, he put on a blankly phony smile and did his best to imitate an apologetic tone. "Forgive me—what did you say your name was?"

"Enver. Çelik Enver. I'm the new senior vice president of investments for this branch."

The empty smile became a condescending smirk. "I'm afraid you must be mistaken, sir. That position is slated to be filled next week by a transfer from the home office."

Radiating anger, Barış replied, "I *am* the transfer from the home office!"

The junior man pressed his palms together as if entreating Barış for patience. "We were told the position was to be filled by Mr. Simpson from—"

"Change of plans." Barış planted his hands on the man's desk and leaned forward. "Simpson got caught with his hand in the till, if you take my meaning. Now you get to deal with *me*. Or didn't you receive Lord Braswell's telegram?" As if by reflex, Barış adjusted the orientation of the manager's stapler so that it rested parallel to the desk's edge.

His invocation of the bank's chairman had put a note of fear in the junior man's voice. "Lord Braswell sent you? I'm sorry, sir, but I didn't see that message, I had no idea, I—"

Barış slapped his supple leather gloves against one palm. "Enough! I have a degree in mathematics from Cambridge, a doctorate in economics from the Sorbonne, and ten years' experience managing this bank's Middle Eastern holdings. So why am I still talking to *you*?"

Called to action, the junior man stood and stretched out one arm toward a pair of doors with stained-glass windows on the back wall of the lobby. "Of course, Mr. Enver, sir. Please, follow me. I'll bring you upstairs to Mr. Wainwright's office, and we'll sort this all out."

"Very good." Barış gestured toward the fancy doors. "Lead the way."

The moment the manager wasn't looking, Barış neatened the papers in the middle of the man's desk. Yasmin struggled not to react. *Get your OCD under control, Barış.*

As the junior man led Barış through the rear doors, across a lobby, and into an elevator, Cade said under his breath to Yasmin, "Put ninety seconds on the clock."

She set down the table's chained pen and checked her watch.

Seconds later, several men emerged through the fancy doors from the elevator lobby. The bulges of holstered pistols under their suit coats caught Yasmin's eye. She recognized one of the men walking behind them as Niccolò, the magician who had nearly killed Cade, Anja, and Briet in the ammunition factory two nights earlier. On his left was a svelte Asian man in an elegant black suit, toting a briefcase chained to a steel cuff on his wrist. Behind them were two more armed guards, and bringing up the rear was another bank executive. They all paused at the rearmost teller's window so Niccolò could sign a stack of paperwork in triplicate.

Yasmin kept her voice to a whisper. "Keep your head down. We've got company."

Cade did as she'd said, and then he pivoted away from Niccolò and his cohort to watch their reflections in the barred windows behind him. Then he muttered, "Well, dip me in shit."

Yasmin reached slowly for her closest knife. "Cade? What the hell's going on?"

He turned back to face the enemy. And he smiled. "We just caught a break."

⌁

Not less than twenty seconds after Barış entered the bank, Anja knew something was about to go wrong. Her first clue was the armored van that pulled up outside the bank's front entrance, and the pair of armed men in dark suits who got out and opened its rear doors. There were no markings on the vehicle, which meant it was privately owned, and not affiliated with the bank. This was no routine pickup or delivery of cash. Something big was happening.

Across Rue du Rhône, Sathit abandoned her charade of window-shopping to eye the van, and then she looked at Anja for instructions. Anja made a V with her index and middle fingers, gestured at her eyes, and then pointed at the bank's front door. Sathit did her best to look calm and inconspicuous as she crossed the busy street. As she neared the bank's door, she reached inside her handbag. In front of the door she artfully fumbled her lipstick case and squatted to pick it up. Anja watched the van's guards; aside from scoping out Sathit's ass, neither seemed to pay her much attention. Seconds later Sathit was on her way, forgotten by the guards.

She hurried her pace as she reached the tram bridge. When she reached Anja, she sidled up to her and pretended to admire the river. "Four more suits with guns inside," she said in a quiet voice. "Plus your friend from the ammo factory and something magickal in a briefcase."

"What is Cade doing?"

"Not sure. But no sign of Barış. He must be upstairs."

Anja's mind raced, and her pulse quickened. "If the guards have magick-piercing bullets, this is not a fight we should choose."

Sathit shot a worried look at the van. "So what now? Bail?"

"You said there was something magickal inside a briefcase?" She clocked Sathit's nod of confirmation. "And Niccolò himself came to retrieve it?" Another quick nod.

What could be so important the Old Man would send his top karcist as a courier? That question nagged at Anja. Her instincts told her there had to be something precious in that case. Perhaps something as important to their fight against the Old Man as the identifying documents she had come here to steal. But there would be no using magick inside the bank, and her team hadn't come prepared to fight this many heavily armed men in the open.

Each passing second made Sathit more impatient. She seemed as if she were about to shake herself out of her skin. "What's the plan? Make a play for the case? Or cut and run?"

"It has to be Cade's call." Anja made a decision. "But he needs you in there now, either as backup or as a distraction. Go, hurry."

Sathit headed for the bank. If she had any doubts or fears about what she was doing, she hid them well. Anja had faith in Sathit's ability to read the situation and take appropriate action in the moment, and she trusted Cade to do the same.

If only there was some way for me to get word to Barış. She considered calling the bank and posing as someone from its London office, but she ruled that out. *I am no good with accents.* Next she thought of identifying herself as Barış's wife, until she remembered that he had gone to his interview not wearing a wedding ring. It was a small detail, but it was the sort of minutiae uptight British bankers might notice—and exactly the kind of slipup that could get Barış arrested or killed.

A stroke of luck: The van's guards ignored Sathit's return, mesmerized as they were by a lissome Nordic blonde approaching from the west side of Place de Bel-Air. As the men filled the morning air with shrill wolf whistles of objectifying appreciation, Sathit slipped inside the bank.

A troubling notion occurred to Anja. *I hope her disguise is enough to keep Niccolò from recognizing her. And that he hasn't noticed Cade or Yasmin.*

It was too late to fix that, now. She put it out of her mind and struggled to focus on how to reach Barış. She was weighing the risks of tying a message to a pigeon's leg, and using her innate gift for communicating with animals to send it to Barış inside the bank, when everything went to hell and the question became moot.

～～～

If ever there had been a moment when Cade lamented being unable to render himself invisible, this was it. He stood at the bank lobby's courtesy table, scribbling astrological symbols onto a series of deposit tickets while keeping his back turned to Niccolò and his cohort, who were embroiled in a polite but tense battle of wills with a junior bank manager just a few meters away.

"Please," implored the manager, "bear with me a moment longer, Mr. Falco. If you could just explain why the client is choosing to terminate his account, I—"

"What difference does it make? The decision is made." Niccolò's voice betrayed his mounting frustration. "I don't see the point of all this paperwork after the fact."

"There are protocols, Mr. Falco. They must be observed. Swiss banking laws are very clear about the need for accurate records."

"So you keep reminding me."

Across from Cade, Yasmin did her best to keep her eyes down and not draw attention while Niccolò's debate with the manager continued. She whispered to Cade, "What do we do?"

"Shh. Pretend you're Swiss and just mind your own business."

She frowned but obeyed, though Cade could see the muscles in her neck tensing. Yasmin was coiled like a spring, eager to strike if only he would give the word.

Cade checked his watch. Sixty seconds had passed since Barış went upstairs. Whatever he was going to do, he'd have to make up his mind in the next thirty seconds.

Meanwhile, at the manager's desk in the lobby's rear corner, Niccolò persevered in his losing battle against Swiss bureaucracy. "With all respect, Signor Keegan, my associates and I are on a tight schedule. Can't these questions wait?"

"I'm afraid not, sir. My superiors will insist on knowing why such a valuable client has chosen to close his account, especially when our security remains impregnable, and his rate of return has been most generous, even by our standards."

Niccolò pinched the bridge of his nose and closed his eyes, as if willing away a headache. "I assure you, *signore,* none of the perquisites of this account are in question."

"Then please help me understand why the client is—"

"I am not at liberty to explain my employer's business decisions—nor should you be questioning them. I am told Swiss banks respect their clients' privacy. Respect it now."

Abashed, the manager broke eye contact with Niccolò and sat down at his desk. "Very well, sir. Please forgive me." He shuffled through the stack of forms he had been holding. "One last detail remains to be set. If you would be kind enough to provide routing and account numbers for the transfer of your patron's funds, we can—"

"Wire transfer? There must be some mistake. My employer wants a cashier's check."

"For so great a sum? That's most irregular, sir."

"But necessary."

"I see." The manager ripped the form he was holding into careful thirds.

Verging on apoplexy, Niccolò demanded through clenched teeth, "What are you doing?"

"Wrong forms." The manager stood. "If you'll grant me just a few moments more of your time, I'll dispose of this and procure the correct documents to draw your check."

Niccolò, his fellow karcist, and their four armed guards stood in a tight huddle as the manager abandoned them. Grumbles of discontent filled their corner of the lobby, but for the moment they all kept their backs to the room—a fact for which Cade was grateful.

Yasmin sidled up to Cade. "What's the word? Go or no go?"

The pressure had him feeling his pulse in his temples. "I'm thinking."

"Sathit stole a look at us on a walk-by," Yasmin said.

"When?"

"Half a minute ago." Yasmin shot a look at the door. "What will Anja do?"

Cade shook his head. "No idea." He slipped his hand inside his jacket pocket and clutched his stainless-steel Zippo lighter. "If I set the fire as planned, Nico and his boys will bug out with the civilians, and we'll lose our shot at the case. But if we go for the case and blow it, Barış could get stuck upstairs, or we could get busted. Worse, innocent people might get hurt."

Yasmin lifted her coat sleeve to reveal her watch. "Time's up. Call it."

Cade had to make a choice, but he felt paralyzed. His ambition was at war with his conscience, his daring tempered by an excess of caution.

Movement at the bank's front door drew his eye. Sathit entered the lobby and paused to peel off her gloves, while standing within arm's reach of a fire alarm on the wall—and the uniformed security guard posted next to it. The pieces all were in position. All that remained now was for Cade to make his move. *I'm done gambling with other people's lives.*

He pulled out his lighter, lifted a deposit slip, and prepared to set it aflame.

Then he saw blurs of motion: Yasmin hurled two long-bladed knives with each hand. In a flash each of the four daggers struck one of Niccolò's four guards in the back of the neck. They all went limp, like puppets with cut strings.

As they collapsed, Yasmin pounced on the nearest two and stole the semi-automatic pistols from their hip holsters before their bodies hit the floor. Then she stood triumphantly over the dead, with her stolen pistols aimed at Niccolò and his Asian colleague.

She filled the lobby with her voice: "Everyone on the floor! This is a robbery!"

The bank guard near the entrance reached for his sidearm. Sathit punched him in the throat and shoved his weapon back into its holster. It discharged, and the bullet blew off the front of the man's shoe—and judging from the blood on the floor, a few of his toes.

Sathit slammed the bank guard's head against the wall, and then she pulled his pistol from its holster and joined Yasmin's impromptu hostage crisis. By the time the lobby's second uniformed guard came rushing back from his visit to the lavatory with his trousers only half buttoned and his belt still undone, Sathit had him covered. At her silent direction, he handed over his SIG Sauer P210 pistol to Cade, who accepted it with a polite nod.

Nodding in approval, Yasmin surveyed the scene with a manic gleam in her eye. "All right, listen up! Do as I say, and no one gets hurt. But if anybody tries to be a hero, I'll make sure every last fucking one of you leaves here with a bullet in your head."

Cade sighed and put away his lighter.

So much for the simple plan.

22

Everything was quiet for the first few minutes after Sathit went inside the bank. Then came the wails of sirens, and moments later Anja saw executives, whom she recognized from her previous day's scouting of the bank's upper floors, running from the building on Rue du Rhône, most likely having used the building's rear exit rather than go through the lobby.

Which meant whatever Cade and the others had done there was bad. Very bad.

The sirens grew louder and resounded in the man-made canyons of stone, steel, and glass. Anja felt her stomach tighten and tie itself in knots. A confrontation with armed police was the last thing she or Cade had wanted.

We were supposed to be gone by now. Anja strained to listen as smartly dressed men and women from the bank's offices hurried past her. Her fluency in Swiss German was rusty, but she understood enough of what she overheard to know the escapees were chattering about an armed robbery on the ground floor. *My plan called for a trash fire. It seems I got one.*

She scowled at the staggered arrivals of half a dozen police cars. Officers scrambled out of the vehicles, which had been parked spread out across Place de Bel-Air. Working in pairs they retrieved rifles and submachine guns from their cars' trunks, and then they used their cars for cover. Half a minute after they'd rolled up, they had the bank's front and back doors covered.

A crowd gathered. Gawkers, tragedy tourists hoping to catch a glimpse of some poor soul catching a bullet. At least, that's what Anja took them for. She found their curiosity morbid, their inclination to herd toward a possible exchange of gunfire as borderline suicidal.

Her mood darkened. *Right now I could say the same of Cade.*

Anja felt desperate for information, for any sign that Cade or one of the others had matters under control inside the bank while everything outside was going to pieces. But the curtains on the bank's windows remained drawn, and sunlight reflecting off the windows of the upper stories made it all but impossible to tell what was happening upstairs.

More vehicles topped with flashing lights arrived, choking the streets and plaza. Vans and trucks, from which leapt squads of men wearing black tactical uniforms and wielding an assortment of military-grade rifles and carbines. They charged inside two buildings on the opposite side of Rue du Rhône and one at the far end of Place de Bel-Air. The very sight of them deepened Anja's already sickening anxiety: in a matter of minutes, at least three Swiss police sniper teams would be in position around the bank.

Looking away didn't help her clear her mind. When she looked toward the river, she saw two police boats cruising toward the bank with their lights spinning and sirens keening—the more distant one from Lac Léman, the closer one from the nearby Seujet Dam.

If they get too close, they will foul our exit strategy.

This job had been planned with such precision, and it had fallen to pieces at the slightest nudge. At a loss to think of a way to get all of her people out of the bank and out of Geneva alive, Anja swallowed hard to suppress a burning swell of acid and fear.

Do not crack. The others need you. Be strong.

She drew a deep breath. Steadied herself. It would have been easier to let herself throw up, but that would only have created a spectacle. Police attention was something she had to avoid if the others were to have any hope of ending this job together and alive.

From the tram bridge behind her, Anja heard the snap of booted feet heading her way. She steeled herself for an impromptu police interrogation—but when she turned it was Briet who greeted her, with anxiety and confusion. "Anja? What happened?"

"You tell me. Your job was to keep the police away."

"My job was to slow down a few cars answering a minor fire call. Whatever Cade just did? It set off every alarm in the city."

Briet's presumption irked Anja. "How do you know this was Cade's fault?"

"Because he was *in charge*. Whatever happens inside that bank is on him."

She was right, and that angered Anja even more. Not willing to press the losing position in a debate, she changed the subject. "We need to get our people out of there."

"Agreed." Briet stole a look up and around, pretending to be just another civilian gawker. "Sharpshooters on the rooftops. Lots of guns in the street. This will get ugly."

Anja pivoted toward the bank. More police arrived each minute. Uniformed officers had formed a cordon around the bank and were shepherding civilians as far back as they could, for their own protection. Plainclothes officers—detectives and commanders, Anja figured—had arrived and formed a command group behind a police truck.

Briet nudged Anja, then gestured with her chin toward the armored car parked directly in front of the bank's main door. "What the fuck is that?"

"Men working for the Old Man are here, taking something of his from the bank vault. Niccolò is leading them." Anja waved toward the van. "That is their ride."

A nod of understanding from Briet. "Let me guess: That's what derailed the plan."

"*Da.*"

"How many of our people are still inside?"

"All but the two of us."

"Fucking hell. We'd better get them out before the *polizei* storm the place."

"Good idea." Anja pondered whether Briet would still sound so condescending with her windpipe crushed. "I am so glad you are here to tell me these things."

<hr />

Cade's first rule of improvisation was that if he hadn't come prepared to dazzle his foes with power, his next best move was to bury them in bullshit.

He shouted out the cracked-open front door, "Hey, cops! Can you hear me?"

A German-accented masculine voice distorted by a bullhorn answered, "*We hear you.*"

"Then pay attention, because I'm only going to tell you this once. I've got ten men in here with me, and we're wiring this heap of bricks with dynamite even as we speak. The side door on Rue du Rhône is wired, and so is the hatch at the top of the elevator shaft." There was no immediate response from the police, so Cade asked, "Did you catch all that?"

"*We did.*"

"Good. Then you also ought to know we have submachine guns, automatic rifles, and grenades. If you try to storm this building, or smoke us out, we'll kill one hostage each minute until you back off. If we run out of hostages, we'll bring the whole place down and knock it into the river. Are my terms clear?"

"*Yes.*"

Cade looked back at the gagged hostages, all seated on the bank lobby's floor with their backs against the long tellers' counter. The bank's employees and customers all looked terrified. Niccolò and a man whom Cade had heard the mage address as Tujiro seethed. Those two knew Cade was lying about possessing dynamite, heavy weapons, and grenades. Based on those false-hoods, they probably had already guessed that Cade had little help beyond his two female accomplices in the lobby. *Now I just need to make sure the cops don't figure that out.*

Mr. Bullhorn squawked, "*What are your demands?*"

That was a damned good question. Not one Cade had been able to consider before now. His primary objective remained mostly unchanged: to hold the line until Barış dug up the client file that would identify the Old Man and perhaps reveal where to find him.

But now Cade had to consider a secondary goal: to acquire the enchanted object secured inside the briefcase locked to Tujiro's wrist. Whatever it was, the Old Man considered it vital enough to send two of his karcist retainers to retrieve it. Now Cade had Yasmin searching Tujiro's pockets—a task that seemed to make him more uncomfortable than it did her—for the key to unlock the handcuffs.

Seconds were bleeding away, and Cade had to tell the police something. Even more critical, he needed to buy time. As much as he could wrangle. He cracked open the front door once more and bellowed into the crisp cold morning air.

"We want two armored vans. Both big enough to carry twelve men and two tons of gold. We want a direct route cleared from here to the airport. We want a Mystere Twenty executive jet, fueled and ready, at the southwest end of the runway. And just in case you're thinking you'll ambush us on the road, or at the airport, we'll be bringing some hostages in each van, and on the jet. When we're safe, we'll release the last of them. Did you get all that?"

"*We did. You should know,* monsieur, *that your list will take some time to acquire.*"

"Then you'd better get started." Cade stepped back and let the door close.

Yasmin finished digging through all the pockets of Tujiro's coat. Then she reached into the front left pocket of his pants, and from there she recovered the handcuff keys. As she unlocked the cuff from his wrist, Tujiro thrashed inside his restraints and tried in vain to shout through his gag, which had been cut from his own suit jacket.

Feigning confusion, Yasmin cupped her hand behind her ear. "Sorry? Didn't catch that." Tujiro went motionless and glared up at Yasmin. She tugged his gag from his mouth. "What?"

"You will pay dearly for this, *gaijin* whore."

His insult put a cocky smile on her face. "I already took the case off your wrist." She drew one of her knives and pressed its cutting edge against the crotch of his trousers. "Got any other dangly bits you want me to remove?" Noting his angry sigh and narrowed gaze, she lifted his gag and pushed it back into his mouth. "Yeah, I didn't think so."

She carried the briefcase to the rear courtesy desk, where Cade was waiting for her. As soon as she set down the case, he said, "Let's see what we've won."

Yasmin unlocked the case, flipped its latches, and lifted its lid.

An unearthly radiance poured from inside the case in hues of gold and violet. With it came a chill in the air, followed by fragrances of lavender, sandalwood, and camphor. It took a few seconds for Cade's eyes to adapt to the brilliant glow. He blinked twice and then focused on the object secured inside the case. It resembled a champagne bottle in general shape, though it possessed asymmetries that suggested it had been crafted by hand. It was a vessel of purple crystal, its surface carved with symbols ancient and arcane, all of it wrapped in a complex mesh of gold, silver, and platinum filigree. The vessel's neck was stoppered with a long cork, which in turn was held in place by thick layers of steel wire.

But the light shining inside of it seemed to float on its own, not touching the sides, its nature inscrutable, its beauty beyond the reach of mortal words.

Cade was still admiring the vessel's myriad details when Yasmin reached out, clearly meaning to pick up the artifact. He caught her wrist. "Don't touch it. It looks fragile. And not just most-expensive-item-in-the-store fragile, but might-be-older-than-human-civilization fragile."

"Relax." She withdrew her hand, and he let her go. "It sure is pretty. But what is it?"

"Beats me." He tilted his head toward Niccolò. "Ask him."

Yasmin didn't hesitate to act upon the invitation. She walked over to Niccolò, pulled out his gag, and put the tip of one blade to his chin while she pointed the other at the glowing artifact. "Do you know what that is?"

"Something that doesn't belong to you."

She surrendered to the obvious: "You're not going to be any use to me, are you?" When he declined to respond, she put his gag back into his mouth.

Cade closed and locked the case as Yasmin returned to his side. "Don't waste your time with him. I've had better chats with brick walls." He slid the briefcase toward her. "Lock it to your wrist. Guard it with your life until we find a way out of here." He clasped Yasmin's shoulder. "I'm trusting you to get this to the safe house in one piece. Can you do that?"

"Yes, Master." She slapped the free cuff onto her left wrist.

The doors at the back of the lobby opened. Sathit returned, nudging along the bank's junior manager in front of her. As soon as Sathit saw Cade, she lifted her chin in greeting, and then she lobbed him the keys to the bank. "The manager was most helpful. The door to Rue du Rhône is locked, and its alarm is reset. If the police try to breach it, we'll know."

"Good work." Cade pointed at the other hostages sitting on the floor. "Put him with the others." He left the courtesy desk to intercept Sathit and the manager. He gave her back the keys. "I'll tie and gag him. Take the keys, go upstairs, and find out what's keeping Barış."

His request seemed to trouble her. "He's not back yet?"

"No, and we can't leave without him. So do me a favor and go light a fire under his ass. I want to get out of here."

"Yes, Master." Sathit hurried away with the keys in hand, through the doors at the back of the lobby. Her running footsteps echoed faintly in the stairwell as she bounded up the steps, and then her footfalls faded to silence while Cade restored the bindings on the manager.

He stood and stepped back from his handiwork to find Yasmin at his side.

She shot a cold look at Niccolò and Tujiro. "We should kill them both now, while we have the chance."

"No." Cade pulled out his cigarettes and lit a Lucky.

Yasmin wore a look of surprise and betrayal. "If the situation were reversed, they would not spare us."

"I know." A long, satisfying drag filled his chest with heat.

"If we let them live, they will tell the Old Man we have his artifact. And his identity."

"Maybe I *want* him to know." He loosened his tie and undid his shirt's top button.

She shook her head. Her fists white-knuckled the grips of her knives. "Let me kill them."

"I said *no*." He faced her and all but willed her to look him in the eye. "They have no magick in here, Yaz. They're as defenseless as civilians."

"So are we." She stared at the pair of enemy karcists, both of whom glared back at her. "But we took them by surprise. Let's finish them."

"They're *prisoners*, Yaz. Tied and gagged. Kill them like this and you'll be a murderer." He grabbed her shoulders, reclaimed her attention. "I taught you better than that. We kill only in self-defense, and only when we need to. Remember?"

She fumed. "This is not how we win wars."

Cade let her go. "If that's our only way to win, we've already lost."

"That's what I'm afraid of." She stalked away from him and the prisoners, perhaps not entirely persuaded but also no longer poised to strike in cold blood. Cade just hoped for all their sakes that Yasmin's instincts didn't turn out to be the right ones.

⚬⚬⚬

Was one lucky break so much to ask for? Barış would not have thought so, but after several minutes spent breaking into filing cabinets packed with papers irrelevant to his search, he was starting to think Fate had a grudge against him. Denied the use of magick while inside the building, he had been forced to resurrect a skill from his misspent youth: lock-picking. It had come as a relief to discover that even half a lifetime after he had last defeated a padlock, his fingers still recognized the subtle resistance of spring-backed teeth inside metal cylinders.

He had spent ten minutes opening all the cabinets on the fifth floor, only to come away empty-handed. No doubt there were plenty of people who would be keen to know the bank's investment strategies for the coming quarter, year, and decade, but none of that mattered to Cade. With every minute Barış squandered on a fruitless search, the more convinced he became that he could feel his master's impatience radiating through the floor.

I probably should have told Cade I cannot read French, Barış mused with regret, while he studied the directory in the bank's fourth-floor elevator lobby.

The first office he ransacked on the fourth floor proved no more helpful than any of those he'd pillaged on the fifth floor. Then he entered a narrow room that ran almost the entire length of the floor. The blinds of its windows were drawn. Overhead, fluorescent lights with long bulbs hummed as they afflicted the room with a sickly cast of green undertones. Along its inner wall stood a long, black steel filing cabinet that stood as high as Barış's neck.

He smiled. *This looks more like a cabinet of client records.*

Barış guided his rake and file inside the lock in the top right corner of the black cabinet. It took several seconds for him to suss out its tensions and negate them. As soon as the entire mechanism was in his control he tried to turn it, to release the catches on the file drawers.

The lock refused to turn.

Relief turned to wrath. *What in the name of* BAPHOMET *. . . ?*

His eyes searched the front of the cabinet for any clue as to what was holding the lock. He saw the culprit at the upper left corner of the black cabinet, roughly three meters away: a second lock. This was no mere redundancy. Only as Barış struggled in vain to rotate the right-hand lock did he see that the cabinet had been designed with a twin-lock system.

To open the cabinet, one would need to turn both its locks at the same time, but they had been placed far enough apart that no human being who had ever lived could reach both of them at once. It would always take two people to open this cabinet, thus ensuring no one person would ever be able to access it without a witness—or an accomplice.

Damn these Swiss bankers. I could understand using twin locks to secure a vault full of gold—but on a filing cabinet? Barış stepped back from the black cabinet and surveyed the room. He looked for anything he could use to pry open the cabinet by brute force. There was no furniture, no chairs to break, nothing but scuffed hardwood floors and dusty venetian blinds.

He stepped back from the cabinet, hands on his hips, flustered. *If I go back to Cade without the Old Man's client file, he will brain me, I'm certain of it.*

On the verge of conceding defeat and going to face his master, Barış caught a blur of movement on his right. Startled, he let out a short whoop and took half a step back before he recognized Sathit, who regarded him with amusement and mock suspicion.

A smirk tugged at the corner of her mouth. "Barış? What was that?"

"What was what?"

"That strange little sound you made."

"Nothing." He shrugged and tried to wave off her query, only to wind up doing halfhearted jazz hands. "I didn't hear anything."

It was clear that she wasn't buying his deflection, but she let it go. "Cade wants to know what's taking you so long."

Barış nodded at the black cabinet. "This. It has twin locks. I cannot pick both at once." He entertained a hopeful notion. "Do you know how to pick locks?"

"I once broke one with a hammer."

That was less than encouraging, but Barış soldiered on. "Good enough. Join me." She met him beside the cabinet's right-hand lock. He slipped his rake and file inside the keyhole and worked at the lock as he spoke. "It is a matter of applying pressure at the right points in the correct sequence, and then holding all the pieces in place while you turn the cylinder. I am nudging each tooth in the lock into its open position." He paused his narration and clenched his jaw while he coaxed the last few bits into place. Then he held the rake and the file each between a thumb and forefinger. "You are going to take hold of each tool, one at a time. When you do, keep gentle pressure on them, each away from the other. Clear?"

Sathit nodded, and then she did as he had instructed. She took hold of the rake first, and then the file. When Barış was sure her grip was solid and her pressure correct, he let go. "Now I'm going to go pick the other lock. When I give you the signal, turn the cylinder clockwise—making sure to keep the tension on the tools the same while you turn. Understand?"

Another nod of confirmation. Worried that Sathit could lose hold of her lock's tension at any second, Barış worked quickly to release the left-hand cylinder. Beads of sweat trickled from the top of his scalp down his forehead and pooled atop his thick black eyebrows. The tickling sensation of moisture on his brow made him want to sleeve it away, but his hands were busy. At last he felt the final tooth inside the cylinder click open. He looked at Sathit. "Ready?"

"Get on with it, Barış."

"Turn clockwise on three. One. Two. Three!" He turned his lock, and she did the same at the other end of the cabinet. From inside its metal housing came the resounding *thunk* of latches being released. Barış gave the top drawer a gentle pull. It slid outward with ease, smooth and silent on well-oiled telescoping tracks. "Well done! Thank you."

She watched him work. From his jacket pocket he pulled a scrap of paper on which he had written down the suspect account number. Fortunately for him, because the Geneva branch of Lloyds Bank observed the same Swiss banking privacy laws as its local peers, the private accounts had been organized by their numbers rather than alphabetized by clients' names.

"Got it!" He found the file with the matching account number not far from the left end of the top drawer. It was among the bank's earliest established accounts, and it was nearly twice as thick as most of the others around it. He hefted the entire hanging folder from the cabinet and tucked it under his arm. Then he pushed the drawer shut and faced Sathit, beaming with pride. "Let's go see how Master Cade plans to get us out of here."

Keeping watch over the hostages wasn't challenging, exciting, or interesting, but it needed to be done. Yasmin wished someone else could have been tasked with doing it.

Cade gave the job to her and Sathit because the two of them had been the first to grab guns when the whole fiasco had started. Or maybe because it had been Yasmin's call to make a play for the briefcase by triggering an armed robbery, and Sathit had elected to back her up. Whatever the rationale had been, it meant that Cade and Barış now were sequestered in the lobby's back corner, arguing in whispers about an escape plan, while Sathit and Yasmin paced in front of the captive employees and customers of the bank, who sat bound and gagged on the floor in front of the tellers' counters. All while hoping the police didn't call Cade's bluff and charge through the doors with battle rifles blazing.

No one had touched the lobby's thermostat, but Yasmin could have sworn the place was getting warmer by the minute. Bullets of sweat rolled down her back, and her face flushed with warmth as the standoff dragged on. She did her best to appear calm and serious, but inside all she wanted was to retreat, to get as far from this place as possible. The muscles in her legs were ready to run. Her nerves and senses were sharp, set to duck and dodge and weave. If only she could get out of this room. Out into the open. If only she could get free.

One small motion from the hostages made her stop and pivot. All her attention landed on Tujiro, who had extended his arms just enough to scratch his thigh. The second he realized he was looking into the barrel of Yasmin's captured pistol, he returned to his previous pose.

It was vital that Yasmin pay extra-close attention to Niccolò and Tujiro. Any of the hostages could present a danger if they were to get free and try to escape, but the two enemy karcists posed the single greatest threat to the survival of Yasmin and her friends. If either of them got outside where they could use magick, all hope of Cade and company surviving an escape attempt from the bank would be lost.

When she looked at Niccolò, he beckoned her with eye contact and a tilt of his head.

She ignored him the first time. When she made eye contact with him again, he repeated the gesture. Apparently, he wanted to talk.

In the corner, Barış and Cade traded whispers with their backs to the room.

Yasmin paced along the line of hostages until she was in front of Niccolò. Then she shot a look at Sathit and signaled her with a gesture to check on the police outside. Sathit nodded and headed for the front door. As she did, Yasmin kneeled in front of Niccolò and removed his gag.

Under her breath she asked him, "What?"

"You don't want to be here. I can tell."

"No one in their right mind would want to be here. What do you *want*?"

"To help you." For a man with his hands tied behind his back, he seemed oddly relaxed. "You are in over your head, *signorina*. I can give you a way out."

She drew a knife and pressed its edge to his throat. "I can offer you the same thing."

"Please, *signorina*. This is unnecessary." His eyes darted toward Cade, and then toward Sathit, before returning to Yasmin. "I can free you from *all* of this."

"Doubtful."

"In the front chest pocket of my jacket I keep an enchanted coin. Take it."

For Yasmin, temptation's magnetic allure was held in check only by the oppressive weight of guilt. She looked over her shoulder at Cade, who remained in deep conference with Barış, and then at Sathit, who continued to study the deployments of the police. Then she reached forward, dipped her fingers into Niccolò's chest pocket, and pulled out the coin. It was made of gold. On one face it bore a demonic sigil that Yasmin didn't recognize; on the opposite side of the coin was engraved an ancient glyph of protection and containment.

While she studied the coin, Niccolò said, "If you ever wish to make contact with me and broker an end to this pointless violence, hold this coin in
your left fist. Repeat *'audite'* three times. Then flip the coin into the air. It will
vanish, and a pillar of fire will rise from your palm. Through the flames you
and I will be able to speak. Do you understand?"

"Yes. *'Audite'* three times, then flip. Got it." She pocketed the coin. "What's
the catch?"

He tried to play stupid. She could tell he was lousy at it. "What catch?"

"Nothing's free. Sure as shit not magic coins. So spit it out: What do you
want?"

"Your masters' grimoires." Niccolò's voice dropped to a soft hush. "The
Iron Codex and all of Cade's new research. I need it all."

"Interesting. Now I think I'll rat you out to Cade."

A smug grin showed his teeth. "You won't."

She put her knife back to his throat. "Why not?"

"Because you long to be free—*and* rich. I can make both those dreams
come true."

On the edge of her vision, Yasmin clocked movement by Cade and Barış.
She put Niccolò's gag back into place. As Sathit turned her way—meaning all
the eyes in the room were upon Yasmin—she punched Niccolò in the nose.
It broke with a loud snap.

The others converged upon Yasmin as she stood and backed away from
Niccolò. For good measure, she spit in his face. "*Kiss ekhtak!*"

She moved to resume her pacing vigil in front of the hostages. Cade
caught her by the shoulder and halted her. "Hey. What did Fancy-pants Mc-
Gee want?"

Yasmin threw a poisonous look at Niccolò, and then aimed a similar glare
at her master. "The same thing every man wants: what he *can't have*."

In a world full of people who longed to be in charge, Barış was one who
dreaded responsibility. Even the idea of being in charge turned his guts to
mud. So when his master had muttered "Keep an eye on things until I get
back" as he disappeared through the bank lobby's back doors and up the
stairwell, Barış had suffered a nauseating flutter of panic.

He turned to face the room. *Please, Allah, don't let anyone ask me anything.*

He hoped Cade wouldn't be gone for long.

Thus began over four minutes of obsessive glances at his watch, in precise fifteen-second intervals. After he had been in charge just shy of five minutes, the doors at the back of the lobby swung inward. Cade returned. Barış breathed a sigh of gratitude that nothing of note had happened during his watch, and that whatever happened next would be Cade's problem.

Cade beckoned Barış, Sathit, and Yasmin to his side. The group huddled in the rear corner, near the manager's desk. Keeping his voice low and soft so as not to be overheard by the hostages, Cade said to the three apprentices, "I know how to get us out of here."

"Thank God," Sathit muttered.

Yasmin looked suspicious. "I dread to ask."

"The key is to be quick. We need to lash all the hostages together, to slow down any escape attempt they might make. Then we need to secure the front doors, and on our way out, we have to lock and barricade the lobby's rear doors."

Barış tensed, and he saw Yasmin and Sathit stand up a smidge straighter. He was the first of the apprentices to ask, "Why? Where are we going?"

"The roof. I was able to signal Anja from a window on the third floor. She and Briet are standing by to join us as soon as we splash down."

Sathit's eyes widened. "*Splash down?* You mean, into the river?"

"Into the clear blue waters of the Rhône," Cade said.

"No," Yasmin said.

Cade nodded. "*Ja,* darling."

"Fuck, no," Sathit said. "Lac Léman is an alpine lake. The Rhône is freezing in the *summer,* never mind *now.* We won't last thirty seconds in water that cold."

"We won't have to." Cade pointed toward the river. "Anja and Bree will jump in as soon as they see us leap. Once we're all in the water, we join hands and Anja takes us home."

"That is not the biggest problem with the plan," Barış said.

His protest drew a pointed look from Cade. "What is?"

"The drop from the roof. This is a five-story building. The roof is peaked, and its edge is probably around sixty feet above ground level. The river's surface is three feet below that. Do you have any idea what a drop like that feels like? Even into water?"

"Yes, I do," Cade said. "When I trained with the Rangers, we made drops from thirty and forty feet. I won't lie: They hurt like hell. But they were training us to survive a jump from the deck of an aircraft carrier, and that's a drop of over ninety feet."

"Into the *ocean*!" Barış took a moment to collect his wits and sound more rational. "Do you have any idea how shallow the Rhône is?"

"Its average depth in this section is about sixteen feet. Enough for what we need."

Barış remained skeptical. "After a sixty-foot fall, it will feel like hitting concrete."

"Not if you hit it correctly." Cade awkwardly mimed a few poses as he described them. "The key is to keep your knees together and your toes pointed. Blade into the water. Most injuries come from making a blunt impact."

Sathit and Yasmin traded looks of disbelief, and then Sathit asked Cade, "Are you kidding? What if we hit the water and break our fucking legs?"

"If you keep your toes pointed, you'll be fine. But just in case, if you have a spirit yoked that lets you do telekinesis, you can shape that force into a wedge beneath you. But make sure you release the wedge as soon as it splits the surface ahead of you—that'll soften your landing but leave you some cushion to slow your fall."

Dismayed, Barış shook his head. "This is insanity."

Cade pointed at Barış. "No, insanity would be staying inside this bank one second longer than we need to. Any minute now the cops are gonna storm this place. We need to be gone *before* that happens, or else we are all *truly fucked*."

Yasmin rolled her eyes. "Fine. Let's get our jumping shoes on, then."

The very notion filled Barış with horror. "You can't be serious!"

"He's right," Yasmin said. "We need to go. Now."

"What about the police? Or Niccolò's men, still outside with his armored car? What if one of them shoots at us during our leap?"

Cade lifted his open palms in a calming gesture. "Relax, Briet's gonna shield us on the way down. We'll be fine."

"Unless one or both of Niccolò's men has magick-piercing bullets," Barış pointed out. "And if they do? What then?"

His warning extracted from Cade no more than a devil-may-care shrug. "If that happens, this gets a lot more interesting." Cade checked his watch. "Time's wasting. Yaz, block the front doors. Sathit, get ready to lock the exit behind us." He turned and walked toward the lobby's rear doors. "Last one to the roof has to jump first."

Sathit and Yasmin hurried to secure the doors.

Barış stood paralyzed by indecision. He had no desire to set foot on the bank's roof, much less be coerced into being the first to jump off of it. Of course, being the last member of the team to jump was no more appealing than being the first. Or the second. Or the third. Worst of all, he was at a loss to picture a scenario that didn't involve jumping from the roof, a notion that made his palms sweat and threatened to empty his bladder against his will.

From the lobby's rear doors, Cade called out, "Barış! You coming?"

Against his better judgment and his instinct for self-preservation, Barış croaked out his halfhearted reply.

"Yes, sir."

23

The plan had been clearly explained. Its details had been unambiguous. Anja had spoken slowly, and Briet had understood and agreed to every word, every step of the way. But now that the moment had come to pull herself over the railing and prepare for a jump into bone-chilling water, her limbs refused to obey. And truth be told, her mind was also in rebellion.

Anja stood on the other side of the tram bridge's railing, her heels perched on a narrow lip of concrete. Below her, the clear blue river coursed, swift and deep. She clung to the metal rail behind her and urged Briet with a sharp whisper: "Come on! We need to be ready."

"I can't." Briet shook her head. "I nearly froze my cooch off talking Cade out of the lake two nights ago. I'm not doing that again." She glanced toward the plaza, where the ever-growing throng of police huddled behind cars and vans, most of them with rifles aimed at the bank's front door. Then she looked up at the bank's roof. "Still no sign of our gang."

"They will be there. Cade will see to it." Anja peeked at the cops. "Climb over. Now."

"No." Briet struggled for ideas but found none. "There must be a better way out of this."

"There is not. Stop bitching and climb."

"The fuck I will. Why not take our people off the roof with a thunder jaunt?"

The question seemed to annoy Anja. "The bank is warded against teleportation magick. That includes the roof. Until our people leave the roof, they cannot open portals or jaunt."

"So they're jumping sixty feet into an alpine river? Do you have any idea how cold that water is? Once we're in, we'll all be in shock within thirty seconds."

"We will be gone in ten. And the police will think we drowned." An icy stare. "Climb."

Briet untied the belt of her trench coat to improve her mobility. She planted both hands on the wide steel railing, and then swung her right leg over it. It took her a moment to find her footing. Once she was stable, straddling the railing, she pulled her left leg over. With careful grace she adjusted her hold so her hands were behind her, and then she, like Anja, was perched with her heels on a narrow edge of concrete with the frigid river rushing past below.

Pitiful dread washed through her. *I will never be warm or dry again.*

As if sensing her trepidation, Anja leaned toward Briet and offered her a wan, conspiratorial smile. "This is not cold. Russian winter is cold. This? Just a cool dip."

"I can tell you're lying to me, because your lips are moving."

Anja seemed content to let the matter drop. Then came the crack of a rifle shot, followed by murmurs of excitement from the crowd behind the police cordon.

Briet looked over her shoulder and saw civilians pointing at the bank's roof. The police covering the building adjusted their aim upward. When Briet lifted her eyes to search the Lloyds rooftop, she saw police snipers on nearby roofs. Every uniformed thug with a gun in Geneva was getting ready to add a few more kills to his official total.

The entire spectacle filled Briet with contempt and alarm. *This must be what happens to people when their country won't let them fight in wars.*

"There they are," Anja said. "Toward the back."

Briet saw Cade and the others peek out from behind the far sloped edge of the roof. How had they gotten up there? An elevator-shaft emergency hatch? An attic access door? A gabled window facing an endless sea of adjacent rooftops? It didn't really matter, she decided—at least, not as much as the dozens of high-power firearms aimed in their direction did.

"Trouble in the plaza." Anja's warning pulled Briet's focus away from the activity on the roof. She looked toward Place de Bel-Air. Two men in dark suits clambered out of the back of a private armored car, both armed with carbine rifles equipped with sniper scopes. "Niccolò brought them. Which means he might have armed them."

In the blink of an eye, Briet engaged the Sight of Vos Satria. The magickal vision revealed the telltale glow of enchantment inside the magazines of their

rifles. Briet's heart sank. "Those rifles are loaded with magick-piercing bullets. All it takes is *one* to break my shield." She looked up at their people on
the roof. "Can you back me up? Give our team a second shield?"

"I must focus on the water jaunt."

Panic made a tempest of Briet's imagination. "Maybe I could blow up one
of the cars, make some smoke, cause a diversion—"

"Not very subtle."

"Since when do we give a shit about that?"

A scathing look from Anja. "Cade said no dead police. Can you blow up a
car without killing a cop?" Briet's eye-roll of angry frustration answered that
question. "As I thought."

If only we weren't in broad daylight, I could blast them to kingdom—

Then she saw it. It was sneaky. Subtle. And just might do the trick.

Bolstered with confidence, she faced Anja. "I have an idea. Tell Cade he's
clear to jump."

***

Cade's first warning there were police snipers on the adjacent rooftops was
the bullet that pinged off the roof's peak a few inches from his head. He
ducked and flinched by reflex. "Stay down," he told his team. Crouching,
he led them out of the gabled access door at the east end of the roof, near
where it met an elevated wall separating it from the next building on the
block.

Yasmin was the last one out the door. As soon as she pushed it closed, the
four karcists squatted beneath an overhang of the roof's peak.

"First," Cade told his adepts, "the bad news: We can't use any teleportation
magick up here. The good news? Now that we're outside, we can use other
kinds of magick to get out of this in one piece." He pointed at Sathit. "Do you
have any illusion talents yoked?"

"Just one. A kind of shimmer effect. It will look like I'm stuttering back
and forth very fast, like I'm in a dozen places at once. Makes me very hard
to hit."

"Can you use that on all of us at the same time?"

"Don't know. I never tried."

"Well, you're about to. For all our sakes, good luck." Cade pivoted toward
Yasmin. "You need to protect the case. It'll make you less aerodynamic, so
before you jump, hug it to your chest. As you jump, conjure your shield,

and in your mind shape it into a wedge with its thin end a meter beneath your feet. Release it as soon as your shield touches the water."

She clutched the metallic briefcase to her bosom. "Got it."

Cade gave his last instruction to Barış. "All we need to do is get enough of a running start to clear the quai, okay? Once you're in the air, pinch your nose, point your toes, and drop like a spike." To the entire trio, he added, "When you hit the water, let your arms rise and slow your descent. Then swim for the bridge. Anja will meet us there and jaunt us out." He held up his hands and asked with uncharacteristic optimism, "Everybody ready?"

Barış looked as if he were about to shit himself. "I can't do this."

"What part of it?"

"Any of it. The jumping, the falling—I just . . . I can't."

It took all of Cade's self-restraint not to throttle his impeccably dressed student. "Barış, I'm going to give you ten seconds to explain yourself before I fucking *throw* you off the roof."

The other man's expression shifted from anguished to guilt-ridden in a matter of seconds. "I'm sorry, truly. But I'm afraid of heights. To be precise, of *falling* from heights."

Cade pulled his hand over his face, as if he could wipe away his glower. "Fuck me. Are you kidding? Because if you are, confess now and I'll only break your fingers."

"I'm serious. Feel my palms! They are slick with sweat. My stomach is a knot so tight, even Alexander's sword couldn't split it. I *cannot* make this jump."

"Goddammit, Barış, yes you can. Because you fucking have to. We all do. If we don't jump, we get caught. If we get caught, we're as good as dead."

Tears welled in Barış's eyes, and he started to tremble. "I know that. I do. And I am so sorry. But my legs won't move. My body won't let me do this." Beads of sweat appeared on the man's forehead, and he wrapped his arms around his own torso.

"Barış! Listen to my voice, buddy. You're gonna be okay." To Sathit and Yasmin, he said, "Grab his arms. Hold him down." From inside his jacket, Cade pulled out his emergency plan. It was a narrow syringe and a short hypodermic needle he kept hidden inside an almost flat leather pouch. It had been prepped and loaded for a quick application. Too many times he had found himself in a tight spot with no way to smooth his rough edges. In the last year or so he had begun making sure he had at least one backup dose hidden on his person at all times.

Before Barış could object on the grounds of his Muslim heritage or a general aversion to narcotics, Cade jabbed the needle into Barış's thigh and pressed the plunger. "This isn't the best way to do this, but in a few seconds you'll feel a fuck of lot more mellow, trust me." He waited until Barış ceased struggling in the grips of Sathit and Yasmin. When a wave of relaxation overtook the man, Cade nodded at the women. "He's good, let him go."

Barış's eyelids drooped shut. Cade gently patted Barış's cheek with the back of his hand to wake him. "Stay with me, buddy. We still have to get off the roof."

"Still don't want to jump."

"But now you might do it anyway, and that's half the battle." To the women he added, "Get him on his feet." Sathit and Yasmin took Barış by his arms and hoisted him. Yasmin draped one of Barış's arms over Cade's shoulder, and from there Cade carried his friend's weight. "Good. When I give the signal, Sathit, cloak us in that shimmer of yours. Yasmin, keep the case close to your body. We'll run for the ledge and jump as hard as we can." Modulating his voice to a soothing tone, he reminded Barış, "Pinch your nose and point your toes."

"That rhymes," Barış said through a broad grin.

"Yes it does."

"Pinch my toes and point my nose."

"Close enough. Okay, everybody set. We go on three. One. Two—"

"Wait!" Barış exclaimed, eyes wide. He grabbed a fistful of Cade's shirt. "I have a better plan!"

Never one to dismiss a good narcotic epiphany, Cade was all ears. "What is it?"

"You told the cops to bring us armored trucks! We wait for the trucks to arrive. Pile inside. And then we drive *the trucks* into the river!"

Cade waited to hear if there was more to the plan. There wasn't. Then he laughed and patted Barış's chest. "That's a great plan, buddy. Except for one small problem."

Standing straight until his friends pulled him back down to hide him from snipers, Barış projected offense and indignation. "What problem?"

Cade had to tell him the truth. "Just like I was bullshitting the cops when I asked for those trucks? They were bullshitting us when they said they would send 'em. There are no trucks, Barış. Never were. The cops are just buying time until they get a chance to shoot us."

"No trucks?"

"Not one."

"Shit!"

"I know. But great initiative, man. Way to think on your feet. Keep that up." He tightened his grip on Barış and steadied the man. "Now, then—ready to go?"

"No."

"Too bad. Count of three. One. Two. Three!"

It all went like clockwork. They ran in unison, close together, but not so close as to do the snipers any favors. Sathit's magickal shimmer turned the quartet into a fast-moving mirage as they darted over the sloped roof, picking up speed for their leap. As they lurched toward the precipice, Barış let off in a slurred shout, "Paint my toes, pick my nose!"

And they jumped.

They soared, and then they flailed, bodies arcing through open air . . . until gravity took hold. Then began the sickening acceleration of free fall. Cold air rushed past, slicing like a knife.

Cade looked down. They had cleared the quai. *Thank fucking God.*

Beside him, Barış pinched his nose and pointed his toes like the disaster prodigy Cade had always known he was.

Stutters of gunfire. Bullets ricocheted off the invisible shield that was following the four of them on their mad plunge toward the Rhône. *Thanks, Briet!*

Below, Anja and Briet were already in the water, and even from a distance Cade could see neither was happy about it.

One rifle's shot cracked louder than the rest. The group's bubble of magickal protection collapsed with an iridescent flash. Next came a brutal punch in Cade's left side, just beneath his ribs, followed by a burning horror that snaked through his guts as he fell—

Red pain turned white deep inside him as his vision blurred.

He was spinning—turning? No, rolling—couldn't tell which way was up—

Voices shouted, but Cade heard only the roar of the wind.

Crushing impact, the wrench of torqued joints, the sickening snaps of cracking ribs—and all the air was slammed from his chest, as if he had been struck by a hammer the size of a truck. Stinging needles of cold engulfed him as everything turned dark.

He couldn't breathe in. Couldn't find the ground, or himself upon it.

The taste of dirty copper filled his mouth. He opened it to spit the foulness out, only to feel water rush in and flood down his throat.

Drowning! Fuck!

He thrashed, twisted, turned, searched for air, for light, for solid ground. All around him was a blur, but when he rolled to his left, he saw the glare of daylight through a curtain of ripples. He tried to kick and pull himself toward it, but every ounce of effort stoked the blaze of pain in his left side and caused him to gasp—which led to gulping down more water. . . .

Then something had him, some force greater than himself. He feared it was gravity, that he was sinking, that he would feel the rocks and gravel of the riverbed at any moment. But contact eluded him. He just kept on moving. . . .

A prisoner of the current, Cade was swept downriver with the rest of the garbage.

⁓

They broke as one through the surface, into the darkness above. Their simultaneous gasps were loud in the enveloping silence, and their clasped hands formed a chain, from Anja at one end to Sathit at the other, with Briet, Yasmin, and Barış between them. Anja made a quick head count, just to confirm that everyone who had started the jaunt with her had finished it. Around them, ripples spawned by their arrival spread across Arthurs Lake, whose black surface shimmered with reflections of the crescent moon high overhead.

Barış was the first to free himself from the chain. Weaving like a drunkard, he staggered toward shore, and toward the lodge house, whose porch light burned like a beacon in the night.

Briet helped Anja shepherd Yasmin and Sathit toward the shore. "Home, sweet home," she said, motioning the two younger women to follow Barış toward the lodge.

Toting a metallic briefcase handcuffed to her wrist, Yasmin stopped in the waist-deep water to confront Anja. "You left him! You forgot Cade!"

Sathit stood at Yasmin's side, a gesture of solidarity. "Why did we leave him?"

Anja was in no mood for this argument. "I had no choice."

"Bullshit." Yasmin stepped toward Anja, her pose aggressive. "There must have been something you could have done. Some way to hold him or bring him back."

"There was no time. The water was too cold. Had we stayed, we would all be dead. Or captured." Her stomach twisted with a raw and terrible grief that she refused to share with the others. "I had to let him go."

"We could have gone after him," Sathit insisted.

Anja shook her head but refused to betray the anguish that was devouring her from within. "No. He was too deep. The current took him. None of us could have reached him."

Yasmin turned her wrath toward Briet. "What about you? You were supposed to protect us!"

"I did."

"Then how did Cade get shot?"

"Magick-piercing bullets!" Briet leaned in to dominate Yasmin. "And if my porter demon hadn't bumped both of Niccolò's gunmen as they fired, they'd have blown Cade's head clean the fuck off. Thanks to me he only got hit *once*. If he's lucky and gets medical attention in the next few minutes, he just might live long enough to *thank* me."

Sathit scowled at Briet. "You mean if he isn't dead already."

Anja closed her eyes and reached out with the magickal senses of PHENE-GREX. She attuned the demon's talent to Cade's life force, an energy whose unique qualities she had come to know as well as her own. In a matter of seconds, she had the truth. She opened her eyes and resumed her march ashore. "Cade lives. He is weak, but not dead."

"Then we go back for him," Yasmin said, trying to sound authoritative.

"*Nyet*. Cade will live." She looked at Yasmin and pointed at the briefcase. "Get that indoors. I want to see what Cade thought was so important."

No one spoke for the rest of their slog through the lake's muddy shallows, their hike ashore, or their trek into the fishing lodge. By the time Anja trudged inside, Barış had already planted himself facedown in the nearest room's unmade bed. Anja noted the peculiarity of his behavior, so she asked Sathit, "What happened to him?"

"He was too scared to jump off the roof, so Cade shot him full of dope."

"Of course he did." She motioned for Yasmin to follow her. "Come. Show me what is in the case." They walked together down the hall and into the lodge's spacious kitchen. Yasmin set the case on the dining table. Unlocked the cuff on her wrist and slipped her hand free. And then she opened the case's latches and lifted its lid.

A surge of magickal energy washed over Anja as soon as the case was opened. Briet swayed at the same moment, as if her chest had been pummeled by an ocean wave. Brilliant hues of gold and violet light shone upward from the object ensconced in the case's bottom half. The air in the room seemed suddenly perfumed with pleasant fragrances, and the chill that had seemed impossible to exorcise from their sodden clothes and weary limbs abated, giving way to a pleasing warmth.

Anja stared into the powerful glow emanating from the peculiar vessel inside the case. It was a bottle of hand-blown lavender crystal, its body broad at the base and tapering at the top to meet a long and narrow neck. The surface of the bottle was etched with eldritch sigils, many of which Anja recognized as Enochian, the language of the angels. A fine metallic mesh had been woven around the bottle, a delicate web of precious metals pulled into hair-thin filigree. Sealing the bottle was a long cork secured with an abundance of tightly wrapped steel wire.

It was a remarkable artifact. Ancient and imbued with powerful magick. But the real prize was, without a doubt, the radiant mass of energy trapped inside of it.

Sathit stared in wonder at the glowing vessel. "It's beautiful."

"Cade didn't know what it was," Yasmin said. "And Niccolò wouldn't say."

Unlike the adepts, Briet regarded the artifact with a combination of reverence and fear. "I've seen one of these before." She looked over at Anja. "And judging from the look on your face, I'd say you have, too."

Anja nodded. "*Da*. I have."

It was like trying to vomit against gravity. Cade's vision was too blurry for him to make out where he was, but he had to be alive, because being dead hurt less. His chest felt as if it were being crushed in an iron tourniquet, and then his stomach contracted, his diaphragm convulsed, and a torrent of cold, dirty water surged up his throat and out of his mouth.

Silt and debris piled up on his tongue and behind his teeth, and his pukewater spilled down his face and into his ears. He wanted to let out a string of vulgarities, but his body was too busy pushing out however many gallons of the Rhône he had swallowed. He ejected the water in roars that dwindled to moans, over and over.

Hoping to speed the process, Cade tried to roll onto his right side, away from the still-bleeding wound in his left flank. Blazing spirals of pain shot through the core of his body and dumped him flat on his back. After his first few gulps of air, a burning flared deep in his gut. He fought to slow his breathing. Whatever had hit him in the air, it was still inside him.

Great. Just fucking great.

His vision started to clear, and the bright blur that surrounded him resolved into the building-lined streets of central Geneva. Then he saw the true scale of his predicament: He was lying on a gurney in the middle of a concrete protrusion of the Seujet Dam, surrounded by uniformed police. His ankles and right wrist were cuffed to the rolling platform.

Fucking hell. I must've floated at least half a kilometer downriver.

Almost by instinct he tried to use the talent of ARIOSTO to unlock the cuffs and free himself as a preamble to an escape—only to find the demon was no longer under his yoke. A more thorough inspection confirmed Cade's grimmest speculation: All of his yoked spirits had fled. He stewed and raged in silence at the demons' predictable malice.

Nothing like a near drowning to set all the hellions free. Shit.

One of the uniformed cops noted Cade's return to consciousness and shouted in French to his superiors. Cade's ears were waterlogged; he couldn't make out a damned thing anyone was saying. All he heard was the roar of the deep, rolling and ebbing in time with his pulse.

Angry Swiss police detectives crowded his gurney and shouted at him in German.

Their volume and the glare of the sun high overhead aggravated Cade's crushing headache. He caught only every third or fourth word the cops were barking at him, but he was able to make an informed guess as to what they were asking him: *Who are you? Where are your partners? How did they escape? Why didn't you actually try to steal anything?* And a hundred other questions Cade didn't plan to answer.

At least, I hope they're asking where my partners are. It occurred to Cade only then that he hadn't actually seen Anja round up the others for a water jaunt. He could only hope they all had made it out alive and unharmed, with the Old Man's artifact and client file safely in hand.

Someone adjusted the top half of the gurney to prop up Cade in a sitting pose. The transition hurt like a motherfucker, as if his intestines were being pulled taut around a hacksaw. Then the movement halted, and the pain abated to a level that was merely fucking horrific.

More questions from the detectives, this time in rapid-fire barrages of French and German. Just to make it fun for Cade, they all talked over one another so he couldn't have figured out what any one of them was saying even if he had wanted to. Which he still didn't.

More water lurched out of his aching chest. A round of hard coughing left him light-headed and gasping like a landed tuna for close to half a minute.

He closed his eyes and did his best to inventory his body's injuries. He sensed the deep pain that infused several of his joints and noted the deep red wells of hurt in his spine, from his lumbar region all the way up to his neck. *Probably some fractures. A few sprains, some torn ligaments.* An attempt to turn from his waist provoked the bullet wound into white-hot jabs of agony that made his eyes water. *Plus this fucking thing. I'd better play this cool. Bide my time and wait for a good chance to slip away.*

He looked around for any sign of his enemies.

Everywhere he looked, he saw nothing but uniforms. The river had carried him away from Place de Bel-Air, half a kilometer west to the Seujet Dam. From this new vantage he had no line of sight back to the bank. *If I'm lucky, Niccolò and his goons are long gone. I just hope they think we all got away clean.*

A few meters from Cade, a tense exchange in at least two languages escalated into an argument. He turned his head toward the ruckus—and his neck vertebrae felt like rusted gears, each one fighting the two on either side of it, all of them hurting like a new brand of torture. The police detectives were trading vulgarities in the local patois with a pair of men dressed in the white tunics and trousers of the medical services, and a third man in a firefighter's uniform, who snapped an order at the men in white as he pointed at Cade.

The debate raged on, louder with each passing moment, as the two medics wheeled Cade away on his gurney, through a gauntlet of pissed-off Swiss police who did as little as possible to clear a path from the riverside quai to the ambulance parked on the street a few meters away. It took all of Cade's restraint not to flip the cops a pair of middle fingers on his way by.

Riverside, the firefighter was still arguing with the detective. Cade admired the tenacity of the Swiss. *They really don't like to let things go. They must get that from the Germans.*

The medics parked Cade's gurney behind the ambulance, facing away from it. He heard them open the station wagon's rear door, and he braced himself for a new round of pain. It arrived as expected when the two medics pushed his gurney inside the ambulance. The stretcher's wheel assembly folded up underneath it as it made contact. The gurney rolled to a halt against the left side of the ambulance's patient bay, and the medics shut its rear door.

It took a second for Cade's eyes to adjust to being in the shade, away from the blinding sun. And then he recognized his two traveling companions in the back of the ambulance.

Seated on squat platforms beside the gurney were Niccolò and his colleague, the Japanese man from whom Yasmin had taken the artifact briefcase.

Niccolò took a moment to straighten his tie, and then he welcomed Cade with a humorless smile. "*Ciao,* Signor Martin. Please permit me to introduce my associate, Signor Tujiro Kanaka." He paused to let Tujiro nod once at Cade. "Are you comfortable, *signore*?"

"I'll feel better once this bullet's out of my gut."

"Don't worry. Signor Tanaka and I will see to that." Niccolò slipped a hypodermic needle into Cade's jugular with the softest touch he had ever felt. With one push of the plunger he sent its syringe's contents rushing into Cade's brain, which welcomed its old friend morphine. The stylish mage smiled. "Do make yourself comfortable."

24

If there was one rule Luis had found to be a constant in the practice of magick, it was that every ritual took longer to prepare and hurt more to perform than he had expected. Case in point: An experiment to conjure a temporary portal, a task he had prepared in less than half a day on several occasions, this time had taken nearly two days to complete. It hadn't helped that the Celestial powers had become even less accessible than usual, or that his request had been made during an unfavorable astrological opposition. He had felt something working against him.

No matter. It's done. Time to go home.

He stood in front of a closed door set within a freestanding frame. It had been crafted of precise specimens of wood, every plank of which had been carved with eldritch symbols, all of it held together with nails forged from pure silver and cooled in a bath of holy water. Now it stood inside a magic triangle, in the old conjuring room of the Monte Albano monastery. Luis saw it shimmering with angelic power, though to the untrained eye it would look quite ordinary.

He looked over his shoulder at the monks of Monte Paterno. "Ready, Brothers?"

Nods of affirmation from all twelve men. Each had come barefoot, clothed only in a cassock. Those who had advanced far enough in their study of the Pauline Art to have made a set of conjuring tools carried them in leather rolls strapped across their backs. The few men who had grimoires of their own each carted them under one arm. At the front of the line was Father D'Odorico, and the others had lined up behind him in the order of their seniority within the occult brotherhood: Father Pantelis, Father Hakkila, Father Malko, and then the others, the young novices whose names Luis had not yet committed to memory.

Father D'Odorico gave Luis a nod. "When you're ready."

Luis took hold of the doorknob, turned it counterclockwise, and pushed the door open.

On the other side yawned the wide sprawl of tall grass that stood between his fishing lodge and the shore of Arthurs Lake. "There it is, Brothers. Our new home."

He stepped through the portal and held it open for the others behind him. The monks traversed the portal single-file and in silence. Luis kept a running count, and just to make certain, he counted heads again after the last man had reached Tasmania. A final look back into the Monte Albano conjuring room confirmed no one had been left behind. Luis closed the door, which vanished without a trace the moment it was shut.

It had been dusk in Italy. Now the monks squinted against a harsh early-morning sun as they trudged behind Luis to the lodge. He sympathized with their disorientation. *My own first forays into teleportation were quite jarring. No cure for it but experience.*

As they neared the lodge's rear entrance, Luis sensed something was amiss within. Even through the closed door he heard the cacophony of voices pitched in argument.

Father D'Odorico pushed in close to Luis's shoulder. "What's going on?"

"I have no idea." He opened the door.

A flurry of profanities washed over the monks, starting with Briet's. "It's a reckless fucking plan, and you know it!"

"It's the only thing that makes any sense," Sathit shot back. "We know they have him. We have to figure he'll break and tell them about this place. Our only hope is to strike now, take out the Old Man before—"

"*Nyet!*" Anja slammed her fist on the table. "They do not want *us*. They want *his* work, and *my* codex. To them, he is just a bargaining chip."

Yasmin folded her arms across her chest. "Fuck bargaining! If we kill the Old Man, all his dickhead magicians are instantly unemployed! Then we can go get Cade. I mean, *fuck*, why are we even *talking* about this?"

Anja seized Yasmin by the throat and pushed her against the nearest wall. "I. Said. No." She tightened her grip, reddening Yasmin's round face. "Briet warned you: Breaking the vessel is *dangerous*. Do you not listen?"

Luis stepped forward to interrupt. "Excuse me?" The gaggle of Goetic magicians looked at him, and then they noted the line of monks behind him. Hoping to defuse the tension in the room, Luis cracked a faltering smile. "Could someone catch me up, *por favor*?"

Anja dropped Yasmin, who fell to the floor, coughing and massaging her bruised throat. "You will act when I tell you to act. Not before." Anja took a deep breath and faced Luis. "We moved against the enemy. A bank job."

Briet held up a sheaf of papers. "We got his name: Konrad Brandt. No home address, though." She pointed at a closed briefcase on the kitchen table. "The real prize is in there."

Wary but curious, Luis circled the table to the briefcase. No one objected as he reached out and opened it. As he lifted the lid, a blinding spray of gold and violet light erupted from inside the case. He had to shield his eyes with his free hand in order to glimpse the enchanted object inside. Within seconds Father D'Odorico was at his side, gazing down in wonder.

"Amazing," the older monk said. "A phylactery, and a powerful one at that."

It was a remarkable sight, but it was painful to look at directly. Luis shut the case. "Do I even want to know whose this—"

"It's the Old Man's," Yasmin cut in. "He sent two of his karcists to get it from the bank. We snagged it on their way out. And now we're *sitting* on it instead of *stomping* on it."

Her remark led D'Odorico to raise an eyebrow. "*Scuse?*"

"She wants to smash it," Barış explained.

Father D'Odorico's eyes widened. "That would be supremely dangerous."

Sathit was spun up with agitation. "But taking out the Old Man—"

"Might serve only to escalate this conflict," Luis said. "We know this Konrad Brandt has powerful allies. His mages also might be bound by vengeance pacts if he is slain." He aimed an inquisitive look at Anja. "Do we know for certain the enemy has Cade?"

Anja nodded. "I performed a divination. They took him from the police in Geneva."

That sounded like good news to Luis. "So, we're positive he's alive?"

"*Da.* But he has no magick." Before Luis could ask why, Anja added, "He drowned for a few minutes. Was dead for maybe one or two. So he had no yoked spirits when the cops pulled him out." She swept a fall of her black hair away from her face. "Now the Old Man holds him prisoner. Some of us"—she indicated herself, Briet, and Barış—"want to trade the vessel for Cade. Others"—she glared at Sathit and Yasmin—"want to break the vessel and sacrifice Cade."

Luis pondered the circumstances. "This is not a moment for rash action. I think that with Cade's life at stake, we should seek to minimize the risks of a bad outcome. Better an exchange followed by an awkward detente than a swift escalation leading to mutual destruction."

His attempt at reason only hardened Sathit's stony countenance. "No, Father. We've already lost enough people in this fight. It's time to put an end to it, by ending the Old Man."

"Please, I know patience is difficult. But expediency is not a path to justice."

Yasmin's features contorted with anger. "Fuck justice. I just want to live through *this week*. And the biggest threat to that goal is Konrad Brandt continuing to draw breath."

Her protest earned no sympathy from Anja. "Too bad. The Old Man has Cade, and I want him back. That means we trade: Cade for the vessel."

"All right," Luis said. "How do we set up the exchange? Does the Old Man have some way to contact us? Do we have some kind of channel to him?"

Everyone in the room eyed all the others around them, but if any of them had ideas about how to reach the Old Man or his people, no one was volunteering what they knew. The paranoid vibe that suffused the room led Father D'Odorico to turn a strange glance Luis's way, but the older monk let the moment pass without explaining his reaction.

"Well," Luis said, "for the moment we seem to be at an impasse." He motioned toward the other monks clustered in the back of the kitchen. "So if you'll excuse us, my brothers and I have had a long few days, and could use some rest." He ushered the monks past him so he could stay behind and take Anja aside to offer her a bit of whispered advice.

"If I were you?" He pointed at the briefcase. "I would lock that up, *prontamente*."

───── ∽∽ ─────

Consciousness returned to Cade before he had the strength to open his eyes. *Probably for the best. I should take a second to listen. Get my head together.*

The first thing he did was assess which parts of him hurt, and to what degrees. He sensed his left side was still tender, but the hideous pain of having hot metal in his guts was gone. Someone had tended to his gunshot wound, just as Niccolò had promised in the ambulance.

How many hours ago was that? He tried to guess, but he had no frame of reference. There was a soft glow beyond his closed eyelids—too dim and ruddy to be sunlight. Too steady to be a fire. It had to be electrical, or perhaps an oil lamp. *So no idea if it's night or day. Shit.*

Most of the deep aches in his joints had abated, as had the grinding sensation in his neck. But his arms were extended behind him. A slight twitch of one hand revealed the presence of steel cuffs on his wrists. When he focused, he felt cuffs binding his ankles to the legs of his chair. He was strapped in good and tight. *At least I'm not gagged or blindfolded.* His longcoat had been missing since he was pulled from the Rhône, but someone had taken his tie, as well as his shoes and socks. *Shit like this is why I left my bomber jacket in Tasmania.*

The scrape of metal across rock, shrill and close enough to make Cade wince.

"You're awake," Niccolò said. "Good. My employer desires a word with you."

The charade was blown, so Cade opened his eyes.

He was in a conjuring room. The chamber was spacious, with a high ceiling, walls, and a floor that all had been hewn from bedrock. Parts of the wall were adorned with old tapestries. The domed ceiling had a rough texture, but the floor had been polished smooth, enhancing the beauty of the natural striations in the gray stone. Occult markings were in evidence all around Cade, as were tapers as tall as a man, though none of them were lit. As he had guessed, the light in the room was being provided by a handful of oil lamps arranged in a circle around him.

Niccolò stood behind the metal chair he had put in front of Cade. "You should feel honored, Signor Martin. My employer rarely meets with anyone."

"Maybe he just got sick of talking to a dipshit like you all day."

A smirk. "Make jokes while you can. As your pupil said in Geneva: You should have killed me when you had the chance."

"I still might."

Crisp footfalls echoed in the circular chamber. A tall figure emerged from the shadows behind Niccolò. A man, imposing in his stature despite his apparent age. His dark three-piece suit was elegant, and the polish of his leather brogues was almost mirror-quality. The Old Man wore his white Vandyke trimmed short, his bowler hat at an angle, and his monocle in front of his left eye. He walked with strength and purpose. When he sat down across from Cade, he did so with poise and balance. The only jarring detail of his appearance was his haircut: shaved on the sides and in back, and a lazy flop of gray at the crown. That style had gone out of vogue decades earlier. It seemed the Old Man was not a slave to fashion.

"Hello, Mr. Martin." His accent was London posh, his voice rich but full of gravel. "What a pleasure to finally make your acquaintance."

"Old-school courtesy? What the fuck? Are we having tea? What do you *want*?"

Behind the beard, the smile of a predator recognizing one of its own. "Straight to business, then. Splendid." He handed his bowler hat to Niccolò, as if the karcist were some mere footman, and then he polished the lens of his monocle as he continued.

"Your former adept Lila suggested I might have misjudged you and your peers. That the three of you—and, by extension, your students—might not be so ideologically rigid as I had been led to believe. I seriously doubt that, but if she turns out to be correct, perhaps we can put an end to this conflict. And, depending upon how reasonable you and your colleagues are willing to be, I might even be persuaded to offer you all significant reparations for harms done and losses suffered." His eyebrow curved upward above his monocle. "Unless, of course, you'd prefer to maintain our current state of hostilities?"

As fervently as Cade wanted to spew venom at the Old Man, this was not the time. This was a moment made for diplomacy—a skill set his late master Adair had never taught to him. Fortunately, Cade had spent two years at Oxford, and several before that in an English boarding school, learning to placate the fragile egos of mediocre men in positions of power.

He smiled and lowered his chin in a show of humility. "Let's talk."

"I hope you'll take this as genuine praise," the Old Man said, "and not as a slight in verbal disguise: You've put up a much better fight than I'd expected."

Suppressing swells of anger and stomach acid, Cade smiled. "How so?"

"You and your adepts proved more adroit in Naxos than I'd thought possible. And in spite of all our reconnaissance, you managed to conceal a tertiary escape method in your basement. Your preparedness exceeded even my most generous predictions."

"I'm glad we could surprise you."

The Old Man's polite nod seemed to mask frustration. "All the same. Now that you have suffered some losses, my hope is you'll have acquired a new appreciation for the precarity of your circumstances."

Cade feigned a humble lowering of his chin. "I think it's fair to say that I have."

"Might you then be amenable to discussing the terms of an armistice?"

Lifting his brow at the Old Man's archaism, Cade nodded once. "We can talk about a truce. But let me be clear: I won't make promises I'm not prepared to keep *and* enforce."

"A sensible position."

"So what do you want?"

"Nothing less than any conqueror wants. I want the world. But I'm not young enough, or deluded enough, to think it can be seized all at once. Far from it.

"An example, if you'll permit me: President Kennedy was too quick to placate the Soviets. Yes, I know his brother really negotiated the end to last year's crisis, and if that had gone sour I would have stepped in. Not much point to being one of the richest men on a radioactive cinder, after all. But the deal Kennedy and his brother struck would have been only the beginning. If he had remained in office, he had a plan for complete global nuclear disarmament before the end of his second term. He would have cost me and my peers billions of dollars in arms sales."

"Not to mention handing international dominance to the Soviets."

The Old Man wrinkled his brow. "How quaint. You still think it matters which countries appear to rule the world. As if that weren't all just a convenient fiction, a grand-scale work of kabuki theater designed to conceal the world's true puppet masters from the masses whose strings they pull." He shifted his weight and leaned forward. "By fortunate happenstance, the murder of Kennedy also set the stage for the elimination of the Americans' Occult Defense Program, and the murder of its supervisor Frank Cioffi—a debacle and a crime for which I have made certain your friend Miss Segfrunsdóttir will take the blame."

"I can hardly wait to see her kill you."

The Old Man did not seem troubled by Cade's warning. "She will die in the attempt." He stood. "I am a patient man, Mr. Martin. My ascension has been a century in the making. If I need to wait *another* century to see my designs come to fruition, so be it."

"You're a karcist?" Cade guessed.

A cryptic smile played across the Old Man's weathered features, and he shook his head. "I prefer to let others soil their hands with the stink of demons."

Cade was confused. "But your monopoly—"

"How many oil tycoons drill their own crude? Have you ever seen a railroad baron drive a spike with a sledgehammer?"

"How can you hope to monopolize what you don't understand?"

"What is there to understand? Magick is a *commodity*, Mr. Martin—one whose supply I mean to control."

"I'll give you credit. You do a good job of sounding like a rational person. You've got the soothing cadence. Even your inflections are spot-on. If I didn't know better, I might not pick up on the fact that you're a deranged sociopath with delusions of grandeur."

"Is there some reason you're trying to provoke me? Or is this just typical American rudeness asserting itself?"

"Let's call it the latter. My tolerance for bullshit is at an all-time low right now."

"What part of my proposal do you dismiss as 'bullshit'?"

"All of it. You talk about a truce, but how can I trust you to honor it? You're the one who attacked me, remember?"

The Old Man sounded apologetic. "I have already confessed to the possibility that I made a tactical error. There is no reason for us to compound it further."

"And we all live happily ever after? I don't think so. You say you'll live and let live, but how's that supposed to work when your real goal is a complete monopoly on magick?"

Cade's criticisms deflated the Old Man's chest and slumped his shoulders. "I'm not a monster. Already I've granted a few of your kind license to continue practicing the Art."

Cade remained suspicious. "Care to name names?"

"Your friend Ballard in Varna, for one. He married last month, in case you didn't know."

"I heard. God help us all if that maniac spawns."

"And even I would rather not tempt the wrath of Dr. Ware."

"Smart. There's a reason they call him 'the Wight of Positano.'"

"My point," said the Old Man, his patience audibly waning, "is that Ballard and Ware were willing to make pacts like businessmen. I'm willing to show the same courtesy to you, Ms. Kernova, Ms. Segfrunsdóttir, and any of your peers for whom you're willing to vouch."

Cade telegraphed his doubt with a look. "In exchange for . . . ?"

"The Iron Codex and your new work of magickal research."

"Not happening."

"You reject my offer of truce, then?"

"Let's just say it doesn't suit my present needs."

"How predictable. And unfortunate." The Old Man took back his bowler hat from Niccolò and planted it atop his decades-out-of-date haircut. "Since you won't relinquish the grimoires my karcists need, we're going to torture you until you give up their location and any defenses you've put in place to protect them. Nothing personal, you understand."

Cade mocked the Old Man's accent. "Oh, of course not, old chap. I say! Bring on the rack!"

"Get your japes in now. You'll soon wish you'd bargained."

"No, I won't, because I know there's no point making deals with fascists. They always end up stabbing you in the back."

The Old Man considered that, and then he nodded. "Yes, I suppose we do."

He beckoned something from the shadows.

Niccolò magickally disposed of the chair he had set before Cade.

The figure in the shadows drew closer. It was a woman of average height and build, pushing a simple metal cart. As she entered the dim ring of light that surrounded Cade, he saw it was Lila. Then he got a look at the top of the cart.

It was packed with implements of torture and mutilation. Blades. Spikes and needles. Hammers. Scoops and wires and tools with saw teeth on one side and a razor on the other.

He looked up at Lila. Her hateful stare made him look away.

The Old Man adjusted his monocle. "I wish I could stay for this reunion, but I have a business to attend." He stopped beside Cade. "In case you're curious . . . Miss Matar asked *specifically* to be the one to perform this task in the event that you *refused* my offer." He lifted a barbed hook from the rolling cart of torture tools and held it in front of Cade's face. "I'm sure all of these implements will be agonizing. But in my experience"—he smiled and leaned in close to whisper his parting words into Cade's ear—"there's no sting worse than *betrayal*."

THURSDAY, NOVEMBER 28

One hour of brutality had bled into the next. Niccolò had seen the worst horrors Hell had to offer, but even so he still found himself compelled to turn away as Lila visited one grotesque torture after another upon Cade. The man's screams had been stomach-turning in their anguish. In spite of the Old Man's direct orders that Niccolò stay and supervise Lila's work, he had found it all but impossible to watch.

Lila's methods were ruthless. She had made use of every tool on her rolling cart, as well as a few magickal punishments that inflicted unbearable pain deep inside the subject.

Her flair for this sort of work disturbed Niccolò deeply. What kind of a sociopath took such glee in this kind of cruelty? Overall, Cade had shown exceptional judgment in his choice of adepts. But Lila? Hers was one of the most vicious, sadistic souls Niccolò had ever seen. How had she fooled Cade into training her?

Every moment he spent observing her felt like a wound in his soul.

She took special pleasure in using magick to partially heal the damage she was inflicting on Cade, only to repeat the injuries or exceed them. Three times already Niccolò had watched her pummel the man's fingers and toes into raw bloody gristle, restore them with a demon's gift, and then hammer them into paste once more. Each time, Cade's howls deepened, grew more desperate. Niccolò knew that music all too well. Those were the cries of a man who knew he was going to die here, in the dark, far from everything and everyone he loved.

They were the cries of a man who had lost all hope.

Under her breath, Lila asked Cade where the Iron Codex was hidden. He spat at her.

Lila's hammer struck again. A sickening wet crunch and a wail of agony.

Niccolò fought the urge to vomit.

Why did the Old Man tell me to recruit her? That question had nagged at him for months now, ever since he had first approached Lila at the Old Man's behest. *Does he really think there's value in employing a brutal sadist?*

Driven by morbid curiosity he looked back toward Lila and Cade. She jammed metal splinters under Cade's fingernails, which tore loose with an ugly sound of shredding wet flesh.

Cade's scream was inchoate, primal, and bloodcurdling.

Lila pressed the fingertips of her right hand to Cade's chest. "Do you feel that? The claws of ZAGAN have hold of your heart. And when I give it a little squeeze"—she pushed against his sternum, and Cade gasped, then seemed to choke on his tongue—"it stops."

His body jerked and thrashed against his restraints. He fought for air, each gulp futile and painful, while his former pupil crushed the last breath from his lungs and laughed in his face. It was a terrible spectacle.

Until tonight, I had thought myself jaded. But I have never seen such hatred, not even from a demon. Niccolò flinched and turned away as Lila plunged a corkscrew-like needle into Cade's gut and twisted it into him with slow, callous turns. *How can a woman harbor such evil toward a man who until a few months ago she had called her friend? Her teacher?*

What must he have done *to her to deserve such pain?*

Nothing Niccolò could imagine was sufficient to answer his questions. But he couldn't listen to one more minute of this medieval horror.

He stepped out of the shadows that concealed the periphery of the conjuring room and interposed himself between Lila and Cade. "Let me have a moment."

She put down a saw-toothed spoon that looked as if it had been made to carve eyes from their sockets. "Make it fast. I don't want to lose my rhythm."

Still cuffed and chained to a metal chair, Cade was a mess, from his disheveled head of blood-caked hair to his crushed and mangled bare toes. His clothes were soaked in blood, vomit, and sweat, and the odors surrounding him made Niccolò suspect Lila's tortures had compromised all of Cade's self-control except over his tongue. Cade looked more like an abused side of raw meat than a human being at this point. Niccolò hoped that meant the man was ready to see reason and start talking before Lila turned his guts into a Jackson Pollock on the floor.

"Cade? Can you hear me?"

Beneath the blood and torn skin, Cade's eyelids fluttered weakly. He lolled his head in Niccolò's direction. For a second he seemed able to focus, but then his pupils dilated and he let his head droop. Bloody saliva spilled from Cade's mouth, over his split lips, into his lap.

Lila picked up a scalpel and stepped forward. "Answer him!"

Niccolò backed her off with a raised hand. He turned back toward Cade and leaned in close. "Please. Do not let this go on. Just tell us how to acquire your work and the Iron Codex." Cade didn't respond, so Niccolò took the silk square from his suit coat's pocket and used it to wipe away some of the blood covering Cade's eyes. Within a few strokes the square was saturated. Disgusted, he cast it aside, and then he resumed trying to get through to Cade. "I beg of you, tell us what we need to know. This? It is barbaric. It demeans us both, Signor Martin."

Tears rolled from Cade's eyes and cut winding paths through the dried blood on his cheeks. With great effort he lifted his head. Focused his eyes. And looked at Lila.

Then he spat at her, rageful to the last. His voice was a slurred roar: "That all you got, *bitch*? Stop pulling your punches."

Calm as could be, Lila palmed Cade's bloody sputum from her face. Then she picked up a boline—a small sickle-shaped blade—that had a serrated edge on its outer curve. Carrying it with the confidence of a knife-fighter, she stepped toward Cade. When Niccolò tried to block her way, she stared him down with a feral intensity. "Step aside or I will gut you *first*."

Unwilling to test Lila's resolve, Niccolò moved away from her and Cade.

From behind him came renewed sounds of flesh being ripped and cut, the patter of blood painting the stone floor, the screams of a man whose entire existence had been reduced to an experiment in the prolongation of pain and desperation.

It was more than Niccolò could bear any longer.

"Do what you must," he called out to Lila, without daring another look in her direction. "Let me know if he breaks."

Her reply was steeped in cruel certainty.

"Sooner or later . . . *everyone* breaks."

⁓

Everyone was exhausted but no one wanted to sleep. To retire to a bed now would be to miss out on any number of revelations, and neither the monks nor their Goetic counterparts wanted to be left out. Not with so much at stake and so many secrets to exhume.

Papers had been fanned out across the broad kitchen table in overlapping arcs. Diagrams, sketches, charts, timelines—everything the dark magicians had learned since becoming targets of the person they had come to know as "the Old Man." They had set out all their evidence for review by Luis and his brothers from Monte Paterno, and the bulk of it had proved to be so captivating that not one of the monks had yet made an excuse to retreat to his bunk.

Buried in the ream of papers on the table was one sheet inscribed with numerous glyphs. Some of them Luis recognized as demonic in origin, but at least one was angelic. He pulled that sheet from the stack and held it up toward Anja and Briet. "Where did this come from?"

Briet squinted at the document. "Those are the glyphs used to make the magick-piercing bullets. Its sigils hail from six demons, one bound to each of Hell's six ministers."

Luis pointed out the anomalous collection of symbols in the mix. "Except this one, which is linked to a major angelic power."

His revelation snared Anja's interest. "How major?"

Father D'Odorico answered, "To be precise, it's the sigil of GAMALIEL. The archangel we were asked to invoke for the defense of President Kennedy."

Anja processed that, and then she seemed struck by insight. "The demon sigils—that is how these bullets break magick shields. But the angel glyph? That is how they killed Kennedy."

Father Hakkila plucked the page from Luis's hand. "That glyph also tells us these magick-piercing bullets, as you call them, were made *specifically* to kill Kennedy."

Briet, whose alertness had been fading, sat up straight, eyes wide. "Explain."

Before Father Hakkila could answer, Father Malko, his longtime partner in magickal studies, snatched the paper from his hand and eyed it up close. "Note the supersymmetries in its design. The way all the glyphs echo or reflect one another. Then consider the parallels and oppositions in the astrological preferences of their respective spirits, and—"

"What my long-winded brother is trying to say," Luis cut in, stealing back the paper as he did so, "is that these bullets must have been designed specifically to kill Kennedy because he had an angelic shield on top of his demonic barrier. And not just any angelic shield: one produced by the spirit whose glyph is scribed inside these cartridges."

"That would make sense for the rifle cartridges," Briet said. "But then why did we find the same pattern inside bullets that were never meant to be used against Kennedy?"

Luis shrugged. "Maybe the architects of this scheme had contingencies. If Kennedy eluded the sniper in Dallas, they might have had plans to kill him in another setting."

A pensive look crossed Anja's face. "Or it was just easy." She noted the questioning looks her remark had attracted. "They made the first bullets for Kennedy. Then said, 'Make more. Just in case.'"

Across the table from Anja, Father Pantelis lifted one hand from atop his belly to stroke at his bearded chin. "But then why leave the angelic sigil in place?"

Anja shrugged. "Why fix what is not broken?"

Her question lingered unanswered. Father D'Odorico looked at Luis. "You know what this means? That somehow the enemy learned of the protections we made for Kennedy."

Wearing an expression of shame, Briet said, "I think that's on me. The enemy was poaching karcists from my program a decade ago. Since your efforts were coordinated with ours, I'd bet it was someone in my division who betrayed your secrets."

"That's as may be," said Father D'Odorico, "but if this is the enemy's template for magick-piercing bullets, it means they all share one serious flaw."

At this, everyone around the table perked up.

Anja looked the old monk in his eyes. "And that flaw would be . . . ?"

"As powerful as those bullets might be, they were made to pierce only *one specific* Celestial shield. So while they might be able to break any *Goetic* shield they hit, there are dozens of Pauline shields against which these bullets would be useless."

The wheels of Anja's imagination turned at speed. "Are you sure, Father?"

The old priest gave Anja a confident nod. "Positive."

"Then *you* should lead the fight against the Old Man."

Luis felt the room's mood shift.

All the monks leaned back from the table, pulling away from the idea of confrontation physically as well as mentally. Father D'Odorico shook his head but seemed otherwise tongue-tied. Luis took it upon himself to explain the matter to Anja. "My brothers have forsworn using magick for violence. The Pauline Art is devoted to the study of divination, healing, and defense. It is an art born not of conflict, but of peace."

Anja seemed unsympathetic to that idea. "This is war. We all fight, or we all die."

"We know that," Luis said. "We cannot and will not fight this war *for* you. But we accept that we *are* at war, and that we have an obligation to defend you as our allies. If that means we must stand beside you in open battle . . . so be it."

Briet and Anja traded hopeful looks.

Briet began, "If Luis and his brothers are willing to act as our front line of defense—"

"—we could focus our power on attack," Anja chimed in.

Both women nodded, jointly approving their new order of battle.

Anja favored Luis with a smile. "This might work."

"Indeed it might." Luis mustered a hopeful smile in return.

"Somebody stop the presses," Briet said to the room. "Who among us ever thought they'd see the day when White and Black magicians would go into battle as *allies*?"

Luis raised his nearly empty goblet of red wine in a toast.

"The Lord works in mysterious ways."

Everyone around him replied as one: "Amen!"

❧

An hour of fresh air had been unable to dispel Niccolò's memories of Lila's torture session. The coppery stink of fresh blood, the sound of metal teeth chewing through bones, the wet crunch of cartilage yielding to the hammer— they all haunted him and turned his stomach. *This is why I send demons to strike at a distance. I prefer not to watch.*

He was alone on the snow-covered deck that wrapped around the top floor of the Old Man's alpine chalet. Behind him, his footprints were the only desecration of the fresh-fallen blanket of white, a straight path leading from the solarium's sliding glass door to his lonesome watch at the railing. Below him, the mountainside fell away in steep grades, with thick evergreens bordering a broad but seldom-used ski trail.

Unlike the other magicians on the Old Man's payroll, Niccolò didn't mind cold weather. The others complained about it ad nauseam, especially Ha-tunde, who was firmly of the opinion that any temperature below twenty-two degrees Celsius was "jacket weather." Only Tujiro had ever shown a tolerance for colder climes, but he too had made it clear that tolerating something and preferring it were not at all the same thing.

As if I need him to remind me of that. How long have I tolerated being the Old Man's lackey? He suppressed his rising gorge with a long, deep breath. Centered, he recalled his mantra. *This is all but the means to an end. Never forget: Hell rewards the agonists.*

He lit a cigarette, hoping it might settle the nerves Lila had rattled. Three puffs into it, he knew it would give him no succor. Its heat in the back of his throat only called to mind the stench of cooking skin and searing muscle that had filled his conjuring room when Lila had spent an hour burning brands into Cade's back. The odor had started to fade while she used magick to heal Cade's blackened flesh, but then she had resumed her repertoire, from the top.

The entire matter stunned Niccolò. *How can any man endure such pain?*

His rumination on Cade's durability was interrupted by a flash of brightness in front of him. It was small. Spinning while also hovering in midair. With each tumble it caught the moon's pale light and turned it golden. After half a second Niccolò recognized it as the coin he had given to Cade's student Yasmin, in the Geneva bank several hours earlier. He reached out, plucked the coin from the air, and held it inside his closed fist. "*Audite, audite, audite.*"

When he opened his fist again, the coin was gone, and tall licks of crimson flame danced on his palm. Within them wavered the fire-drawn image of Yasmin's face. He greeted her with a pleasant expression and a welcoming tone. "Lovely to see you again, *signorina*."

She cast furtive looks over her shoulder, as if she feared being overheard. Accordingly, she spoke in a voice barely above a whisper. "*Your offer at the bank? Will you honor it?*"

"Of course. I am a man of my word, Signorina Elachi." He let her see his amusement at her anxiety. "Though, to be frank, that is not the bargain I expected you to seek."

Her fearful mood turned sullen. "*Why? Because you took Cade?*" Her mouth curled into a frown. "*That's his problem. Anja wants to trade your boss's doodad for Cade's life.*"

"And you?"

"*Couldn't care less. All I want is the money. So, how much are they worth to you?*"

"You're the vendor in this transaction, *mia cara*. Set a price."

"*All right. Two million dollars, American, for the Iron Codex and Cade's manuscript.*"

Her demand was steep but not necessarily untenable. "And for the artifact?"

"*You want that, deal with Anja. I swore off playing the middleman when I left home.*"

"I am prepared to double your request if you bring me the artifact, as well."

"*You're lucky I'm bringing you the books.*"

He regarded Yasmin with suspicion. "And why are you? Is it really just greed?"

"*Pure spite. Cade nearly got us all killed in Naxos trying to save his stupid book. He cares more about it than he ever did about me.*" Through the flames, a cruel smile. "*I just wish I could see the look on his face when he finds out it's gone.*"

"Very well, *signorina*. Two million American dollars, in cash." He tested her resolve once more. "Bring me the artifact. I'll pay you five million for that alone."

She shook her head. "*No way. There are magicians all around it, and Anja won't let it out of her sight. I can't get anywhere near that thing.*" Pointing at Niccolò, she added, "*And I need you to swear, on pain of your instant deliverance into the tortures of your Infernal patron, that you won't try to ambush me or double-cross me, and that once our business is done, I get to walk away scot-free. No reprisals, no grudges, no debts. Agreed?*"

"Agreed. I swear to abide by these terms, and to bind my peers likewise." He took a short puff of his cigarette, half of which had turned to ash while he had conversed with Yasmin, and then he flicked its long gray cap into the snow at his feet. Exhaling, he continued. "Where and when do you wish to make the exchange?"

"*How soon can you have the money?*"

"I work for one of the wealthiest men on earth. I can produce two million dollars in two briefcases within the hour."

"*Good. I presume that when our conversation ends, your coin will return to me?*"

"It will."

"*Then go and get the cash. I'll hail you again in ninety minutes, after I'm safely away with the codex and Cade's papers. We'll set the details then.*"

"As you prefer, *signorina*. I look forward to it."

Niccolò closed his left hand, snuffing the ruddy tower of flames. Wherever

Yasmin was, the tongues of fire weltering in her hand had just vanished in a furious twist and a flash—leaving Niccolò's gold coin in her palm once more.

He took a final drag off his cigarette, and then he flicked it into the darkness. Coils of his smoky breath unwound behind him as he walked back inside the chalet. On his way to the guest suites to wake his colleagues and recover his wand, he checked his watch.

Ninety minutes from now, Signorina Elachi will be quite rich. He smiled. *And I will be just one step away from becoming the most powerful karcist the world has ever seen.*

26

Kizkalesi stood dark and silent, surrounded by the placid waters of the Mediterranean Sea. The abandoned fort a few hundred meters off the southern coast of Turkey had been the loneliest place Yasmin could think of, making it the ideal place for a clandestine meeting. Now she stood on its rubble-strewn shore, gazing up at it in wonder. Despite being over a millennium old, the walls of the vaguely triangular fortress were in excellent condition, save for a few ragged breaches. A pair of sixty-foot-tall circular towers anchored the ends of its northern wall.

This should keep things nice and private.

She had told Niccolò to meet her inside the fort, but caution had compelled her to finish her jaunt outside its walls rather than risk dropping into an ambush. Trudging through a broad fissure in the western wall, she was thankful to be back in her own clothes—fatigue pants, a loose shirt and jacket, and combat boots. The boots gave her better footing as she made her way over heaps of broken stone. She needed all the traction she could get, thanks to the weight of the Iron Codex and Cade's bundled pages of research, which she toted in a large backpack.

At the wall's inner threshold she paused to scout the vast courtyard within. It was impenetrably dark; heavy clouds had blotted out the moon and stars. Yasmin employed the Sight to reveal the fort's details, which her magickally aided vision rendered in sepia tones.

The fort's inner structures were long gone and had left only the footprints of their former domains. Jagged slabs of broken rock littered the wide-open space. Here and there, a few skinny saplings had grown, each one a testament to nature's tenacity.

Hovering several meters above the field of desolation were Niccolò and two of his associates, Hatunde and Tujiro, whom he had told Yasmin to expect. They were spread out from one another. Niccolò was in the middle. Tujiro was to Yasmin's left, Hatunde to her right—and they each held one large briefcase. Niccolò, by contrast, held only his wand.

He beckoned her with his free hand. "Please, *mia cara*. Join us."

Yasmin emerged from the wall's accidental passage and walked slowly toward the trio. With each step she took a mental inventory of the knives hidden on her person—and closed her hand around the device concealed inside her coat's front pocket.

Fifteen meters from the men, she stopped. Around them, an eerie stillness. No wind moved inside the ruins. Barely audible were the lazy waves lapping against rocks outside.

Niccolò raised his hands. "The moment of truth."

She slipped free of her backpack. Unzipped it. Angled it toward the trio so they could see the codex and Cade's bound documents. Then she zipped it shut. "Now you."

Small nods from Niccolò prompted Tujiro and Hatunde to open their respective cases. Both appeared to be packed solid with American hundred-dollar bills.

The lids closed with soft clicks.

An unseen force tugged on the backpack. Yasmin resisted. "Not yet." Her refusal had come out sharper than she'd intended. She had hoped to play this cool, but now she had no choice. She put her right hand in her coat pocket. "You don't get the pack until I get the money."

Tujiro regarded her with naked condescension. "And if we take it anyway?"

Yasmin removed her hand from her pocket to reveal a detonator, whose shoe she had already clutched into the firing position. "Deadman's switch. Half a kilo of C-4 in my bag. If I let go? Or you cut the wire? *Boom*. Kiss the codex and all of Cade's work good-bye."

Niccolò dipped his chin, his expression incredulous. "Overkill, *signorina*?"

"Call it insurance."

In a deep voice with a smooth accent, Hatunde said, "Trigger that, and you'll die."

"Get rich, or die trying." She beckoned with her free hand. "Let me check the cases."

"The cash is all there," Hatunde insisted.

"Forgive me if I don't take you at your word. If they check out, I'll hand one of you the trigger. After I'm gone, pull the detonator from the charge in the bag. Done."

No one raised any objections. Niccolò assented with a nod. "Pay her."

Hatunde and Tujiro let go of the briefcases, which floated over to Yasmin and came to rest in front of her. With her free hand she opened each case, riffled through the stacks of bills to make sure they weren't padded with blanks or rigged with traps. A quick survey of the cases using the Sight confirmed there were no enchantments upon them or the cash inside them.

She closed the cases and locked them. "Okay. Who gets the switch?"

No one volunteered. With mild exasperation, Niccolò made a decision. "Tujiro."

The order earned Niccolò a dirty look from his colleague, which he deflected with an urgent tilt of his head in Yasmin's direction.

Compliant but unhappy, Tujiro floated to the ground, made a soft landing, and walked to Yasmin. He held out his left hand. "Carefully, please."

"No shit. I don't want to get blown up any more than you do." Yasmin extricated her hand from the deadman's switch and relinquished control of the trigger to Tujiro.

They were halfway through the handoff when, from behind Yasmin, Anja's voice resounded inside the courtyard. "Who do we kill first? The traitor? Or the vermin?"

From another direction, Briet answered, "Kill them all and let Hell sort it out."

Yasmin froze, and then she looked up and back. Anja stood atop one of the fort's great towers, her wand out and ablaze with green fire. Pivoting, Yasmin found Briet perched on top of a different tower, her wand crackling with tendrils of violet electricity.

Their arrival actually brightened Niccolò's mood. "How nice of you to join us!"

Pack and trigger in hand, Tujiro stepped back from Yasmin.

A bolt of lightning from Briet scorched the sand into glass at his feet.

"Not another move, asshole." Briet aimed her wand at Tujiro.

Anja kept hers pointed at Yasmin. "You. . . . How could you?"

"You made it easy." She shifted her footing to stand over the two briefcases, and snuck her left hand into her coat pocket. "I'm done being your pawn."

"Better my pawn than my enemy." Anja flourished her wand, a preface to a strike—

Yasmin plucked an enchanted pearl from her pocket and hurled it at her feet.

It exploded with an emerald-green flash, and a smoky portal opened beneath her. She and the briefcases fell through it, gone in a blur—and landed half a second later on a gentle slope of deep sand, with the portal still swirling overhead. She drew her wand from beneath her coat and pointed it at the portal. "*Claude ostium!*" The rip in space-time snapped shut, leaving behind a trace of greenish vapor that evaporated in the cool night air.

A clean escape. Nice.

She stood. Dusted herself off. Took in her surroundings.

A few hundred meters to the northeast stood the Pyramid of Menkaure. Behind it loomed the far larger Pyramid of Khafre and, largest of all, the Great Pyramid of Giza. Beyond the trio of ancient wonders, the lights of Cairo glowed like a beacon.

Yasmin mentally instructed her demonic porter Ravok to collect the cases, which vanished into its custody. Unburdened, she began her slow plod down the hill of loose sand.

Her next order of business would be to find clothes befitting a proper Muslim woman, so as not to draw attention once she reached Cairo proper. But after that . . . ?

I'm a free woman with two million American dollars in cash. I see a hot bath and a long massage in my future.

<hr />

The moment Yasmin escaped, the showdown at Kizkalesi went from tense to clusterfuck.

Briet struck first. A fistful of lightning at Tujiro. He knocked it aside, into the dirt.

Anja hurled a plume of fire at Hatunde. He turned it away by filling the courtyard with a sandstorm and placing himself and Niccolò safely in its eye.

As the tempest sped up, Niccolò parted his hands, tearing Yasmin's backpack in half. The Iron Codex and Cade's books tumbled free and shot through the maelstrom into Niccolò's hands.

The C-4 brick landed at Tujiro's feet.

As Niccolò caught the codex and manuscript, Briet fired another stroke of lightning at Tujiro—but cut the wire to the deadman's switch instead.

In a tenth of a second, she saw it all in slow motion: the churning dust funnel twined with licks of orange flame . . . the bomb bouncing as it hit the ground . . . Niccolò conjuring a spiral of blue sparks in midair . . . Tujiro twitching in the grip of wild blue lightning—

A searing flash. Bright as the sun, louder than thunder, it rattled Briet's teeth inside her head and filled her ears with pain. It shook the earth and poisoned the wind with the stench of singed hair, cordite, and burning blood. Black smoke filled the fort.

After the roar . . . silence. The conjured sirocco died out, but not before it tattered the dark fog, revealing that Niccolò and Hatunde were gone, and the magickal texts with them.

A wide swath of the ground was painted with blood and shredded viscera. Tujiro's body had been blown to pieces, all four limbs parted from the trunk. Half his head was missing. What remained look like a charcoal briquette. Coils of intestine hung tangled in tree branches. The entire grisly mess smoldered; pockets of fat inside the mangled torso were still burning.

Stunned by the speed with which the confrontation had unraveled, Briet stared down at the carnage and shook her head. When she saw Anja levitate down from her tower to the courtyard, she used PALARA's gift of telekinesis to float herself down to meet her.

She found it hard to read Anja's expression as the woman nudged one of Tujiro's arms with the tip of her boot. Briet sidled over to her. "Fucking hell. What a mess." Clocking her grim ally's sidelong look, Briet added, "I ordered this medium-rare."

"You think this is a joke?"

"It's not? Let's review, shall we?" She made a show of counting with her fingers. "Cade's still a prisoner. Yasmin's in the wind with two million dollars. The enemy has the Iron Codex and all of Cade's research. And we're knee-deep in this fucking guy's pancreas. Yeah, I'm really *loving* this plan, girlfriend. You've outdone yourself."

Bitter silence festered between them.

Anja sighed. "Could be worse." She noted Briet's prompting glance. "Could be raining."

Thunder rumbled. Seconds later, the sky unleashed a storm of biblical proportions.

Torrential rain flattened their hair and filled their shoes.
Briet scowled at Anja. "You just *had* to say it, didn't you?"
Anja stared at the sky. "Could be worse."
"Don't you say another fucking word."

27

Lila was the last of Niccolò's surviving peers to join him in the chalet's library. He, Hatunde, and the Samuels sisters noted her arrival with varying degrees of annoyance. Two steps into the library Lila paused and backpedaled half a step, instantly defensive. "What?"

Niccolò tapped the face of his watch. "I said this was urgent. Where have you been?"

"Washing my hands and changing my shoes. But if the Old Man doesn't care whether I track blood through his house, next time I'll just come running."

With a large hand to Niccolò's chest, Hatunde preempted a verbal escalation. "It's done. She's here. Let's get on with it." He met Niccolò's stare with perfect sangfroid.

"Very well." He motioned for Lila to join him and the others at the library's long table. Upon it rested the Iron Codex, a massive grimoire with heavy outer bindings of wood banded with iron, and a collection of newer papers tied together with strips of silk and twine. "I am pleased to report our campaign against Signor Martin and his cohort is at an end." He gestured at the two occult treasures. "We have obtained the objects of our desire."

Around the table, eyes went wide with avarice. Anorah reached out with a gloved hand to touch the cover of the Iron Codex. "Is it true this can help yoke angels?"

"*Sì.* And that is the least of its wonders." Quick movements of Niccolò's fingers directed a demon's hand to undo the bindings on Cade's papers. "The Iron Codex contains protective sigils more powerful than any previously known. And sources Below tell me that Signor Martin's research has uncovered links to rituals that will change forever the way we practice magick. By combining these two great works, we five will harness a new kind of power."

Adara leaned back, her face a mask of doubt. "Not the first time I've heard *that* line. This will get you killed." She signaled her sister with a backward nod. "Let's hit the road."

"Not yet. I want to hear this." Anorah caught her sister's angry look and mirrored it.

For the first time that Niccolò could recall, the sisters were not in accord. It was too soon for him to know whether that was an omen of good or ill. Still, this was an opportunity not to be wasted, and if he hoped to make the most of it, he would need four tanists inside the great circle. Which meant he needed to persuade both sisters to stay and see this through.

To his left, Hatunde spread the pages of Cade's research across the table. "This all looks promising." He met Niccolò's gaze. "But I want to hear it from you. What *is* this? What did my friend die for tonight?"

"Tujiro gave his life so we could make the first major advance in the practice of the Solomonic ritual in more than two thousand years." Niccolò unfastened the bindings on the Iron Codex as he continued. "Think of what we all were told when we began our studies, however many years ago. There are six ministers of Hell who sign pacts with mortals. We are permitted to choose only one of those six as our patron, and through it gain access to all of its subordinate spirits, forsaking access to those of the other ministers."

Nods of understanding from the others. A good start.

He opened the Iron Codex. "Then our masters taught us that those six ministers answer to two greater spirits, PUT SATANACHIA—also known as BAPHOMET—and BEELZEBUTH, who reign over the ministers in the Infernal Descending Hierarchy, three ministers to each greater spirit. And those two greater spirits answer in turn, to one power only: the Emperor of Hell, SATAN MEKRATRIG. Those three constitute the unholy trinity, none of whom can be summoned to appear on earth, nor be compelled to sign pacts with mortals."

Niccolò let a knowing smirk manifest on his face.

"What if I told you that was a *lie*?"

Now he had the other karcists' undivided attention. "By fusing the protections found in the Iron Codex with new rituals detailed in Cade's papers, my patron assures me we will be able to conjure either of the greater spirits we desire—and compel them to sign pacts."

Lila looked as if larceny and terror were vying to dominate her soul. "If I sign a pact with one of the greater spirits, would that mean . . . ?" She seemed to lose track of her question.

"It would give you the right to strike subpacts with the three ministers under its control," Niccolò said. "And through them, you would have access to all of their subordinate spirits. Your potential range of talents would triple instantly." He turned toward Hatunde. "And where your first patron spirit promised you seven hundred years of life? Now you can get fourteen hundred more from two more ministers—and another thousand from the greater spirit they obey." He looked into the eyes of the doubting sister. "Imagine that, Adara! Three *thousand* years of life!"

Anorah, perhaps dreaming of new powers, seemed giddy. "Could we strike pacts with both greater spirits?"

"No," Niccolò said, but then he corrected himself. "Or, I should say, not yet. We all would need to choose one or the other . . . for now. But with three thousand years to plumb the secrets of Heaven and Hell . . . we might one day learn to bind even Emperor SATAN to our will."

Marveling at Cade's handwritten pages in his hands, Hatunde said in a hushed voice, "Think of all we could do in three millennia. Imagine all we could learn."

"Now you understand, *amici miei*. We stand poised to become not just the greatest karcists in the world but the most powerful who have ever lived. And with these tomes to guide us, we will be forever without equals. But I will need all four of you to make this work."

He felt the electricity in the room. The anticipation. The rising will to power.

"So? Are you all with me? Hatunde?" The rugged scholar nodded his agreement. "Anorah? Adara? What say you?" The twin sisters conferred briefly and in whispers. Then they both gave him slow nods of accord. Which left only the master's newest retainer, the cold-blooded sociopath who made demons look tender by comparison. "Lila? Are you in?"

Her dark brown eyes studied the grimoire and the papers but betrayed nothing.

Then a single nod. "I'm in."

"Splendid. Now, we need to prepare the conjuring room, but we have no further need for Signor Martin. Signorina Matar? Please go downstairs and kill your former teacher."

Lila acknowledged the order with a subtle bow of her head.

"Yes, Master."

The moment the book was opened, BELIAS flew free. Undetected by the five mortals convened around the tome within which it had been bound, the fallen spirit resisted the temptation to spread its wings and shatter the room with thunder. Not out of caution or mercy, but fear.

Sworn to silence and invisibility am I. Forbidden to shed blood.

Because in truth, BELIAS was not and never would be free. Merely released from one cage or another to serve on a long leash, in accord with fearful instructions. Its only genuine concern was avoiding fresh torments and escaping the material sphere of the Eve-spawn, to once more seek refuge in the consuming fire of the Pit.

So long have I burned within that flame, its temper has become my temper. Its fiery embrace now feels as soft as it once was severe.

Hovering against the library's ceiling, BELIAS was forbidden to touch any of the mortals gathered beneath it. It could not peel the tender skin from their faces. Break their bones. Grind their guts into paste and savor the heady draughts of terror to which the human heart was heir.

It had instead a simple set of directives, the first of which was to act without delay or detour. Compelled to obey, BELIAS departed the library and passed through its walls like a sparrow through a bank of fog, impelled by an engine of hatred at the core of its being.

The arrogance of humans. These fragile, fleeting bags of blood think themselves worthy to command my kind. I beheld the shattering of the cosmic singularity. I have seen billions of great races born only to die. Always the same story. Pride—and then the fall.

The spirit moved like the faintest of breezes through the chalet. Down starkly lit corridors, up long stairs, through rooms as empty as they were cold.

In the upper rooms of the mountain retreat, a man of advanced years sat at a desk reviewing pages full of numbers, while paying no mind to the canine companion lying on the floor at his feet. His own kind would think him old, but to BELIAS the earth itself was young, and so even the longest-lived humans were nothing to the demon but a blink in the stare of eternity.

Even if BELIAS had been willing to give in to temptation and defy the orders of its sending, it could not touch the Old Man. The elderly human had been tattooed with several sigils of protection, including one from BELIAS's master, ASTAROTH. One of the man's sigils had recently been negated, perhaps by the death of the karcist who had bestowed it. With effort BELIAS discerned that, of the six ministers' sigils, the only one missing was BELIAL's.

Its curiosity sated, the spirit moved on at the speed of thought.

Deep in the hewn bedrock beneath the chalet, in its capacious conjuring room, the demon discovered that which it had been sent to find and liberate: the karcist Cade Martin.

Being in any kind of proximity to Cade was painful for BELIAS. Just like the karcist who had sent BELIAS, Cade was a *nikraim*, a human whose soul had been fused before his birth with the immortal essence of an angel. The human radiated angelic power in spite of his disheveled state. To bear witness to such energy after having been cut off from it billions of years earlier was agony for BELIAS, but it had its mission. Pushing through the cold burn of angelic light piercing its spectral form, the demon removed the bindings from Cade's wrists and ankles.

Unbound, Cade stood from his chair and massaged his wrists. He looked around and sniffed at the air. "Show yourself."

To make itself heard by the human's ears, BELIAS forged a voice from the endless roar of the deepest sea. I AM HERE.

"Did Anja send you?"

SHE DID.

"With what instructions."

FIND YOU. FREE YOU IF YOU LIVE, AND OFFER TO BRING YOU TO HER.

"And if I refuse to go?"

RETURN TO HER AND REPORT THE LOCATION OF THE IRON CODEX.

"Then do that. Because I'm not leaving here until I settle a few scores."

AS YOU DESIRE.

The demon made its exit from the chalet before Cade had a chance to change his mind. It made no difference to BELIAS whether the karcist accepted rescue or rebuffed it. Whether he lived or died. *If he wishes to die here, so mote it be.*

With all but the last of its obligations honored, the spirit raced through the dark, toward the coming dawn, eager to finish this mission and be returned to its Infernal repose.

Let me be safe in Hell's embrace once more, the spirit begged of a God that no longer heard its prayers or cared for its fate. *And let me dream of the death of Man.*

The demon was gone, but its sulfuric odor lingered in the conjuring room, sharp in the sudden cold that the spirit's departure had spawned. Cade was well accustomed to the stink of demons after more than two decades of using them for magick, but being familiar with an unpleasant thing didn't make it any less noxious.

Cade massaged his wrists as he skulked to the door. From the other side he heard men's voices. Two of them, making small talk in German.

Guards. So much for just walking out.

He looked around the oval room, seeking fodder for a distraction. Beside the wall to his right stood a table and some shelves loaded with a variety of laboratory-style glass—beakers, phials, measuring cups. All handmade by Niccolò or his fellow karcists, just like all other major implements of the art. Impending mischief put a smile on Cade's face. *Perfect.*

He walked over to Lila's cart of torture tools.

Picked up the hammer and a dagger. Carried them both back to the door.

He flung the hammer with all his strength at the table full of glassware.

It struck dead-center with a bang, followed by an unholy clamor of shattering glass.

At the sound of bolts being retracted and keys turning in the door's lock, Cade stepped to the hinged side of the door and waited. It swung inward, concealing his position.

The first guard through the door, a tall man with a shaved head, let his semiautomatic pistol lead the way. Cade let him pass and waited for the second guard to enter behind him. The backup man was Cade's height but barrel-chested and bearded.

Cade seized the second man by his hair, yanked his head backward, and stabbed him in the throat. Warm blood jetted from the wound, drenching Cade's arm. The dying man couldn't scream, but the sound of the knife piercing his flesh and his frothy gurgle were enough to make the first man turn around—only to be struck in his throat by Cade's thrown dagger.

Staggering backward, the tall man fired one shot, which ricocheted off the floor to the left of Cade. The guard fell on his ass and sprawled like a child making an angel in the snow.

Cade kneeled over the tall man and retrieved the dagger. Wiped it clean on the guy's shirt. Tucked the blade under his belt. He took the dead man's pistol from his hand. It was a Walther P1, a reliable weapon. Cade ejected its eight-round magazine. Six rounds of 9 mm Parabellum left, plus one in the chamber. He pushed it back into place, engaged the Walther's safety, and tucked the pistol behind his waistband. A quick search of the previous owner yielded one spare loaded magazine. Cade stuck it in his right pocket.

Next he searched the second man, from whom he took a Zastava M57 semiautomatic pistol. Unlike the Walther, the Yugoslavian-made Zastava fired 7.62 mm Tokarev rounds from a nine-round magazine. He put the spare clip for that weapon in his left pocket.

Got to make sure not to mix those up. That would be bad.

Then he made his most important tactical acquisition: the second man's boots and socks. To Cade's relief, the boots were a snug but passable fit.

Once more properly shod and armed, Cade left the conjuring room with the Zastava held low but ready for action. He had no yoked spirits and therefore no magick, but he was still a former U.S. Army Ranger and MI6 assassin, with loaded weapons and a plan.

His confidence was high. It was time to go hunting.

28

Goetic karcists and Pauline monks sat in a variety of poses on the periphery of the grand circle in the fishing lodge's conjuring room. A pall hung over them, a mood like that of condemned prisoners dreading the hangman's summons, or frontline troops awaiting an order to advance upon an invincible enemy target.

Representing the razed Monte Paterno sanctuary were its former director, Father Bernardo D'Odorico, and three of his senior practitioners: Father Malko, Father Hakkila, and Father Pantelis. D'Odorico had passed the slow hours reflecting on the Psalms. Fathers Malko and Hakkila had spent the same time arguing in whispers about matters spiritual. Father Pantelis had devoted the lacuna to somber reflection and silent prayer, and he alone had made the effort to light a few sticks of pleasing incense, to purge the room of lingering demonic fumes.

Their Goetic counterparts had made other uses of the brief downtime. Sathit had taken it upon herself to instruct Briet, Anja, and Barış in the rudiments of a card game called bridge. After more than two hours of listening to Sathit expound upon such ideas as "passes," "bids," "tricks," and "trumps," as well as players reduced to compass directions, Anja still had no idea how to play this ridiculous game, and she had no idea why she would ever want to learn.

Luis sat apart from both groups, thumbing through a book he had told Anja he had read several times in the past few years, a dog-eared copy of Jack Kerouac's *On the Road*.

They all were freed from the shackles of anticipation when a tower of green fire rose from the bounding circle inside the thaumaturgic triangle to the south of the great circle. As the flames licked at the ceiling, the monks and Goetic magicians got to their feet. With obvious reluctance, Luis folded a corner to mark his place in his book and closed it in one hand. Then he, too, stood to hear the report of the demon that Anja had sent abroad hours earlier.

Anja stepped to the edge of the circle and drew her wand, in case BELIAS chose this occasion to indulge in a fit of pique. "What news, spirit? Speak, I command thee!"

THE IRON CODEX IS OPENED, the demon answered in a voice of crackling flames and the sound of ashes blown by the wind. IN THE CHALET ABOVE FAFLERALP, SWITZERLAND.

Anja felt her hopes rising. "And is Cade there?"

HE IS. AND HE LIVES. BUT HE REFUSED MY PASSAGE.

"Very well. Spirit, provided thou harm no one, I dismiss and discharge thee. Return directly to thy Infernal repose, and appear to me when, and only when, I call for thee. Begone!"

The demon let out a low growl but said nothing. The floor inside its bounding circle vanished, revealing a black void—starless, lightless, soundless—into which the beast of flames plunged. As soon as the last lick of flame from its head was through the opening, the floor reappeared, and all trace of BELIAS save its odor was gone.

Anja raised her voice to make sure the whole room heard her. "Our target is a chalet above Fafleralp, Switzerland. Whatever preparations you need to make, see to them now."

Briet moved through the conjuring room, checking on each person as she went. She, too, spoke in a voice for the room around her. "Secure your things. Your weapons. Your grimoires. Leave nothing precious with a porter demon. If you're wounded and the spirit abandons you, it will take at least half and maybe all that you have entrusted to its care."

Casting off an outer robe, Sathit revealed she was garbed from head to toe in black fatigues. Tucked under her belt was the SIG Sauer pistol she had captured at the Geneva bank. In addition, she had acquired from Anja's demonic porter a pump-action twelve-gauge shotgun, for which she had donned a bandolier loaded from end to end with shells.

More sensibly, in Anja's opinion, Barış and Briet had armed themselves with military-grade rifles: Belgian-made FN FALs, 7.62 mm automatic weapons with thirty-round magazines. Each of them also had their wand hidden securely inside their overcoat, ready for quick-draw should Anja's planned assault devolve into a magickal duel.

The monks all were busy saying final prayers of cleansing, so she left them be. Luis, meanwhile, cast aside his copy of Kerouac, took a deep breath, and cracked his knuckles by weaving them together and making a single flexing stretch of his arms.

Anja stopped in front of him. He had come a long way from being the man who had refused to get involved when she had needed to save the world almost a decade earlier. But she still harbored doubts. They both were Gray magicians, but Luis leaned far closer to the Pauline side of the spectrum, while Anja, in spite of being able to wield angelic power, had continued to favor a more Goetic approach to the Art. Could she really count on him to stand with her in war?

She waited until she caught his eye. "Are you sure you can do this?"

He nodded. "Positive."

"Because if you balk when the fighting starts—"

"I won't. I have a wide repertoire of talents, including one I think you'll love." He took heed of her inquiring look. "It's called a 'spirit hammer.' It's an angelic talent. If I'm strong enough, I can use it to sever all of a karcist's bonds to their yoked demons." He smiled. "I can literally smack the Hell out of them."

Overhearing him, Briet moved closer. "Maybe we should put *you* on point."

Luis shook his head. "Don't. I can use the hammer only once, and then it's gone."

"In that case? Choose your target wisely, Father."

Anja moved into the middle of the room and raised her hand, drawing everyone's focus. "This is the order of battle: Each Goetic magician will be paired with a Pauline monk. Monks provide defense. Karcists press the attack." She pointed everyone into their pairings. "Father D'Odorico, with Briet. Father Malko, with Sathit. Father Pantelis, with Barış. Father Hakkila, with me. And Luis . . . ?" Looking him in the eye, she felt unworthy to give him orders.

Taking her cue, he said, "I'll be right behind you, guarding all your backs."

That was good enough for Anja.

She used her wand to draw a triangle of blue fire in midair. When the pattern was complete, a wash of indigo flames passed over its interior, which faded to reveal a snow-covered mountainside bathed in moonlight—and then the flames around the edges faded away. "Time to move."

Briet herded the group toward the fire-edged portal. "All right, people.

Next stop, Switzerland. Don't forget your gloves and tuques, because I promise you it is *cold* out there."

Their ragtag magickal army trudged toward the portal. The monks led the way. As Father Pantelis stepped through, he muttered just loud enough for Anja to hear, "I hate snow."

That was when she remembered that all the monks, because of their vows of poverty, were barefoot. And she was sending them into knee-deep snow in the middle of the night.

As she followed them onto the Swiss mountainside, she feared this plan might not be as ready for execution as she had hoped. But by then it was too late.

The attack had begun.

———

Certain indignities came with being the one at the bottom of a hierarchy, the last in a pecking order. Drudgery. Scut work. Menial tasks. So it came as no surprise to Lila when Niccolò paused in his explication of his plan to use the Iron Codex and Cade's research to expand their magickal access to Hell's legions, to send her on a dull errand.

"To better explain this," he had said, "I will need to compare the relevant sections of the *Pseudomonarchia Daemonum* and the *Grimorium Verum*. I believe there are copies of each in the reading room on the first floor. Lila, be a dear and fetch them for us, please."

Not a request, but a command disguised with a pleasantry.

There had been no point to protest. Lila was the newest of the Old Man's retainers, at least until a replacement was found for Tujiro. That meant she had to endure being treated like the help. Such were the dynamics of nearly any group, any organization. One was expected to eat shit, to pay one's dues as a demonstration of obeisance. In that respect, the Art was no different from any other subculture. To be new was to be abused.

She buried her resentment and left the library, betraying nothing as she went. If the others had snickered or taken any pleasure in her being treated like a servant, they had hidden it well. *At the very least, they held their tongues until I was out of the room.*

That was more than she could have said for some of her childhood peers.

Her steps echoed in the empty corridor. She always felt conspicuous inside the chalet. It was so austere, its spaces so devoid of furnishing or inhabitation that it seemed more like a museum than a home. With no carpeting to muffle steps or voices, every little sound carried from one end of the mountain retreat to the other, resounding ad infinitum.

Down the stairs to the first floor. Like so much of the house, the staircase had been designed to feel open and airy. It had no backing and no walls, just wide steps suspended on its frame. A narrow handrail was all that prevented people from tumbling off and crashing down one floor after another all the way to the basement.

The chalet's first floor was dead quiet. Its only background sound was the low hum of the refrigerator in the kitchen. No one lived on this floor, and most of its rooms had never seen a guest, despite being adorned with priceless works of art and the most stylish of furniture.

Lila quickened her pace. At the far end of the house from the library was the reading room—an architectural choice she found questionable at best. She opened its door, stepped inside, and conducted a quick search. Just as Niccolò had said, copies of two of the world's most important works of magickal scholarship, the *Pseudomonarchia Daemonum* and the *Grimorium Verum,* had been left on a low table in front of two armchairs with matching ottomans, all tastefully arranged facing the hearth, in which a banked fire now smoldered.

She gathered up both books and hurried out of the reading room.

A few steps shy of the stairs, a powerful hand seized the back of Lila's shirt and pulled her into the shadowy environs of the kitchen. She dropped the books and struggled, but her assailant had an arm around her neck in a flash. Then her head was forced backward, and she felt the cold bite of a knife's steel tip against her throat.

The next voice she heard was Cade's.

"Not one fucking sound, Lila."

She stopped fighting and relaxed. He let her go, and she spun to face him.

"Fucking took you long enough," she berated him. "Where the *fuck* have you been?"

He sighed. "Long story."

Six Months Earlier. . . .

Teeming crowds shuffled past the open-air café in various directions, not a soul among them paying any heed to Cade and Lila sharing a small table.

He found that surprising. Attitudes in Marrakesh tended toward the provincial at best, and in most cases leaned toward the ultraorthodox. Though Lila wore a black burqa and niqaab, as was customary for adult Muslim women in Morocco, it was decidedly unusual for her, a young unmarried woman, to be without a chaperone while in public with a Western man.

A waiter dressed in flowing white linen trousers, a matching shirt, a dark paisley vest, and a red fez brought their Turkish coffees in hand-decorated porcelain *kahve finjani* cups. As usual, Lila had ordered hers *sade,* or unsweetened, while Cade had asked that his be served *orta,* with a couple of teaspoons of sugar. Though they had not ordered any food, the waiter brought a small plate of dark chocolates and two glasses of tepid water. Cade recalled from gut-wrenching experience that the chocolate was safe to enjoy but the water was not.

As the waiter departed, Cade lit a Lucky with his Zippo, and then he tucked the lighter back into the pocket of his bomber jacket. He took a long drag while Lila sipped her java—a delicate operation that involved lifting the lower part of her niqaab away from her chest and sneaking the *kahve finjani* beneath it.

Cade exhaled smoke. "Has anyone followed you lately?"

"No." Lila's voice was clear despite her face being hidden by her niqaab. All that Cade could see of the young woman was her dark brown eyes.

"Some of my students have seen people tailing them." He studied the pedestrians in the street and the clientele inside the café for spies and eavesdroppers. "And I've had old friends tell me people have been asking after me and Anja. About my research, and the Iron Codex."

Lila set down her cup. Picked a morsel of chocolate from the plate. "What people?"

"In Europe, an Italian man who likes fancy suits. In South America, a well-spoken Nigerian man. In the United States, a pair of blond twin sisters. In Asia, I'm told, it's a Japanese man with no sense of humor."

Lila lowered her voice. "Have you fought any of them?"

"Just one. A high-strung Dane. Anja helped me kill him in Stockholm two nights ago." Savoring another slow drag on the Lucky, Cade considered how much to tell Lila. "He didn't tell us much. But I think this is where you'll come in."

She swallowed a demure nibble of chocolate. "I don't understand."

"The man we took down was a karcist. His patron was ASMODEUS. Same as yours."

"So? A patron can sponsor any number of karcists."

He could tell she was becoming defensive. Softening his tone, he tried to set her at ease. "No one's accusing you of anything. What I'm saying is, Anja and I think that all of the people looking for us have been karcists, each one sworn to a different patron, but all of them working for the same person or organization here on earth." A roguish grin. "We're hoping we just made a job opening. One the enemy will ask you to fill."

Her posture straightened, telegraphing her discomfort. "Why would they ask me?"

"Because they've been watching us. All of us. Looking for clues to our strengths. Our faults. Our allegiances. If they're on to you at all, they'll have figured out you're one of the world's most talented Goetic karcists sworn to the sigil of ASMODEUS."

She feigned offense. "*One of?*"

"I'm glad you have a sense of humor about this. You're gonna need it." He flicked the ash from the end of his cigarette. "If Anja's right, these people move fast. They might approach you tonight for all we know."

"If they ask me to betray you, I will cut out their tongues."

"No, you won't. Listen to me, Lila. These people, whoever the fuck they are, have shown themselves to be filthy fucking rich, dangerously well-informed, and strongly motivated. And the biggest threat to us right now is we have no idea what they want, or who they serve. We can't risk you taking a stand against these people. Rebuffing their invitation could be fatal."

"You *want* me to betray you?"

"It's called being a double agent. You tell them you'll work for them, but the whole time you'll be gathering intelligence for me and Anja. Think you can do that?"

Beneath the niqaab, an anxious nod.

"Okay, good. If we're right, and you get approached by recruiters for some rich mystery outfit, take the job. Get as deep inside their operation as you can. Dig up secrets. Earn their trust at any cost. Find me a way to take them down or keep them in check."

"How do I tell you what I find?"

"No idea. You'll have to look for gaps in their security, find a way to get a message out. We'll be counting on you to give us an advance warning if the enemy moves against us."

Lila tried to take another sip of her coffee, but when she picked up the fragile cup, her hand trembled so violently that her bitter drink splashed across the table. Embarrassed, she set down the cup. "Why me? You have other students sworn to ASMODEUS."

"None as powerful as you. They won't attract the enemy. You will."

"How can you be sure?"

"Because two men are watching us from the café across the street right now." Cade flicked away the stub of his first Lucky and lit a fresh one. He exhaled through his nose. "The brown-skinned gent with the shaved head, and the Japanese fellow in the white seersucker suit. They don't know they've been spotted."

Cade watched Lila to see how she would react. Would she give away their advantage? Freeze at the first sign of threat? Flee and leave Cade to mop up the mess?

Lila enjoyed another demure sip of coffee beneath her niqaab. She adjusted her pose to steal a surreptitious look at the mirrored wall behind their café's bar. Reflected in it, between bottles of watered-down scotch and bootlegged Russian vodka, were the two figures Cade had described. Neither seemed to realize Lila had just clocked their presence.

She set her cup on its saucer. "What now?"

"Bait the hook. Look up quickly, as if I've said something horribly rude. Then stand and slap me in the face as hard as you can. And make it hurt—we need to sell this."

Fear churned in Cade's gut. If he was asking too much of Lila, he might be about to get her killed. And even if this harebrained scheme worked as intended—

Lila played her part to perfection. Her recoiling suggested deep indignation. Then she bolted from her chair, cocked her arm, and delivered a full-hand slap to Cade's face that snapped his head halfway around. When the echo of the smack faded, Cade became aware of the sudden hush that had filled the café, the weight of a crowd's gaze falling upon him, and the burning sting of Lila's violent contact with his left cheek.

Feigning shame, he stood with his eyes downcast and dropped a few bills of local currency on the table. "Well done," he whispered. "Wait for them to come to you. Good luck."

There was no time to say more. He turned his back on her and walked out of the café, praying that one day he would see her again, and that neither of them would have to regret the terrible gamble he had just made.

～

Lila took hold of Cade's arms and bowed her head. "I am so sorry. Please forgive me, Master."

"You've done nothing wrong, Lila."

Tears fell from her eyes. "Yes, I have. I tried so hard to do as you asked. But they watched me *all* the time. I never had a free moment."

"Lila, your warnings are the only reason we had half the defenses we did. If you hadn't told us a major attack was coming, I never would've built an escape portal in the villa's cellar."

Grief contorted her features, and her voice caught in her throat, as if she were choking on each word. "But . . . all those lives! The other students." She shut her eyes and fought to keep herself from breaking down. "My mirror. Niccolò used it to destroy all of yours." She inhaled through gritted teeth. "Leyton. Mira. Mel. Gathii. Yong-Mi. All dead because of me."

Cade pulled her into a consoling embrace. "It wasn't your fault. I tried to save them. So did Anja. But this is war. And the truth is, we can't save everyone."

"But I opened the door."

"They were coming for us no matter what. I told you to earn their trust at any cost, and you did. Now we just need to make that gamble pay off."

She stepped back, out of his arms. Pulled herself together. "Are the others coming?"

"Count on it. Anja had one of her bond-spirits smuggled in with the codex."

"That explains how you got free. Even with my illusions faking your torture, those bonds were as real as Hatunde could make them." Once again, her countenance dimmed. "I wish I'd known what they'd planned for your friend Miles. I would have covered for him, too. Instead all I could do was call in the anonymous tip to his people."

Her news filled Cade with both sorrow and gratitude. "When I heard he'd been rescued, I figured that was you. . . . Thank you."

"Don't. If I had seen what was happening sooner—"

He lifted a hand to stop her. "Don't second-guess yourself. It'll drive you crazy."

"But I can't stop thinking about it. About what they did to him. And I just *stood* there." Again her eyes brimmed with tears. "Because I was afraid."

"Lila, listen to me. There's no shame in being afraid." She glared at him, as if she were angry that he would try to console her with such an obvious lie. He pressed on. "I'm going to tell you something I've never told anyone. Not even Anja."

He waited until he was sure he had her attention. "When I made the landing at Pointe du Hoc on D-day, there was a moment, just after I hit the beach . . . when I froze. I scuttled into a crater and curled up and started shaking. I was crying and wanted to hide, and I knew that I might shit myself at any moment. All I heard were bullets screaming past my head, and shells going off, and grenades blowing up—and Lila? I just fucking *cracked*. Right there on the beach. I thought I was gonna die, and part of me just gave up." He paused, realizing his own eyes were now wet with tears born of a horror he wished he had long ago left behind. "And I would've died there. Except another soldier told me to get off my ass. My buddy Dutch. He told me I wasn't hit. Then he told me to get my fucking ass up the rope. So I did."

He looked into Lila's frightened brown eyes. He saw that she didn't understand.

"I know what you're feeling, Lila. It's called 'survivor's guilt.' I've watched friends get killed, and yet I live on. I've had to live with knowing that dozens, even hundreds of people have died so I could go on drawing breath. And I can't even count how many times I've asked myself, 'Why them and not me?' Or, 'Did Fate make a mistake?' I wonder if I deserve to be here." This time Lila looked down at her feet. Cade had struck a sore spot. "I won't lie to you, Lila. The pain never goes away. Neither does the doubt. It just waits for its next chance to cut you down."

She looked up at him, a portrait of sorrow. "How am I supposed to live like this?"

"You try to live a life worthy of their sacrifice. And you hope if the day ever comes when you need to do the same, that your courage won't let you fail." A bittersweet memory of a heartfelt conversation beside the Thames returned to him. "Or, as my late master Adair used to say, 'You get up. You go on. And you *burn brightly.*'" He gave her shoulder a brotherly clap. "So what do you say? Ready to go out in a blaze of glory?"

"No."

"Good. That's how people get killed." Cade drew his stolen pistols, one in each hand. "Draw your wand. We need to find the Old Man, pronto." Moving with soft prowling steps, he tossed his next words over his shoulder. "Because the second our friends get here . . . we're gonna light this bastard up."

29

Barefoot monks and booted magicians moved in pairs through a dense cluster of old evergreens. They were ankle-deep in snow as they trudged up the alpine slope toward the Old Man's chalet. Briet had hoped the snow would be light and powdery, but it was heavy and wet, like fresh cement. The wind slashed at their faces as if it bore them a grudge.

The cloudless sky was salted with stars, and the waxing moon was more than three-quarters full and as bright as limelight. Low in the west, it cast long shadows across the slopes and valleys of the Alps. Briet checked her watch. By her reckoning, in just under three minutes, the moon would vanish behind the slopes of the Birghorn, leaving everything from the Breithorn to the Sattelhorn steeped in true darkness. Then it would be time to strike.

Behind her: the soft crunches of running feet compressing snow; the muted rattle of well-secured weapons and gear bounding off moving bodies. Briet crouched behind a fallen tree and looked back. Barış and Sathit leaped through Anja's portal into the woods. Unlike many such magickal rips in the fabric of space-time, this one had no telltale glow around its edges on this side, no frame of fire or lightning to betray its presence.

Anja must have spent years looking for that, Briet marveled. Recalling that she and Anja had the same Infernal patron, she considered asking her—after this battle was done and they were back on safe ground—what demon had granted her such a portal. *As if she would tell me. Karcists guard their secrets even more jealously than stage magicians.*

She turned her eyes toward the Old Man's chalet, a few dozen meters upslope from her position in the woods. There were lights on inside, in spite of the hour; it was nearly two o'clock in the morning here. Beyond the windows' gauzy drawn curtains, a dance of shadows suggested someone was home and awake. Engaging the Sight courtesy of her yoked spirit Vos

SATRIA, she searched the woods. She saw no roaming guards, either human or animal.

Odd. No perimeter defenses? Despite a declared state of hostilities? When she looked back at the house and perceived its robust magickal protection, she chalked up the absence of patrols to overconfidence. *The Old Man and his karcists think the house is impregnable. Which means it's up to us to prove them wrong.*

She looked back toward the portal, only to find it had vanished. Briet's focus was drawn by a blur of motion on the edge of her vision, but then it, too, darted away. She assumed it had been Anja. *A Russian who fought in the Winter War? I'm lucky I saw that much of her.*

Another glance at her watch. Two minutes until the moon dipped out of sight.

Briet hunkered behind the fallen tree, alone in the cold with her memories and her regrets. *I should have known not to go home. I could have sent a telegram. Or a message hidden in a box of flowers. Hell, I could have written "RUN" with pepperoni on a pizza and sent it to them. Instead, I led a golem to our door.* She wiped rageful tears from her cheeks. *But I can't just blame myself. I didn't send that monster. These evil pricks did. And now it's time to make them pay for what they did to Hyun and Alton. For what they did to Frank. To my life.*

She pictured in her mind the thrill of seeing this stilted alpine chalet come down in a storm of fiery chaos . . . and she smiled. That was why she had come.

I want to see the Old Man's face when I turn his house into kindling.

Father D'Odorico's tall body was awkwardly stooped as he hurried from the forest to join Briet behind the fallen tree. He settled in beside her with a nod, which she returned. Then she checked her watch. One minute until assault.

Briet squinted to see the disk of the moon through the trees. It sank fast, swallowed by the overlapping slopes of the Alps, its light fading like a drowning man succumbing to the sea.

Then it was gone.

No more shadows in the woods. No more frosted light to limn the trees. The snow, which moments earlier had seemed aglow as if from within, now looked like dull gray stove ash.

Only one light source drew the eye now in the fathomless black beneath the Breithorn: the chalet. It spilled warm golden light in every direction, a beacon for attention. Looking upon it with a heart full of hate, Briet wanted nothing more than to extinguish the chalet's fires forever.

She nudged Father D'Odorico. "Ready?" He gave her a quick nod.

Briet broke from cover and vaulted over the fallen tree.

The priest followed several paces behind, losing ground with each step.

Sprinting upslope, Briet felt her heart slam inside her chest, and her breaths grew short and desperate in the rare mountain air. Her FN FAL rifle slammed against her back even though she had cinched its strap tight across her chest. Comforted by its weight, she fantasized about putting a bullet between the Old Man's eyes the moment he climbed free of his splintered house.

I hope he begs for mercy. It will make his death so much sweeter.

She reached her next point of cover, a snow-frosted boulder. There still was no sign of a patrol, and what little activity she noted inside the house was languid. Relaxed.

We have the element of surprise. Good.

Father D'Odorico scrambled into position behind her and crouched.

She snapped her fingers once to signal she was ready. The sound carried in the crisp silence. A few seconds later she heard two finger-snaps in quick succession—the signal that Anja was ready to attack—followed by the snap-pause-snap signal from the two apprentices. Everyone was in position. It was time to take this fight to the enemy at last.

Briet stood and threw back the hood of her parka, to let her red hair whip freely in the cold wind. It felt like freedom.

From the chalet, the echo of footsteps on wooden planks. A single sentry walked beside the railing of the upper floor's sundeck. Briet was close enough to the chalet that with the Sight she could discern the man was young, fair-haired, and lanky. He gazed into the distance as he ambled across the deck, his mind on something or someone very far away.

A rifle shot scattered his brains across the side of the chalet.

Score another kill for Anja the Stalingrad sniper.

At her feet, Father D'Odorico tensed as the shot echoed off the mountain-sides. He looked up at her and did his best to conceal his fear. "Did it work?"

She turned an ear toward the chalet and listened. From inside came a din of shouting voices, the hustle of running feet, the clangor of armed men scrambling into action.

"It worked." In one smooth motion, she unslung her rifle and raised its stock to her shoulder. "Brace yourself, Father. Now comes the messy part."

———

Tapping the relevant passage in the pages of the Iron Codex, Niccolò admitted to his colleagues, "I have no idea where we're meant to find the death mask of an angel, and this formula for the tribute demands the inclusion of *Viola cryana,* an herb that's been extinct for thirty—"

A muffled crack of gunfire from outside. Everyone in the library tensed.

Alarm bells resounded throughout the chalet.

Looking around, and then noticing the time, Niccolò noted with anger and suspicion, "How long has Lila been gone? Where is she?"

His implication dismayed Hatunde. "Surely you don't think she—"

Major Rico Corocho, a commander in the Old Man's company of mercenaries whose chief claims to notoriety were having once killed a bull with a knife and his expulsion from the French Foreign Legion, threw open the library's door. Holding an automatic rifle in his left hand, he snapped at the assembled karcists, "We're under attack! By *your* kind!" And with that the man was off and running, scrambling to load a fresh magazine into his weapon on the fly.

A grim intuition put Niccolò on alert. "This is it. The enemy is here." He drew his wand. "They have come for Cade."

The other three magicians looked bewildered. Adara drew her wand, but then she wavered in place like a small animal caught in a car's headlights. "How did they find us?"

From outside came the stutter-buzz of rifles on full auto. Thumps of detonation. The battle was underway. "All of you, prepare to fight. Protect the Old Man at all costs. Defend the house if you can, but his life above all." He waved his wand toward the door. "Go."

The twin sisters left first.

Hatunde and Niccolò met at the doorway. As usual, Hatunde struck an optimistic note. "Perhaps Lila sounded the alarm, and is outside, holding the line."

"Maybe," Niccolò conceded. "But if she betrayed us, she dies tonight."

———

Bullets ripped through tree bark and peppered Anja's face with stinging bits. She and Father Hakkila stood a few meters apart, their backs to broad trees, both trying to stay cool as six mercenaries from the chalet strafed their position from outside the woods. In less than a minute the air had turned sharp with the stench of gunpowder.

It made her crave a cigarette.

"You were right," Hakkila said. "They're firing magick-piercing rounds. I feel their sting through my shield." He glanced in the direction of fire. "How long do we wait?"

"Let them get close." Anja felt the need to conjure an attack as if it were an itch in her soul. "We need their weapons."

Staccato bursts of gunfire churned up the snow between them, ostensibly a warning of what to expect if they tried to charge their attackers. Hakkila listened as more guns chattered in the dark. "What do you think? Kalashnikovs?"

An explosion of smoldering bark from Anja's tree made her lean left, away from the burst. "Chinese knockoffs. Type Fifty-six."

"Must be how the Old Man became a billionaire: cutting corners."

She turned a questioning look at the middle-aged monk. "You know weapons?"

"What are you saying? I can't have a past?"

Thunder came with a flash of white light, followed by the rapid patter of shrapnel.

"Grenades," Hakkila muttered, as if Anja needed the explanation. Another peek around his tree, and then he added, "They're in the woods."

Anja conjured the barbed whip of VALEFOR and set it ablaze with the fire of HABORYM. "Full shield, now." Hakkila shifted his weight onto his back leg, and with a flourish raised both his open palms to project a massive curved wall of angelic protection between them and the approaching mercenaries. Anja brought her demonic whip to bear. It passed through the monk's invisible barrier and snapped into one merc's chest, ripping him open from liver to larynx.

The other five soldiers-for-hire in his unit opened fire at Anja. Their vaunted magick-piercing bullets flared against the monk's angelic shield—but failed to break through.

A sweep of her arm hectored the squad with LERAIKAH's poisoned arrows. Two more men fell. The other three scurried for cover.

Anja ferreted out the last three men with forks of green lightning that bent around trees to find their targets and reduce them to quivering masses of fried nerves and smoking flesh.

She signaled Hakkila to stay low and quiet.

There were no more mercs active near her, but she heard the muffled sounds of the apprentices ambushing a second merc squad in the woods farther upslope.

"Clear." She moved toward the dead mercs and beckoned Hakkila to follow. "Stay low. Get their guns." They scampered through the underbrush to the mercs, whom they disarmed one man at a time, making sure to grab reload magazines for their rifles.

"You were right," Hakkila said, holding up a rifle. "Type Fifty-sixes."

Piercing the darkness with the Sight, Anja caught sight of shimmering forms racing down the slope from the chalet and swiftly closing in on the woods. "We have a new problem."

Hakkila followed her eyeline—and then he froze, eyes wide.

Prowling between the trees, skulking toward their position, were two dozen spectral wolves invisible to anyone not empowered with magickal vision. Green flames danced from the beasts' eyes, and noxious glowing poison spilled from between their bared fangs.

"Hellhounds," the monk grumbled. "The Old Man's magicians are in the fight."

The phantomlike wolves spread out, flanking them, and then surrounding them in two circles moving in opposite directions. Snarls filled the air as the circles contracted.

"Let them come." Anja braced her stolen weapon against her shoulder.

Hakkila braced his own rifle, and then he put his back to Anja's. "Count of three." The hellhounds pressed inward. "One."

She set her eye behind her rifle's targeting sight. "Two."

His finger curled around his trigger. "Three." He picked his first target. "God help us."

He fired, and their world became a fury of bullets, fangs, and fear.

So much for the plan.

Briet didn't fear the mercs' magick-piercing bullets. Father D'Odorico had kept his promise of a shield that could stop them. The pack of hellhounds unleashed by the Old Man's magicians? That was proving more of a challenge.

There were dozens of the fiends. They charged in waves down the slope and then—just as they were almost within range of her attacks—they darted with preternatural speed and grace into the trees, using them as cover to evade Briet's best strikes of lightning and fire.

The Old Man's mages must be directing them. Hellhounds aren't this smart on their own.

Cracks of rifle fire resounded from high overhead. Briet searched for the source but couldn't find it, even with the Sight. *An invisible shooter, has to be. But on whose side?*

Huddled behind the fallen tree, she put her trust in Father D'Odorico's shield as she stood to pick off a few more hellhounds emerging from the woods behind them. She skewered two with the unerring javelin of MEZA-MALETH, blasted a third into vapor with the flames of PYRGOS.

The next three veered wide in a flanking run. Briet channeled the frost-shaping talents of EGROS and turned the snow on the slope into spears of ice that erupted beneath the hellhounds and hoisted them into the air. Impaled, they whimpered and then dissolved into mist.

Flush with confidence, Briet filled her hands with fire and looked for fresh targets. Indulging a reckless urge, she taunted the enemy: "Is that the best you've got?"

Then the snow around her and D'Odorico sublimated into fog, and then the mass of swirling vapor became an army of specters, charging at them from all directions at once.

I had to ask.

Luis raced out of the dark and stopped in front of her. He held his arms wide and his palms up as he bellowed, "Get down and shut your eyes!"

She shut her eyes and dived into the snow. Even so the flash was blinding, hot and white as if she were staring into the soul of the dawn, and with it came a roar like a jet engine and a wind that made whips of her hair and fluttered her great coat above her prone form.

The light faded and Briet dared to open her eyes.

The legion of phantoms was gone, and Luis helped Briet stand. "Are you hurt?"

"I'm fine." She brushed snow off her clothes. "What the fuck was that?"

Luis seemed unable to hide his satisfaction. "The sword of URIEL."

Recalling the monk who years earlier had balked at the notion of using force, Briet met his news with approval. "You've come a long way, Father."

Her compliment left him abashed. "Too kind." He pointed upslope, toward the quartet of enemy karcists who had emerged from the chalet and were on their way to intercept them. "But we still have a little farther to go."

One of the enemy karcists hurled a flurry of indigo lightning. It struck something high overhead, halfway between the two groups. In a flash of violet, a figure with a woman's shape fell from the sky, slammed through the snowy boughs, and vanished into the forest.

From a distance Briet couldn't tell who it was, but a sick feeling in her gut told her it must be a member of her team. Whoever she was, she was alone, hurt, and vulnerable.

Briet shouted to D'Odorico and Luis, "With me!"

And before they could reply, she abandoned caution and charged into the woods.

Once the bullets started flying, it no longer mattered how many times Sathit had told herself to be brave. Her reflexes took over and put her into a fetal crouch behind the broad trunk of a tree.

The monk's shield will hold. It has to.

A few feet away, Father Malko flinched as incoming fire peppered his invisible wall of angelic power. The White magician had also taken cover behind a tree—no doubt an instinctive reaction, but not one that filled Sathit with confidence.

How does war keep finding me? A battlefield was the last place Sathit wanted to be. She had hoped never to see combat again after Cade helped her flee the Hmong guerrillas who had pressed her into service at the start of her country's civil war. All she wanted out of life was to be a painter; all she wanted from magick was a chance to peek beyond the veil that separated life and death. *I don't want power, or money. I just want answers to questions science can't even ask. But here I am again . . . dodging bullets and holding a rifle. Fighting someone else's war.*

She tightened her grip on her shotgun as her guts churned like a pool of hot mud.

I didn't ask for this. But if it's a war the Old Man wants—

The reports grew louder, the echoes shorter. The mercs were close, inside the forest. Sathit caught Malko's attention and signaled she was ready to strike. He nodded his assent.

One clean pivot out from cover and Sathit had a clear view of three riflemen.

They all snapped toward her. Their muzzles flashed with fire, and Sathit felt her heart skip a beat in terror as she unleashed the flying blade of ORIAS. Swerving and spiraling, the demon's spectral knife left a blur of light in its wake as it sped around trees and slashed the mercenaries' throats. Two of the men fired off wild bursts as they fell. The third dropped face-first into the snow. When the echoes of gunfire faded, Sathit was relieved to find the monk's shield had performed as promised. The magick-piercing bullets had been countered.

Sathit scrambled toward the fallen men. Malko hesitated, but after a second of fearful indecision he scrambled into motion behind her.

She reached the point man, took his rifle, and searched him for spare magazines. At her side, Malko performed last rites over the fallen man. She glared at him. "What are you doing?"

"What my faith demands."

"Survival demands you grab a weapon."

The monk shook his head. "I cannot."

Sathit pocketed the two magazines she had found on the point man, and then she stepped over him, to his nearest fallen comrade. She thrust the next man's rifle at Malko. "Take it."

"I don't know how to use it."

She ejected its magazine and showed it to him. "Two-thirds full. About twenty shots, plus one in the chamber." She slammed the magazine back into the rifle. "Safety's off. Point at center-of-mass and pull the trigger. When it's empty, press this to eject the magazine. Put in a fresh one. Then keep shooting." This time she forced the weapon into his hands.

"I will not take human lives."

"The next thing coming for us isn't human."

She saw the telltale flicker of magickal light in Malko's eyes as he engaged the Pauline equivalent of the Sight—which meant he, too, saw the approaching pack of hellhounds, their eyes aflame and their teeth glistening with poison.

"Keep your shield up, and lay down suppressing fire to drive them toward me." She invoked the gift of ASARADEL to launch herself into the air, while at the same time using the talent of FORAS to render herself invisible.

"I don't know what that—" His voice trailed off as Sathit soared above the treetops.

She tucked her stolen rifle's stock against her shoulder, set the weapon for semiautomatic fire, and trained its scope on one of the hellhounds.

Time to see if this thing really is loaded with magick-breaking bullets.

Bam! One shot vaporized a hellhound on contact. *Oh, yes.*

Hovering above the battle, Sathit put her sharpshooting skills to use, picking off one hellhound after another. Down below, Father Malko ducked and recoiled from the echoes of gunfire whose origin he seemed unable to discern.

The hellhounds, single-minded terrors that they were, pushed relentlessly forward. Either the beasts failed to notice their numbers shrinking beneath Sathit's expert sniping, or they were too dumb to care. As the last hound exploded into green mist that dissipated in the span of a breath, an eerie silence descended upon the mountainside.

Then it all went to shit.

The moment Sathit caught a glimpse of the four magicians walking down the slope from the chalet, one of them wrapped her in a bolt of lightning that felt like burning barbed wire. Paralyzed and biting her own tongue, she felt as if she were erupting in flames from the inside. She plummeted through snowy boughs that snapped beneath her, and then she hit the ground like a sack of meat. It took her a second to realize she had sunk a few feet into the hard-packed snow, and then she struggled in vain to draw breath.

Half buried, unable to breathe or stand, she listened in terror as the woods filled with the roaring of flames, mad sizzles of lightning, and dull thuds of demonic fists meeting angelic shields. Then came the horrific crack of a tree snapping like a toothpick, followed by the wet crunch of breaking bones and a grotesque cry of pain that Sathit recognized as Barış's.

～～

The plan worked right up until the moment it didn't. Barış had a perfect vantage from which to strike at the pack of hellhounds. It didn't matter that the creatures had surrounded him and Father Pantelis. With the monk's angelic shield in place, Barış had been free to pick off the Infernal vermin at will, and he had almost started to enjoy this rare opportunity for target practice.

He wielded PERIKAEL's lightning as if it were a lasso.

Its crackling loop of blue sparks filled the air with the scent of ozone, and when it closed around a hellhound's neck, it severed the beast's head and sent its essence back to Hell. One fortunate throw had snared two of the hellions at once, and with a single pull on the line's slack, Barış cut them both in half. As their bodies turned to sickly green vapors, he yanked his line of sky-blue electricity back behind the monk's shield and readied it for his next throw.

The hellhounds leaped and snarled at the invisible holy barrier that kept them at bay.

Just four of them left, Barış noted with rising hope. *As soon as I finish them, we can head upslope and sneak behind the Old Man's—*

The hellhounds' next lunge brought them to within striking distance. They were too close for Barış to risk using a fireburst, and he wasn't sure he could snare them at point-blank range with his demonic lasso without entangling himself. He called over his shoulder, "Father? What's going on?" There was no reply. He risked a quick glance backward.

Father Pantelis was on his knees, his face a mask of agony, his right hand clutching at the left side of his chest. His left arm hung limp at his side, and his usually pale round face was flushed almost violet. Most telling of all, in spite of the freezing air and the fact that he was barefoot in the snow, the heavyset monk's bald head was coated in sweat.

The strike team had prepared for every kind of attack except a heart attack.

Father Pantelis's eyelids fluttered shut, and he collapsed facedown in the snow.

The hellhounds sprang in unison and slammed into Barış with stunning force.

A deafening crack filled the air as they snapped his spine and broke the trunk of the tree against which they'd pinned him. Terror clouded his mind as each of his wrists was caught in a hellhound's viselike jaw, and one of his legs was torn in half at the knee by a third.

All Barış could do was scream . . . until the last beast sank its fangs into his throat.

A hand reached into the snow and seized Sathit's wrist.

Briet pulled Sathit to her feet and then into motion. "Come on! Run!"

Being upright and moving helped Sathit inhale, and she felt a surge of relief as she drew a full breath. Then she broke away from Briet, who had been dragging her toward Anja's last known position, and darted toward the ski slope. "Cover me!"

There was no time to argue or talk tactics. Sathit knew what she had to do.

On the run, she ejected the empty magazine from her rifle and loaded a fresh one.

Forks of lightning arced around trees, clearly trying to find a path into her back. Fireballs came up short against tree trunks, setting swaths of the mountainside on fire. Demonic whips cracked like thunder, shearing away whole stands of trees with one strike. The enemy was near and getting closer by the second. Sathit reached the ski trail and ran to its center.

I only get one shot at this.

She took a knee. Raised the rifle. Peered through the scope.

At the peak of the slope stood the chalet. Peering down at the battle from one of its top-floor windows were the Old Man and his dog.

Sathit set her targeting sight on the Old Man. Put her finger on the trigger. She exhaled. Felt her body go still in the space between heartbeats.

Then she fired six shots in three seconds.

The first made the magickal shields around the chalet flash and shimmer.

The second made them crackle with lightning.

The third popped them like a soap bubble.

The fourth cracked the window and made the Old Man run for cover.

The fifth shattered the window into a million fucking pieces.

The sixth put out the ceiling light in the room beyond the window.

Sathit pivoted, expecting to face the Old Man's hired-gun karcists. Instead she was met by Briet. Father D'Odorico and Luis were close behind her, and she saw Anja and Father Hakkila sprint out of the woods to join them.

"The chalet's shield is gone," Sathit told her friends between gasps.

"Good work," Briet said. She frowned. "Where are Barış and Pantelis?"

Sathit's downcast eyes and dark expression told everyone the bad news.

"Cry later," Anja said, turning to face the four enemy mages. "Now we end this."

* * *

Seven on one side, four on the other, they halted twenty meters apart on an open field of knee-deep snow between the ski slope and the chalet.

Anja was on point, several meters in front of her comrades. Behind her to the right was Briet; on her rear left was Sathit, with Father Malko at her back. Father Hakkila haunted Anja in the same fashion, and Father D'Odorico hewed to Briet as if he'd become her shadow. Only Luis stood alone, lurking several meters behind the rest of the group, out of sight on the slope below.

Facing them, in a line with the chalet at their backs, were four karcists loyal to the Old Man. One of the identical-twin Samuels sisters stood at the far left. Next to her was Niccolò. Hatunde held the third place in the skirmish line, with the other twin sister on the far right.

A tense silence settled over the field.

Tiny licks of flame danced on fingertips. Tendrils of electricity crept between digits on karcists' hands. The cold swirling breeze turned rank with sulfuric fumes. Magick was in the air.

Niccolò and his mages attacked, all at once.

He focused his assault on Anja, pummeling the invisible shield provided by Father Hakkila with a swiftly changing array of forces: cones of fire, brute-force energy assaults that dimpled the angelic shield almost to its breaking point, multipronged forks of lightning that quickly ripped holes in a barrier Anja had thought impenetrable. Within seconds he had her and Hakkila both fighting to avoid being pushed backward down the slope.

From the flanks the twin sisters hectored Sathit and Briet.

The one on the left unleashed from her wide-open mouth a jet of frost and needles that grew into a vortex surrounding Sathit, and then she skewered the snow devil with indigo rays projected from her eyes.

The twin on the right enveloped Briet in darkness and then barraged the lightless sphere with everything she could muster: a flurry of daggers, cascades of lightning, deafening thunderclaps spawned by the flapping of a demon's wings.

Hatunde aimed his attacks at the monks protecting Anja and the other Goetic karcists. He conjured an orb of lightning above the karcists' heads and then used it to launch strikes at the holy brothers. When that failed to breach the monks' defenses, he harried them with flights of ghostly arrows wreathed in hellfire. All his missiles ricocheted into the night and vanished.

Then he conjured a long spear topped with a fearsome blade.

The moment Anja saw it, she knew it was the spear of SKOVOG—a shield-breaker. Her late master Adair had conjured it once during the Great Patriotic War. Fear took hold of her.

Hatunde threw the spear.

Anja tracked its arc. Reached for it with the hands of BAEL.

The spear's blade slashed through her demon's grip and stung her hands with sympathetic pain. It pierced the shield of Father D'Odorico. Slammed through his chest and staked him to the ground with his lifeless eyes staring up at his dead God.

Seeing their mentor fall was all it took to distract Fathers Malko and Hakkila for a fraction of second—which was all the twin sisters needed to overcome the monks' defenses and cut them down in gruesome whirlwinds of demonic power.

Now the battle was four against three, because Luis was nowhere to be seen.

Anja's fear became a swelling tide of despair.

Niccolò tilted the odds further in his favor. With a silent command, he filled the vast space behind him with a legion of spirits. His horde of demons rose like ghosts from the snow, charged past him like berserkers, and filled the night with monstrous, bloodcurdling shrieks.

The blond twins both attacked with demonic whips, cracking them at Briet and Sathit.

Briet caught her foe's whip and set it aflame with the power of PYRGOS. Hellfire surged up the bullwhip, shot through the blonde's shield, and set her ablaze in the blink of an eye.

The other twin broke Sathit's shield. She coiled her whip around Sathit's neck. Sathit retaliated with a fireball, but the blonde swatted it down into the snow at her feet.

With a violent jerk on the whip, the blonde broke Sathit's neck with a loud snap.

Hatunde threw a curving stroke of lightning over the horde at Anja.

She opened a portal with its entrance facing the electrical strike—

—and its exit facing the second blonde's back.

It slammed into her spine and burned through her heart before she had time to realize she had been cut down by Hatunde's attack.

Her smoldering corpse fell, twitching and electrocuted, face-first into the snow.

Anja cursed under her breath. *I meant to open that portal behind him.*

Niccolò's phantom legion was just a few strides from striking distance.

Anja marshaled the exorcising talents of her yoked angel CADRAEL.

Bluish-white energy shot from her raised palms. Ribbons of energy impaled and linked every demon in Niccolò's Infernal legion. In a cerulean flash, his entire army of ghosts vanished.

Smoke and steam rose from the eerily quiet battlefield.

From the nearby woods, braying howls preceded the appearance of the last four hellhounds. The beasts charged toward the standoff, growling with wild—

Anja fired a single pulse of CINISAEL's black disintegrating energy from her left hand and reduced the hounds to smoke and echoes, both of which quickly vanished into the night.

Hatunde and Niccolò regarded the pair of women facing them with clear respect. "I suppose," Hatunde said with a hint of humor, "it's a bit late to call for a truce."

Briet tilted her head until the crick in her neck released with a pop. "Afraid so, sport." She aimed her wand at him.

Anja raised a hand to stay Briet's attack. She said to the men, "You want to surrender? Take back your sigils of protection for the Old Man and walk away."

Her demand seemed to intrigue Niccolò. He tucked his wand under his belt and sank his hands into his coat pockets. "And if we refuse?"

"We kill you both. Your sigils die with you. And then we—"

Reacting to a shift in Niccolò's weight, Briet leaped in front of Anja. Something went *bang*. Then she fell at Anja's feet, writhing and clutching her bloodied gut with both hands.

A second shot shattered Anja's shield and banished AMYNA from her yoke.

Smoke rose from a fresh bullet hole in the pocket of Niccolò's overcoat.

He pulled a semiautomatic pistol from his pocket and aimed it at Anja.

"Forgive me, Signora Kernova. You were saying . . . ?"

30

Five minutes earlier . . .

Moving like a ghost through the darkened halls of the chalet, Cade did his best to keep pace with Lila. The confidence of her movements—knowing where to pause, where to expect ambushes—made it clear she had spent her time undercover learning this place's secrets.

Sounds of gunfire and magickal combat echoed off the mountainsides, making the house feel as if it were surrounded by conflict. Cade kept dreading the appearance of a demon, a hellhound, or some other minion from Below to block him and Lila from reaching their goal. As they climbed the steps to the chalet's top floor, he felt exposed. There were no walls and no backing to the steps, making them seem to be suspended in the air. Which meant, in spite of the darkness, that he and Lila were visible as they hurried up one flight after another.

They reached the top floor, and Cade let go of a breath he'd been holding without having meant to do so. His pulse raced and thudded in his ears, and clammy sweat clung to his back like a morning frost. Meanwhile, Lila looked untroubled as she led him down the hallway.

"Hurry up. The library's down here."

She led him into a luxurious room packed with dark wooden furniture, floor-to-ceiling shelves lined with tomes ancient and arcane, and well-upholstered chairs. Dominating the middle of the room was a long conference table. Spread out upon it were his three books concerning the Mystery of the Dead God. In the middle of them was the Iron Codex, left open to an arbitrary page a third of the way from its end.

"Jackpot." He pointed at the window curtains. "Pull one of those down, and get the cinch rope. Let's wrap this to go."

Lila hurried to the window and tore down one of its dark blue curtains. Cade gathered the scattered pages of his magickal research back into some semblance of their proper order. By the time she returned to him with the curtain folded in half, he had tucked the loose pages under the heavy front cover of the Iron Codex and secured its bindings to keep them trapped inside.

She spread the curtain across the table. He set the codex upon it, pulled up the fabric around it to form a sack, and then he used the cinching rope to tie the bundle closed. "There," he said, satisfied the precious works were ready to travel. "Now we—"

"Leave that right where it is," the Old Man said from behind Cade.

Together, Cade and Lila pivoted to face the Old Man. The well-weathered billionaire stood tall in the open doorway with a vintage revolver in his hand. Cade masked the sick feeling of dread churning in his gut by feigning a nonchalant interest in the weapon. "That wouldn't happen to be an 1885 forty-five-caliber Colt Peacemaker, would it?"

"You've a good eye for firearms, Mr. Martin." The Old Man raised the weapon to eye level and steadied his aim. "Care to guess the nature of its ammunition?"

"I'd be very surprised if it wasn't the magick-piercing variety."

"Right again! Both of you, toss your weapons to the back of the room."

Not daring to blink or take his eyes off the man, Cade discarded the pistols and the knife he had taken from the conjuring room. His mind raced in search of a strategy to stall the Old Man and concoct a plan of escape, retaliation, or both.

Lila turned out her pockets. "I'm not armed."

The Old Man tilted his head. "That doesn't mean you aren't dangerous."

Thunder roared from the Peacemaker. Blood erupted from Lila's back, spraying out of a massive exit wound, spattering Cade's face. He winced reflexively as she was thrown backward into his arms. Her weight and falling momentum knocked him to the floor—where his mask of bravado shattered. "Lila? Lila!" She was dead weight in his arms. There was no life in her eyes, no breath in her lungs. One shot had stolen everything she was, everything she might have been . . . all that Cade had loved in her. Soul-broken, he wept into Lila's hair.

He had no words, only rage and a scream that shook the rafters.

Unmoved, the Old Man stood at a distance and kept his revolver aimed at Cade.

If only I had a demon. He'd be dead already. Through his tears Cade saw the Old Man's outline in the doorway, his aim sure and steady. "You fucking prick! *Why?*"

"Don't be naïve, Mr. Martin. She swore oaths in bad faith. Spied on me. *Betrayed* me. And she was about to help you steal treasures for which I have spent and sacrificed more than you can imagine. If anything, you should be grateful I made her death quick and painless."

"A favor I promise I won't return."

"I know your reputation well enough to take you at your word." He gestured with his pistol for Cade to stand. "Come. I have a negotiation to settle with your wife." Noting the look of apprehension on Cade's face, he added, "You don't think I've spared you out of some sense of mercy or fair play? I need you alive so I can trade you for the artifact you stole from me."

Feeling sick and hollowed out, Cade eased Lila's corpse to the floor. He stood to find his shirt soaked with her blood. Bile climbed up his throat, driven by hate and revulsion. He choked down the horrid sensation and recovered what little composure he had left.

In the doorway, the Old Man was eager to be underway. "Quickly, please. It's not as if I have all day to bring my soul safely back under lock and key." He backed into the corridor and continued to maintain a safe distance behind Cade, who let himself be shepherded down the hall.

"Just so you know, *Mr. Brandt,*" Cade said, seething as he emphasized the Old Man's real name for effect, "once I'm free there won't be anywhere on the face of the earth where I won't fucking find you. And when I do, I'll make you suffer for what you've done."

"Maybe you will . . . someday. But I assure you"—he cocked the hammer of the Peacemaker—"today is not that day."

⁓

"Forgive me, Signora Kernova. You were saying . . . ?"

Anja's stomach turned as she stared, defenseless, down the barrel of Niccolò's pistol.

On the ground beside her, Briet kept one hand over the gunshot wound in her gut while she used the other to push herself up to a sitting position, her teeth gritted with the effort.

Anja kept her expression blank as she made a mental command to her demonic porter. *Give it to me.*

Courtesy of DANOCHAR, the phylactery appeared in her hands.

Its swirling inner glows of gold and violet light cast eerie hues across the bloody trampled snow between herself and Niccolò. She held the artifact at eye level, a clear counter to his threat. "I hold this in a demon's hand. Shoot again, and I will crush it."

The pistol remained steady in Niccolò's hand. "Are we negotiating?"

"*Da*. Cade's life for the Old Man's soul."

"And what if I—"

"Down!" Hatunde jumped in front of Niccolò and threw a blue fireball downslope.

A barbed net of smoke shot past Hatunde's fireball, into his face.

Hatunde's flames engulfed Luis, broke his shield, and set him ablaze. Luis's screams and the flames on his cassock were both extinguished as he tumbled away, down the snowy slope.

At the same time, Luis's barbed net enveloped Hatunde, tightened until it cut into his flesh, crushed his throat, and diced him alive beside Niccolò, where he fell in a bloody heap.

Through it all, Niccolò's aim had not wavered.

The smug bastard arched an eyebrow at the sudden carnage. "Well. That was a pleasant distraction. But back to business. As I was saying: What if I don't wish to trade?"

The Old Man answered Niccolò's question.

"I don't think that's your decision to make, Mr. Falco."

The first figure to emerge from the darkness behind Niccolò was Cade. For a moment Anja hoped he had magickally imitated the Old Man's voice as part of an ambush.

Her heart sank as she saw the Old Man appear several steps behind Cade, with a large revolver in his hand. A quick look with the Sight confirmed Cade had no aura of yoked spirits; he was without magick of any kind, which meant the Old Man, whose weapon radiated the same deadly enchantment as Niccolò's, now held the advantage.

Anja held the delicate glass-and-filigree artifact higher. "Close enough."

Cade stopped a couple of meters behind Niccolò, and the Old Man remained roughly five meters behind Cade.

Now that Cade was within range of the artifact's uncanny illumination, Anja saw the fresh bloodstains on his shirt, and the shadow of grief in his eyes. Dreading his answer, she asked in a faltering voice, ". . . Lila?"

He shook his head, his eyes downcast. "We found the books in the library. Had them ready to go." He jerked his head toward the Old Man. "And then this asshole shot her."

Briet looked up at Anja, a glimmer of her fighting spirit rekindled. All that Anja could spare her ally was one glance and a nearly imperceptible dip of her chin.

Then she focused past Niccolò to look the Old Man in his monocled eye. "Terms."

"Put down the artifact and take five steps back."

"And then you shoot Cade? No deal."

"I assure you, Ms. Kernova, I honor my contracts."

"We have no contract. Just hostages. You can have yours when I have mine."

The Old Man moved closer, his revolver still pointed at Cade's back. "And how are we to set this exchange in motion without a gesture of trust?"

She lifted her chin toward Niccolò. "First, he stands down."

"Fair enough. Mr. Falco, toss your weapon, please." When his mercenary karcist hesitated, the Old Man said with more steel in his voice, "Do it *now*, Mr. Falco."

With reluctance and resentment, Niccolò hurled his pistol into the dark. It vanished into the snow with barely a sound.

"Now step back, Mr. Falco. Behind me, please."

Seething, the magician obeyed his master.

"Splendid. Ms. Kernova, please step forward and set the artifact down *gently*. Then take five steps back. Once you've done that, I'll holster my weapon and send Mr. Martin to you."

"And then?"

"The two of you and Miss Segfrunsdóttir will be free to leave. With any luck, none of you will ever see me or Mr. Falco again."

From the ground at Anja's feet, Briet mumbled, "Sounds good to me."

The Old Man lowered his revolver. "Shall we get on with it?"

Anja nodded her assent and walked toward him. Five steps through the snow, until she was just beyond arm's reach of Cade. She set down the artifact with tender care.

The Old Man holstered his revolver. Satisfied, Anja took five steps back.

"Mr. Martin? You can go. But not too close to the artifact, please."

Cade walked toward Anja and Briet. Steered himself just beyond arm's reach of the artifact as he passed it. He was five steps from Anja. Five steps from freedom.

Niccolò fired a blast of crimson light from his hand.

It slammed into the phylactery at Cade's feet.

A blinding shock wave flattened everyone to the ground, including the Old Man—but not Niccolò, who stood safe behind his magickal shield.

Anja looked up. A prismatic flood shone from the artifact. It brightened to blinding as a rising whine split the air. The artifact was about to explode and kill them all.

Then the rainbow glow vanished and the shriek was muffled—by Cade.

He threw himself on top of the device—just as the Rangers had trained him to do.

Anja opened her mouth to cry out his name—

An explosion like Armageddon.

A sphere of orange fire lifted Cade into the air like a rag doll, its spread contained by a shell of heavenly white light—the essence of the angelic spirit that existed as part of Cade.

Then the glow faded. Cade's broken body slammed onto the charred patch of earth and lay there, smoldering in a pool of his own blood, a sacrifice signed in crimson.

Anja sprawled in the snow, in shock, trembling, paralyzed by grief.

Just meters away, Briet lay stunned and silent.

The detonation echoed off the surrounding mountains in the dark.

A sphere of magickal light appeared above Niccolò, who loomed over his stricken former employer. The Old Man lay supine in the snow, racked by violent seizures. Moments ago he had appeared vital in spite of his antiquity. Now all that remained of him was a bent, ghoulish figure with rheumy eyes sunken into cavernous sockets, his skin as brittle as onion paper. His hands were shriveled like dead spiders, and his once-arch voice had been reduced to a rasp. Shaking with either terror or palsy, he wept as he asked Niccolò, "Why?"

"Because I'm done serving in Hell." The karcist drew his wand, and with a flourish he extracted a glowing stream of energy from the Old Man's decrepit body, leaving the dying man in an even more wretched state. "Mine was your last sigil of protection. And I just revoked it." He shifted his wand to his left hand. "Give my regards to the Devil, Signor Brandt."

He flicked his wrist.

The Old Man's neck broke with a wet snap.

Revolted and startled, Anja sprang to her feet and reached for her wand.

Niccolò extended his right hand, and the pistol he had cast away flew back into his grasp. Holding it at eye level, he aimed it Anja.

"Time for *me* to be king."

31

"I should thank you, Signora Kernova." Niccolò used his wand to direct a demon to scribe the symbols of a portal gate into the snow around him. "I have never been keen to share power." He gestured with his pistol at the dead bodies littering the torn-up snow around them. "Thanks to you, I no longer have to. *Grazie mille*."

"You want to thank me? Shut up and go."

"In good time." A final series of movements with his wand, and his magick circle for teleportation flared to life. "But before I go, I—"

A vapor appeared before him, tenuous and almost invisible, its presence revealed by the condensation of his breath. The voice of SEIR, his most recently yoked demonic porter, intruded upon his mind like the scrape of a shovel through an oven packed with hot ash. *THE BOOKS AND PAPERS YOU SENT ME TO COLLECT ARE NOT IN THE LIBRARY.*

That was news Niccolò didn't want to hear. His ascension hinged upon those texts; his entire future depended on them. Alarmed and confused, he looked around, and then toward the chalet as he snapped at the demon, "Then where *are* they?"

NOT IN THE HOUSE. THEY ARE BEYOND MY PERCEPTION.

Sprawled beside Anja and marinating in her own freshly spilled blood, Briet fixed Niccolò with an evil smirk. "Looking for the books you stole?"

Her taunt stoked his fury. He aimed his pistol at her. "Where are they?"

"Safe. And far from here."

Anja narrowed her eyes. "Did you think we would let you *keep* them?"

Horrified realization took root. Rage followed on its heels: "*Vaffanculo, zoccole!*" Death by cursed bullets would be too quick for these two. He wanted this to *hurt*.

Death magicks swirled around him, a growing storm conjured by his fury: the fires of ANDRAMELECH, the cold lightning of AZALETH, the cursed blade of SAVNOK, the paralyzing breath of LEVIATHAN. He gathered them all into one strike that would give the witches the lethal punishments they had so richly earned, and raised his arm to throw it: "*Muori, puttane!*"

A surge of white light bashed into him like a freight train.

For a moment that seemed to last forever, he felt weightless but paralyzed. An unearthly brightness blinded him even with his eyes closed, and stinging needles of heat seared him to his bones, as if he'd been thrown into the heart of the sun.

The glare faded. He opened his eyes to see he was surrounded by a different kind of tempest: one made of demons. Misty specters circled him, roaring and moaning in dire voices older than the earth. Some fought to reach him, but jolts of lightning forced them away. They spun faster with each revolution, until they formed a vortex that lifted him off the ground.

The howling gale tore the pistol from his hand and launched it into the forest.

He squinted at the terrifying faces in the wind—only to realize these were his own yoked spirits, violently freed of their servitude, their unholy vengeance against him kept in check by the same force that had ripped them from his control.

A declaration by the monk Luis Pérez set the horde to screaming.

"Flee, beasts of the Pit! I banish thee one and all directly to Hell! By the power of the names most holy: ELOHIM, SHADDAI, JEHOVAM, JEHOVAH TETRAGRAMMATON, and by the power of the archangels MICHAEL, GABRIEL, and URIEL, I command thee! *Begone!*"

The whirlwind of demons climbed into the night sky and dissipated.

The wind ceased, and Niccolò fell to the ground.

He landed on his palms and knees in the snow, shivering and nauseated.

This must be what a fish feels when it's gutted. His portal and his sphere of light were gone, extinguished with the rest of his magickal talents. It took his eyes a moment to adjust so he could see by the feeble light of the nearby chalet.

Several meters away, Luis lay prone on the downward slope. Only the burnt monk's head and one arm peeked over the top, but that had been all he'd needed to work this cruel trick.

Fearful and furious, Niccolò shouted at him, "What have you done?"

Anja stood half lit, half in shadow. "He took your spirits. You were a karcist. Now you are just a man." She drew her athamé from her belt. "Time to see if you can *die* like one."

His pistol was gone. His magick torn away. His allies slain.

And a Red Army–trained killer was prowling toward him with murder in her eyes.

There was only one thing to do.

He staggered toward the chalet and prayed to reach the conjuring room before Anja caught him—because its hidden escape portal was his only hope of getting off this mountain alive.

The coward ran, and Anja let him. The last person who truly meant anything to her lay broken and bloody in the midst of a scar on the mountainside.

She tried to make herself go to Cade, but her legs refused to obey. In her heart she was afraid to see what was left of him. But she had to know. Had to see with her own eyes.

In faltering steps she went to him. Kneeled beside his charred, unmoving form.

Extending her senses with the gift of PHENEGREX, she felt the last fading spark of life in Cade's body. His soul still clung to his shattered mortal frame, no doubt thanks to the strength it gained from being united with the essence of an angel.

Tears filled her eyes and her breath caught in her throat as she rolled him over. His eyes were open but distant. Could he see? Or hear?

Her voice trembled: "Cade?"

He didn't react. Anja rested her right hand upon what was left of his chest—much of his torso had been torn open, his internal organs exposed by the blast. She channeled the healing talent of BUER, hoping to fan the ember of life that continued to smolder inside her husband.

As she invoked the demon's power, it resisted her.

His wounds were wrought by great magick. I cannot heal this.

Rage churned through her sorrow. *I know you cannot save him. Just give him back to me for a moment.*

As thou commands.

The spirit let Anja funnel all the vitality she could into Cade's body.

His eyes fluttered, and he looked up at her as she cradled him in her arms.

". . . Anja?"

"*Da,* my love."

"Is it over?"

She nodded. "Soon."

"You . . . okay?"

Her tears fell onto his forehead. "You saved me. Saved us all."

His gaze lost its focus. Through the senses of PHENEGREX, Anja felt Cade's soul part from the essence of his bond-spirit and begin to fade away.

She touched his cheek with her fingertips and turned his eyes to look into hers.

As Cade's last ounce of life force shrank to a dying spark, he gave Anja a weak smile. His voice was like a cold wind through dry leaves.

"Leave a light on for me."

She could barely see his face through her tears. "I will."

A soft gasp escaped his mouth. . . .

From that moment to the next nothing seemed to change, but Anja felt the difference, and she knew that everything had. Cade's eyes were still open, but they no longer saw. The warmth was still in his flesh, but it would soon be gone.

Life had become death cradled in her arms.

Racked by sobs she fought to hold in, Anja laid his body down, and then she shut his eyes with a soft pass of her hand.

Her body trembled with a terrible, inchoate sorrow. Tears rolled from her eyes, so she squeezed them shut, only to feel her pulse throb in her ears. She felt as if she had swallowed an ocean of grief and had no idea how to spit it out, no idea how to find her way back to herself.

Her sorrow was a tourniquet around her throat.

Then she let out a roar of such anguish that the mountain itself quaked in terror.

She had been rendered hollow. Aimless. Adrift. She wanted to tear herself to pieces, surrender to her loss, submerge into mourning, and follow her husband into the darkness. . . .

But that is not my way.

Eyes open, she knew what had to be done.

She stood and looked toward her friends. Briet and Luis had crawled to meet each other. Anja walked to them, set her hands upon their shoulders, and blessed them both with all of the healing charms BUER could offer. Their wounds closed, and their strength returned.

Briet stood and took stock of her restoration. "Thanks."

"You were lucky. His bullet went through. Had it lodged inside, magick would not heal you until it was out." She offered Luis a hand, but he waved it off and stood without aid. "How do you feel, Father?"

"Done for the night."

"You fought well. Rest." She turned toward the chalet as the fleeing Niccolò retreated inside of it. "Let me finish this."

Briet stepped forward to stand at Anja's side. "Let *us* finish this."

Anja accepted the offer with a nod. *She deserves her revenge at least as much as I do.*

Behind them, Luis blessed them with the sign of the cross. "*In nomine Patris, et Filii, et Spiritus Sancti.* Amen. . . . Go. Do what must be done. And God be with you."

Briet frowned as Anja started her march to the chalet.

"Father, I don't think God wants to see what we're gonna do next."

The witches walked shoulder-to-shoulder across a blighted field of snow. Their destination, a chalet aglow with golden electric light. Their mission, revenge.

The wild things of the mountain all fled as fast as leg or wing could take them. Anja emanated her silent warning, one made possible by the angel fused to her soul, and saw to it that nature's innocents would not be caught in this cross fire.

A German shepherd scrambled out an open door on the side of the chalet. Whining and yelping in dismay, the dog bounded into the forest with its tail tucked between its legs.

The chalet was just a few dozen meters away. Through its great walls of glass, and a few breezeways between its different wings, Anja spied a number of vehicles behind the building. Snowmobiles. A Sno-Cat treaded vehicle. And, on a circular pad, a sleek helicopter.

Five strides from the front door, the witches began their assault.

With demonic hands they lifted one snowmobile after another and hurled them at the house like steel missiles. They crashed through the chalet, fracturing its wooden frame as if it were made from toothpicks. Anja hurled the Sno-Cat through the house's roof. Briet launched great boulders through its side walls. Anja used BAEL's fist to demolish the chalet's exposed interior, while Briet tore off its wraparound deck and scattered its pieces down the mountainside with the casual cruelty of a vandal breaking windows.

When they ran out of small vehicles and natural ammunition, Anja hoisted the helicopter into the air and then brought it down like a hammer on the mangled mess of splintered wood.

She felt Niccolò's life force. He was still alive, somewhere beneath the debris.

She sniffed the brisk night air, which had been fouled by the chemical odor of spilled gasoline and aviation fuel. And she smiled.

Briet gave her a conspiratorial look. "Do it."

Anja snapped her fingers, invoking the hellfire of HABORYM inside the petrol-soaked ruin of the house. One demonic spark set the entire property ablaze in a matter of seconds. Yellow-white flames climbed into the night sky as the witches walked forward, both protected from the inferno by fire demons. Briet stayed behind Anja, who followed her senses through swirling walls of flame, and then down burning steps into the chalet's basement.

Emerging from a corridor of fire, Anja and Briet stepped inside an oblate conjuring room excavated from the bedrock under the chalet. On the far side from the entrance, Niccolò was busy pulling down a heavy tapestry that concealed a large, iron-banded oak door. One glimpse with the Sight revealed it to be incandescent with magick.

It had to be a portal.

Anja would not let that save him. That, or anything else.

With the hands of BAEL, she pulled Niccolò away from the hidden portal, into the center of the room. Briet used a demon's strength to pin the panicking *skotolozhets* to the floor, faceup.

Anja stepped over Niccolò and stood with one foot on either side of his hips.

Briet struck the same pose over his head, facing Anja.

Hot gusts from the burning chalet made Anja's long black hair and Briet's coppery tresses whip about them like angry serpents, as if they were daughters of Medusa.

Anja eyed Niccolò with contempt. "I was going to have a demon gut you. But then I remembered: All we need for that"—she and Briet drew their athamés—"*is a knife.*"

He screamed as they descended like the Furies, their hearts cold and their consciences silent. Briet tore open his throat. Anja disemboweled him with one savage hack after another. Together they carved out his organs and watched the light in his eyes fade to black.

They kept on cutting long after he was dead.

The chalet continued to burn as the witches marched out of it, new sisters reborn in blood and flames. They returned to stand on either side of Luis, and then Anja looked back to watch the last remnants of the mountain house collapse, consumed by the blaze.

"Time to go."

Briet stared into the flames. "Not yet." With a dramatic sweep of her arm, she called down from the sky a bolt of indigo lightning greater than any Anja had ever seen.

Unearthly in its blue-black radiance, it fell from the heavens with a gut-shaking crash and a flash of light brighter than the dawn.

Rumbles of thunder—not from the sky but from the peak above. The mountaintop's glacier had fractured like fine crystal hitting a slate floor, and now it was bearing down on them with a vengeance.

The entire mountain shuddered under their feet.

Luis shot a nervous look at Anja. "This might be a good time for a portal?"

"Hold," Briet said. "I want to see this."

It felt like an earthquake. God's fist roared down the mountain in the form of a million tons of snow, ice, rocks, and mud. Wild tremors coursed through the bedrock and turned the slope's packed snow into a loose fluid that shivered around the trio's legs, as if it had come alive with the anticipation of being imminently swept away.

A shock front of displaced air traveling ahead of the slide scattered the chalet's burning remains in a great cloud of fiery debris and hot ash. Gray, thunderous, and unstoppable, the leading edge of the disaster Briet had wrought bashed into the smoking ruins of the chalet and buried it, hurling tons of lethal rubble through the air, straight at her, Anja, and Luis.

Briet deflected every piece of it to one side or the other.

Hunks of rock, metal, and wood ricocheted into the dark as Briet swatted them with demonic hands, and a slurry of liquefied snow detoured around them, as if they were immovable objects islanded in a sea of destruction, three blessed souls untouched in the midst of calamity.

Anja looked back, over her shoulder. The avalanche slammed down the mountainside, shearing away trees at their roots like a razor slicing through stubble.

And then it was over. The mountainside was silent.

Where the chalet had stood, nothing remained but snow tainted gray with ash.

Briet lowered her hands and exhaled. "*Now* we can go."

32

The young monks stood on the shore, watched, and waited.

Nine had left the lodge. Only three returned.

Come midafternoon a portal opened, an impossible oval window framed in silver light. Its crackling energies scattered the mosquitoes of Arthurs Lake and cast a pale and weltering light across the waving grass. Two women carried Father Luis through the tear in space-time.

No one spoke and no one smiled. There were too many empty spaces around them. Places where friends had stood an hour before but never would again.

The last three had come home drenched in blood. Blackened with soot. Torn, bruised, and broken. All their faces betrayed their mission's result. The life the nine had gone to save had been lost. If this was by any measure a victory, it was a hollow and costly one.

Dismayed and at a loss for words, the young brothers of Monte Paterno took the burden of Father Luis from the women. He was their leader. Their responsibility.

All the same, they offered succor to the female karcists. Both refused.

Rendered into the arms of his loyal acolytes, Luis remained mute. Most of the damage to his flesh had been made whole, but the truth was in his eyes: he bore a soul-wound, one that had no name but would linger for months, or years. Maybe the rest of his life.

None of his brothers dared to ask what had happened.

They cleared his path. Saw him safely to his bed. Washed his feet and hands, set a cool cloth upon his fevered brow, laid a warm blanket over his shivering form . . .

And prayed that one day the man they called *teacher* would awaken.

The fight was over. The enemy had fallen, but nothing had been won.

Back at the lodge, Briet craved escape. Release. Anything to quiet the voice of guilt that nagged at her. She had quelled her yoked demons by banishing them all the moment she had set foot back in Tasmania. But their absence had given her no peace.

Neither had half a bottle of cheap vodka. It wasn't enough.

She retrieved Cade's spare gear from under his bed. There wasn't much dope left.

Alone in her room with a dead man's kit, she prayed to Hell Below and Heaven Above that it would be enough to let her sleep, even if just for one night.

She prepped the needle. Fixed it to the syringe. Set the plunger forward.

Next came the cook. A spoon, a few drops of vodka, the chalky powdered heroin.

A Zippo lighter stood on the rough wood floor, cap open, flame dancing. Above it the bowl of the spoon. The powder released its bounty as the vodka sublimated. A pinch of clean cotton as a filter kept the particulate out of the needle as she drew it full.

She tied a leather strip around her biceps. Probed the pit of her elbow for a vein.

The drugs hit her arm like a wave of golden heat.

She emptied the syringe into herself and then leaned back, waiting for bliss to arrive. Speeding her ego into the void, Briet hoped to shed not just her grief and her regrets, but her memories, her identity, her whole fucking consciousness. She wanted to bundle her soul in old newspaper and chuck it out a window, just another piece of trash on the road.

It was a beautiful dream. A perfect plan. Except that no matter what she cast away, when she awoke she would find it waiting to greet her on sobriety's bleak shore.

But not tonight. For tonight, at least . . . she would sleep.

With every passing moment, Cade's death grew more real, more concrete in Anja's memory.

She sat on their bed in the lodge, with his bomber jacket in her hands. As she felt time burn away, stealing him farther into the past, further out of her reach, she grew more despondent—and more enraged.

The Old Man had died, but not by her hand.

Niccolò had robbed her. Stolen her revenge. And she had made him suffer for all he had done. But it was not enough. She wasn't sure anything would *ever* be enough.

Anja fought to quiet her mind.

The papers her friends had taken from the Old Man's bank would give up more of his secrets and the names of his peers. She was certain of it.

When she was ready to weep, she would. But in her own time, on her own terms. After that, the allies of the Old Man would need to learn the bitter lessons of regret.

Those were lessons Anja was uniquely qualified to teach.

I will swallow my grief. Eat my sorrow. Turn my tears into fuel for my rage. And when I find the Old Man's allies . . . I will burn them all to the ground.

1964

APRIL

"Smile! You're going home today!"

Such cheery parting words, uttered by the gray-haired nurse who had wheeled Miles out of the hospital and delivered him into the hands of his long-suffering and exquisitely discreet other, Desmond Spencer. The woman had been utterly bereft of any sense of the depth of Miles's grief, even in the face of objectively good news.

My best mate is dead. Gone forever.

He had put on a brave face and a classically British stiff upper lip. After all, it wasn't as if he hadn't been living in constant dread of that exact news for the better part of a decade. But to have it confirmed, and to know Cade's end was the product of a conspiracy that could never be exposed or answered . . . it filled Miles with a sense of hopelessness.

Back in our Exeter days, I'd have sworn Cade and I could conquer the world. And after I learned about the powers he'd gained, for a moment I thought we might even give it a go. He sat next to Dez in the front of his Bentley and watched the London suburbs blur past. *Now I'm numb from the waist down. A bloody invalid.*

Miles studied the road signs they passed. He didn't recognize them. "Dez? Where the bloody hell are we going?"

"I couldn't refit our old flat to accommodate your new needs." Dez guided the car through a turn onto a lovely tree-canopied lane. "So I had to sell it and invest in something a bit more *pliable.*" Halfway down the block, he steered the car toward the curb and brought it to a stop in front of a rock wall that fronted a charming stone cottage festooned with ivy.

"Welcome home, my love." He reached over and gave Miles's hand a gentle squeeze.

In spite of his intention to retain his composure, Miles felt his eyes mist with grateful tears. "Is this really ours?"

"All ours. Thanks to a few judicious investments and a frugal lifestyle." A glimmer of mischief lit up Dez's expression. "Though I might have splurged a bit on a wine cellar. And a fair quantity of wine."

Miles admired the house from the car's passenger seat while Dez got out and retrieved the wheelchair from the car's boot. When Dez opened the door for him, the new conveyance was already unfolded and waiting. "Shall we?"

"Might as well." Miles let his lover help him out of the car and into the wheelchair. Once he was settled, Dez pushed him in the chair up the drive, toward the ramp that had been built to ease their approach to the cottage's side door. The fair-haired solicitor moved ahead, opened the door, and then returned to guide Miles inside their new home.

Half the countertops in the kitchen had been lowered to heights that would be convenient for Miles in his chair, and most of the doorways had been widened. There was no carpeting in the house, as Miles discovered while wheeling himself through it. All the floors were tile or hardwood, and wherever there once had been steps there now were shallow-grade inclines. Even the bath and the WC had been rebuilt to offer him handholds, to ease his transitions in and out of his chair. Miles had never seen or heard of anything like it.

Dez appeared behind him while he was staring verklempt at the bath. "Will it do?"

"It's brilliant." Miles smiled over his shoulder at his beloved. "Positively splendid, Dez. I couldn't have asked for more."

"I'm glad." He gestured for Miles to follow him. "Come. You've got mail."

Curious but apprehensive, Miles asked, "From whom? Please tell me not from work."

"No, no." Dez led Miles through the house to the sitting room, where a space had been cleared for Miles to park his chair between the hearth and the front window, with a quaint end table dutifully standing ready to hold his tea. Once Miles had secured his chair into its place of pride, Dez reached inside his tweed jacket and pulled out a sealed envelope. He handed it to Miles. "It came by courier, a few months back. The sender asked me to give it to you once I thought you had recovered."

Miles regarded it with suspicion. "You've read it?"

"Heavens, no. It was marked for your eyes only, love."

Reassured, Miles opened the envelope by quickly tearing a thin strip off its end. Then he shook it and coaxed out the single folded sheet of paper inside. The message it bore was brief and dated December 1963.

> *Miles—*
>
> *By now I suspect you have learned of Cade's death. If not, forgive me for being the one to tell you. Know that your friend died to save others and to bring the corrupt to justice. He did not die in vain.*
>
> *It will be best if I vanish for a while. Maybe years. Perhaps forever. It is impossible to say. But let me leave you with something I know is true: Cade loved you like a brother. And I will never forget how you loved and honored him in return.*
>
> *Our paths will cross again one day, Miles Franklin. Until then, may the Hand of God stand between you and harm.*
>
> *Your friend,*
> *Anja Kernova*

Miles folded the paper shut and tucked it into the pocket of his cardigan. From the sofa, Dez asked, "Everything all right?"

Maudlin but buoyed by fond remembrance, Miles nodded. "Couldn't be better."

"Good. Can't have you moping about for the next two weeks, now can I?"

The arbitrary deadline made Miles sit up. "What happens in two weeks?"

"You go back to work, you old sod. I negotiated your return to HQ. With a promotion and a bump for hazardous duty." Dez teased Miles with a lift of one eyebrow. "You didn't really think I'd let you sit here gathering moss the rest of your days, did you?"

Miles had to laugh at his lover's optimism. "I suppose not. So . . . I return to Her Majesty's service in two weeks, do I?"

"You most certainly do." Dez got up and moved to stand beside Miles and caressed the back of his neck. "But until then, my unsung hero, you're all mine."

"Only until then?"

"Then and always."

Miles pulled his wonderful man into a kiss that said *thank you,* and *I love you,* and *I would be lost without you.* "Always and forever."

That earned a grin from prim-and-proper Dez. "You'd better bloody believe it."

With another kiss Miles knew that he was, at last, truly home.

JULY

In the hidden acres of an old-growth redwood forest, far from the gazes of the curious, the world's richest men had gathered, as they did for two weeks every July. The Russian River Valley was known to many people as the heart of Northern California's wine country, but the world's economic and political elites knew it better as the home of Bohemian Grove.

The luxury campground was kept private by a gated road and a platoon of armed security. Only a few of the club's most senior members were aware that magick played a role in its defense, but any competent karcist would be able to feel the resistance of its warding glyphs from miles away. Its strongest charm of protection came from the towering owl-headed statue of its patron spirit MOLOCH, a subordinate of the Infernal minister BELIAL. At the start of each annual gathering, the all-male congregants sacrificed to the demon an effigy dubbed "Dull Care," in a ceremony they called *The Cremation of Care*. It was meant to symbolize the shedding of everyday concerns, but it didn't take an occult master to recognize the Goetic ritual hidden beneath the Bohemians' pantomime and gibberish.

Despite its official motto of "Weaving spiders come not here," some people who knew of Bohemian Grove and its gatherings tended to speak of it with suspicion. A few fringe types were convinced that, sequestered from the media and the rest of society, the richest of the rich met inside Bohemian Grove to plot cruel schemes against the poor, engineer vast conspiracies, rig national economies, and strategize the destruction of their enemies.

But from all that Anja had seen, the chief reasons that titans of industry, world leaders, banking tycoons, and the occasional celebrity came to Bohemian Grove were to spend two weeks in the forest with their own rarefied breed of the rich and famous, get shit-faced drunk, tell dirty jokes or give long-winded self-important lectures, and piss on thousand-year-old trees.

She was not usually one to judge, but she found the spectacle quite juvenile.

Breaking through its magickal defenses had been tedious. Anja had spent months casing the campground, testing its perimeter, and evaluating the skills of its security personnel. Under normal circumstances, she would not have considered mere access to be worth this much effort. But these were not normal times, and this was the one place she knew she would find all four of her targets together. For decades this had been the annual meeting site of a body she had only very recently come to know of as the Shadow Commission.

Konrad Brandt had been its founding member. Now that he had been dealt with, Anja had decided it was time to face his remaining peers.

Creatures of habit, they did not disappoint her. The members of the Commission, smartly dressed one and all, sat at a round table on the shore of the camp's man-made pond. Dinner was long since over, the dishes cleared away by a service staff that had been dismissed for the night. A few bottles of wine and scotch stood open on the commissioners' table, most of them crowded in front of its one empty chair—the one left vacant in memory of Brandt. In the table's center was an oil lamp with a darkly tarnished glass chimney. Hunched inward, the commissioners looked as if they were trying to hoard its soft orange glow.

The other Bohemians gave the commissioners a wide berth. No one sat close enough to eavesdrop on the four men—or to stop Anja as she walked out of the woods, directly to the table. "Gentlemen. And I use that word loosely."

Wide-eyed shock, stunned silence. Anja understood their surprise. The men saw this as *their* place. *Their* sacred domain. They had likely never imagined a woman being here.

The first to break his silence was the youngest-looking of them, the Russian. "How dare you violate this sanctum, you *shlyukha*!"

"Shut up, Comrade Kolnukov." Anja savored the Russian's horrified recoiling at the sound of his own name. Apparently, the members of the Commission had been too long accustomed to anonymity. "Yes, that's right, Yuri, you *skotolozhets*. I know your fucking name."

She let her gaze pass from one commissioner to the next, around the table. "I know *all* your names. Pieter Kerzner of Cape Town. Martino Tarella, Buenos Aires. Saleem al-Zahra, Riyadh. I know where you live. How you made your billions. And I know that each of you is much older than you appear.

You all got rich late in the last century—before you learned how to make your names and your fortunes invisible."

Martino, a fair-haired man with blue eyes, glared at Anja. "You should stop talking."

"I am just getting started." She began a slow orbit of the table, the wand in her hand clearly visible as a warning. "I know how well-protected you all are. Each of you bears six sigils of protection, one from each minister of Hell." She tapped her wand against her left palm. "You four must be the wealthiest people on earth. You would need to be, to keep no fewer than six master magicians, one sworn to each minister, on your permanent payrolls." She made a small snort of derision. "Even Rockefeller can't afford to keep more than two at a time."

Pieter said with scorn, "Rockefeller is a dilettante."

Amused, Anja nodded and continued her journey around the table. "Yes, you would think so. But how is it that men as rich as you do not appear on lists of the wealthiest people? None of you sits on any corporate board. Holds any corporate title. Occupies any elected, hereditary, or appointed office. And yet . . . you are the spiders at the center of a global web, with control over dozens of the world's most profitable and strategically important industries. How?"

"Good planning," quipped Pieter.

Anja returned to her point of entry, behind the empty chair. "I do not think so."

Yuri sneered at her. "What is the point of this *performance*?"

"Simply this. Men who have as much as you do, have that much more to lose. And I plan to make sure every one of you loses all you have. Every last cent. And only after I topple your empires, burn your fortunes, and break you all in both flesh and spirit, will I show myself to each of you one last time—when I part your head from your neck."

Pieter, arrogant bastard that he was, laughed as if he had nothing to fear. "You don't want to go down this road, Ms. Kernova. You made your point with Konrad. And you had every right to do so. But know when to cut your losses. After the debacle of Fafleralp, the four of us agreed to let you and yours walk away. You ought to show us the same courtesy."

With a mental command, Anja wreathed her wand in green fire. "Konrad was one of you. *His* plans were *your* plans." She leaned forward, her glower like steel, her heart like ice. "Cade and I were supposed to have seven hundred *years* together. *You* took that away. And I will not rest until you all pay for every *second* of my love you destroyed."

Her threat was met with stern silence.

Out of the corner of her eye, Anja saw a security team approaching in a hurry.

An evil smirk tugged at the corner of Saleem's mouth. "You *will* regret this, Ms. Kernova. You have made a terrible enemy today."

Anja regarded the commissioners with a murderous stare: "*So have you.*"

The security team charged at Anja and lunged—only to sprawl like fools across the commissioners' table as she vanished—without a word, an effect, or a trace.

35

Anja shook off the dreamlike state that accompanied astral projection and blinked against the glare of headlights. Her friends' long rest stop appeared to be coming to an end. Folks were folding up their blankets, returning musical instruments to their cases, and dousing the twigfires they had been using for light, warmth, or a hot roadside snack.

It was a beautiful night in the New Mexico desert. The rasping songs of insects seeking mates filled the warm air. Just beyond the horizon, a city's streetlamps gave the sky a peach-colored glow. A three-quarter moon shone high overhead, its soft halo erasing the nearest stars.

Part of Anja wished she could go with her friends on the bus. But that wasn't possible. They all had no choice now but to keep moving. Always moving.

Briet walked toward her. As a disguise, she had dyed her coppery hair a light brown and adopted a wardrobe cobbled together from Native American garb, tie-dyed fabrics, and garments imported from India and Sri Lanka. "We're heading out. Are you coming with us?"

"*Nyet.*" Anja closed her ruck. "Better if we split up." She lipped a Lucky from her half-finished pack, and lit it with Cade's old stainless-steel Zippo. "Where do you go next?"

"Ken didn't say. Guess we're going where the road takes us."

Anja imagined she and Briet made for a mismatched pair. Briet was all long legs and flowing hair and rainbow colors, while Anja, half a foot shorter, was decked out in blue jeans, military-surplus combat boots, and a plain black shirt. Her sable tresses had been hacked short on her right side, but were still long enough on the left to drape like a curtain over the scar on her cheek. Her gray eyes she kept hidden behind black sunglasses, even at night. As she resigned herself to getting back on her motorcycle for another long solo ride, she shrugged into the last piece of her ensemble: Cade's leather bomber jacket, its exterior well-weathered after decades of adventure, its map-illustrated silk lining as soft against her skin as his touch once had been.

The bus's driver honked its horn twice, summoning the passengers. With a sigh, Briet hefted her duffel over her shoulder. Exhaust fumes, invisible but noxious, choked the air around the bus—a refurbished school transport painted in psychedelic colors and patterns, and whose hand-lettered front destination placard read simply *Further.*

Anja walked with Briet to the bus, where Yasmin stood waiting for them. Not having been willing to embrace the "hippie" aesthetic with the same enthusiasm Briet had shown, Yasmin had given up her trademark wardrobe of olive drab and camouflage fatigues in favor of long, flowing summer dresses and simple frocks. Despite this, she still managed to conceal no fewer than eight bladed weapons on her person at all times—a trick Anja secretly envied.

Just as Anja had hoped when she and Cade had sent Yasmin to deliver their magickal Trojan horse to Niccolò, the quick and resourceful young woman had made a near-perfect getaway after the handoff. Even more impressive to Anja, Yasmin had kept her word: She had refrained from spending all but a trivial amount of the fortune they had scammed from the Old Man and his minions. They had split the haul three ways, but only because Father Luis still honored his vow of poverty and had refused to accept so much as a cent of the stolen cash.

"It was good to see you," Yasmin said to Anja. "Sure you can't join us?"

Anja shook her head. "Too dangerous. We need to lie low. Stay quiet."

Briet looked worried. "For how long?"

"Years. Maybe longer."

Yasmin cocked an eyebrow. "Why'd you have to be in such a hurry to declare war? You couldn't let us live a little first?"

"They would have come for us, war or no war. But I wanted them to know: If they hit *us,* I can hit *them.*"

"Well," Briet said, "since you just put all our cards on the table, we'd better start working on a plan. After all, us witches only live for seven hundred years." She tapped her bare wrist. "Clock's ticking."

In spite of herself, Anja was starting to like Briet. Or at least not hold her in contempt. She shook the woman's hand. "We will take our time. Do this right. And bury them." Taking Yasmin's hand, she continued, "As my late master always said, 'The war never ends.'"

The bus driver leaned long and heavy on his horn, signaling his impatience.

"Guess we'd better go," Briet said.

Yasmin cracked a mischievous smile. "'When shall we three meet again? In thunder, lightning, or in rain?'"

Briet scowled at the invocation of *Macbeth*. "Put a sock in it, First Witch."

"*Da*. Just get on the bus."

Before Briet and Yasmin could board, the bus's owner and de facto tour leader, a young writer named Ken Kesey, leaned out the door. "What's the holdup?" He did a double take as he saw Anja. Cigarette dangling from his mouth, he stepped off the bus, reached out, and pinched a bit of her bomber jacket's sleeve. He admired it with a slow nod. "Nice leather." Then he cocked an eyebrow. "It's a little big on you, isn't it?"

She pulled her sleeve free of his hand. "I plan to grow into it."

While he chewed on that, Yasmin and Briet boarded the bus and found an empty seat to share. Around them, Ken's migratory band of artists, musicians, writers, and scholars—a troupe he called his "Merry Pranksters"— packed themselves in like cargo. Ken bid Anja farewell with a jaunty salute and got back on the bus.

The driver shut the door, gave Anja a quick double honk as a farewell, and pulled off the dirt shoulder onto the blacktop. The rattletrap school bus rolled down the black desert highway, free of schedule or agenda.

Anja hoped fate would reunite her with her friends someday.

Do svidaniya, comrade sisters.

For her part, she was traveling light. She had shed every trace of responsibility she could. Cade's great work, his magnum opus of the dead God and the Devil who dreamed of rebuilding Him, had been entrusted to Luis. Her last two friends were off the radar, at least for now. And though she had just declared war against the four most powerful people in the world, she herself had only one plan in mind for her future: going dark.

She secured her ruck behind the seat of her 1962 Royal Enfield Interceptor, a fast and reliable motorcycle that so far had carried her halfway across America. She still missed her long-lost 1953 Vincent Black Shadow, but the Interceptor was a serviceable steed.

With a kick of its starter and a twist of its throttle, the Interceptor thundered to life.

Anja put on her helmet and riding gloves. Lowered her visor into place.

Pulling onto the highway, she didn't know where the road would take her. She knew only one thing for certain: that the night would welcome her with open arms.

As it always had.

As it always would.

GLOSSARY

adept—*n.*, an initiate into the Art of ceremonial magick; often used synonymously with "apprentice." The lowest level of adept in magick is a *novice*; a journeyman adept is an *acolyte*; a master-level adept is a *karcist* (see below).

Art, the—*n.*, capitalized, a shorthand term referring to Renaissance-era ceremonial magick.

athamé—*n.*, a black-handled knife with many uses in ceremonial magick.

dabbler—*n.*, karcists' pejorative for an amateur or a poorly trained adept of ceremonial magick.

demon—*n.*, a fallen angel; demons provide the overwhelming majority of magick in the Art, with the remaining small percentage coming from angels.

Enochian—*n.*, the language of angels; *adj.*, related to or originating from angels or their language.

experiment—*n.*, in ceremonial magick, technical term for a ritual involving the conjuration and control of demons or angels.

familiar—*n.*, a demonic spirit in animal form, sent to aid a karcist and amplify his or her powers.

grimoire—*n.*, a book of magickal contracts between a karcist and the demons with whom he or she has struck pacts in exchange for access to them and the powers they grant.

incubus—*n.*, a low-level (i.e., nameless) demon, a creature of pure meanness and spite, whose function is to seduce mortals or, in some cases, act as their sexual servant; an incubus can take any of a variety of masculine forms. When so desired, it can assume a feminine form; in such an event, it is referred to as a *succubus* (see below).

Kabbalah—*n.*, a system of esoteric theosophy and theurgy developed by Hebrew rabbis; it is considered a system of "White Magick," though it has a "Black Magick" component known as *Sitra Achra*.

karcist—*n.*, a master-level adept in the Art of ceremonial magick.

lamia—*n.*, a low-level (i.e., nameless) demon summoned to act as a domestic servant; though lamiae can be compelled to behave in a manner that seems docile or even friendly, they must be carefully controlled, or else they will turn against those who conjured and commanded them.

Llull Engine—*n.*, a divination tool, often consisting of overlapping wheels made from stiff paper or cardboard, that can be called upon without invoking either demons or angels.

magick—*n.*, when spelled with a terminal "k," a shorthand term for Renaissance-era ceremonial magick, also known as the Art. Not to be confused with theatrical or stage magic, which consists of sleight of hand, misdirection, and mechanical illusions. All acts of true magick are predicated on the conjuration and control of demons or, in rare cases, angels.

nadach—*n.*, a human being whose soul has been spiritually bonded prior to birth with the essence of a demon; such a union persists for life and often confers one or more special abilities.

nikraim—*n.*, a human being whose soul has been spiritually bonded prior to birth with the essence of an angel; such a union persists for life and often confers one or more special abilities.

operator—*n.*, in the Art, the adept or karcist leading or controlling an experiment.

patient—*n.*, an antiseptic term of the Art for the intended subject (often a victim) of a demonic sending (see below) resulting from an experiment.

rabble—*n.*, karcists' nickname for the world's non-magickal majority of people.

rod—*n.*, in the Art, a wand; used to impose punishments on demons and direct magickal effects.

scrying—*n.*, a term for remote viewing, or clairvoyance (i.e., witnessing events in faraway places) by means of magick.

send—*v.*, in the context of magick, to dispatch a demon by means of an experiment, with orders to perform a specified task. Such actions can include, but are not limited to, murder, assault, recovery of valued objects, and the acquisition of information.

succubus—*n.*, a low-level (i.e., nameless) demon, a creature of pure meanness and spite, whose function is to seduce mortals or, in some cases, act as their sexual servant; a succubus can take any of a variety of feminine forms. When so desired, it can assume a masculine form; in such an event, it is referred to as an *incubus* (see above).

tanist—*n.*, a karcist, adept, or other person who acts as an assistant to the operator during an experiment. Most experiments are designed to be performed either by a lone operator or by an operator with two or four tanists.

ward—*n.*, a glyph, seal, or other sigil, whether temporary or permanent, that serves to protect a person, place, or thing from demonic or magickal assault, detection, or other effect.

yoke—*v.*, to force a demon or angel into the conscious control of a karcist. Yoking a demon often incurs deleterious side effects for the karcist; such effects can include, but are not limited to, headaches, nosebleeds, nightmares, indigestion, and a variety of self-destructive obsessive-compulsive behaviors.

THE INFERNAL DESCENDING HIERARCHY

SUPERIOR SPIRITS AND MINISTERS OF HELL

SATAN MEKRATRIG

PUT SATANACHIA (BAPHOMET)			BEELZEBUTH		
LUCIFUGE ROFOCALE	ASTAROTH	SATHANAS	PAIMON	ASMODEUS	BELIAL

Mortals cannot strike pacts with the Emperor of Hell (SATAN MEKRATRIG) or the other two superior spirits (BAPHOMET and BEELZEBUTH).

A karcist makes his/her first pact with one of the six ministers (governors) of Hell; subsequently, his or her future pacts are limited to the subordinate spirits of that minister, and no others. It is possible for a minister to act as patron to many human karcists at once. None of the six ministers (aka patron spirits) can be yoked by a mortal karcist.

The ministers, ranked in terms of power and influence, from most to least, are:

> LUCIFUGE ROFOCALE (666 legions)
> PAIMON (200 legions)
> ASMODEUS (72 legions)
> BELIAL (50 legions)
> ASTAROTH (40 legions)
> SATHANAS (38 legions)

The fortunes and influences of the spirits fluctuate as the demons vie for power in the Infernal Hierarchy. A karcist most often makes compacts with his/her patron spirit for such benefits as wealth, longevity with slowed aging, and immunity to disease.

ACKNOWLEDGMENTS

I wish to thank Marco Palmieri, the editor who acquired the Dark Arts series for Tor Books, and who oversaw the editing of its first two volumes. I also am grateful to editor Jennifer Gunnels, who took over editorial responsibility for this, the series' third volume, and who responded with grace and patience when I asked to pull back the first draft I had submitted to her so I could rewrite its entire second half again from scratch.

Also due a debt of gratitude is the series' cover artist, Larry Rostant. Thank you for putting such great images on my books' North American editions, Larry.

Thanks are owed to Nicolas Oberson of the Geneva, Switzerland, Fondation Genève Tourisme & Congrès. He was forthcoming and helpful when I needed precise details and obscure historical facts about his lovely city.

This book would not have been as good as it is without the input of my beta reader, Aaron Rosenberg, and my historical consultant, Scott Pearson. Thank you, gents!

Lastly, I wish to praise the makers of Stolichnaya vodka. It is because they do what they do so well that I am able to do what I do at all. *Spasibo.*